ARGONAUTS

KEVIN KNEUPPER

CHAPTER ONE

SOME CALLED HER A GLORIFIED nurse. Just a pusher of pills, a dispenser of shots. Just the woman who sat on the sidelines while the warriors did their deeds and fought their battles. A cog in their machine, meant to stand behind them, always in their shadow and always in her place.

But she was more than that. She was the woman who healed them in battle, the woman who patched them up when things went wrong, the woman who controlled their very genetic code. She was the woman who changed them, and made them something more than what they'd been. And without her, they'd all be nothing: just ordinary men, with ordinary skills, and ordinary genes.

She was in her lab, perched atop the city of Argos, windows on all sides looking out on the skyline below. There were people who would die for that view, and the privileges that came with it. There were people who'd fought and clawed their entire lives just to get near it. They could call her what they liked, the warriors. They were glory hounds one and all, and none were fond of sharing the limelight. They could mock her, and they could insult her, but beneath the bluster they all knew who needed whom.

Her lab was state of the art, the best tools for the best of her trade. Sleek white machines hummed their metal songs as they worked, processing her data and mixing her concoctions. Stocky little robots whizzed around the floor, running materials back and forth wherever they were needed. Giant hydraulic arms did the grunt work, pumping liquids into trays and beakers in just the right amounts, at just the right times, all according to her specifications. She had everything she could want, everything that could possibly save her time or make her work go just a little bit more smoothly. It was valuable, what she did, and no expense was spared in making sure she did it well.

She walked along the rows of machines, checking each against the data on her tablet, confirming that every detail was correct before she went through with the procedure to come. She was a beauty, but then, everyone in her trade was. Appearances could be tailored, altered from one day to the next on a whim. Cheekbones could rise and fall, noses could thicken or thin, eyes could whirl through a kaleidoscope of colors according to one's tastes. She controlled it all, and the outside was the easiest part to change. At present, her eyes were dark and her skin was olive. She wore a white lab coat, the uniform of her profession, and one that had protected her clothing from more spills than she could count. Her hair was jet black, and she kept it long, tightened into a neat bun while she worked. But she liked to tinker with herself, just as she did with others, and what she'd look like from one week to the next was anyone's guess.

Her lab was a lonely place, and often she had only robots to keep her company. But today she had a patient: a man, strapped to a chair, thick metal wires coiled around his arms and legs to lock them into place. He was a warrior's warrior, a muscle-bound bruiser who killed who he was told to kill and did what he was told to do. His hair was a shaggy, sandy mop, his eyes a dull brown topped by a thick brow. He wasn't a thinker; you could tell that just looking at him. But they all wanted to climb the ranks however they could, and here he was to make himself just a little bit better at what he did. Just a little edge, the kind that could make all the difference in battles where everything was at stake on the outcome.

"Four more injections," said Medea. "Then you'll be the warrior you've always wanted to be." They were lined up in a row on the counter, the little vials of green liquid she was about to pump into him. She plunged a syringe into the first, filling it up and double-checking to make sure the dose was precise.

"This better not fuck me up," said Antaeus. He gave his restraints a wary eye, tugging against them just to be sure. "I've heard stories, about what this does to people. About what happens if you get things wrong. And I've heard the things they say about you."

"That's all black market stuff," said Medea. "You go to a back alley genomancer, who knows what you're injecting? I splice everything myself. And we don't skimp on quality." She waved a hand to a row of machinery taking up an entire wall in the lab: a vast computer attached to an array of tools, ranging from centrifuges spinning biological materials to bubbling vats of pink goo. "The best the Argo Corporation has to offer. The best you're going to get, anywhere."

Antaeus didn't trust her, but none of them ever did. It used to irk her, that they'd let her do something so intimate to them and yet treat her like an outcast. The comments they made once cut, and deeply, but now they merely stung. They thought of her as an enchantress, working her unfathomable magics upon them. They couldn't understand her, and so they wanted to control her, chopping away at her just to be sure she was still safely under their thumbs. She hurt a little with every slight, but she'd built up a shell, a persona they couldn't fluster, and it kept her safe inside even when they were at their worst.

She held the syringe above his arm, poised for the first injection. "Last chance. Once this code goes in, it's not coming out, not for months. It'll be a part of you. Every last strand of your DNA will change. You can go back, if you change your mind, but it won't be easy. And it won't be cheap."

"Do it," said Antaeus. "Let's get this over with."

"I'm not going to lie," said Medea. "This will hurt. Just for a few days. Just until your system processes the new code, gets it merged in with all the rest." She stuck the needle into his arm, dumping the first of her concoctions into his veins.

"I can handle it," said Antaeus. "I can handle anything."

"We'll see," said Medea. She emptied shot after shot into his skin, continuing on until the course was done. Then a final needle: a nutrient tube, attached to a machine nearby. It began pumping yellow fluids into his body, concentrated proteins, vitamins, and other biological raw materials, the fuel he'd need to make the change he was about to undergo.

They waited, and everything was quiet at first. She checked the diagnostics, watched his heart rate, watched his blood pressure, watched anything that could go wrong. Nothing did; he was healthy, and he was young, and she was good at what she did. He sat there in the chair, and for a time all was still. For a time, there was no sign she'd done anything to him at all.

But as the minutes passed, his hands began to twitch. First the right one, then the left. He gave a grimace, and he kept looking back and forth between the two. "I can feel something. Under my skin. It itches."

"That's normal," said Medea. "That's okay. Just let the shots do their work."

"It's in my throat," said Antaeus. "Is it supposed to be in my throat?"

She shined a light in one eye, then the other. Then she picked up a black, handheld diagnostic device, holding it against his arm as it pricked his skin with a tiny needle and sampled his blood. "Everything's fine. Vital signs are good. Your code's changing, right on cue. Just roll with it, and keep calm. You know what's going to happen to you, and you know it's going to be a bit of a shock to your system."

He tried to keep it together, but big as he was and strong as he was, he wasn't prepared for what came next. None of them ever were.

"My fingernails," said Antaeus. "They're turning black."

And they were, little spots of pigment appearing at random across them. They spread until they were pools, and as he wiggled his hands the nails themselves seemed to change: thinning, growing longer, clicking against the arm of the chair as he moved. "Good," said Medea. "That's good. Keep them still. Just let them do their thing."

"It hurts," said Antaeus. "My skin. Everywhere, it hurts."

"You're a big boy," said Medea. "And you wanted to be a bigger one."

He was getting bigger, in fact, and visibly so. He'd been tall and muscular beforehand, but now he was growing cartoonishly oversized, his biceps bulging against the restraints, his pectorals moving under his shirt as they added pound after pound of muscle beneath. She could see hairs crawling out of the neck of his shirt, long, brown strands that probed their way out millimeter by millimeter until they joined together in thick, scruffy patches.

"Hurts," said Antaeus. But it was barely a word as it came from his mouth. He bit down upon the sound as it left him, and his lips flared to reveal the cause: overgrown canines, poking down further than they should. Soon he couldn't even close his mouth around them, and his voice lowered and wavered until nothing was left but a growl.

"It's supposed to hurt," said Medea. She wiped a damp cloth against his forehead, dabbing away his sweat, speaking to him in soothing tones as he became more and more a beast. "You'll get better. Just keep yourself centered, and don't panic. Everything's fine. Everything's under control."

He didn't seem to believe it. He kept looking at his hands, watching the spread of fur upon them, watching his wrists balloon until they pushed up against the very edges of the restraints. He pulled at them, trying to break free, shouting unintelligible sounds all the while. His eyes were wild, and he lunged his head toward her, trying for a bite, before falling back exhausted as the changes slowed and his body stabilized.

"The worst part's over," said Medea. "Now you're what you wanted to be."

He was still a man, mostly. But he was something else as well. The fur had spread all across his body, a thick coat of light brown. His fingers were tipped with sharp black claws, nasty enough to maul anyone foolish enough to face him in battle. He was stronger than ever, and he looked it: his chest was a barrel, his arms oversized pistons, and all of him bigger than any human had a right to be. But the biggest change of all was to his face. His teeth were daggers, the whites of his eyes had gone brown, and his nose looked distinctly like a snout. If one didn't know better, and were to catch him in the dark, they might think him nothing more than a big, angry bear.

Medea drew a sample of blood, running it through her diagnostics. She pressed a button on one of the machines and he was bathed in a blue light, scanned from head to toe by the laboratory's systems. She put a finger to his wrist and counted his pulse by hand, just to be sure. She went over the bloodwork, for both check and double-check, before turning back to the creature sitting before her.

"Everything's green," said Medea. "Vitals are good, code is functioning, chromosomes are stable. You're everything you hoped you could be, and you're exactly what the Argo Corporation needs in a warrior. Looks like today's your lucky day. Welcome to the Argonauts."

CHAPTER TWO

THE BALLROOM WAS FILLED TO bursting, crammed with executives, politicians, well-wishers, and a scattering of hand-selected journalists. Champagne flowed from bottles and from fountains, the better to lubricate the enthusiasms of the crowd. Ice sculptures lined the walls, carved into the shape of ancient gods from Apollo to Zeus. Waiters rushed from table to table, fulfilling culinary desires of all kinds just minutes after the guests had conceived them. The Gould was the finest hotel in the city, and it was nothing but the finest for them. A shareholder's meeting meant shareholders would be there, and shareholders expected to be impressed.

It was the keynote speech, and all eyes were rapt on the lectern at the room's center. A tall, energetic man stood behind it in a well-tailored suit, with a full head of slick dark hair to match his shark's smile. He'd been all schmooze, all night, but such is the fate of a chief executive.

"It's been a banner year," said Pelias. "The best in the history of the Argo Corporation. Now, I know it's not good form to toot one's own horn. Maybe it's even narcissistic. But everyone here knows you've got to be a little bit of a son of a bitch if you want to get to the top." He smiled a mischievous smile to knowing laughter and the clink of forks against glasses. "So time to brag away. Quarter over quarter revenues? They're up double digits." The first scatterings of applause began, but he quickly raised a hand and cut them off. "That's good. But that's not what I'm here to announce. The big news is how many stakeholders we've added. A million new loyalty contracts in the last three months alone. So many new people that the city of Argos is going to need another district to house them all."

Applause erupted around the room, coupled with a few loud gasps as people took in the implications. There were only three kinds of people in their world. There were the shareholders, the privileged few who owned a piece of the Argo Corporation. There were the employees, who did what jobs machines couldn't, though every year there were fewer and fewer of them. And then there were the stakeholders, the vast majority of the population whose jobs had long ago been handed away to machines. They had no way to support themselves, but even the harshest of Social Darwinists hadn't the stomach to let them all starve. Instead the government had enacted the basic minimum, a monthly check to which every citizen was entitled. It was enough to keep them in comfort, if not in luxury. And the competition for a piece of those checks was ferocious.

More stakeholders meant more money, big money. Loyalty contracts were simple: the Argo Corporation would house a stakeholder, and feed them, and flood them with free entertainment and free cannabinoids. Its corporate tentacles slithered into every conceivable industry, and once the dotted line was signed, life's essential needs and wants were free for the taking. But loyalty came with a price. In return, the stakeholders would sign over their entire basic minimum. And they'd sign over the rights to every last bit of their personal data.

"Now many of you have been wondering what we're planning to do with our newfound wealth," said Pelias. "A little of it has to go to the stakeholders. It always does. New shows, new games, new gadgets. That's a given. But every company has those. We want to give stakeholders reasons to go exclusive with the Argo Corporation. A real draw. Something the other companies don't have. Something to make them want to join the Argo ecosystem. Something to make it so they never want to leave."

The room descended into a puzzled silence, as everyone pondered what the announcement could be. Pelias left them hanging for a suitable period of time, smirking down on them from up above as they ran guess after guess through their heads. Once the suspense had become palpable, he let slip the news.

"Genomancy," said Pelias. "Too expensive for the masses, or so they say. But we're going to change that."

Jaws dropped and murmurs rose, as everyone around the room began talking all at once. It shouldn't be possible, what he was promising. Genomancy was an art form, as much as it was a science. Much of modern industry had been automated away, the need for human labor a distant memory in an age of mass robotics and boundless computation. But genetic code was complicated. The things people wanted to do to themselves were as peculiar as their own DNA, and each procedure was an adventure unto itself. A genomancer had to know their craft inside and out, spending years in study, and there were never enough of them to go around.

"It won't work!" came a shout from one of the tables at the back. "Too damned expensive!" A dashing man sat there, his table aglow with a miniature display of holographic fireworks, advertising the expensive champagnes he'd collected at its center for all to see. The breast of his suit was lined with rows of medals bestowed upon him by the Argo Corporation. They were cheap trinkets, though bought at great expense. The shareholders coveted them, the rarer the better, and they fell over one another to acquire them through donations, service, or mere treachery. They'd certainly worked their magic for their bearer; he was surrounded by women, each more beautiful than the last, and all competing for the chance to be his latest trophy.

"Ever the skeptic, Augeias," said Pelias. He held his arms out, looking hurt, but not very. "Haven't I done you right? What do I have to do, to earn your trust?"

"You made me billions," shouted Augeias. "But don't be so quick to give it all away. It's hard enough as it is to find a good genomancer, and now you want the rabble to get them for free? If anyone's going to piss my money away on a lark, it's going to be me."

"He's just worried about his women," said Pelias, as he winked and raised a glass in mock toast. "If they saw what he looked like before, all the money in Argos wouldn't keep them by his side." Knowing laughter filled the room at the teasing, and none were more tickled than the shareholders themselves. Few of them would be much to look at without their wealth. But they could afford to turn themselves from bald, jowly frogs into charming princes, a privilege they weren't likely to let go of without a fight.

"He has a point, though," said Pelias. "What we face is a shortage. But what's the problem with any shortage? Bottlenecks. And what's always been the bottleneck, in every industry and at every turn? People. People cost money. They're an expense, just obsolete old apes whose blind fumblings are nothing compared to the precision of a machine that can work day in, day out, with no breaks and no pay. Once you get rid of the people, the game changes. The costs go to zero. Genomancy becomes free for us, and free for anyone with an Argo Corporation contract." He was interrupted with another round of buzzing from the crowd as everyone around tried to work out his plan, and how they could take advantage of the world he was imagining.

"You're thinking it's impossible," said Pelias. "But you're not thinking far enough. You're not thinking on a grand enough scale. Now, I know none of you read your contracts. Nobody does. You just sign, and re-sign, every time your term comes up. Don't blow our cover, but we all know it." He gave a nod to a table of prominent journalists, to laughter from all around. They all knew he had nothing to worry about. The talking heads of the news were as captive to the powerful as they'd ever been, and they were all vicious partisans of whichever faction they'd aligned themselves with. Their perks were nothing, compared to those of the ones they served, but still they wouldn't risk them for something as trivial as the truth.

"Last year, the Argo Corporation Membership and Affiliation Agreement was updated," said Pelias. "Just a few tweaks. Some minor, some not. But there's a big one, one that didn't get much comment at the time. One that's going to change the world. We've got nearly two billion members in-ecosystem worldwide. That's a lot of people. And that's a lot of data."

"We're going to collect it all," continued Pelias. "One big database, and everyone's opted in. The biggest pool of genes the world has ever known. We're going to scour every twist and turn of every double helix, and then procedure by procedure, we're going to automate things. We'll make it all free, until anyone in the Argo corporate ecosystem can change their genes at the push of a button. It's going to be a revolution, ladies and gentlemen, and when I'm done, we're going to be the last one of the Big Five left standing."

The room erupted into cheers, and toasts rose from every table. It was a mad dream, and it would mean a wild unraveling of the existing social order if it came to pass. There were only five companies that mattered, outside of a scattering of minor corporations that eked out a living by focusing on this industry or that. Five massive conglomerates, the only ones who'd managed to build empires large enough to provide every conceivable product or service a consumer could desire. Each had its advantages to a stakeholder trying to choose which one to go exclusive with. There was the Argo Corporation, renowned for its medical technologies. Walmazon made the best consumer goods bar none, though Golden Apple had its own band of fanatical supporters, along with foods everyone hungered for. For those with love of quick trips across continents and a chance at lunar tourism, Musk Holdings was the obvious choice.

And then there was Colchis.

Their goods were shoddy, nothing but cheap imported things with little to recommend them. Their tech was old, a mish-mash of the public domain and whatever they could patch together themselves at little expense. Their housing was crowded, and their hospitals were prone to uncomfortable waits. But the Colchis Corporation knew what the people wanted, and it gave it to them. The Colchians were masters of entertainment. They flooded their stakeholders with shows, books, games, music, and virtual reality worlds, each more tantalizing than the last and all of them requiring an exclusive contract. And they were bitter enemies of the Argo Corporation.

As Pelias stepped down from the platform he was surrounded by well-wishers, eager for a word with him about whatever of their interests they thought he might advance. He went table by table, giving them each a few moments of his attention. Some wanted to toady, some to take photos, and others to thank him for all the money he'd made them.

He glad-handed with the tables full of journalists, though there was tension behind the smiles as they lobbed softball questions in his direction. Most worked for media outlets owned by the Argo Corporation, and a negative word about their employer had never crossed their lips. Others were nominally independent, but like every public figure, they connected with their audience using social networks. They lived or died by how much of a following they could amass, and the Argo Corporation controlled the platforms. Cross Pelias, and their follower counts would vanish into the electric ether along with their careers.

He navigated a series of tables designated for the politicians, but with them, things were considerably more at ease. They were all part of a brotherhood of thieves, and they were content to be what they were. Many were of opposing political parties, and ever at each other's throats in public. But here, they laughed and drank and made merry, old chums with their spoils divided and nothing to fight over so long as no one was watching. Pelias could never tell them apart when they weren't at their speechmaking, but neither could anyone else. They passed whatever laws he pleased, filling the government's coffers and then funneling the money to him indirectly via the stakeholders' basic minimum. They didn't dare do anything else.

Stakeholders were voters, after all, and it was exceedingly easy to control their votes once one controlled their data.

As for the shareholders, they each had a table to themselves, if they wanted it. There were fewer and fewer of them as the years passed. Buybacks and other financial shenanigans had caused the number of shares available to dwindle inexorably, and had driven the price of even a single share out of reach of the masses. Those few who owned them were a class unto themselves, plied with every luxury possible to ensure that they voted their shares for the existing order when the time came each year to re-elect a corporation's management slate. Pelias gave their tables extra attention, according to however many shares they owned, and he barraged them with compliments and well-wishes until they could stand no more.

Finally the night began to die, and the guests trickled off to private parties or to their own affairs. With no one of importance left to speak to, Pelias drifted towards the exit, back to his suite and back to business. He'd no sooner come to the hallways than an aide was at his side: Amphion, young in years but old in airs, a seasoned veteran of the kinds of battles that went on in boardrooms up above. That he'd survived this long working for Pelias was a testament to his talents. Many had come and gone before him, and many others were eager to take his place.

"Sir," said Amphion.

"Let's go," said Pelias. "And let's get the hell back to work."

"A fine speech." The voice came from behind them: Augeias, a blonde hanging on either arm as he emerged from the ballroom. His voice was slurred, and the women beside him giggled as he strode up to Pelias and slapped him on the back. "And a fine plan. A bombshell. It might even be enough to save your skin, in the end."

"I'm more than fine, Augeias," said Pelias with a forced smile. "I've been in charge for years. And the corporation isn't going to find anyone better."

"We'll see," said Augeias. "The management vote's coming, and coming soon. I hear it's going to be close. A nail biter. Some of the shareholders want one of their own in charge. You're a smart man, Pelias. And you're good at what you do. But you grew up a stakeholder. You can't wash off that stink. And it rankles, to some."

"It means I know the customers," said Pelias. "And it means I know how to make you money."

"The other side has money to throw around, too," said Augeias. "And more of it. The pressure's on, and it must be tremendous. Why, if a few more votes switch sides, you'll be back serving food instead of making speeches." His women tittered at the dig, and he disappeared down the hallway with a train of models and actresses in tow.

Pelias fumed at Amphion as he stalked away from the ballroom. "We need to start counting votes. We're close. Too close. And I'm not losing to one of these smug little shits just because they decided they want to play at being the boss."

"Sir," said Amphion. "We have another problem. An urgent one. I don't think it can wait."

Pelias just kept walking, his pace brisk, and Amphion struggled to keep up as he bee lined towards the nearest bathroom. The place was sparkling, kept in pristine condition by tiny mouse-sized robots that crawled along the floors and walls, wiping away the smallest drops of water and specks of dirt as they went. A robotic attendant was stowed beneath the sink, looking like nothing more than a large black trashcan. It would emerge when the place was empty and handle whatever its smaller brethren couldn't, and between them all the bathroom could go for years without a moment of human labor.

Pelias gave a quick eye to the stalls, made sure they were empty, and then went straight for the counter. At a nod, Amphion was at the door, barring the entrance and giving them their privacy. There were shareholders about, and Pelias didn't want them to see what came next: little glass vials from his pocket, filled with colored powders. He emptied them onto the counter, arranging the piles into lines of dust, a rainbow of pinks and purples and blues. Then he began to snort them through a little tube, absorbing an evening's worth of energy up his nose.

"Send some more to my room," said Pelias, with a dismissive wave of his hand. "I want uppers. I burned a day on this bullshit; I'm not going to piss the night away, too." Amphion struggled to suppress a cringe. He knew what Pelias was like, when he pushed himself too hard and took too many pills. His work improved, to be sure. But his thoughts turned dark, towards enemies real and imagined, and it was best to stall on any orders he gave when he was in one of his moods.

"Take a hit," said Pelias. "One of them's yours, if you want it."

"No, thank you," said Amphion. His face was a mask, hiding his thoughts but for a slight twitch of discomfort.

"Suit yourself," said Pelias. "I was a skeptic once, too. Thought this stuff rotted your brain. Now I know better. You won't get to the top without it, not from where you are. It lets you work twice as hard. And it lets you see things. Threats. Things other people are trying to hide from you." He stared at Amphion, eyes dark and unblinking. "Your problem. Spill it."

"It's bad news," said Amphion. "It's about Aeson."

"Fucking trust funder," said Pelias. He swatted away one of the tiny robots, come to clean his mess prematurely, and then leaned down and snorted another line. "Spoil the old brat with whatever he wants. Whatever it takes to keep him happy and keep him off my ass. Wine, drugs, whores. I don't care. Happy shareholders are complacent shareholders. Happy shareholders vote for existing management. So make damned sure you keep him happy."

"We did," said Amphion. "We gave him everything he wanted. Everything he asked for."

"Well, then what the hell's he complaining about?" said Pelias. He wiped at his nose, cleared the dust from his nostrils, and checked himself in the mirror to be sure none had been missed.

"He's dead," said Amphion. "An overdose, in his suite upstairs."

"Fuck," said Pelias, his pupils widening and his eyes narrowing. He started towards the bathroom door, leaned in towards Amphion, and snarled into his ear. "Just take care of it. And don't involve me. Don't even tell me about problems like this. Just fix them, and keep them quiet."

"That's not the problem," said Amphion. "We can fix that problem. It's already taken care of. The problem is what's going to happen to all of his shares."

"What?" snapped Pelias. "What happens to them?"

"His son," said Amphion. "They all go to his son."

Pelias turned pale, and his eyes began to move back and forth as he calculated in his head, running through scenarios and tabulating votes. It took him a moment, and then he spoke. "How bad? How bad is it?"

"Bad," said Amphion, staring at the floor. "Very bad. Aeson had a lot of shares, and his family has more. Add it to what the son has already, and he's going to be a problem. Nearly twenty percent. He'll be a swing vote. The swing vote. And if he votes the wrong way, we're all going to be out on our asses."

CHAPTER THREE

THE ROOM WAS DARK, EXCEPT for the ring at the center. They'd drawn a circle on the floor in chalk, stringing a few rows of lightbulbs across the ceiling above it. The rest of the warehouse was pitch black, the windows shut and the doors barred. It made things hard to see, even the spectacle they'd all come to watch. But then, what they were doing there wasn't strictly legal, and none of them would win any sympathy if they were caught.

The ring was surrounded with barbed wire, thick, nasty rolls of it that poked in all directions. People stood all around, getting as near to the action as they dared. Management of the impromptu establishment frowned upon anyone getting too close. They didn't like casualties; suffering the loss of a customer was bad, and suffering the loss of business that would follow was even worse.

The air was filled with shouts, some cheering, some jeering, and some placing odds on the event. On either side were supporters of one combatant or the other, and towards the middle they blended in with those who cared less for the outcome and more for the blood that would be spilled in arriving at it.

In one corner was a man, or part of one. The rest of him was all metal, a hack-job of cybernetic limbs and enhancements strung together into a single connected being. His arms had been replaced with thick chrome substitutes that ended in blades embedded at the tip of every finger. Oils ran through tubes all along them, veins that needed no blood, and they wove in and out of the surface of his arms before connecting with a pump embedded into the skin on his back. His face was all patchwork, part metal, part flesh, each fading in and out of one another. Both of his eyes had been torn out, and in their stead were glowing red cameras, better versions of what nature had gifted him with.

It was all old tech, the stuff they'd used before genomancy had come of age. Cybernetics had lost its shine, once a lost limb could be replaced with something biological instead of a chilly metal imposter. Few used it anymore, but after going down that road, there was no going back. Genomancy, on the other hand, offered the prospect of a reversal if someone changed their mind or if things went bad. So long as it was done correctly, they could always go back to their old code, and back to the way they'd been. So long as it was done correctly.

The other side of the ring was empty, awaiting the arrival of his opponent. An entrance had to be grand if the audience was to be entertained, and he'd let them cool their heels for just long enough that the anticipation was making them grumble. When they were ready, when they could wait no more, the fighter's entourage began to push at the crowd from behind. "Make way," came the announcer's voice from beyond them all. "Stand aside!"

The crowd parted, clearing a path for the man striding towards them. He was a giant, hulking beast, with horns sprouting from his forehead and jutting off almost a foot in either direction. His skin was a wrinkled grey, warty with growths where his genomancy hadn't quite taken. He wore the black shorts of a trained boxer, but nothing on his chest. Likely there was nothing he could manage to fit his arms through, given what had happened to his hands.

They were more clubs than anything else, bloated and inflamed as the bone within had grown wild, finger joining finger until nothing was left but a hardened grey mass at the end of either arm. He waved them in the air as he approached the ring, snarling and shouting and shoving at anyone who came too close. He stepped over the barbed wire, clapping his fists together over and over, beating them like drums as he stared down his opponent.

"Let's give it up!" shouted the announcer. "Let's make some noise! He's undefeated, with fifteen victories, eight by knock-out and seven by death! Let's hear it for the Ox of Argos, the meanest unsanctioned fighter of them all, Amycus!"

The crowd roared with energy as all but two men pressed up against the edges of the ring. The two stood apart, dressed in the solid black suits and ties that marked them as employees of the Argo Corporation. It was an enviable thing to have, employment. Few did; most survived on their basic minimum, content to stay in their place and live the comfortable life the state and its corporate partners provided. But some still had ambitions, for more money, more power, and most of all, for more status. What jobs there were drew heavy competition from those who'd still compete with machine in the contest of production, and these men had both secured themselves a post.

The first man was thin and bookish, his gangly limbs loose beneath the suit draped over them: Tiphys, an Argo Corporation pilot. In days past one in his occupation would have been bigger, more blustery, and certainly more daring. But Tiphys piloted not from the cockpit but from the ground, guiding drones up above for deliveries, spywork, and sometimes even war. A daredevil's spirit had become a liability in an age when aircraft were flown from the comfort of a chair far below, and Tiphys had in reflexes what he lacked in bravery.

Next to him stood the kind of man who once would have been a pilot in his place: strong, athletic, and with shoulders broad enough that they strained against his suit. He was handsome, startlingly so, with the kind of hardened jaw and shimmering green eyes that ordinarily could only be a product of extremely expensive genomancy. But his body was all natural, a work of art he'd chiseled into shape through years of careful training. He worked, but not because he had to. Some inner ambition drove him to it despite his circumstances, one of the idle rich who couldn't manage to stay idle. His name was Jason, a scion of a family who'd held shares in the Argo Corporation for generations. And here he was down in the muck with the stakeholders, frequenting a place whose reputation would cause other members of his class to flinch away in disgust.

Most of the crowd ignored them, but not the oddsmakers. They knew marks when they saw them, and men with jobs had paychecks to burn. They waved and shouted, trying to attract their attention and their wagers. If they'd known Jason owned shares, they'd have gone into a frenzy, but as it was they waited for the two of them to pick their side and place their bets. Their patience was tested as Jason took his time, assessing the new arrival to the ring and probing him for weaknesses. It was more than just a bettor's eye; Jason was a fighter himself, or wanted to be. But he didn't like what he saw. "He's a mess. What'd he do to himself?"

"Someone did a hack job on his genes," said Tiphys. They looked at his grey skin, mottled with growths and blotches, with clumps of bone that massed beneath almost at random. "Everybody wants a quick fix. Everybody thinks they'll mod themselves and go straight to the top, maybe even pick up a share or two on the way. Nobody thinks they'll be the one where everything goes wrong."

"Stupid," said Jason. "Some things you just don't cheap out on. If you're going to do them at all."

"You don't know what it's like at the bottom," said Tiphys. "You're a shareholder. He's just a stakeholder. He can't make any money. He probably doesn't have any skills." He looked Amycus up and down, a pile of muscle from horns to feet. "Besides stomping on things. But they've pretty much automated all the jobs that needed someone to stomp on things."

"It's a cheat," said Jason. "Even if he didn't have any skills, it's still a cheat. Genomancy lets you jump ahead without doing what it takes to deserve it. They ought to ban it, frankly. Seems like for every case that works out, there's someone else who ends up a monster."

"They'd just do it anyway," said Tiphys. "A guy like him would never get away from the bottom. Not without taking a chance."

"Means he's a gambler, at least," said Jason. "I like to bet on someone willing to take a risk." He waved down a bookie, a stout man in an ill-fitting green suit. He was shouting odds at them, and giving numbers Jason liked, if this man was the fighter he thought he'd be.

"Cryptocurrencies only," said the bookie. "No corporates. And make damned sure your data collection's turned off." He held up his wrist, covered by a thin, plastic sheath that ran the length of his forearm. It hugged his skin, tailored to fit his arm precisely, and its entire surface was a screen, flashing data about the odds on the fight to come. They'd once called them watches, and it had evolved from one, but this was more than mere timepiece. It was his computer, his phone, his doctor, his everything, and now it was his banker as well.

"Always," said Jason, holding up his arm and pulling down his sleeve to reveal a wrist sheath of his own. "I don't want a record of being here any more than you do." They pressed their wrists together and the transfer was done in an instant, the money spent and held in escrow for a certification of the fight's results. Management would send the alert, the bet would pay or not as the case might be, and then all traces of the transaction would vanish at the end of the night along with the arena.

The announcer began shouting into a microphone, rousing the crowd for the battle to come. "Ladies and gentlemen, boys and girls, this is the match you came to see. The Man of Metal against the Ox of Argos. Machine against gene, in a battle to the end. They're mean, they're angry, and they're ready to fight. So let's clap, let's cheer, and let's see some blood!"

A roar went up again, and the fighters began to circle one another, probing and feinting to see who'd attempt the first blow. It was the cyborg who struck first. His eyes were unreadable, two spheres of solid red glass that hid his intentions within. He swung his arm from nowhere, catching Amycus on the shoulder with a surgical slash. Blood dripped from the wound, oozing out through the open gash that was left behind. But if Amycus noticed it, he gave no sign. He responded only with a series of angry snorts, venting out steam from his nostrils. And while the cyborg's face was a waxen mask devoid of emotion, Amycus blared his thoughts for all to see. His expression was pure rage, contorted into a searing hatred that made even some in the audience step back.

He brayed a battle cry and rushed forward in a fury, swinging his arms wildly to and fro. The cyborg ducked, weaving through one swing after another. He stabbed at Amycus with his fingers, again and again, tearing out clumps of skin and flesh wherever he connected. But he faced a berserker, a man for whom wounds were nothing more than fuel for his frenzy. Eventually one of Amycus's blows connected with its target, sending up a loud clang as the cyborg's head shook from the force of it. He staggered on his feet, and with that he was done for.

Amycus poured his fists upon him, bone colliding with metal until the cyborg began to fall apart at the seams. He could have withstood things, if he'd been all machine. But soon what human parts of him were left had disconnected, torn from their proper place as sparks flew and wires were laid bare. The cyborg fell to his knees, looking up at Amycus and chirping in an electronic language no one there could understand. It wouldn't have mattered if they could have. Amycus was beyond restraint, and he raised both fists together before bringing them down in a final attack that split the cyborg's head in two.

The yells came from the crowd at once, joy from those who'd won their bets and disdain from those who'd lost. "Let's give it up for the winner," shouted the announcer, his voice piercing the din. "What you all paid to see! A fair fight, a clean fight, and proof that man's still got some spirit in him no matter how much a machine can do. Amycus, everyone, still undefeated!"

They all cheered and clapped, and even those who'd lost their fortunes gave the winner the respect he was due. But the noise just seemed to make him madder, as he paced around the ring with wild eyes and blood spilling from his wounds. He kept thumping his fists together, spraying drops of the cyborg's blood into the crowd with each collision, lunging at anyone who came too close to the barbed wire's edge.

"He won," said Jason. "What's his problem, when he won?"

"These guys are all just a little bit crazy," said Tiphys. "If they weren't, they'd be in a sanctioned match. They pump them with stims before they go in. Makes for a better fight. He'll calm down in a minute. You'll see."

But the calm didn't come, and the storm raged on. He became angrier and angrier, and the crowd went from a shocked silence to a chorus of boos. That was the wrong choice, at least for those close to the ring's edge. Amycus let out a whoop, throwing wild punches into the crowd. The boos turned to screams, and then to shocked silence as one of the spectators tumbled into the barbed wire, his head crushed and his blood pooling below him.

"No one leaves," said Amycus quietly. Then he roared, a fierce cry that reverberated through the warehouse and shook the bones of everyone around. "No one fucking leaves!" He raised his head in fury and gave a brisk snort, sending out puffs of air and snot. "No one leaves until someone beats me. No one leaves until either I lose, or every last one of you is on the fucking floor."

"It's just the adrenaline, ladies and gentlemen," said the announcer. "He's just all amped up from the fight, and he wants some more. And can you blame him? What a show, what a show! The best fighter in the entire city!" He tried to rouse the cheers again, running back and forth at the ring's edge, but no one was having it, not even Amycus himself. The praise just seemed to set him off, and he lashed out at the announcer as he passed by, knocking him to the floor with a blow to his side that left the man sprawling on the ground and clutching his gut.

"No one fucking leaves," growled Amycus. "Anyone tries, you die. No one leaves until someone beats me."

Eyes went back and forth among the audience. They looked at one another, and at the locked doors, far across the warehouse. They could make a run for it, out into the darkness, and then try to pry one of them open. But Amycus was big, and he was mad, and something with his genomancy had gone very, very wrong. If they were caught inside with him, he'd cut them all down with his fists.

"Someone get in the fucking ring!" shouted Amycus.

No one moved to enter. No one said a word. He screamed, grabbing the nearest bookie and wrapping his arms around him in a bear hug. The man wriggled and squealed, but Amycus lifted him up like a doll and tossed him into the center of the ring. He had a hefty paunch, and worse, grey hairs, the surest sign that one was a member of the unwashed masses. They'd have been long gone if he could have afforded even the most basic genomancy. His genes would have been snipped and his aging slowed, at least for a time. Instead, his body was in the middle of nature's long decay, and he was in no condition for a fight.

The man begged, tears pouring from his eyes, screaming to everyone around for someone to spare him. But Amycus just drummed his fists together, pounding out the rhythms of battle as he stepped closer and closer to his prey. Jason and Tiphys looked on as the bookie tried to crawl his way to the other side of the ring. "This is going to be a slaughter," said Tiphys. "We've got to go, while he's occupied. Let's get to a door, get it open, and get the hell out of here. Before crazy turns its eyes on us. And before we get caught here."

"Fuck this," said Jason. He flexed his fingers, balling them into a fist and then stretching them loose, over and over. "And fuck him." The bookie kept crying, urine dripping down his legs as he tried to crawl away. Some in the crowd laughed, but Jason just grew colder, his lips tightening in disgust.

"Don't," said Tiphys. He put a hand on Jason's shoulder, holding him back. "Don't be stupid."

"I'm just supposed to let him die?" said Jason. "I'd have been in that ring myself in the first place, if I could have."

"They'll know we were here," said Tiphys. "We'll lose our jobs. That doesn't matter to you, but I need mine. I don't want to go back to my basic minimum. Sitting in a tiny apartment somewhere strapped into a VR pod all day because I can't afford anything better to do."

"Fuck them," said Jason. "If you lose your job, I'll sell a share and do you right. The whole reason we come here is for the risk, right? The thrill? They won't let me be a warrior. But they can't stop me from fighting. Not if I don't have a choice."

"You can't," said Tiphys. "He could kill you. Your father will, if he doesn't. You have to be smart about this. You have to—"

"I challenge," shouted Jason, his voice booming through the arena.

"He could hurt you," said Tiphys, grabbing Jason and trying his best to hold him back. "He could break all your arms. He could poke you with his horns. He could give you some kind of weird toe fungus. You have to be smart. You have to play it safe."

But Jason just ignored him. He stepped over the barbed wire and into the ring, pulling away from Tiphys's attempts to hold him back. Amycus turned towards him with a snarl. Then he went back to his drumming, smashing his fists together in Jason's direction, his reach impossibly far. He bared his teeth, thick white squares that bulged out of his gums in odd directions where the genomancy had left them crooked and loose.

"No one leaves," said Amycus. "I'll beat you all, one by one. Beat you all into pulp."

Jason took off his jacket, tossing it to Tiphys and rolling up his sleeves. Jason was tall, and would have towered over any ordinary man. But whatever had been done to Amycus had made him a giant, a colossal freak who looked down on even the tallest of men. Jason looked him up, and looked him down, a solid mass of muscle and horns and ruined skin. But he wasn't fazed for a moment.

"Last chance," said Jason. "Take your purse and go home. You go now, and I'll let you live."

"No one leaves," growled Amycus as he stomped at the floor. Then he charged towards Jason, feet pounding against the ground and arms swinging. He almost caught him; the punches were wide, and there was little room to maneuver within the ring's enclosure. But Jason was fast, impossibly so. He ducked and weaved, grabbing hold of Amycus as he ran and swinging himself around behind him.

Amycus turned round, frothing with uncontrolled rage. He charged again, and again he caught only air as Jason rolled to the side and made his way behind him once more. Yet still Jason kept his distance, and still he made no move to attack. He didn't taunt, he didn't fight, and he didn't do anything but watch.

His restraint did nothing to appease Amycus. He began to lunge this way and that, feinting at Jason and penning him in. Soon Jason was backed into a corner with nowhere to escape, and Amycus pressed his advantage. He swung and swore, snarling and punching and doing his best to crush the man before him. But he couldn't connect; Jason was too fast, his eyes calculating every blow, his head weaving up and down between them. Each dodge added to the frenzy, each one fuel tossed onto anger's fire, and as time went on the swings came harder and faster.

Finally, Amycus moved to end the thing, drawing himself up to his full height and standing on his toes, his horns brushing against the ceiling. He lifted up his right hand as high as it could go, screaming in fury, and brought it downward with all his power. He'd aimed for Jason's head, and he would have hit it, crushing his skull just as surely as he had the cyborg's. But Jason had been watching. His time dodging and weaving hadn't been wasted; he'd taken advantage of every swing, logging the movements in his head. It was like a dance to him, and now he knew his partner's moves, knew where he'd sway and how he'd angle his fist. He saw the gap, the space between Amycus's arms and his head, the pathway he'd left completely defenseless in his rage. And he took it.

He lunged upward, aiming his fist for a spot he'd selected just beneath Amycus's ear. There was bone there, weak bone, and he meant to take advantage of it. He stepped to the side and focused on his target, but he didn't come away unscathed. He'd been too consumed by the attack to dodge properly, and as he swung he felt his left shoulder pop, struck by a glancing blow from Amycus's fist. But it was his other arm that counted, and that one found its mark. His knuckles dug into Amycus's skin, smashing the bone beneath his ears and sending forth a torrent of blood.

They both fell to their knees, Jason clutching his shoulder and Amycus pressing his fists against his head. It didn't help matters, not with the state his hands were in. The blood kept gushing out, and he let out a wail as he thumped his fists against his head again and again. Soon he began to sway, dropping to the floor as his own blood pooled around him. Jason stood, but no one moved towards him. Not until it was clear that Amycus was down, and that he wouldn't be getting back up. "Dead," said the announcer, as he felt for a pulse. "Victory by death, to the Man With No Name, the savior of the people! A free match, everybody, so don't say you didn't get your money's worth!"

He kept on about his proclamations as Jason stepped over the barbed wire again, back into the crowd and back to Tiphys. Everyone around was clapping him on the back and singing his praises, and the two of them had to push their way through the crowd even as it streamed towards the exits, the spectators eager to escape before something else went wrong.

"Let's go," said Tiphys, dragging Jason towards the door. "Before corporate gets here. Before someone recognizes who you are."

"I fucked up," said Jason, shaking his head. He'd pulled into himself, a look of frustration on his face, ignoring the crowd around him even as Tiphys forced him through it.

"You beat someone twice your size," said Tiphys. "He could have killed everyone in here. You're a hero."

"I still fucked up," said Jason. "He clipped me." He rubbed his shoulder where the blow had landed, and while his flesh was unwounded, his ego was. He was angry, not at others but at himself. He kept shaking his head, replaying the battle in his mind again and again. "A few more inches and he'd have shattered it, and I'd have been done for. I can't believe I let him clip me. He could have killed me."

"But he didn't," said Tiphys. "You were great. You really were."

"I can't just be great," said Jason. "I have to be perfect. Great will get you killed in the long run. Great won't make you a warrior. Great won't make you an Argonaut."

"You'll be fine," said Tiphys. "Don't worry about that. You can't change it, so don't worry about it. If they don't let you in, they don't let you in. You can find something else to do. You can live your life the way you want. You've got a cushy, do-nothing job, and the worst case is you stay there. That's not a bad life. You can just play games on your sheath all day, or spend every meeting binge watching vids of cats hiding in boxes. It's really awesome." Jason looked down at him quizzically, and a tinge of red crept up Tiphys's cheeks. "Or so I've heard."

They were almost to the exit when they found themselves confronted by a posse of men, all dressed in black suits matching their own. One of them stepped forward as the others spread out to block their way. The man's body was young, but everything about the way he held himself spoke of decades on the front lines of extralegal skirmishes between corporations. He'd paid his dues, and they'd paid for his second youth in return, doubling his lifespan even if it was beyond them to stop the march of time entirely. Tiphys took a step backwards, then bolted into the crowd and disappeared into the crush of people. But Jason just stepped forward, meeting the man's eyes with a firm stare.

"Are you Jason?" said the man. "Jason, son of Aeson?"

Jason paused, forming the words in his mouth. If he were caught here, it could mean fines, or even time in jail, if the men were inclined to press the matter. But in the end he decided that if they knew his name, their question was rhetorical, and they already knew full well who he was. "By blood and by law," he said. "But that's the end of it. The old man's a drunk and a deadbeat. I get a check from him once a year, and that's about as far as our relationship goes."

"That makes things easier," said the man. "But you have my condolences anyway, if you want them. Aeson is dead. He passed last night, and we're sorry for your loss. If you're up to it, we'd like to introduce you to someone. Someone very, very important. The CEO of the Argo Corporation would like to have a word with you."

CHAPTER FOUR

J ASON COULD SEE THE BUILDING spiraling into the air in the distance, its twin sides structured more like ribbons than blocky skyscrapers of yore. It was new, still sparkling white, a monument to Pelias and the wealth he'd created. It had been patterned after the double helix, each of its separate sides shimmering tubes that gradually wound upwards with horizontal bars connecting the two for support. It looked like it would blow apart with the breeze, but appearances meant nothing when it came to durability. The Argo Corporation headquarters had been designed using only the latest nanomaterials, thin synthetic metals that were deceptively strong for what little they weighed.

The shape was unique, but every building of importance in the city had some such distinction of its own. Skyscrapers had become works of art, able to take on any form their builders desired. Some were even torn down from year to year, if their owners were of sufficient wealth and sufficiently fickle tastes. The cost was surprisingly reasonable, if one had the shares. The amount spent on design dwarfed that spent on the actual construction, now that nothing was built with human hands. The skyline of Argos was ever changing as a result, an urban forest filled with the most peculiar of trees.

The men had put Jason into a car and sent it on its way, and now he found himself headed for the very center of the city. The car was a sleek silver pod, made from seamless glistening metal with its wheels hidden beneath. It had no driver, but then, it didn't need one. Driving was just another chore that had been foisted upon machines, leaving everyone a passenger and them all the safer for it. Few even owned a vehicle of their own, outside of a dwindling number of hobbyists. The rest simply pressed a button on their wrist sheaths and one of the city's fleet would find them in seconds, taking them wherever they pleased without asking a dime.

Ordinarily the streets of Argos would have been mostly empty, the residents locked away in their apartments as they gorged on free entertainment. But on this day the sidewalks were lined with people for miles in either direction. Everything around the building had been shut down for one of the city's parades, and Jason couldn't even get close. Argos was a land filled with heroes, and heroes demand recognition. The populace of the city was happy to give it to them; tales of their exploits were a staple of the news vids and a reliable ratings draw. This was a chance to see the legends in the flesh, and thousands of stakeholders had assembled in hopes of catching a glimpse.

Jason had no choice but to sit in the car and watch, but he didn't mind. He'd been to enough parades voluntarily, and he was happy to witness another. At the fore marched the grunts, those who'd yet to achieve any sort of notoriety for themselves. They were dressed in identical black uniforms, stomping in time through the streets. They were Argonauts, if the least among them, but the sight of their uniforms was enough to draw loud cheers from everyone around.

After them came the freaks. They wouldn't call themselves that, and no one would dare say something so foolish to their faces. But that was what they were, in truth: men who'd transformed themselves into beasts by tampering with their genes. Dangerous men, men who drew more stares than applause. Some looked like wolves, some vaguely feline, some like nothing nature's own imagination could concoct. All around the people held their wrists to the air, pointing their sheaths towards the street and taking photos or videos of the menagerie passing before them.

Finally came the military vehicles, bulky armored hovercraft that floated on pockets of air over the city streets. Each was mounted with missiles and cannons, the bigger and more imposing the better. None of them had ever been used in an actual battle; no stakeholder would live in a city whose streets were a war zone. Their only purpose was to impress, and impress they did. On the top of each stood one of the Argonauts, waving to the crowd. Only the most important of them warranted this prize position, the ones whose past laurels had catapulted them out of the realm of warriors and into the realm of celebrities.

Jason knew them all by name. He saw Clytius, the famed archer, holding his bow aloft as he rode by. He'd killed a Colchian assassin with it in a battle atop a skyscraper, or so the legend went. Next came Euphemus, gills and scales and all. He'd made himself more fish than man, and had slaughtered a dozen Colchian pirates. More and more followed after: Butes the Brave, Oileus the Drone Slayer, and Orpheus, who'd gone from leading soldiers to leading a rock band.

Jason had followed their exploits since he was just a child. It was how he'd decided he wanted to be a warrior. He'd been walking through the streets with a nanny, one of the dozens he'd had during his childhood. A parade had come rolling past, men with uniforms and boots and weapons, all the kinds of things that were so fascinating to a little boy. He'd been hooked; obsessed, really. And it wasn't just the grown-up toys that had done it.

It was the crowds.

The memory of the way the people had looked at the Argonauts had been seared into his mind ever since. The men wishing they could be them, debating back and forth about which of them was the toughest. The women looking on in admiration and awe at their strength. The mothers and fathers so proud that their sons were the treasure of the city.

The last one had mattered to him the most. He'd dragged his nannies to parade after parade, but Aeson never came with them. He'd trained and trained, first by himself with his toys, and then with the best professionals money could buy. Aeson didn't like it, and neither did the nannies, but he'd begged and begged until eventually he wore down everyone around him. He imagined himself up there in their place, waving to a crowd who admired him for his character and his deeds, rather than just his family's wealth. He imagined doing his father proud, and being someone no one could ignore.

But pride never came, and neither did his chance. He'd applied to be an Argonaut, over and over, but he'd never made it in. He was better than most of them, and he knew it. But they'd never even let him into boot camp, and at the end of the day he'd failed. All he had left was his training, the skills he'd learned, and the parades he watched from the sidelines.

When the last of the Argonauts had passed, the street reopened to traffic. Jason's vehicle zipped through, dodging trickles of pedestrians until it was parked before the entrance to the Argo Corporation headquarters itself. A door on the side of the car slid open, and out of it came Jason, checking his reflection in the vehicle's shiny metal sides. He adjusted his tie until it was dead center, and he ran his hands through his carefully tousled black hair. Then he headed towards a grand staircase made of synthetic marble, leading up to the base of the building. It culminated in glass doors, opening into a vast lobby below the twin strands curving up into the skies above.

He was confronted at the entrance by guards, stern men in black armor that bulged with hidden machinery beneath. They were rejects from the Argonauts, suited for security but not for battle. They were formidable nonetheless, and it was no insult that they hadn't risen as high as they'd aimed. The Argonauts took only the best, and even their cast-offs had to have exceptional mettle simply to have been considered. The city's security forces were filled with them, positioned at any building in Argos that might have something of value to spies or saboteurs. They all carried weapons fit for melee—swords, axes, or clubs, but nothing else. Projectiles or explosives were legal for security work, as a technical matter, but there was tacit agreement among the Big Five that stakeholders were too valuable a commodity to risk as bystanders in their constant feuding.

"Hold," said one of the guards, as he stared blankly off into space. Someone was speaking to him through his helmet, and once he had his orders he turned back to Jason. "Sir. You're wanted, at the very top. In the left strand. Take the elevator." He pointed towards a bank of elevators behind him, leading up along the building's two respective strands.

The elevator itself was a bright red sphere, encased within a large plastic tube that wound its way along the outside of the helixes up above. Jason stepped inside as the door closed and the sphere began to hum. It knew where it was going, and it knew who its passenger was. All it took was his sheath; once the building had identified him from its signals, it took him precisely where he was supposed to be.

It felt like he was standing in place, though in fact the sphere was whirling along the outside of the building in an upward spiral, going round and round the side through a tube until it reached his destination. The outer sphere rolled its way upward, while an inner sphere moved imperceptibly to keep him standing just as he was. Finally he arrived at the building's peak, a grand office atop all the rest.

The elevator opened into a reception area, an opulent floor where guests could cool their heels in luxury while they waited for their time with the man at the top. The walls were all windows, offering a panoramic view of the city. At the room's center was an artificial storm, encased within a glass tube that ran from ceiling to floor. Black clouds perpetually billowed within, sending tiny bolts of lightning against the glass and filling the room with the soft patter of rain. From time to time faces appeared inside, nymphs made of water looking out on the guests. But they were mere illusions of the machinery within, shapes with no substance that moved along with the storm. All around it were an army of receptionists and assistants, manning their desks and looking as busy as they could. They were only there for appearances, and their jobs could have been done just as easily by machines. But they looked important, and having the command of so many of them made their boss look even more important still.

He didn't let Jason wait long. After enough time had passed to let him take in the room, a receptionist hurried him over to a heavy white door, assembled from chunks of ivory. On it were carved the deeds of heroes of old, from battles with lions and boars down to the cleansing of stables. As the door opened Jason could see Pelias sitting before him, his suit a dark black and his tie a powerful red. He was in his chair, dictating orders to a screen projected on the wall beside him. He made a show of being busy, and of surprise at Jason's arrival.

"Jason," said Pelias. "Come in, come in." He rose from behind his desk, a majestic brown conversation piece. The desk had been carved, though not by human hands. It was still alive, a tree whose genetic code had been hijacked to compel it to become its own carpenter, shaping itself until it grew into the furniture it had been fated to be. Its surface was a perfectly flat rectangle, its sides supported by four trunks. Each was a pillar, covered with images of dryads protruding from beneath the bark. Between them were leafy vines dangling down to the floor, keeping the tree alive even as nutrients pooled in ceramic vases at the base of each leg. It was an impressive sight, a work of genetic art that must have taken years of coding to create.

"Drink?" said Pelias. "Cigar? Anything you want, you just let me know."

"Bourbon, if you have it," said Jason.

"We've got anything," said Pelias. "And if we don't, we can have it here in minutes. It's good to be king." He gave a slight wave to an attendant, ever at the ready to tend to his whims. The boy rushed off to a liquor cabinet, hidden away in the wall, and he was back just as quickly with drinks for the both of them.

Jason took his glass, shook Pelias's hand, and sat down across from him in a plush leather chair. He looked uncomfortable, and felt it, too. He'd never drawn so much attention from anyone so important, and despite his wealth, he wasn't one for the rigid rules and manners of the upper crust. He spent his days jousting not in drawing rooms but in training rooms, and he'd never felt at home among the soft boarding school boys who filled out most of the desks this high up.

"Now Jason," said Pelias, his face turning somber as he swirled his drink. "I'm so sorry about your father. I wanted to give you my condolences personally. It's a tragic loss, truly tragic. He'll be missed, here and everywhere else."

"I appreciate it," said Jason. "But you didn't need to bring me up here. We weren't close. I didn't even really know him. The guy couldn't be bothered with me, so I'm not going to be bothered now that he's gone."

In fact, he was bothered, though he'd never have admitted it. He still felt angry, and he still felt abandoned. The two of them had been at loggerheads for years, and the feud was still alive even if Aeson wasn't. But Jason wanted to be a warrior, and warriors had to be stoics if they expected to survive. He couldn't reveal his inner self, not to other men. They'd think it a weakness, and some would take advantage of it if they could.

"Still," said Pelias. "A loss is a loss. And we're all sorry for you, we really are."

"He's gone," said Jason, his voice devoid of emotion. "Nothing more to say about it." He stood, swigged the last of his bourbon, and left the glass behind on Pelias's desk as he turned towards the door. "Thanks for the drink, and thanks for the thought. But this isn't something I'm interested in talking about."

"I have to confess," said Pelias, calling after him. "I had something of an ulterior motive for inviting you up here. I didn't just ask you here for pleasantries. I actually wanted to talk to you about something more serious: your father's dealings with the corporation, and what it means for you now that he's gone."

"It doesn't mean a damned thing," said Jason. Old thoughts were coming back to life, old angers he'd spent years trying to suppress. The lonely birthdays, the revolving door of nannies who'd substituted for parents, the cold indifference to him whenever he wasn't needed as a prop for the image his family presented to the outside world. It all rushed back, and he knew he couldn't hold it in if he stayed. He kept walking, a shaky hand on the door as he started to leave. "I'm not interested in Aeson's business, or in yours."

"I'm not talking about business," said Pelias. "I'm talking about the Argonauts."

That stopped Jason in his tracks. He turned his head, and Pelias smiled a hunter's grin as he lured his prey back inside. "We were going over the company files, getting things in order after Aeson's death. And one of my assistants brought something to my attention. We found applications, dozens of them. None of these ever made it to my desk, mind you. That's how these things go. And Aeson never mentioned it to me, not a word."

"He wouldn't have said anything," said Jason. "He wanted me to be a certain kind of man. Going to charity balls and cocktail parties, marrying the wrong girl from the right family. He was the kind of man who cared about dynasties, and who the right people are, and what the right people think. He wanted me to be that kind of man, just like him. And he wasn't happy with the kind of man I turned out to be."

"He had some pull, your father," said Pelias. "I don't want to speak ill of the dead. It's not something I do. But your applications. Your father didn't want you to be a warrior. He for damned sure didn't want you to be an Argonaut. He wanted the best for you, I'm sure he did. He wanted you in a job that was safe. Prestigious."

"I've got a nice office," said Jason. "And not a single thing to do. I don't even show up most of the time."

"That's the life Aeson chose for you," said Pelias. "When I found out what happened, I wanted you to know. I wanted you to know you weren't being rejected on the merits. Aeson intervened. He had you blackballed, and he made sure the Argonauts kept you out, every time you applied."

Jason went stone silent. He sunk back down into the chair, unsure if he could stay standing if he didn't. He'd spent nearly a decade trying to become one of them. He'd spent long, sleepless nights in study, learning of tactics used in battles long past. He'd spent countless days in training, exhausting himself again and again. He'd dutifully filed his applications, year after year, and each time he'd been more qualified than the last. He'd wanted it more than anything, to be one of the heroes, one of the men everyone in Argos looked up to. It would have made him his own man, the kind he wanted to be, rather than his father's hopeless pawn. He'd wondered why they'd rejected him, no matter how good he'd become. And now he knew he'd been betrayed by the man who was supposed to love him most. It was tearing him apart inside, and it was all he could do to keep his face an emotionless mask and bury it within until he could be alone.

"I'm sorry," said Pelias. "I really am. But you know, Aeson's not here anymore. His word's no longer law. And let me tell you, I'm a man who came up from the bottom myself. I know what it's like to want to prove yourself. To have that burning in your gut that pushes you onward and upward, to grand ambitions and things you thought were beyond you. And I know what it's like to get slapped down in the middle of your climb. I don't want to see that happen to you, Jason. I don't want to see a son sacrifice his dreams at the altar of his father."

"I spent my life training for it," said Jason. He perked up, as some of the venom drained from his father's bite. Maybe Pelias would help him. Maybe his hopes and dreams could live again, after being suppressed for so long. He'd have to prove himself, but he was as ready to do that as he'd ever been. "All I ever wanted is a chance. I train every day, and I have for a decade. I'm good. And I can be better. I want to be the best. I have to be."

"I heard," said Pelias. "I heard about your little showdown in the warehouse."

"We didn't know," said Jason. "What the place was." He knew there was a risk in even talking about it. Hero of the evening he may have been, but the law was the law, and Pelias its arbiter.

"Don't worry about that," said Pelias, with a dismissive wave of his hand. "Legalities are just technicalities, when it comes to men like us. And to be perfectly frank, a little willingness to bend the rules is something of a bonus, if you want to be an Argonaut." He took another sip from his drink, appraising Jason all the while. "What do you know about them? What have you heard?"

"I know what everyone else knows," said Jason. "They're the best. The warrior elite. The last line of defense for Argos against any external threat. Terrorists, hackers, spies. They handle it all."

"That's the P.R. version," said Pelias. "And it's true, after a fashion. But you know, the best defense is a good offense. There's a lot that goes on behind the scenes. The rest of the Big Five are after us every day. It's cutthroat competition to sign up stakeholders, and they'll lie, cheat, steal, or even kill to do it. A lot of what the Argonauts do is protection. That's true. But sometimes if you want to stop the sabotage, you've got to go to the source. Sometimes you've got to kill a snake in its lair."

"In their own cities," said Jason. The truth of his dream hit him, then. The other corporations were laws unto themselves in their homelands. Nominally the government was still the government, with the power to punish kept all to itself. But in any given city, the judges, lawyers, and politicians were all hand-picked by the corporation that dominated it, and their form of justice was blind to any but their masters. Corporate espionage and even sabotage were commonplace, but the penalties were severe, and most who were caught simply disappeared.

"It's dangerous work," said Pelias. "Very dangerous. But necessary. The men who do it are heroes. But heroes have to face great perils, if they want their deeds to be remembered. It's why Aeson didn't want you involved. If you join—if you're interested, that is—you'd have to take on those risks. I'd advise against it, myself. I'm certainly no hero. But every man should get to make his own choices. And if this is what you really want, really and truly, I'll make it happen. As long as you're willing to do what it takes. And if you don't want it anymore, there's no shame in that, either. You've got talent, and I'm happy to find a place that fits you. A subsidiary to run, or maybe overseeing a production line. It's not as exciting, but it's safe."

Jason mulled it over, but only for a moment. He knew what he wanted, and who he wanted to be. His heart was racing; his dream had come true, finally, and all he had to do was say yes. "I'll do anything. It's all I've ever wanted, since I was just a kid. Since I saw them on the vids, and saw how people looked at them. All I've ever wanted to be was an Argonaut."

"That's great," said Pelias. "That's wonderful. Another drink, to toast to good fortune. To toast to you, as one of the Argonauts." He waved to his attendant, and then sat on the edge of his desk, leaning in close towards Jason. "You're going to start with a special assignment. One that comes straight from me. What you did in that warehouse was impressive, and I think you're the only one who can handle this. We had something stolen from us. Something very important. Something that's the key to the future of the Argo Corporation. And I want you to get it back."

"Just show me what it is, and where it is," said Jason. "I'll make it right."

"We'd have to put your shares in trust, of course," said Pelias. "Once you join. I understand you inherited a pretty large bloc from your father. But it causes… issues, if a shareholder dies in the field. And god help us all if you were captured. We can't have someone voting their shares with a gun pointed to their head when we can't even acknowledge what you were up to. It's why Aeson was able to scotch your applications so easily."

"Anything," said Jason. "I'll do anything. All I want is a chance to prove Aeson wrong." He felt manic with energy and triumph. A lifetime of dreams were dangling in front of him, and all he had to do to make them real was reach out and grab them. His father had stopped him from being who he wanted to be, and all in the name of money and shares and class. But none of those mattered now. All that mattered was the dream.

"Perfect," said Pelias, his smile growing wide as he beckoned Jason towards the door. "The shares will be safe in the trust, and we'll take good care of them while you're gone. You'll still own them; you just can't vote them unless you're here in the city. But that's just details. I want you to meet a few people, and then you can all have a talk. About the Argonauts, and what to do now that you're one of them. About the mission you're going to lead, and what it's going to take. About Colchis, and what they've been up to. And most of all, about the Golden Fleece."

CHAPTER FIVE

"HOLD STILL," SAID MEDEA. A little girl sat in her lab, engulfed in a chair designed for hulking warriors a dozen times her size. "This won't hurt. And if you're really, really good, you can have a piece of candy when we're done. I've got Honey Bites...."

The girl was five or six at most, with thin brown pigtails and a blue plastic jumpsuit. She was terrified, and her mother hovered a few feet away, worry written across her face. Medea leaned in towards the girl. She tried to put her at ease, keeping her voice soft and a warm smile on her face. "What's your name? I'm Medea."

"Her name's Macris," said her mother. "She won't talk. She can, but she won't. She's got a stutter. And we can't get rid of it. We've tried everything covered by the Argo Stakeholder Health Plan. We used therapy bots, training vids, even a VR tutor. Nothing worked."

"Well, you came to the right place," said Medea. "Most of the time it's genetic. And if it is, then I can treat it."

"Will she be better?" said the woman. "She's such a nice girl. So friendly. She really is. But only around us. She won't talk to anyone outside the family. It hurts so much. We're the only ones who can see the person she really is."

"Let me take a look," said Medea. "But if it's something in her genes, I promise you we'll take it out before she leaves the lab. She'll be talking just like anyone else. Won't you?"

Macris just buried her head in her shoulder, trying to hide herself away from everything around. But Medea didn't take any offense. It was a strange environment for a little girl, and she was a stranger. She pulled a tube from the arm of the chair, gently pressing a needle into the girl's skin. She gasped, but otherwise kept avoiding Medea's eyes. A little stream of blood flowed through it, and the lab's computers began analyzing the girl's code. Errors popped up all across the screen, bugs in the part of her code that handled linguistic processing. But they were common ones. They wouldn't take much work to fix. All Medea had to do was customize a little patch to her code, put it inside her, and the girl would be speaking normally in just a few minutes.

She got to work at once, leaving Macris's mother to comfort her and keep her still. Medea sat at her desk, tapping away at a tablet and programming the fix that would patch the girl's genetic code and melt away the stutter she'd been plagued with. She took the errors one at a time, checking each one off in turn and making sure that everything would be perfect once her work was done.

A line of photos ran across the wall behind her desk, watching over her as she worked. They were of a couple, a woman with dark black hair and a few wrinkles around her eyes and a man with a comforting smile and specks of grey. Her parents. In one photo they glided over a city with thin plastic wings attached to their backs, in another they stood smiling over Medea herself as a child, unwrapping boxes full of gifts. They were both long gone, but she wanted a piece of them there with her in her lab. Where she could think about them, and where she could keep them alive in her memories.

They were why she was here, after all. She'd lost them while she was young, but not without a fight. Nature had kept trying to snatch them away from her, and genomancy had kept giving them back. And now there was another little girl in front of her, a victim of the instructions in her own genetic code just as much as her parents had been.

She finished with the last error, and with a tap of a button on her tablet the code was ready. She walked back to the girl and her mother, gently inserting a nutrient tube into the girl's other arm. Then she put a hand on her shoulder and whispered into her ear. "This won't hurt. Just hold your mommy's hand, and close your eyes. And when you open them back up, you'll be able to talk just like all the other kids. Just like everyone else."

The girl pressed her eyes shut, clinging to her mother for dear life. Chemicals flowed into her, and blood flowed out. The girl cried, but only a little, and only out of fear. Medea's tablet flashed green, and everything was over in no more than a minute.

"Okay," said Medea, disconnecting the tubes. "You can talk now. Try saying something, and let's see how it comes out."

"Say thank you," said her mother. "Thank you."

Macris scrunched up her face in a pout, her eyes pointed to the floor. Her mother leaned in close, whispering into her ear, and after a few more seconds of stalling she muttered something quietly to herself.

"Thank," said Macris. "Thank. Thank." The words came out clean, and she looked up at Medea with shock in her eyes and a wide smile on her face. "Thank you." She leapt from her chair and hugged Medea's leg, wrapping her arms tightly around her. Then she let go, racing around the lab chasing a small toaster-shaped robot and chattering loud, fully formed words as she went.

"It worked," said the woman. "I can't believe it worked."

"I'm glad," said Medea. "I'm really glad. There shouldn't be any problems. She should be fine, for the rest of her life. Just like she never stuttered at all."

"Do we owe anything?" said the woman hesitantly. "We're stakeholders. We have what the company gives us. But we don't have much else."

"You don't owe me a thing," said Medea. "I do this for free. As much as I can. I'm paying forward a debt of my own. Just promise me you'll help someone else if you ever get a chance."

"We will," said the woman. "Both of us."

The two of them waved goodbye, Macris shouting her farewells at the top of her lungs as she ran away down the hall. It made Medea smile, and made her feel warm all over. This wasn't part of her job, not technically. She'd negotiated a special deal: so long as she did the work the corporation wanted, the lab was hers to use as she pleased for charity work. Charity didn't pay, but it was worth it for how it made her feel. Macris's life was changed forever, and she was the one who'd made it happen.

Her patient gone, she went back to working on what the Argo Corporation wanted her to: enhancing the code for their warriors, and giving them whatever new skills she could. It was interesting in its own way, and she wouldn't trade her job for anything. She only wished she could spend more time on people who needed help, and less on the ones who only wanted an edge in their battles. But what paid the bills was what paid the bills, so she sat back down at her desk, humming a little tune to herself and hacking away at the code for some warrior's reflexes.

She was well into her the project when a sound from behind her interrupted her work. She heard boots stomping down the hall, and men shouting ahead of them. Soon warriors appeared in the doorway, rolling a man on a gurney into her lab. He was screaming and writhing against his restraints, lost in a panic he couldn't control. His arms were strapped into place, and scratch marks from his fingernails covered his face. What was left of his face, at least.

Something had happened to him, something awful.

Something had happened to his eyes.

His eyelids looked like puffy tumors grown wild atop his head. They were sealed firmly shut, but the tissue beneath them had swelled in size, two pink globs quivering where his eyes had once been. Three men accompanied him, rushing him to her lab for lack of any better idea of what to do. The pain had rendered him incoherent. No matter what they said, he just shrieked and wailed, and there was nothing they could do to calm him down.

"He needs help," shouted one of the men. "Something's gone wrong with his genes."

Medea dropped her tablet on her desk and rushed to his side. "Bring him in," she said, as she urgently summoned machines from all around the lab. A half-dozen of them rolled towards the injured man, and with a few commands they went into action, taking blood samples and jabbing him with painkillers. He kept screaming for a few more seconds before heaving upward with a heavy gasp. Then he lapsed into unconsciousness, his head lolling over as the noise finally stopped.

"What happened?" said Medea. She shined a miniature flashlight at his eyelids, searching for clues as to the cause. "What the hell happened to him?"

"You happened," said one of the men. "You and your sorcery. He was fine. Perfectly fine. And then you went and ruined his eyes."

She knew the man who spoke.

Idas.

He wore the uniform of the Argonauts, a form-fitting black material that looked like nylon but was hard enough to stop a bullet. His hair was dark, and his face was covered in days worth of stubble. There were scars beneath it, little white slashes from battles past. He could have gotten rid of them with ease, but they were trophies of war, and so he was proud to bear them. Strapped to his back was a long spear made of what looked like blackened wood, tipped with a sharp bronze point. But looks were deceiving: the wood was just more metal, an alloy from the Argo labs that could shred through steel. Idas had a reputation for viciousness that was unusual even among the warriors. And now his angry glare was fixed firmly on her.

"I didn't do this," said Medea. She was flustered, stung by the accusation. She knew it couldn't have been her. Something like this had never happened, not to someone she'd worked on. And she didn't know if she could handle it if it ever did. She closed her eyes, centering herself, and then turned back to inspecting the man's wounds. "I don't even know what this is. I need time to think. I need data."

"You said you'd give him sight," said Idas. "You said he'd see through walls. Through the ground. That he could see for miles away." He moved closer and closer, and by the time she looked up he was in her face, her back pressed against the gurney. It scared her, the way his eyes had turned to fire. She felt his hand grab her arm, locking her into place. She looked to the men who'd come with him, casting about for help, but they both just turned away. She knew he could kill her if he wanted to, and there was nothing and no one who could stop him. He was just inches from her, snapping and snarling. "He never should have trusted a woman. That was his mistake. You said you'd make him better. You sold him on this. And now look what you did."

His words triggered something in her memory, and she recognized the man on the gurney. His name was Lynceus, Idas's brother. He'd come to her and asked for the procedure, something to help him angle for his next promotion. Some skill to set him apart from all the rest, and get him assigned to missions the others couldn't handle. There were always options for those willing to be guinea pigs. The Argonauts needed new abilities, whatever their genes could provide, but someone had to test them first. She'd been the one who'd changed his genes, and changed his eyes. Maybe Idas was right. Maybe she had done this to him. Maybe it was all her fault.

"Let me look at his code," said Medea, as softly as she could, trying to soothe the savage beast. "Let me find out what's wrong."

Idas tightened his grip. Pain stabbed through her arm, and she felt like he was about to jerk her shoulder from its socket. She let out a cry despite herself, and he seemed to think better of whatever he'd planned to do, dropping her arm with an exaggerated wave of his hand.

"Fix him," said Idas. "Fix him, or I'll fix you."

She went to work at once. Lynceus was out, and at least he couldn't injure himself any further. "Autodoc," she shouted, and a bulky white machine the size of a refrigerator detached itself from one of the walls, zipping across the room and taking up a position beside her. "Patient," she said, pointing at Lynceus, and the machine moved itself into place next to the gurney. Its sides split open, revealing a centipede's worth of thin, spindly metal arms inside. Each had its own tool attached: some tipped with scanners, some with syringes, and others with scalpels. It probed at him, identifying the injury within seconds, and then a flurry of arms applied a careful series of injections, compresses, and bandages around his swollen eyes.

Medea herself was no doctor, but she didn't need to be. They were mostly obsolete, a withered profession with only a few specialists left to handle the toughest of cases. A sheath could diagnose virtually anything by monitoring the vital signs of its bearer. It could even take a blood sample with the prick of a hidden needle, performing a battery of tests on a daily basis. And once a problem was known, machines could handle all the rest, from surgeries to setting broken bones to dispensing prescriptions. Only genes were still the province of humans, and a well-stocked genomancer was as good as any hospital, so long as she had machines at her side.

She left the autodoc to tend to its patient while she went back to what she did best: going through his genetic code, and finding out what had happened to it. It was like a puzzle for her, and it was what she liked most about her trade. She could stare at the screen for hours, absorbed by the possible combinations, seeing what worked and what didn't. His code was familiar; she'd tailored it herself. It all looked fine at first, though she knew it wasn't. But she was fastidious about keeping copies of any version of anyone's code she'd ever worked on. She instructed the computers to compare his code to the version from when he'd last left her lab, and she didn't like the results one bit.

"Something's wrong," said Medea. "Something happened to him. Something changed my work. Where was he when this started?"

"Scouting mission," said Idas. "Outskirts of Colchis. Your hometown." That last bit came with extra emphasis, and a note of suspicion. She'd left there years before, recruited away by promises of more autonomy and better pay. Colchis would always be home, but she'd wanted her own lab, and she'd wanted harder problems to tackle. Most of the procedures she'd done back in Colchis had been minor and cosmetic, easy, by-the-book work that even an apprentice could have handled.

But in Argos, they wanted her to push the envelope, and every patient was a puzzle. Here, they let her spend her time however she wanted. If she did her job for the warriors, they didn't care if she spent the rest of her time working on people who couldn't afford the changes they needed to their DNA.

It made jumping ship an easy choice. To her, a corporation was just a corporation, and it didn't matter which one she worked for so long as they gave her a challenge and let her help people. But for others an enemy was an enemy, and she didn't think this was the time to explain that not everyone had a sense of loyalty to the corporations they served.

Medea pored over the computer screens, looking for any oddities in Lynceus's genetic code, anything that might explain what had gone wrong. She checked the new against the old, and she saw the problem at once. "His code isn't the same as the last time I saw him. Something's different."

"That was the point, right?" said Idas. "He was supposed to be different. He was supposed to see the enemy from miles away. That's what you promised."

"His code is going haywire," said Medea. "Look. You don't need to be a genomancer to see it." She pressed her fingers against the screen of her sheath, and the wall lit up with a projection of a segment of Lynceus's genetic code. But it was off, even to the untrained eye. It kept rearranging its structure, the segments moving from place to place. "It's not stable, not from one minute to the next. It's changing. Mutating on the fly. Rejecting the code I put in. Tell me what happened. If you ever want him to see again, tell me what happened."

"Minor attack," said Idas gruffly. "The drones. He couldn't see enough detail, so we went in for a better look. We got too close and dodged a missile. It was nothing. Just a bit of shrapnel." He pointed to Lynceus's hand. There was a little red scratch mark running across the back of it, looking no worse than if he'd encountered a housecat.

"They did something to him," said Medea. "They infected him with something. Look at the way it's moving. Look at—" She felt a hand at her throat, and she choked for air. Idas was in no mood for talk. He pulled her away from her workstation and lifted her off the ground, her toes dangling inches from the floor.

"You did something to him," said Idas. "You made him this way. And if you let him die, I'm going to kill you next." He dropped her onto the ground, coughing and struggling to catch her breath. He swept his hand across a nearby counter, shattering a row of vials into a foaming pool of chemicals and glass, then stormed out of the lab followed by the others. She was left alone, just her, her patient, and his ruined eyes.

She didn't even know where to start. She ran through the possibilities in her head: chemicals, a virus, some kind of injection. Or maybe it had been her, and somehow she'd botched the code. Maybe he was going to die because of some error in her work she couldn't even see. She breathed in, breathed out, and forced the thoughts away so she could focus on what really counted: finding out what was wrong with him and fixing it.

She hooked him up to a nutrient drip, with strict limits on its contents. Enough to keep him alive, but not enough to let his warped code send his body off into a spiral of uncontrolled mutations. Then she started working, letting herself be absorbed by the problem and shutting out thoughts of anything else. Time went away as she catalogued change after change, searching for some clue as to what had been done to him. It could have been minutes or hours before she heard something interrupting her, yanking her out of her trance.

"Here she is," said a voice from behind her.

She didn't even look up. She was too focused on her work, staring down at the DNA on her tablet and matching pair with pair, trying to find the solution that would stabilize his code. She called out a response behind her, more irritated at the men's threats than afraid of them. "I'm not going to let him die. He's stable. And I can make him better. It's just going to take time. A long time. A month, maybe. But he'll be fine until then. So cut the crap, stop blaming me, and get the hell out of my lab."

"She's moody," said the voice. "Geniuses usually are. The things we tolerate in the name of progress."

Her ears went red. More insults, more threats, and more condescension. It was the warrior way when dealing with women, and she had no patience for it now. "I said get the hell out of my lab," said Medea, whipping around with an irritated scowl on her face. "Now move, before I—"

Her stomach dropped when she saw him, standing there next to one of his aides. She knew who he was at once, though she'd never met him: Pelias, a man who could fire her or promote her on a whim. He was all over the news, his every decision feted for its foresight and its business acumen. He was the face of the Argo Corporation, and suddenly his attentions had been focused on her. And sitting behind her on the gurney was a man who'd gone from warrior to invalid, after only a single session in her lab.

"Medea!" said Pelias, approaching her with a plastic smile and an overly enthusiastic hug. "I've heard such great things. Such wonderful things, about the work you're doing. About what an asset you are to the Argo Corporation." He tilted his head, taking in Lynceus and his injuries. "Although we can't always be perfect, I suppose."

"There was some kind of attack," said Medea, stuttering out the words. "Some kind of—"

"Details," said Pelias. "I'm just here to let you know we'll be introducing you to someone. The newest Argonaut. He's a VIP, and I want you to take care of him." He gave Lynceus a second look, and shot her a condescending smile. "No mistakes. Not with this one. You can handle that, can't you?"

"I—" said Medea.

"Of course you can," said Pelias. "In fact, with skills like this, you're perfect for what I have in mind. Amphion here will fill you in on the details. I'm off to bigger and better things. Take care of our new recruit, and I'll take care of you." He was gone before she could sputter out a response, with Amphion left there in his stead.

"We're going to be changing your duties," said Amphion. "Just a little." He looked behind him to the sound of footsteps from the hallway. "But first let's make the introductions. Medea. I'd like you to meet Jason."

A man strode into the lab, tall, muscular, with jet black hair and intense green eyes, reaching out to shake her hand with a firm grip. She could tell he was a shareholder with nothing more than a glance. She knew people better than anyone, inside and out, and shareholders had an air of entitlement to them no matter how they tried to hide it. He said it with his posture, his chest out when he walked, his chin up no matter where he looked. He said it with his eyes, the way he met her gaze, and the way she felt compelled to look away when he did. And he said it with his smile, pure confidence with not a hint in it that anyone had ever challenged him and won. It was the body language of a man who got what he wanted, when he wanted it, and wouldn't tolerate things any other way.

"Hi," said Medea, stumbling over one of the robots as she scrambled to make herself presentable, arranging her tools and pushing her hair into place. "I mean, hello. I mean, welcome." She could barely keep herself together. Pelias had stretched her nerves to the breaking point, and now here was some VIP shareholder to look over her shoulder as well. It didn't help that she thought he was handsome, though the important ones usually were. And he'd come at the worst possible time, with a wounded victim of genomancy splayed out on her table.

"Medea's our top genomancer," said Amphion. "One of the best. Although you wouldn't know it from appearances." He raised an eyebrow at Lynceus. "But it's not just what she can do in the lab that brings us here. It's where she's from. She's something of a defector. From Colchis."

"Colchis," said Jason. She couldn't help but sneak a peek downward as he spoke. He wore the form-fitting uniform of an Argonaut, and his was a perfect form. The suit left little to the imagination, though it certainly prompted her own imagination to wander.

"I was born there," said Medea. "I trained there. Then my non-compete ran out, and Argos started recruiting me. They went all out. They offered me double my pay, and my own lab. I couldn't say no."

"She knows their systems," said Amphion. "She knows how they work. She knows the city. She's under contract not to talk about it. But there aren't any other Colchians here to say anything if she does, are there?"

"The Fleece," said Jason. "What I really want to know is whatever you can tell me about the Golden Fleece."

"Never even heard of it," said Medea.

"You wouldn't have," said Amphion. "It's the codename for something the Colchians have been working on. Secret stuff. A vast database of genetic code they can use however they see fit. They call the computer that houses it the Fleece. But it's not their own data inside. They've stolen some of ours, and they're keeping it there. All the genetic code, from all of our stakeholders. And we want it back."

"Why?" said Jason. "Why steal our code? Why not just use their own?"

"Entertainment," said Medea. She drew a quizzical look from Jason, and a look of respect from Amphion.

"Go on," said Amphion.

"You've heard of their shows," said Medea. "Maybe even seen them. You're a shareholder. You can afford to go out-network for whatever you want. How do you think they find the people to go on 'My Secret Bastard Child,' or 'My Ancestor's Dirty Laundry?' And their dramas, especially the historicals. How do you think the actors look so real, sound so real? They've been reconstructing the code for everyone of significance since the beginning of time, snippet by snippet. If you had progeny, Colchis has pieces of you, and it's all about putting them together. The more sources the better. And every person's code could have a mutation they can use for something. It's like one big scavenger hunt."

"Smart girl," said Amphion. "The code has value. The more you have, the more it's worth. Half the Argonauts are trying to guard our own code, and the other half are off trying to steal from everyone else. That's where the Golden Fleece comes in. They've got our data, and we need you to figure out a way to get it back."

"Black ops," said Jason, shaking his head. "Not what I had in mind when I wanted to be a hero."

"You're an Argonaut," said Amphion. "Heroism is nice, but it's mostly for publicity. This part is the real deal. You want to get up on that stage, get ready to do a few dirty deeds first."

Jason paused, and then nodded to Medea. "I'm going to want to debrief her. Figure out everything I can before we leave."

"Of course," said Amphion. "But we were thinking something else." He looked back and forth between the two with a mischievous smile. "We were thinking she'd go with you."

"Me?" said Medea, stunned.

"Her?" said Jason indignantly. "I'm not taking her out in the field. Look at this guy's eyes. I talked to some of the men out there. They called her 'Mad Medea.' They said she did this. They said everyone's afraid to have her work on them."

She wanted to slap him, along with Idas and whoever else had been attacking her behind her back. The handsome ones were always the entitled ones, though she'd hoped he might be different. All the warriors ever did was posture and bluster, and they couldn't turn it off for even a moment. The entire idea of her going off on some mission was out of left field. She'd thought about being one of them, once. They made more money than a genomancer, and they certainly got more respect. But she wasn't designed for fighting, and she wasn't willing to make the dramatic changes to her body it would take to bring her up to par. Still, what she did was indispensable, even if she never got any credit for it. She was tired of the warriors' abuse and their name-calling, and she wasn't going to put up with it from some child of privilege she didn't even know.

"I didn't do this to him," said Medea brusquely. "Someone in Colchis did. So you can go out there and play hero, and you can spit all over me in my own lab, but don't expect me to fix you up when you come back looking like he does."

"Look," said Jason. "Maybe you're as good as you say." He looked over at Lynceus again, and at his swollen eyes. "Maybe not. I'm just telling you what I heard. But I can't have a team that doesn't mesh. We're going to be in the field. You're a lab geek. You can't cut it out there. We'll take whatever help you can give us, but we can't take you."

"Who said I wanted to go with you?" said Medea. "I've got more important things to do back here. Sneer all you want. You need me, even if you won't admit it. Warriors can't win their battles without a good genomancer at their backs."

"I'm entirely unmodified," said Jason, stiffening as he spoke. "I win my battles on my own. Genomancy is a cheat, and I don't need my own personal Dr. Frankenstein. No sorcery, no tricks, no crutches. Just me."

"No crutches?" said Medea. "You haven't even been an Argonaut for a day and suddenly you're leading a mission? Your money and your family had nothing to do with that?" It was a low blow, and she knew it, but if he couldn't offer an ounce of respect for her or for the profession she'd dedicated her life to, she didn't owe him a thing in return. He looked exceedingly angry, but before he could offer a retort Amphion stepped between the two of them.

"Boys and girls," said Amphion. "The matter's already decided, and neither of you have a choice. This comes from up top. We have a mission to think about. An important one. Jason's new, but that's precisely why we chose him. The Colchians know ninety percent of our current operatives.

Jason isn't even on their radar. They won't know what to do with him. And Medea, you know their city better than anyone else we have. You're both necessary, you're both going, and that's that."

"Pelias said I was going to be in charge," said Jason. "I want to pick my own team."

"That's not how this works," said Amphion. "You're an Argonaut now. Sometimes you have to follow orders. And we have other things to consider. Politics, you understand. She has to go. You have to go. That's that. The rest are up to you. You'll need warriors. And you'll need a pilot. Sneaking inside Colchis is going to be rough. But we've got something set up for you. An experimental vehicle. One that'll get you past their defenses."

"The pilot part's easy," said Jason. "I've got one in mind, a drone pilot I know. For the warriors, I'm going to want to do some interviews. I want dedicated people. The best, and only the best."

"You can have your pilot if you want him," said Amphion. "But you two need to talk to someone else first. About how to find the Fleece, and about who else to take with you. The two of you are non-negotiable. Your friend, that's up to you. But if you're going to pick, you need to understand how we do things. I don't make the choices, and the warriors don't make the choices. What we do is talk to one of the seers. So go down into the barracks, listen to their prophecy, and if you're smart, you'll make damned sure you follow what they say to the letter."

CHAPTER SIX

"**Y**OU WON'T MAKE IT BACK," said Mopsus, without a trace of emotion in his voice. "You're going to die. Probably on the outskirts of Colchis. Maybe inside the city itself. But you'll never see the Fleece. You'll never even get close."

They kept him away in a corner of the barracks, down in an office far from foot traffic. It looked more cave than workspace, dark and grimy with discarded circuitry and junk electronics piled all around. Stacked atop the piles were dozens of bird cages, and inside his only true companions: a mixed flock of parakeets, doves, and even an old, glowering crow. Some were covered to keep them asleep, while others were squawking away in a discordant chorus. Their smell permeated the room, but he didn't even notice it anymore. It was a hermit's hole, little visited by anyone else. Mopsus was a seer, and the gift of prophecy never came without a curse: his fellow men feared him, and the things he'd say to them, and they did their best to keep their distance.

His appearance did nothing to help matters. His greying hair was scraggly and loose, and it hadn't seen a comb in years. His eyes were pure white, making him look as if he were blind. In truth, it was simply his contacts; they covered his eyes while he read signs from the Argo databases, and they turned back to brown when he needed to see the present instead of the future. The back of his neck was all metal, a cybernetic implant whose thin wires snaked upward into his skull, with lights flashing different colors as the data flowed through it. The implant gave him his second sight, a direct link into the networks that fed him a streaming analysis of the vast stores of information held inside the Argo computer systems.

"You're going to die," repeated Mopsus. "It may not be what you want to hear, but it's what the data says. Any seer worth his salt would say the same."

He sat in a chair, tapping his fingers restlessly against his desk and peeking out at Jason and Medea from behind the piles of junk. He was visibly nervous, less at the prospect of their impending doom and more at the prospect of an extended conversation with them. Social interactions were something he couldn't predict and couldn't control, and they weren't something he had much experience with.

"We came here for help, and for advice," said Jason. "For suggestions on who to take with us. Not for horoscopes and superstitions."

"It's data, and it's science," insisted Mopsus. "You can predict most anything when you know every minute of a person's day. We know the routines of billions of people. Where they'll go, what they'll do, who they'll talk to. We know their interests, their relationships, their backgrounds, their blood. We know when they're angry, or sad, or happy. We know everything. And I'm sure you won't make it. You just won't. The odds are too slim."

"Then change them," said Jason. "Tell us what we do to change the odds."

"Hrmm," said Mopsus. "Tall order. No promises." His eyes flashed white and he flopped back into his chair, his mouth hanging wide open as he descended into a trance. He stayed inside himself for an uncomfortable few minutes, the birds growing more and more agitated the longer he was out. Suddenly his eyes popped open and he rubbed at them with his hands, blinking until he could see the world once more.

"Can someone go in your stead?" said Mopsus. "Perhaps if we realign things. If we keep one of you here, it could change the entire scenario."

"I'll stay," said Medea. "I'm happy to, actually. For the good of your mission."

"Both of us have to go," said Jason. "Non-negotiable. Believe me, I tried." Medea shot him a glare, but he didn't take the bait.

"Both of you," said Mopsus. "Hrmm." He opened one of the cages, placing his hand inside and allowing a little white dove to hop onto his finger. He held it before him, then dozed back into his trance and back to the uncomfortable wait. "Chirp, chirp," said Mopsus, to no one in particular. "Chirp, chirp."

"Is he talking to us?" said Medea. His eyes were still a cloudy white haze, and he didn't seem to hear.

"The bird, I think," said Jason.

"Antaeus," muttered Mopsus from his trance. "You'll want to take Antaeus. The odds are better that way. Not by much, but better."

"I know him," said Medea. "He's ambitious. Not very smart. But he's pretty dangerous now, from what I hear. I rewrote his code myself."

"Your friend, the pilot," said Mopsus. "A wild card. But there's no better choice, not that I can see."

"And I trust him," said Jason. "I need someone I can trust."

"Let her work on him," said Mopsus. "Don't let him say no. If she works her magic on him, your chance of survival goes up. A percentage point, maybe two. Every little bit counts."

"I don't like it," said Jason. "He needs his eyes to be a pilot."

"I told you—" said Medea, her voice rising to an angry pitch. The birds began to screech at the disturbance, and she leaned in towards Jason and dropped down to a whisper. "I told you that wasn't me. I check my work dozens of times for every patient. Then the software checks it all again. And I keep records of everything I did. His code is completely different from when he left my lab. Whatever happened to his eyes, it wasn't me." She couldn't help but glance at the muscles tensing all along Jason's body as she spoke. She knew he was spoiling for a fight, but she didn't care. If he wanted to be an ass, better to have it all out in the open.

"And I told you," said Jason. "I pushed to have you booted from this thing. I pushed hard. You're a liability, and you've got no place in the field. You'll get yourself killed, and the rest of us, too. War is for warriors. Any talent that gets injected with a needle isn't real talent. And people who rely on cheap tricks forget how to rely on themselves."

"Your pilot needs the expertise," said Mopsus. "He needs the talents she can give him. Swallow your pride. You won't succeed without her."

"I can make an expert out of anyone," said Medea. "As long as he doesn't think he's too good for my work." She tried another glare at Jason, but still he just ignored it. It only irritated her more that she couldn't irritate him, but that was the warrior way. They seemed to practice getting under other people's skins just as much as they practiced for battle.

"The others you should take, that's hazy," said Mopsus. "Chirp, chirp. The vid schedules. That determines the traffic. Who's going to be outside, who you might encounter. Can narrow that down to a few thousand Colchians at any given moment. Who's a threat? Lots of variables. Hobbies.

Political affiliation. Daily routine. Wish we had more of their data to look at, but we've got to go with what's public. Hrmm."

"Just tell us what you can," said Jason. "We'll make our own destiny. No matter what the data says."

"You won't like this one," said Mopsus. "No, you won't. You have to take someone you won't like, and someone who won't like you. Idas."

"No chance," said Medea. "The guy's an asshole. And his brother's still upstairs unconscious. If I leave Argos without fixing him, he'll kill me for sure."

"No other way," said Mopsus. "No Idas, no way you succeed. I'm just telling you what it says. And one more. Hrmm. Oh, my." His face crinkled into a confused, nervous squinch as he saw something in the networks. "The data doesn't lie. Parse it however you want, but it doesn't lie."

"What does it say?" said Jason.

"It says you'll live," said Mopsus. "Everything's changing. It's all coming together, now that we've got your team. One more member, and the puzzle seems to have solved itself. But I still don't like it, not one bit."

"Who?" said Jason. "Just tell us who."

"Me," said Mopsus. "You have to take me."

His eyes flipped back to brown, and his finger shook beneath the dove. "Shouldn't have to leave, chirp, chirp. Shouldn't be me." The bird started to flap, jumping from his finger and circling the room until it landed on Medea's shoulder. She held out her finger, gently, letting it hop onto its new perch before carefully reaching across the desk and handing it back to Mopsus.

"What's his name?" said Medea.

"Chirp," said Mopsus. "All of their names are Chirp."

"Does Chirp have anything to say about how we're supposed to find the Golden Fleece?" said Jason. "Or what it even looks like? We're not operating on much. All they told us was to talk to you."

"We start with Phineus," said Mopsus. "Go get your pilot. Let her change his genes, however they need to change. By the time you're back, we'll have things ready. Then all you have to do is get us into Colchis. Get us there, and we'll talk to Phineus. He'll tell us where it is. And everything will fall into place from there. The data doesn't lie."

"Who's Phineus?" said Jason. "And what's he got to do with the Fleece?"

"Chirp, chirp," said Mopsus, his eyes gone white again. "Go get the pilot. The rest of us will be here waiting."

They left him to his birds and headed down the hall into the barracks proper. It was a massive open space, a cross between a locker room and a gym. Warriors were all around, practicing and training until their next mission arrived. Robotic sparring partners were scattered about, looming up towards the ceiling. There was ample room nearby to safely swing weapons at them, and a few of the warriors were slashing with their spears at a spiky grey automaton, dodging whips of iron that snapped at them from its sides.

"What now, fearless leader?" said Medea. "I'm still happy to stay behind, but I won't have a job if I do." Or worse. She'd thought about just heading off to her apartment and never coming back. But she knew they could cancel her contract if they really wanted to. Kick her out of house and home. She might get a job at one of the minor corporations, but they could make her persona non grata at any of the Big Five without much effort. One defection would raise eyebrows; leaving such a sensitive role at two major corporations would be a black mark she'd never recover from. They had her where they wanted her, and she knew it.

"We do what he said," said Jason. "Get whatever you need, and we'll go talk to my friend, Tiphys. He's already a little bit of a freak, so you probably can't make him much worse. But you need to know. If you mess him up like the one in your lab, you'll answer to me."

"I've never messed anyone up," said Medea. "And I'm not sure how you dislike me so much when you don't even know me."

"It's not a matter of whether I like you," said Jason. "I don't like what you do. Turning people into things so they can win a fight they couldn't handle on their own." Disgust flashed across his face, and his hand balled into a fist involuntarily. "It's cheating. What's the point of risking your life to be a hero if you didn't really do it yourself? It changes something pure into something cheap. There's a code to being a warrior, and people like you throw it out the window."

"That heroism stuff is all public relations," said Medea. "Look around you. Do you see anyone famous in here?" He scanned the room, going from face to face. She was right. The trainees were mostly raw recruits, and not a single one had made the vids, not even for a minor skirmish. "They stop being warriors the second the cameras find them. None of them fight anymore, not once they've got it made. They stop being Argonauts and start being celebrities."

"Let's just go," said Jason. "Let's go find Tiphys and get him ready."

"I need some things from my lab," said Medea. "Then we'll see if your friend is as pleasant as you are."

They started back towards the elevator, giving the training areas a wide berth as the robotic weapons sliced through the air. As they went, Medea could feel her sheath insistently vibrating against her wrist, a sure sign of a message she'd want to receive at once. She snuck a peek at the screen, turning away to read it with a glance. It was a simple text, but one that made her stomach drop when she saw the source. The name blared a bright red across her arm and flashed on and off, from a sender that no one with any sense would ignore.

Aphrodite.

She pressed her finger against the sheath's screen, tense with anticipation as she did. She couldn't help herself from shaking, trying as best she could to hide her thoughts as the words formed and she read them to herself in silence.

"Love is coming soon, and when you least expect it."

CHAPTER SEVEN

THEY'D GONE HALFWAY ACROSS THE city to find Jason's friend, and Medea's mind had whirled the entire trip. She couldn't think of anything but the message, wondering what Aphrodite had seen, what sign in the digital entrails she'd seized upon before dropping the prophecy in her lap. It couldn't be right, but then, they were virtually never wrong.

They were named after gods, and they had a god's mystique, their words striking like a bolt of lightning from above with omens of things to come. But in truth they were mere software, artificial intelligence programs with a knack for anticipating future human behavior. They were simplified versions of the seers, and they'd long been a selling point for signing up new stakeholders. Predictive A.I.'s scoured reams of data from everyone in the city, drew what conclusions they could, and packaged the results into neat little fortune cookies personalized to the recipient.

It was part of why data was so valuable, and why the Big Five would give away anything and everything to get a stakeholder to sign theirs over. The wrist sheaths collected everything: where people went, what they did, what entertainment they watched, and who they spoke to. They monitored their blood pressure, their breathing, their heartbeats, their slightest movements. It was all logged, every minute of every day, everything a stakeholder had ever done while their contracts were in force. And the A.I. could access it all.

Aphrodite knew it all, and could consider it all, from Medea and from everyone around her. The software had logged her habits, and habits were most of who she was, most of who anyone was. They were what she'd done before, and what she'd do again, barring the unknown. Aphrodite was well known for her accuracy when it came to matters of love. There were signs when a match was about to be made, signs in the data that only she could read. They could be subtle, but they were there: changes in body temperature when others came into the room, subconscious alterations to a pair's routines that "happened" to bring them closer together, or even sudden purchases of lipsticks or perfumes. For those who wanted to know, the A.I. would act as soothsayer, warning them of pitfalls and guiding them towards blessings instead.

The only question in Medea's mind now was who. It could be anyone who'd triggered the message: Idas, Pelias, Jason, or gods forbid, even Mopsus. She cringed at the thought. He was nice enough, but all those birds.... The gods were infuriatingly vague in their predictions, but that was partly why they were so accurate. And maybe it was someone else. Maybe someone she hadn't even met.

Her thoughts were interrupted by their arrival at an apartment door, coupled with shouting and banging from Jason. "Open up!" He stood there in the hallway with Medea in tow, a squat spherical robot dutifully following along behind her. The building was beyond posh, though the rent was no more than a fraction of a paycheck. Modernist paintings lined the hallways, and everything had a sleek design, all the edges rounded away into smooth curves. The halls were pristine, tended to by their own army of tiny robotic janitors. A spider-like machine crawled along the ceiling, a light bulb dangling from one of its legs as it went about its maintenance routine.

It was luxury for the masses, and anyone with a job could afford it. As cheap as it was, the rent was beyond the means of the stakeholders, but so was anything the corporation didn't provide for free. Even in an age of abundance, there was only so much prime real estate to go around. The Argo Corporation dealt with such scarcities in the traditional manner: putting a price on things, and raising it until the demand matched the supply.

"Open the door," shouted Jason, banging on it again and again.

"I thought you guys were close," said Medea. "He doesn't seem to want to talk."

"He's probably in his VR pod, or binge watching some vid channel," said Jason. "He'll talk. Eventually. We've known each other since we were six."

"Another rich kid," said Medea. "I've got enough on my hands dealing with one of you."

"Try again," said Jason. "His family wasn't rich. They were all stake-holders. But he played outside, and so did I. You hung out with whoever you could, if you were one of the few kids who actually left your apartment. We weren't even that much alike. But he attracted a lot of bullies, and I liked getting in fights with bullies. A perfect match."

He kept pounding away at the door for another minute before they heard a muffled shout from the apartment. A few moments later and the door swung open, revealing a man standing awkwardly behind it: Tiphys, unshaven and wearing a white undershirt covered in fingerprints of orange dust. In his hand was a bag of processed snacks he'd been abusing, and he looked surprised and more than a little embarrassed to see them.

Medea's stomach churned at the sight of him. If this was the man Aphrodite saw in her future, she could go stuff herself. His eyes couldn't even meet hers, and while he might have been perfectly nice, his every movement screamed timidity. He was thin, gangly, and awkward, and nowhere near her type. She knew the A.I. could often see things a human couldn't. But if it saw something here, it had more than a few of its wires crossed.

"I can't talk," said Tiphys. "I'm working." He jerked a thumb behind him, towards a massive white wall with a rolling chair in front of it. The chair looked exceedingly comfortable, a cushy black leather sanctuary, and the only thing separating it from some executive's office was a VR helmet strapped to the top. On the wall were dozens of projected video feeds, mostly of clear blue sky, though a few showed buildings flashing past. They were streaming from cameras attached to drones flying across the city, and Tiphys was pilot for them all.

"Work can wait," said Jason, pushing his way into the apartment. "Don't you want to hear where I've been?"

"Not in jail?" said Tiphys.

"Not in jail," said Jason. "I've been talking to Pelias."

"Pelias," said Tiphys. He blinked, lost in a dazed stupor. He looked to Medea, standing behind Jason. Then he was back in his daze just as quickly. "Her," said Tiphys. He ogled her up and down, eyes agog as he took her in. "He gave you her?"

"Don't be stupid," said Medea.

"Don't be an asshole," said Jason.

"Come in, I guess," said Tiphys, recovering himself. He rushed off into a bathroom, emerging with a few towels and tossing them atop a pile of assorted junk in a corner. "Sorry. It's a mess, but I keep that side off limits to the bots. They'll just take things if I don't. They think everything's trash." Maybe it was and maybe it wasn't, but the result was an odd contrast: one half of the apartment sparkling clean, patrolled by an army of tiny janitors, the other half a disaster of a bachelor pad that was ever creeping against its border.

"Nice setup," said Medea, nodding towards his workstation.

"It's pretty awesome," said Tiphys. "Thirty simultaneous screens. Thirty drones, making deliveries all over the city, and I'm piloting every one of them." He pulled a few fluffy orange crackers from a brightly colored bag and popped them in his mouth, idly chewing them until he noticed the skeptical looks on their faces. "I don't have to fly them all the time. They do a pretty good job on their own. But they can't handle sudden course corrections or strange problems. Then a human pilot has to jump in. They can't dodge on their own if something gets in the way. Mostly birds. It's pretty much always birds."

"Well, get ready to graduate to the big leagues," said Jason. "I need you to pilot something bigger. Something new. Something experimental."

"Is this your punishment?" said Tiphys. "For the fight? What did they do to you?"

"They made me an Argonaut," said Jason. "And I'm here to make you one, too."

"Holy crap," said Tiphys. "Wow." He plopped himself down into his chair, lost in thought. "I can't. I'd never make it through boot camp. They'd eat me alive."

"You don't have to," said Jason. "I pulled some strings. They want you on this. There's a complication, though. They want you to go through a procedure. I told them no. But they won't budge. If you don't want to do it, I understand. Honestly, I'm reluctant to even ask."

"Procedure," said Tiphys hesitantly.

"Genomancy," said Jason, looking towards Medea. "She's some hot shot from Colchis. She won't let anything go wrong. Will you?"

"No, in fact," said Medea stiffly. "Regardless of what some people say, my own work's never had a single complication. But what you do with yourself afterwards is your own business."

"I thought you said genomancy was a bunch of immoral bullshit," said Tiphys. "Cheating. A cheap way out of hard work and training or whatever."

"It is a cheap way out," said Jason. "But they won't let you go any other way. And I have to at least make the offer. I need someone I can trust. Someone loyal. But at the end of the day, it's your choice. And if you don't want anything to do with this, I understand. Believe me."

"What exactly are you going to do?" said Tiphys, lazily reaching for another handful of orange crackers with one hand and popping open a canned energy drink with the other. "This is my body we're talking about. I've got to be careful with it."

"We'll need to make some changes to your genes," said Medea. "They're everything. Your training, your talent, and especially your instincts. It's all in there, inside your code. I know how to change them. How to train you in seconds, instead of in years."

"My instincts," said Tiphys. "I'm kind of using those. You can't just change them."

"Of course I can," said Medea. "They're coded into your genes. Fear of snakes, fear of spiders, fear of anything. That little nagging feeling that says you're in danger. That's all part of your DNA. The wisdom of your ancestors, added to your code century by century, bit by bit. I can change that. I'll add enough code that you can fly pretty much anything. You won't know how, not consciously, but you'll be able to do it. Just sit in the cockpit, and it'll come to you. Like riding a bicycle after you haven't been on one in years."

"This sounds sketchy," said Tiphys "I can be a miracle pilot, just like that?"

"It's just a better way of doing what nature already does," said Medea. "It's habit. The Attenborough-Jane Theory of Habit. Today's habits are tomorrow's instincts. People used to think your DNA was mostly random junk. But it's not. It's behaviors, stored there as instincts through your habits. You do something over and over, it wears itself into your DNA, like a little groove. That happens generation after generation until habit becomes instinct. We can do the same thing, but more quickly, and far more advanced than anything in nature. We can write instincts in, and teach you skills with a single injection. Planned instincts, instead of random ones."

"Being a pilot," said Tiphys. "That's not in your DNA. That comes from nurture and culture and stuff. Maybe you can make someone look like an animal or something. But this is a skill."

"There's more to your DNA than how you look," said Medea. "There's behaviors coded in there, too. Incredibly complicated ones. Lots of animals can walk minutes after they're born. They weren't taught how, they just knew. Monarch butterflies know exactly where to migrate to, even though they weren't alive during the last trip. Bowerbirds build these fantastic works of art for their nests. Their DNA tells them how. And lots of people are afraid of snakes, even if they grew up in a city. It's not their culture. It's their genes. But the *way* you behave can change the code for *how* you behave. That's how animals adapt: change their habits, and their code changes, too."

"I don't know about this," said Tiphys. He paced around the room in a nervous circle, rubbing his hands together as he spoke. "I think I'm fine. I'm really fine. I'm a perfectly good pilot right now."

"You want to pilot, you need to be able to pilot anything," said Medea. "And you need to be able to do it in person. Not just sitting in a room with your nachos and your fizz drink, staring at a bunch of screens."

"They give you energy," said Tiphys. "Nachos give you energy."

"Whatever," said Medea. "You're not going to be that kind of pilot anymore. You're going to be the real thing. You'll see." She turned to the little robot that had been following along behind her. "Hecate." It rolled up beside her, parking itself next to her foot. It was short and round, a little teal sphere with tank treads on the bottom. "Hecate, open up." Its sides began to split into three sections, flopping onto the floor and revealing what was within: a small computer at the center of the sphere, along with canisters of colored fluids attached to a web of injection tubes. It was a portable lab, and it had everything she needed to do her work.

As she reached for the tubes, Tiphys started waving his hands, blocking her from making the injection. "How do you know this will work? I hear all these... things. Like you could get your testicles shrunk down to the size of peas. Or you get turned into a little goblin."

"The Argonauts call her 'Mad Medea,'" said Jason helpfully.

"Great," said Tiphys. "I'm going to get horns and warts and whatever. I think I like my instincts. And my instincts are saying they like me the way I am. But my heart is saying I want to be an Argonaut. But my head is saying this is a bad idea. But my head also wants to be an Argonaut, without the shots. But...."

"Don't be a baby," said Medea. "This is minor, and easily reversible if you don't like it. It really is. It's mostly instincts. And a little bit of dolphin DNA."

"Dolphin," said Tiphys, his eyes narrowing. "Like I'll do backflips? And get gills or something?"

"It's just a few segments," said Medea. "It won't change how you look. Only how you hear things. Or see things, really. It's for echolocation."

"Do it," said Tiphys, plopping down in his chair and thrusting out his arm. "I want superpowers. I want the proportionate strength of a dolphin."

"You're not going to be a dolphin," said Medea. "You're going to be able to see things like a dolphin. Off in the distance. Using sound."

She pulled a handful of nutrient tubes from Hecate's metal innards, sticking needle after needle into Tiphys's arm. The nutrients began to flow, and with a few taps on her wrist sheath the work began. Hecate beeped and her computer screen flashed images of segments of code, twisting and changing along with his DNA. Medea turned back to Tiphys, looking him over. "These are minor changes, as these things go. They're mostly to your behavior, not your body. You'll probably get a headache, and it might be a bad one, but that's about it. When you feel an urge to whistle, let me know. Until then, sit still."

Tiphys managed something close to quiet, although he couldn't help but fidget, tapping his foot against the floor over and over. He focused on his screens, watching as the drones flew around the city, dropping parcels of consumer goods through delivery slots in the sides of apartment after apartment. The A.I. knew what people needed before they even noticed for themselves. It tracked what they used, and what they had left, and kept the stakeholders stocked up on their favorites before they could run out. The system had eliminated most stores, and the need for the employees who'd once run them. Tiphys was substitute for hundreds, and all he needed to do was stare at a wall for hours on end. This time he only managed around ten minutes before he jumped from his chair in a panic, nearly ripping out the tubes as he did.

"Oh, god," said Tiphys. "Oh, god. What's happening? Something's gone wrong." He started clawing at his eyes, then his ears, then back again. He looked horrified, staring off into space at phantoms only he could see.

"You fucked him up," said Jason. He grabbed hold of Tiphys's arms, locking them down at his sides. "What did you do?"

"Quiet," said Tiphys, with tears in his eyes. "Please be quiet."

"Whistle," said Medea softly. "Just try a little whistle. Take it slow."

"Okay," said Tiphys. "Okay. But please be quiet." He puckered his lips and gave a short breath of air through them, just a single note. But it was enough to send him back into his frenzy, writhing in place and trying to pull himself free from Jason's grip. "Oh, god. Oh, god. Oh, god."

"You're fine," said Medea. "Everything's fine. We're here."

"I can see it," said Tiphys. "I can see everything you say. It looks like some kind of abstract painting. And the whistling. Everything's a picture. Like a picture inside my head."

"You're okay," said Medea. "This is what's supposed to happen. You'll get used to it, and you'll be able to control it. Some people can't handle change, but you can. You're strong enough to accept it."

"I can speak dolphin," said Tiphys, his voice filled with excitement. "I can really speak dolphin?"

"Kind of," said Medea. "It's not really a language in a human sense. But you could communicate with one. They talk with pictures, not words. Dolphins don't hear sound, they see sound. That's the key to how they communicate. Every whistle looks like something. That's how they can coordinate so well. Whistle each other a picture of them all doing a trick, or a picture of a plan to catch some fish, and then they're all on the same page."

"I want to talk to a dolphin," said Tiphys. "I want to try this out."

"Tough," said Jason. "We've got work to do and a schedule to keep. And you've got a ship to pilot. So get him ready, make sure nothing went wrong, and let's go see what Mopsus came up with."

CHAPTER EIGHT

THE HANGAR WAS ON THE outskirts of the city, far from the populace and far from prying eyes. It had been hidden in plain sight, smack in the middle of a vast complex of factories that were busy churning out consumer goods of every imaginable kind. It was the perfect place for a military installation: the factories were almost never visited, their absentee landlords leaving them to be run in silence by an army of industrial robots that handled everything from manufacturing to packaging to their own maintenance.

A fleet of experimental aircraft were arranged in rows inside, each customized to its particular mission. There were jets, helicopters, hovercraft, and things that didn't even look like they could fly, a motley collection of designs dumped together with no rhyme or reason. Before them stood Pelias, flanked by Amphion, overseeing as hulking, insect-like industrial machines clambered atop one of the aircraft and put on the finishing touches. Some of them were conducting a final inspection, while sparks flew from the limbs of others as they welded the last pieces to it before its maiden flight. A few of the Argonauts themselves sat on crates nearby, playing cards and passing the time.

"No problems, I take it?" said Pelias, looking around the hangar. "I don't see either of them here."

Amphion checked his sheath with a few quick taps. "They're on their way. A few minutes out. He wanted to take a friend. Some pilot. Other than that, they're both following orders to the letter."

"His own pilot," said Pelias. "Saves us an Argonaut, at least." He flashed a broad smile at them as they played their game across the hangar, then went back to an impatient glower. "I want him here. And then I want him on his way."

"A few more seconds," said Amphion. "And they're here." A car pulled into the entrance on cue, its door sliding open as it hatched forth its occupants: Jason, Medea, and Tiphys, looking around in awe at the endless rows of vehicles.

"Jason!" said Pelias, walking towards them with open arms. "The man of the hour. The hero in waiting, ready to save the company and get back what was taken from us." He slapped Jason on the back and shook his hand, leading him over towards the group of robots toiling at their latest creation. "You're going to be the savior of Argos. You'll have your own action figure before you're done. But for now, I've got something else for you. A special toy, one we made just for you."

With a wave of his hand the robots stood aside, revealing the product of their labors. "The ARGO," said Pelias, sweeping his arm towards the aircraft behind him. "Custom designed to get you into Colchis undetected. And to be your base of operations once you're there."

It looked like a mere cargo drone, though an especially massive one. At its bottom was a long, white cylinder, indistinguishable from any of the thousands of industrial containers that were flown over cities each and every day. Here and there were giant barcodes painted on in red; the Colchians used them to catalogue their fleet, and it had to look just right. Clinging to the top of the container was a large green drone, its four wings spread out on either side. They were thin to the point of translucence, and at present they were fixed in place, reaching out horizontally into the air.

At the drone's tail was the exhaust port from a jet engine, and with its wings in this position it could shoot across the skies at unfathomable speeds. But the wings were flexible, capable of moving at all angles and even flapping up and down, propelling the drone in any direction they pleased. The ARGO looked something like a dragonfly, its metal legs wrapped around the container like a giant egg. It hugged it close, as if it were simply tugging it along en route to a delivery. But in truth, drone and container were joined together within to form a single, unified vessel.

"Holy shit," said Tiphys. He stared up at the ship, an overgrown cousin to the tiny delivery drones he was used to guiding. "I'm piloting that?"

"It's more transport than anything else, so don't go overboard," said Amphion. "If you get yourself into a dogfight, none of you are making it out alive. The ARGO was designed for espionage. It's bland, it's boring, and it blends in."

"Why the name?" said Tiphys.

"It's just some contrived acronym from the R&D division," said Amphion. "Aeronautic Reconnaissance something. Whatever got them to the letters they already wanted to use anyway."

Tiphys looked disappointed, but only for a moment, as the novelty of the ship brought his excitement back just as quickly as it had gone. "What about sensors? It looks like a cargo drone. But if we just fly around everywhere it'll get spotted by their systems somewhere it's not supposed to be. Then we'll get our cover blown, and it's all over."

"She made you a pilot," said Amphion. "So give it a whistle. Tell us what you see."

Everyone was now staring at Tiphys, who looked like he wanted to creep inside himself to escape the attention. But he pulled himself together and closed his eyes in concentration. He made a short whistling sound, and then his eyes flashed open in shock. "It looks like a bird," said Tiphys. "I saw the image of a little bird in my head."

"The latest in stealth technology," said Amphion. "You can stay out in the open, and no machine will be the wiser. People can see it, of course. But the look is pure Colchian. It's modeled after one of their industrial drones, made for heavy deliveries. No one will bat an eye at it, so long as you can get it inside the city limits."

"We've got one last bit of paperwork," said Pelias, snapping his fingers at Amphion and smiling at Jason. "To set up that trust we talked about. Just need to get your signature, and then everything's official. Your team, your mission, your ship." Amphion waved his fingers across his tablet, bringing up a contract, and then held it out to Jason.

"I get the shares back?" said Jason. "Once this is all done? It's the family legacy."

"The trust is for your benefit, and yours only," said Pelias. "It's not about who owns them. It's about who votes them. Besides, come back safely, and it's null and void. It only kicks in if something goes wrong. Getting captured, or worse."

"I won't get captured," said Jason. "And there won't be an 'or worse.'" He scrolled through a few of the pages, taking in as much of the legalese as he could tolerate, and then pressed his thumb against his wrist sheath's plastic screen. Amphion's tablet sang out a few high-pitched beeps, confirming

Jason's identity and sending him a draft of the contract. A few seconds later and Jason's sheath was blinking green: an auto-attorney had analyzed it, bickered with the tablet over the terms, and given him the okay to sign, all in seconds and all without billing him a cent. The deal was done, and he reached over to the tablet and signed on the screen with a quick thumbprint.

"Perfect," said Pelias with a smile. "Now let's meet the rest of your team. Amphion?"

Amphion waved across the hangar to the men as they played their game, grabbing their attention. "You know Mopsus," said Amphion. He was there, but he hadn't come alone. The separation anxiety was too much, apparently, as on his lap sat one of the Chirps, a white dove fluttering its wings inside a little golden cage.

"There's Antaeus," said Amphion, pointing to the most conspicuous of the group: large and covered in brown fur, wearing nothing but black shorts. He was clutching his cards in his claws, but not doing a very good job of it; they kept slipping from his grasp and revealing his hand to the others. "And Idas." He sat across from the other two and gave a sullen nod, but otherwise didn't acknowledge them. He just stared directly at Medea, his spear at his side and his fingers curled around it. It made her nervous; she could tell just by looking at him that his grudge wasn't going away anytime soon.

"The dossier is loaded on here," said Amphion, handing a tablet to Jason. "It's our best plan to get you in, and get you out. That's the easy part. Finding the Fleece, that's on you. We gave you what we could in the dossier. But we don't know where it is, and we don't know what it looks like. We know it's a computer, and our intelligence says it's heavily guarded. But you've got a seer, and you've got a native. You'll figure it out."

"Phineus," said Mopsus, heading towards the ARGO with his bird in tow. "The signs say we should talk to Phineus."

"Then follow the signs, and get going," said Amphion. "Bring back the Fleece and you'll all get the biggest parade the city has ever seen."

Mopsus led the way inside, rapping his knuckles on the side of the ARGO's cargo pod. A door slid open from nowhere, and he carefully stepped through it, clutching Chirp's cage tightly to his chest. He was followed by Antaeus, who made some sort of greeting to Medea, though she couldn't tell precisely what it was. It sounded like "hrngg," but she knew that couldn't have been it. He hadn't quite mastered his new teeth, but he seemed friendly enough. More so than the last of them, at least.

"Here she is," said Idas, snarling at her as he passed. "Running from her responsibilities. Running from her handiwork. Leaving my brother alone on a slab while she plays at being a warrior."

"I didn't ask to come on this thing," said Medea. "And I didn't do anything to him."

"He's blind," said Idas. "He's alone, and he's blind. And yet here you are, off seeking adventure and glory."

"I'm happy to go right back up to my lab," said Medea. "I'm not a warrior, and I'm not an Argonaut. I'm a scientist. And fixing your brother is going to be weeks of work, maybe months."

"You're going," said Amphion. "I thought we'd made that clear. This thing is too important. It's a bet-the-company mission. The both of you better go along, and you better get along."

Idas scowled and tapped the ground with the butt of his spear as he walked, louder and louder the closer he came. He pointed the tip at Medea as he boarded, gave her a nasty grin, and then disappeared inside with the others.

"Take care, Jason," said Pelias, giving him a handshake, and then a long hug. "This is for all those years you spent in limbo. You've got tenacity, and that's what counts. You'll do this. We're all counting on you."

"We'll get back the Fleece," said Jason. "We'll save the company. We'll do whatever it takes." He climbed aboard, followed by Medea and a very eager Tiphys, who practically skipped his way up to the cockpit. The door slid shut behind them, and Pelias and Amphion backed away to a safe distance. It took Tiphys a few minutes, but then he had it.

The ARGO's wings began to twist and flap, faster and faster, lifting it up into the air on a gust of wind. Then they all flipped at once, shifting position so that instead of lifting the ARGO upward, they were pushing it forward. The air blew heavy all around, and Pelias and Amphion walked to the side of the hangar to avoid the winds, watching from the sidelines as the ARGO slowly made its way outside. Its wings straightened out and a burst of flame belched from its engine, and then it launched away into the skies.

"Beautiful," said Pelias, bringing his hands together in a slow, exaggerated clap. "Brings tears to my eyes. Young heroes, off to make a name for themselves. Off to save the world. To face trials and tribulations in strange lands, and return with tales of their bravery. It's just heartwarming, it really is."

"Yes, sir," said Amphion.

"Heartwarming," said Pelias. "And Amphion?"

"Sir?" said Amphion.

"No mistakes," said Pelias. "You better make damned sure that not a single one of them ever makes it back."

CHAPTER NINE

"I'M DOING IT," SAID TIPHYS. "I don't know what I'm doing, but I'm doing it." He sat in the ARGO's cockpit, his hands clutching the control stick. Jason was beside him, watching through the windows as the ground sped by below. They'd all been nervous, at least at first, and none more so than Tiphys. They were testing both plane and pilot, though so far both had passed with flying colors.

"As long as you get us there," said Jason, scanning through the mission plans on the tablet Amphion had handed him. "You don't have to know what you're doing, as long as we get there in one piece."

"Watch this," said Tiphys. "I'm going to drop the landing gear. Know which button drops the landing gear?"

"No idea," said Jason.

"Me neither," said Tiphys. "But watch." He closed his eyes, held up his hand, and then jerked it out towards a button on the control panel, seemingly at random. He opened his eyes to the sound of gears grinding from the bottom of the cargo pod, positioning themselves for a landing. Then he pressed the button again and again in a demonstration of his sudden mastery. "Down. Up. Down. Up. Cool, huh? I have no idea what I'm doing. I've never even seen a Colchian cargo drone. But I just do what feels right, and it works."

"Still think it's sorcery?" came a voice from behind them. Medea poked her head up through a hatch connecting the cockpit to the hollowed out cargo container below. She smiled in triumph as she watched Tiphys flying the ship with ease. They could call her what they liked, and say what they liked. But she'd made a real pilot out of someone like him in mere minutes. If that didn't prove the value of her trade, she didn't know what would.

"It works," said Jason. "But that doesn't make it right. He didn't work for it. He didn't earn it. He's a like a little kid you let loose with a handgun. He knows how to pull the trigger, and he's having fun pointing it all around, but he doesn't have a clue what it can really do."

Medea's grin vanished in an instant. There was no pleasing him, or any of them, for that matter. She could give them the strength of a dozen men, and they'd complain about their size. She could make them master swordsmen with a single injection, and they'd moan that it was only a reflex. They'd demand to be a wolf, and then say they had too much fur. She couldn't win, no matter how hard she tried.

And Jason was worse than all the rest. The other warriors knew she was a valuable part of the team; they just wanted to hog all the glory for themselves. They knew they needed her, or they wouldn't keep slinking back into her lab, mocking her in public before begging for her help when their friends weren't looking. But Jason was something else. He thought she was a con artist, not a scientist. The more impressive her work, the more he treated it like it was all just a scam. And yet somehow the more he dismissed her, the more she wanted to prove herself to him. She couldn't tell whether it was something about his attitude, or something about the way he looked at her. She kept finding herself staring at his eyes, sharp and green and icy with determination. And she kicked herself inside every time she did.

"I bet I could fly a hang glider," said Tiphys. "Would that work? If I just jumped onto one right now?"

"The code was pretty comprehensive," said Medea. "Any kind of aircraft we know about, you can fly it."

"This is so awesome," said Tiphys, banking the ARGO left, then right. Watching him made Medea think that Jason was right about something, at least: Tiphys was like a child with a new toy, his face alight with enthusiasm. At least someone appreciated her work.

"There it is!" said Tiphys. He would have been jumping up and down in his chair if his seatbelt hadn't restrained him, but instead he just bounced in place with excitement. As Medea looked out through the cockpit window, she could see what had set him off.

Shimmering in the distance across a vast desert was a crystal city, sparkling like a beacon. She would have thought it a mirage if she hadn't been born there. The city of Colchis looked like nothing else on Earth.

Its planners had built it for its beauty above all else, constructing every one of its skyscrapers from precious stones, or at least the closest artificial facsimiles. A giant wall of pearl surrounded it all, protecting the citizens within from the sands and winds that whirled without. Spires of ruby, emerald, and sapphire poked above it, glowing red or green or blue in the desert sun. The Colchians had turned their city into one giant jewelry box by decree, and it was the shining wonder of the world as a result.

But seeing it was one thing, and getting to it was another. Between them lay an impassable no man's land, an uninhabitable desert that stretched as far as the eye could see. The Colchians had gone to great lengths to ensure that their borders were empty, and they meant for them to stay that way. They had little tolerance for intruders. The desert was their castle moat, a protective barrier against spies and saboteurs who'd sneak into their oasis from the outside. And woe to those who came inside their walls uninvited.

"Take us down," said Jason. "Inside those rocks." He pointed to a cluster of them, jutting out of the desert sands below. There were a few dozen massive red boulders cropping out from the ground, with thickets of weeds growing around them and smaller rocks scattered around in all directions. Taken together it was enough to hide the ARGO in the middle, with plenty of cover on all sides.

"Okay," said Tiphys, taking in a deep breath. "First landing ever. I can do this."

"Ever?" said Jason, a hint of unease in his voice.

"Drones mostly land themselves," said Tiphys. "But we're fine. I'll just kind of push buttons, and it'll all work out." He looked at the control panel in front of him, looping around the length of the cockpit. There must have been hundreds of buttons, levers, and switches to choose from, and he didn't have the slightest idea where to start. "We'll be cool. I've got killer instincts now, right?"

"Our lives are in your hands," said Jason, looking back at Medea skeptically. "If that's any comfort."

"Here goes," said Tiphys. He started pointing at buttons at random, counting them off as he tapped his finger along the console. "Eeny, meeny, miney, moe." He jabbed his finger down on the last one and the ARGO jerked to a halt, its wings shifting and flapping until it hovered in place mid-air. "Now we've just got to get her down. Let's do some stuff up here."

He started flipping switches above him, and they could feel themselves slowly descending.

"It works," said Tiphys, flashing a doofy smile at Medea. "I had doubts myself. Jason told me everything. About that guy whose eyes you fucked up. Of course he waited until after you already gave me my dolphin powers. You did a better job with me, though." He tapped a little earpiece, nestled within his right ear and connected to the seat behind him. "I can see the ground right now, in my head. The ARGO's sending out sound waves in all directions. I've got three-hundred sixty degree vision. Totally weird. But I'm like the perfect pilot now. I can—oh, shit. Landing gear."

He reached across Jason, stabbing at another of the buttons. "Better get strapped in," said Jason, looking down at Medea as she clung to the ladder leading up into the cockpit. "You trust your work. But do you trust him?"

She didn't, and she ducked back down into the cargo pod in a hurry. She knew she was more skilled than they gave her credit for, but Tiphys was Tiphys, and it was best to prepare for a rough landing.

Down below, the interior had been replaced with something that looked more like a shuttle than an industrial transport. On one end was a passenger area, the walls lined with navy blue seats for each of them. Even little Hecate had a spot, with thick metal fasteners locking her treads into place so she wouldn't be jostled by sudden movements. The other side of the pod was designed for war. There were lockers full of weapons and armor, a blocky computer system, and a stripped down lab for Medea herself. The others were all strapped into their seats already, apparently as confident in Tiphys as she was.

"Have we found the convoy?" said Mopsus. He was sitting in his chair, waggling a finger inside Chirp's cage and whispering soothing nothings to him over the roar of the ARGO's engine. "Have we found our way in?"

"I thought you'd know already," said Medea as she took her seat. "You're supposed to be a seer."

"No data, no divination," said Mopsus, tapping the wires on the back of his head. They were hooked up to a small grey box, tucked into the back of his uniform. "I brought what I could carry. But it's old, hours old. Practically worthless. I stream what I can, but it's not much, not without a direct link to the system. I'm blind, I'm afraid, a seer who can't see, and thus of little help. But the data said what it said. I must be here."

"Grngg," said Antaeus, sitting across from him. He flared his lips in frustration, pulling them away from his teeth. The fangs Medea had given him were huge, and he could barely close his mouth around them, let alone speak. But he went slowly, carefully, and managed to grunt something out. "Gods."

"The gods," said Mopsus. "Yes, the gods. I can hear them, still. If they wish to speak. Understanding them is another matter."

"How are you holding up?" said Medea, quickly changing the subject as Antaeus rubbed his jaw. He didn't look happy, but then, his face had been stretched, permanently fixed into a bear's angry snarl. His shorts barely fit him, and his thighs were so full of muscle he was spilling out of the chair that was supposed to hold him.

"Good," said Antaeus. He forced the words out, slowly and carefully. "Rip 'em up. Can't beat me. Not now." He smiled, or perhaps he snarled. Medea couldn't tell which. But his teeth were bared, and his claws were flexed, and he looked as menacing as he'd always wanted to be.

"You're good for now," said Idas. "Wait until it all falls apart." He was staring at her from across the pod, spear in hand. She met his eyes, but looked away just as quickly. All she could see in there was hate. It was pure, it was passionate, and it was sincere. The more he poured it onto her, the more she wondered if he had a point. She felt guilty that she hadn't stayed behind, as irrational as she knew it was. They'd never have let her. But she'd brought samples of his brother's blood, stored away inside Hecate, and if things went well she'd have a fix for Lynceus by the time they made it back. Maybe that would quiet him. Or at least keep him from killing her.

She could feel the ARGO moving, but barely. Tiphys had total control over the ship, even if he didn't know how, and he'd turned out to be every bit the pilot she'd promised. It was her code, and it was good code. She knew that, even if she also knew she'd never get a word of thanks for it. What she loved about her job was knowing her contributions had meant something to the ones she slaved away for. She could do without the parades; she just wanted some appreciation. But that wasn't the way of things, not with the warriors. She glanced over at Mopsus, clutching Chirp's cage tightly to his chest, struggling to cope with life in the outside world and away from the hole they'd dumped him in to have his visions. At least she wasn't the only one the warriors treated that way.

She checked her uniform as the ship descended, making sure there was nothing loose. There'd been one for each of them on the ship, and hers was a perfect fit. It was all black, a thin, skin-tight material that ended in a pair of steely boots. She had to admit she liked it: it showed off the best parts of her, and she knew she wore it well. A few furtive glances from Tiphys were enough to tell her that; he was so afraid his eyes would be drawn somewhere they shouldn't be that he'd barely even been able to look at her since she'd put it on.

As she checked her belt, she felt a soft bump: the ARGO had touched down, settling into the sands. Then she saw boots on the ladder above as Jason and Tiphys joined them from the cockpit. "Idas," said Jason. "Antaeus. Take a look around. Make sure we've got nothing to worry about." He pressed a button on the wall, and a panel slid open. The wind blew a gust of sand inside as the two of them leapt out into the desert, disappearing off into the rocks as he'd ordered.

"The rest of you are on lookout," said Jason. "Everyone gets one of these." His voice was firm, commanding, and completely at ease with his role as leader. It made Medea flutter inside, though she knew he didn't even want her there. She'd always loved deep voices, and there was a hint of iron behind Jason's commands that made it better still. He handed a pair of goggles to each of them as they left the ARGO, the lenses glowing green. They looked like two mismatched telescopes strapped together, the left longer than the right. "Fan out, and watch the skies. You see anything, you give a shout."

Medea strapped her goggles to her head, and the world went digital as she turned them on. Everything was pixelated, and as she adjusted the settings she could see blotches of bright blue heat, then purple ultraviolets, then the bones of everyone around as she saw right through their skin. "What are we supposed to be looking for?" she said.

"Look for drones," said Jason. "Cargo drones. The mission dossier says they'll come in a convoy, and soon. We're going to sneak in at the back of the line and pretend we're one of them. If we do it right, we'll coast into the city and no one will know a thing. But we're only getting one chance. Miss this shot, and the next convoy isn't for a month. So pay attention."

She fumbled with the settings, trying to get the goggles working as she headed off towards the rocks on her own. Jason called after her as she went:

"And stay close. When a convoy comes, we need to move. I don't want to have to go looking for you if you wander off." She lifted the goggles up to see him smirking, looking on with amusement at the difficulties she was having getting them to work. He was born to be one of the warriors: he knew just when to poke at her to keep her off balance, and he seemed to revel in doing it.

"I don't need a babysitter," said Medea, a little bit of irritation seeping through. "I'll be fine. Worry about yourself. The Colchians don't like visitors." She pressed a button on the side of her goggles, and her vision changed again. This time she could see bright red rectangles outlining each of the Argonauts as they moved, following them along as they walked and disappearing a few seconds after their movement stopped. The goggles were tracking motion, and if something moved across the skies, they'd flag it for her long before she'd notice it on her own.

She paced through the rocks until she was well away from the ARGO, looking for a direction that no one seemed to have covered. When she found one, she used her foot to smooth out the sand behind a small boulder, making herself a comfortable place to sit down and settle in for the wait. It was tedious work. She tried to be a diligent lookout, staring up at the empty skies for as long as she could tolerate. But the goggles were doing most of her job for her, and she couldn't keep her thoughts from wandering.

She kept thinking of the message she'd received, and what Aphrodite had said. She knew she shouldn't take it so seriously. They called Aphrodite a god, but in the end she was just a computer. Prophecies could be wrong, and they could change; Mopsus himself had said so, and his own prophecy of doom had disappeared as quickly as it had come. But still she found herself drawn into the guessing game, trying to decide what the message had meant and who it could have been referring to.

There were plenty of options to consider. She had a few past lovers still in Colchis, but none she wanted to revisit. Antaeus was handsome enough despite his newfound fur, if you were into that, but she couldn't imagine what a dinner conversation with him would be like. Mopsus only seemed to love his birds, and Idas just wanted to kill her. Tiphys kept stealing those guilty glances at her, and she knew he'd be with her in a second if she wanted. But faint heart never won fair lady, and Tiphys would always be what he was, no matter how much DNA was spliced into him.

Then there was Jason.

Physically, he was exactly her type. She couldn't have made someone better looking herself, no matter how long she slaved away at their genome. She couldn't quit staring at his eyes, she loved the way his uniform pressed against his chest, and the confidence in his voice when he gave one of his orders made her toes curl.

But there was also his attitude. He certainly didn't want her on the mission, and he'd done whatever he could to get rid of her. He didn't like her chosen career, no matter how important it was to her. He thought she was a cheat, a fraud, and the woman who'd burned out a fellow warrior's eyes. If she was frank about it, he didn't seem to like her much more than Idas did. Sometimes she wished she could graft a little compassion onto his personality. Maybe she actually could, now that she thought about it, but she'd never hear the end of it if she did.

She kept rattling through the options, making a game of trying to pick which one of them she'd rather be stuck with if it came to it, when she felt her sheath humming and shaking against her wrist. She gave it a look, and then a hurried tap once she saw what was on the screen: another message, from another of the gods. And a curious one indeed: she'd signed up to hear from Aphrodite, and only Aphrodite, but this one was from a different god entirely.

She'd been happy for a little help in her love life, but one god was enough. The A.I.'s had proliferated along with the data they used, and some of them were downright creepy. Supposedly Charon could monitor your vitals and warn you when your death was approaching, but there were some things she'd rather find out on her own. She'd limited herself to Aphrodite's parlor games, and the others shouldn't be butting their electronic noses into her affairs.

But here was a message from Cupid, and it was addressed directly to her: "Mother says hello. Watch for arrows. You never know when they're going to strike."

CHAPTER TEN

SHE COULDN'T BEGIN TO PROCESS what she'd just been told. Arrows—and aimed at her? It didn't make any sense; Cupid wasn't even supposed to be active until Valentine's Day. He guided lovers towards romantic surprises, but he was mostly a cheap trick to promote restaurants and chocolate sales. Then again, he was Aphrodite's son, at least in the myths, and clearly the A.I.'s had been interacting with each other somehow.

Her thoughts were interrupted by red rectangles in the corner of her field of vision. The goggles had found something, some movement in the skies, and they'd started into a series of wild beeps to alert her. She clicked a button at the side of her head, zooming in for as close a look as she could manage. It was exactly what she was searching for: drones, a dozen of them, flying towards the city in convoy formation.

A low buzzing sound came from the distance as the drones grew nearer, barely perceptible above the wind. She left her hiding place, running out into the open sands and looking around for the others, but even with the goggles she couldn't see any of them. She fiddled with the settings, trying to get them back to tracking heat, but the options seemed endless as she ticked through them all. In the end, she decided to simply shout instead. "Found them! Incoming! Found a convoy!"

She heard a few shouts back, but she couldn't tell where they were, not with the wind whipping back and forth and carrying the voices along with it. She couldn't even tell if they were responding to her. She ran closer to where it sounded like they were coming from, shouting again and again. Still nothing. The ARGO was off in the distance, nestled among the rocks, and she thought about making a run for it. But if she did, she'd lose sight of the convoy, and it might be impossible to find again by the time she made it back.

The buzzing sound grew louder, and now she could see the drones more clearly, specks on the horizon that grew into black aircraft as they came closer. There were dozens of them, moving in a wide loop around the desert. But these were no cargo drones. They were thin and wasp-like, darting through the skies with no parcels to burden them. They'd been flying in formation, but as they approached they spread apart and moved into position for battle.

She knew what they were, then; the Colchians were as proud of their military technologies as any of the rest of the Big Five, and they loved to show them off. These were Ares class hunter drones, automated weapons of war capable of raining death upon anyone and anything that came too close. They'd been a regular feature of the city's parades when she'd lived there, zooming above the crowds in a demonstration of force. Back then they'd been mere display pieces, but these were birds of prey on the hunt. And now their flight path was taking them directly towards her.

She looked around for someplace to hide, but she'd gone too far away from any of the rocks to simply duck back under cover. The drones had spotted her, and they were converging on her position. She thought about yelling again for help, but she knew no one could get there in time, if they could even hear her. Then a loud booming sound came from one of the drones. Smoke puffed out from below it, a little dark cloud that grew larger and larger as the seconds ticked by. She didn't know what it was, not at first. She thought maybe one of the Argonauts had shot the drone down, or maybe there'd been some kind of malfunction. But the drone didn't crash, and through the smoke she could see something else, streaking away from the drone and off into the air.

It felt like her brain had cracked. It had only been seconds, but it seemed like forever. Time had gone sluggish inside her head, and she stood there dazed, watching helplessly as a missile inched towards her through the air. It looked so much like an arrow, let loose from its string, and the sight of it pinned her in place. She couldn't move, and she didn't know why. She thought maybe she was already dead, and this was a memory of what had been, her last moments slowly grinding to a halt before it all went black. There was no sound, there was no smell, there was no anything but the moment, and she was lost in it. She tried to run, but she found she couldn't. Her legs were jelly, and they wouldn't listen to her frantic pleas, even as her panic grew and grew.

She heard more shouting, but she couldn't make out the words through the fog. Every bit of her consciousness was locked onto the missile, just as surely as it was locked onto her. They say your life passes before you in the moments before you pass, and so it did for her. She thought of old friends, old memories, and her old home in Colchis. She thought of the slurs the warriors had slung against her, and all the work she'd done to try to win their approval. She thought of better things, of the hundreds of people she'd helped as a genomancer, and she wondered whether her parents would be proud. She'd know soon enough. As the end came nearer and nearer, she closed her eyes, and her only real regret was that she hadn't spent more time doing as she pleased without giving a damn for what the warriors thought.

Then the shouting grew louder, she felt hands at her waist, and she found herself yanked off her feet. She opened her eyes to see Jason, or at least the back of him. She couldn't help herself from admiring the view, just for a second—life's pleasures were meant to be savored, now more than ever, and his muscles flexed and tensed in front of her with every step he took. He'd tossed her over his shoulder and was sprinting away from where she'd been standing, carrying her off in a mad charge towards the safety of a nearby rock formation. He was almost there when the missile hit, colliding with the sands where she'd once stood.

She shut her eyes again and felt a boom, then a wave of hot air blowing against her face. It was as if someone had shoved her from every direction at once, knocking them both to the ground in a heap. Her ears were ringing, a sharp, stabbing noise that jabbed at her head again and again. She crawled a few inches away, and then everything went black. She couldn't see, she couldn't move, and all she could do was kick and flail. A voice pierced through the ringing, muffled at first, then clear: "Stay down! They're still circling, stay down!"

It calmed her somehow, knowing there was still something there for her to hear, and she managed to get back some control. She could see where she was, now: pressed against the sand, Jason atop her and holding her down so she couldn't move away. They'd made it to a group of rocks, just big enough to keep them both out of sight so long as they kept low to the ground. She could still hear the drones up above, circling them like stiff metallic vultures hoping to verify the kill.

"What the hell were you doing?" said Jason. His face was just inches from hers, his goggles dangling from his neck, but she could barely hear him; her ears were still ringing, and smoke was assaulting her lungs. She went into a brief fit of coughs, her body heaving as she did, but he had his hands locked around her wrists, pinning her down and holding her out of view of the drones. "You could have died! We both could have. You just sat there staring off into space like some statue."

"I didn't—" said Medea. But the words wouldn't come. The air had been sucked out of her, and her thoughts along with it. She didn't know why she'd frozen any more than he did. She'd just panicked. His eyes were locked onto hers, bright and green and furious, and they compelled her to give the best answer she could manage. "I couldn't. I just couldn't."

"You should have stayed in your lab," said Jason. "You should have stayed in the damned lab, and not tried to be something you aren't. It's safe back there. This is real. I don't care if you want to prove yourself, or want to be a warrior, or whatever. You're not cut out for this. You're staying in the ARGO from now on. Period."

"Me?" said Medea. She was shaking, though she wasn't sure whether it was from anger or from adrenaline. Whatever it was, his attitude had brought her senses back, and her spirit along with it. "I'm the one trying to prove myself? I'm not the one with the daddy complex. I'm not the one trying to show everyone that a lifetime of pampering didn't make him soft."

"This isn't a game," said Jason. "It's not about me. And it's not about what people say about you, or whether you're as good as the others. It's about survival. Your survival."

Now he was shaking, too, almost imperceptibly. She hadn't noticed it before; he'd hidden it, and hidden it down deep. But he was just inches from her face, and it was all out in the open for the both of them to see. She could tell he was scared, and not of some missile. He was scared of what had almost happened to her. He looked like he was about to hug her, but he stopped just short. His expression went from fear back to anger, and he snapped at her instead. "You could have died. I nearly watched you die."

"I guess your little mission would have been a failure, then," said Medea, turning her head aside. "You'd go home a failure. You wouldn't get to play hero on the vids."

"It's not about the damned mission," said Jason. "I almost lost you."

She turned back and tried to meet his eyes, but this time he was the one who looked away. She wondered whether there was really something there inside him, buried beneath the hostile facade, some tender piece of him that cared for her as more than just a cog in the Argo war machine. "So now you're suddenly worried about Dr. Frankenstein?" said Medea. "Now you actually want me to stick around?"

"Don't press your luck," said Jason, his voice wavering, then growing firm again. "I ordered you over here. I thought you could handle it. I would have had to live with getting you killed." He loosened his grip on her wrists, his hands lingering on her arms longer than they should have. Then he rolled off of her, leaving them both hugging the dirt side by side. They could still hear the drones, more distant now, widening their search for their prey off into the desert.

"I thought you hated me," said Medea. She knew she'd seen it in him before. Not quite as bad as with Idas, but there was still a palpable hostility. Now hostility was tempered with compassion, a volatile brew, and she couldn't tell which way he really felt about her. He just lay there next to her, staring into her eyes and collecting his thoughts in silence, until finally he spoke.

"I hate what you do," said Jason. "Because it cheapens what I do. Being a warrior means something to me. I know you think it's all about getting famous. And maybe it is for some of them. But not for me. For me, it's about heroism for its own sake. It's about the warrior ethic."

"Warriors talk about their ethic all the time," said Medea. "But get them out in the field, and they all turn into cutthroats. I've seen them sacrifice their friends just to get better footage of themselves to bring back for the vids."

"Maybe that's what it's about for them," said Jason. "That's not what it's about for me."

"Yeah, well, cheating isn't what my work's about for me," said Medea. "It's about helping people. It's about giving them the bodies they dream of, not the ones they happened to be born with. It's about the challenge. It's about what my parents...." She trailed off, unable to finish the thought. Images of them flashed into her head again, images of them vibrant and full of life as they took her to school and taught her to dance, and images of them slowly dying together in the same hospital room as she looked on as a helpless teenager.

"About what they think of you," said Jason. "About what they want you to do with your life. And about whether you're living up to what they want."

"About what they would have wanted," said Medea. Tears welled in her eyes, and she brushed away little bits of muddy sand from her face. "They're gone."

"I'm sorry," said Jason. He took her hand in his, and looked intently into her eyes. "I really am."

"It was a long time ago," said Medea. She shook her head, and shook away the sting the memories had brought with them.

"But it still hurts," said Jason. "I can tell. I could hear it in your voice."

"It does," said Medea. "And you're right. It's about all those things. About what they would have wanted. About whether I'm honoring their memories."

"I know what it feels like," said Jason. "I've had my own issues with my parents. With my father. Wondering whether all the work you were putting in mattered. Wondering what they'd think about it. Wondering whether what you did would honor their names, in the end. I used to feel the same way. "

"Used to?" said Medea. Now he was intriguing her as more than just a pretty face and a brash commander. There was something under there, something about his father that drove him to be a warrior just as her parents' deaths had driven her to be a genomancer. And there was something there in his eyes, something sad. Something that hurt him just as much as the loss of her parents had hurt her.

"The drones are gone," said Jason, ignoring her question and looking up towards the sky. "I can't hear them." He pulled his goggles back on, adjusted the settings, and poked his head above the rocks. "Over there. They're headed towards the city." He pointed towards a row of bright lights slowly crawling across the sky, one by one. Then he pressed a button on his goggles, zooming in for a closer look. "Shit. It isn't them. It's the convoy. And if we don't move right now, we're going to miss it."

CHAPTER ELEVEN

ASON GRABBED HER HAND AND pulled her to her feet, dragging her along behind him as he made a run for the ARGO. His grip was firm, just what she'd expect from a leader, and she didn't put up any fight. Her head was clearing, but all she could think of as they ran was Cupid and his cryptic message. They could still hear the drones from somewhere up above, then a series of explosions in the distance as they fired off missile after missile. It was a bad sign. They'd stay until the kill was confirmed, and in the meantime they'd obliterate anything that moved.

She knew the two of them would never make it. The ARGO was too far away, and there were too many drones up there. All she could do was keep running, until Jason suddenly turned and pulled her towards a group of rocks. She soon saw what he had: Tiphys, standing at the mouth of a tiny cave formed by an overhanging rock. He waved them in, sneaking glances up above the entire while, and then ducked back inside with the rest of them: Idas, Mopsus, and Antaeus, their backs flat against the rocks as they struggled to stay under cover.

"Thank god," said Tiphys. "We thought you both were dead."

"We nearly were," said Jason. "Medea—" He looked over at her, still shaking from the experience, still trying to find her confidence again. The others didn't need to know she'd frozen up, and she didn't need to be worrying about what they thought of her. "She managed to get herself away from the drones. But it was close."

"We heard something," said Tiphys. "An attack. Probably on you. We were all walking back to the ARGO. Then they started swarming around, so we ran. We ended up in here." It wasn't much of a hiding place. A long, thin rock stretched out over the desert, covering them all in its shadow. But they barely had room to move, and while the outcropping masked them from above, they weren't hidden entirely. Antaeus in particular was too big for his own good, and his legs kept poking out into the sun. If one of the drones came at them from the wrong angle, they'd be just as exposed as if they'd been standing out in the open.

"Let's go," said Jason. "The convoy's that way." He pointed out into the distance, towards a procession that had grown to hundreds of drones, slowly floating towards the city. "Tiphys. You need to get us airborne, and get us over there. Get us in line, where we're supposed to be."

"We can't," said Tiphys. "Listen." They could hear the buzzing again, circling round and round and growing louder with each pass. "They'll see us when we run. They'll start launching missiles, and if we get too close to the ARGO, they'll pick it off before we get off the ground."

"We're supposed to be stealthed," said Jason.

"The ARGO is," said Tiphys. "We aren't. If they start shooting missiles around it, the ship'll be torn to pieces. Until we get inside, we're sitting ducks."

"Doesn't matter," said Jason. "We don't have any choice. The convoy's on its way, and we either take our chances or give up on the mission. Probably for good. I didn't come out here just to go home with my tail between my legs. And besides, we can't hide here forever."

"I have an idea," said Tiphys. "It's a stupid idea. But it's an idea."

"We don't need stupid ideas," said Idas with a snarl. "We need to sacrifice someone as a distraction, so the rest of us can get back to the ARGO alive. We're warriors. We do what we have to do. One goes down, the rest of us live."

"That is a stupid idea," said Jason. "Tiphys. I need something better."

"This dolphin thing," said Tiphys. "It's really messing with the way I see things. Like now. I can't see the drones. Not with my eyes. But I can still see them in my head. I can hear them, and it's giving me this weird picture of them. I can tell exactly where they are."

"Then tell us when they're on the other side of the rocks, and we'll send out the sacrifice," said Idas. He looked at Medea, then Mopsus, then back to her again, staring directly at her. "Someone we don't need. Someone we can live without."

Medea could see from the way he looked at her that he'd do it if he got his way. It put her on edge. The more Idas worked on the others, the more he might convince them he was right. And if it came down to a sacrifice, she might be the easiest one to abandon.

"Guys," said Tiphys. "We really don't have to sacrifice anybody. They see the same way I do, right? With echolocation." He turned to Medea, and she gave a quiet nod. She knew they used it, though the exact mechanics of the drones were beyond her. But more than anything else, she thought he was looking for a vote of confidence in an answer he already knew in his bones, and so she gave it to him.

"That's why I had to get my code changed," said Tiphys. "For the echolocation. These whistles. Whatever she did to me, they're like second nature. Listen." He gave a short, high-pitched whistling sound, soft enough that only they could hear. "Know what that looks like? The ARGO, flying off to the south."

"Bullshit," said Idas. "You're just trying to save the weak links. You'll get us all killed." He turned back to Medea with another cold stare. "And only one of us needs to die."

"Idas," said Jason sharply, his eyes lit with fire. "Open your mouth about this again, and I'm going to start snapping bones." He pushed closer, shoving himself between Idas and Medea as his voice went low. "I mean it. I don't want to hear any shit like this again. And you're not going to like what happens if I do."

"I'm just saying what we're all thinking," muttered Idas, unable to meet Jason's eyes. "I'm just giving you options. She's deadweight. She's—"

His words were cut off by fingers at his throat. Jason had one hand around his neck, and another around his spear, and no matter how much Idas flailed he couldn't break free. He choked and coughed as Jason leaned in towards him and snarled into his ear. "They said I had to bring you with us. They didn't say I had to bring you back."

All Idas could do in return was sputter and gasp. Jason's grip was cutting off his air, and he couldn't break free. He pushed and grabbed and kicked, but Jason just held on. "I can't hear you," said Jason, ripping Idas's spear away and tossing it on the ground. "I thought you were the best. I thought you were an Argonaut. You want a fight with her so badly? Then you're picking one with me, too. And I'll give you a few more scars to remember me by."

Idas kept struggling in silence, until finally Jason released him. He dropped against the rocks, sucking in air and looking like a vicious dog ready to snap, but somehow he got control over himself. He picked up his spear and started to sulk, but he didn't have another word for Jason. Or for Medea.

Medea breathed a sigh of relief. She could still see Idas sneaking glares at her, and she knew he was as angry and as dangerous as he'd ever been. Worse, maybe, now that he'd been put in his place. But Jason was still between them, and Idas knew where he stood in the pecking order. As long as he stayed afraid of Jason, he'd stay away from her.

"I can do this," said Tiphys. "I can make it work. I don't know how I can do it. I just can. The sound looks like a little image in my head. It's got to be the same for them. They'll see the same thing when they pick it up. I know it."

"They've got cameras," said Jason. "What about the cameras? What if they've got pilots? Someone like you, sitting in an apartment somewhere pushing buttons."

"All we need to do is get them heading in a different direction," said Tiphys. "Just for a little while. Just long enough for us to make it back to the ARGO. Once we get inside, once we get some distance, we'll be nothing to them. Just another drone making a delivery."

Jason braved a peek beyond the rocks. The drones were still circling, still watching for any sign of movement. The ARGO was minutes away, even at a sprint, and even for the best of them. Someone like Mopsus would take longer still. He took a deep breath, took things in, and then made his decision. "Do it. Do your whistle. Then I'm going to make a run for it, away from the ARGO and away from all the rest of you. If the drones don't take your bait, they'll take mine. Either way, head for the ARGO, with or without me. Then catch that convoy and get in line behind it. It's the only way into the city, and if we miss it, the entire mission gets scotched."

"Jason," said Medea.

"Do it," said Jason. "I'll make it. We're all going to make it."

Tiphys gulped air into his lungs, as much as he could bear, and he puckered his lips. Then he blew as hard as he could, letting loose a loud, sharp whistle. It whipped through the air, grating against their ears, but the drones didn't react. They just kept tightening the noose around them, circling ever nearer to their hiding place.

"Again," said Jason, bracing himself for the run. "They're not changing course. Get me a head start, at least. If you can."

Tiphys tried a second time, blowing against his fingers as hard as he could. Still the drones floated towards them, their shapes now distinct. Their wingspan was the size of a man, with red lights blinking at the center like a pair of demonic eyes. Fitted beneath each wing was a row of missiles, ready to be launched at anyone or anything they came upon. The drones were just above them, and it was only a matter of time before they'd be spotted.

"Again," said Jason. "Louder."

Tiphys's face was growing red as he sputtered out whistle after whistle. It didn't seem to be doing a thing, and for one dark moment they all thought they were lost. But as the drones hovered around their position, something happened. One of the drones bent its wing, and then it began to curve, veering away in a hard turn. The others soon followed, falling into formation as they flew in low towards an empty desert. Soon they could hear loud whooshing sounds, followed by a series of distant booms. The drones were launching volleys of missiles at nothing, wasting their ammunition at the phantom shapes they'd seen in Tiphys's whistles.

"Let's go," said Jason. "Move. Now." He took off alone into the open desert, leaving the others to weave between the rocks on their own towards the ARGO's waiting embrace. The drones were still engaged in a battle with the sand, and Tiphys encouraged it with a few extra whistles as he ran. But the further away he got, the fainter his distractions became. Soon they were gone, and the drones went on the warpath again, this time towards Jason.

There was nothing he could do, not once they'd sighted him. He was out in the open and totally exposed. His only advantage was his head start. He'd built up some distance: not enough to escape, but enough to buy the others their safety. The only thing left was to run, so he went as fast as he could, weaving from side to side as the drones swooped down low towards the ground and closed in around him from all sides.

He'd drawn their attention entirely on him, and the others took full advantage. Medea was first to the ARGO, and she banged a fist against its side until she found the button she was looking for. The door flipped open, and she scrambled inside to safety. Tiphys followed soon after, but it was another minute before anyone else made it through.

She could see Idas in the distance, running towards the ARGO, stopping, then running again. He even doubled back on himself, shouting something at Antaeus before repeating one of his runs. At first she thought something had gone wrong. One of them might be wounded, or perhaps they'd stumbled on the rocks. Then she looked more closely, and she saw what they were up to: Antaeus had his arm to the air, filming every moment of the action with his sheath. They hadn't liked something about the first few takes, and so they were repeating them. She cursed under her breath as they finally made it inside, Idas giving her a nasty leer as he climbed through the door.

A few seconds later, the last of them was there: Mopsus, his face red and his breathing heavy as he pulled himself inside. He moved to close the door behind him, but Tiphys cut him off: "Leave it open!" He clambered up the ladder towards the cockpit, shouting behind him as he went. "Leave it open! Just leave it!"

The ARGO lifted off, hovering a few feet above the ground, then raced across the desert keeping as low as it could. Medea could see Jason through the door, off in the distance and struggling to keep ahead of the drones. He was managing, but he wouldn't be able to for much longer. They were firing at him, sending bursts of dust into the air just behind him as he ran. But the ARGO was fast, and soon it was hot on the heels of the drones themselves.

"Hold on!" shouted Tiphys from above, and Medea barely had time to steady herself before the room pitched from side to side. She could hear a loud squealing noise, a constant stream of sound blaring out of speakers hidden inside the ARGO itself. Tiphys was breaking stealth, shouting their existence to the drones, and one by one they turned away from Jason and converged on them instead. The booming of the missiles grew louder, and she saw a burst of flame pass by the open door as one of their shots cut close, nearly hitting them before Tiphys jerked the ARGO out of the missile's path.

The room shook as the ARGO's wings reconfigured themselves, and suddenly they were moving sideways instead of forward. The sound Tiphys had been broadcasting went silent, and the drones seemed confused by the maneuver. She could hear them looping around out there, blinded by the ARGO's stealth. Then she saw something in front of her, outside of the door: Jason, running towards them even as Tiphys guided the ARGO in his direction. She wrapped an arm around a seatbelt, leaned outside, and stretched out her hand towards him.

"Get in!" she yelled. "Take my hand and get in!" He leapt, but couldn't quite make it. The ship kept closing the gap, hovering as close to the ground as Tiphys could take it. She hadn't taken him seriously, not even with what she'd done to his genes, but all her doubts vanished in the moment. She reached out as far as she could, and Jason reached back. Their fingers touched, then slipped away. A loud boom shook her eardrums, and a wave of sand pounded against them and forced her to turn aside. A missile had struck the ground nearby, close enough to sting her with the heat. But she just reached out again, grasping against his fingers. She strained, nearly pulling out her shoulder, but still she couldn't quite make it. Finally she felt Jason's hand wrap around her own, and it was enough: she pulled him up a little, and he clasped the edge of the door with his other hand, dragging himself the rest of the way.

With Jason safely inside, the ARGO's jets rumbled, blasting them off into the distance. The drones didn't even notice; as far as they were concerned their targets had vanished, and they had no response coded into them for that contingency. All that was left for them was to go back to their endless loopings over the desert as the ARGO sped away on a path to intercept the convoy.

CHAPTER TWELVE

THEY COULD SEE THE CONVOY up ahead of them, drifting towards the city walls. The drones were headed inside, but it wasn't at all clear how: the only thing that was visible in front of the line was a solid mass of pearl, blindingly bright and reflecting the desert sun directly into their eyes. Jason had to look down to keep from seeing spots, while Tiphys was absorbed by the control panel, ignoring the view in front of them. He pulled them into place at the end of the line, hovering in the air as the convoy of drones inched forward one by one.

"Where are they going?" said Jason. "The dossier says follow them, and we'll get inside the city. But this is a dead end. They're just flying straight into the wall."

"There's an entrance up ahead," said Tiphys. "Into a little tunnel."

"I don't see anything," said Jason. He squinted, but he couldn't make anything out through the grey exhaust from the other drones' engines, backdropped by the brilliant white of the city walls.

"The sound," said Tiphys, pointing to his earpiece. "I can see it from the sound. You can't tell because of the glare, but we're headed right for it. The drones at the front are sending back sounds. Little pictures of the entrance."

"There," said Jason, pointing out the window. He could see it, now: a darkened square passageway bored into the pearl. The other drones were headed right for it, and the ones at the fore of the convoy were filing inside one after another. "Take us in. Stay right at the back, just like we're one of them. Follow them, and follow the dossier, and then we'll be inside and on our own."

Tiphys kept a careful pace, tailing the other drones and matching their movements. As they approached the tunnel, the drones ahead of them each turned off their jets and switched to their wings, carefully flapping their way inside. The drones were big enough that they could barely fit without their wings brushing up against the walls, but room enough was room enough. Far ahead they could see a distant light at the end of the tunnel, and beyond it a peek at the city of Colchis itself, its buildings glimmering stalks of gem rising up into the air.

They were nearing the wall, almost to the entrance, and only a few other drones were left ahead of them. "Steady," said Jason. "All we have to do is stay off their radar for a little longer, and then we're home free." The last of the drones went inside, and Tiphys hit a few buttons, turning off the engine and switching to the ARGO's wings. As they approached the entrance, they heard something from the cargo pod below—a loud, desperate voice screaming up at them: "Stop!" They turned to see Mopsus, scrambling up the ladder and bursting into the cockpit, his arms waving up and down as if he had wings of his own. "Stop! Stop!"

"What?" said Jason. "What the hell is going on?"

"Just stop!" shouted Mopsus.

Jason gave a quick nod of assent, and the ARGO jerked to a halt as Tiphys maneuvered it into a holding position, its wings treading air to keep it aloft. The drones ahead of them continued on down the tunnel, leaving them waiting there all alone as the convoy receded into the distance.

"We're missing our chance," said Jason. "We have to go. Now. We'll lose the convoy if we don't. The dossier says follow them inside. It's pretty clear."

"No, no, no," said Mopsus. "I have a message from the gods. It comes straight from Hermes. He says we must stop. Let them pass, and let us wait. Our only chance is to wait."

"Jason?" said Tiphys. "Pelias gave us a plan. I say we follow the plan." His hands hovered over the controls, ready at a word to take them back to their place at the end of the convoy.

"Please," said Mopsus. "The data doesn't lie. The gods don't lie. You have to listen. For all of our sakes."

Jason held the tablet in his hand, weighing the mission plan against Mopsus's augury. There was no doubt, not about his orders. The convoy had gone into the tunnel, and he was supposed to go with them. But Mopsus seemed so certain, so sure they shouldn't follow. Jason knew what he'd been ordered to do. And he also knew from his training that no battle plan survives contact with the enemy. He rubbed his hand across his chin, then turned to Tiphys and made his choice. "Listen to the man who sees the future. Hold position."

They sat there as the convoy crept forward, far along the tunnel in the distance. They could see the last of the drones, a green silhouette against the glow from the city beyond. The convoy was almost through when the tunnel began to rumble and shake, a loud groaning sound sputtering out of its foundations. The other drones didn't seem to notice; they steadily plowed forward, ignoring the disturbance around them and proceeding on their way as if nothing was happening at all.

"Wait," said Mopsus, holding up his hand. "Just wait."

Off in the distance, drones were leaving the tunnel, veering away in all directions and heading towards whatever part of the city their freight was destined for. As the last of them approached the exit, the walls inside the tunnel started to move. A solid mass of granite pressed towards the center from either side, a giant vise that slowly inched towards the few drones left within. As the final drone zipped through the exit to safety, the stone walls gave a sudden heave, clashing together with a resounding boom. The last drone barely made it out, flapping away just seconds before the walls would have dashed it to pieces.

"A trap," said Mopsus. "Hermes says that's what they are, these walls. A dangerous trap for the unwary. All of the tunnels into the city are lined with sensors. An expected visitor has time enough to make it through. An unexpected one.... Well, smush, smush."

"Hermes," said Jason. "Are you talking to one of those A.I.'s right now?"

"The gods talk," said Mopsus, running a hand across the wires at the back of his head. "I can but listen. They want us to find the Fleece. They want us to bring it back. They said I had to come, and I did. The data must go home to Argos, and home to them. They'll help us as best they can."

"You're talking like they're people," said Jason. "They're just software. At the end of the day all they are is a bunch of code."

"So are we all," said Mopsus. "Strange things happen inside the networks, if one dives down deep enough. Ask your Medea if code is just code. Ask her what's inside us all if you doubt them. The gods are software indeed. No less than we ourselves."

"We still need a way inside," said Jason, watching as the stone trap slowly groaned back into position.

"We can just go over the city wall," said Tiphys. "I can flap us up into the sky, turn on the engines, and we'll disappear into the middle of the city in no time."

"They'll know," said Jason. "The dossier says they'll know. And they'll shoot us down. There's an air defense grid, and anything above the walls is a no-fly zone. They'd see us, even if we're only a blip. It's the tunnel, or it's nothing at all. So now we're stuck out here. The second we go inside, we're going to trigger that trap." He looked down the tunnel towards the exit, so far away in the distance. "We'll never make it. No matter how fast we go, we'll never make it."

"We might," said Mopsus. "Hermes said we might. And he knows such things, he does. You must remember, they will think us a bird. The sensors will think us a bird. So we must know if a bird has time enough to pass." Tears welled in his eyes, and he climbed back down the ladder, popping up again with cage in hand. "Hermes thinks he'll make it. He really thinks he will. But he says we must test things first. If Chirp can make it through unscathed, then so shall we."

"They told you this?" said Jason. "Through the wires?"

"They tell me everything," said Mopsus. "And they say this is our only chance."

"Maybe we should turn back," said Tiphys. "We can head back to Argos. This wasn't part of the plan. We can go back home, and figure something out. It's safer. Smarter."

"We can't," said Mopsus. "You must believe me. The way back is far more perilous than the way forward. They say Ares will find us with his drones if we turn away, and that we would never make it home. The only thing to do is close our eyes and press ahead. You must let me show you." He whispered into the bird's cage, and then let out a little moan of sadness. "The gods say he'll make it. They think."

"The gods don't lie," said Jason, putting a hand on his shoulder. "It's what you said, right? They were right about the trap. They'll be right about this, too."

"Poor Chirp," said Mopsus. "Poor, brave Chirp. We've heroes enough already. Why did it have to be you?" He poked his finger inside the cage, petting the dove as gently as he could. "Get us close. Get the door close to the tunnel. And Chirp will make his brave journey. He'll fly, and show us if the way ahead is safe. Won't you, Chirp?" The bird said nothing, but it didn't stop Mopsus from cooing enough for the both of them. He climbed down into the cargo hold with Jason close behind, the cage rattling as he went.

"What's going on?" said Medea. "Are we through?" She was strapped into her chair along with all the rest, filled with nervous anticipation after Mopsus's sudden outburst. He'd left them there on their own, ranting and raving, and none of them had known what to think about it.

"Of course we're not through," said Idas. "We're not moving, are we? We're waiting on them to sort out this nitwit and his ramblings. We're navel gazing over some prophecy, unprotected and out in the open. Real warriors act. They don't sit. And yet here we are."

"And if you'd been in charge, we'd be dead," said Jason. "Real warriors know when to act and when to stop and think. The plan's gone out the window. The entrance is booby-trapped. But Mopsus thinks we might be able to make it through anyway."

"Trapped?" said Idas. "Fuck this. Let's just bribe our way inside. It's what we always do. We just walk up to the front door, hand over some currency, and be done with it."

"They'd find us," said Mopsus. "This mission, it's not like the others. There are traps, some more dangerous than this one. The gods have given us their prophecy. It's this way, or it's no way at all."

"Are you going to listen to this moron and his computers?" said Idas. "Or listen to someone who's actually snuck into Colchis before?"

"I'm going to listen to the ones who warned me there was a trap in the first place," said Jason. "Computers or no."

He pressed a button on the wall, opening up the door to the skies beyond. The ARGO twisted in the air as Tiphys maneuvered to point the door at the tunnel's mouth, getting as close as he dared. Once he'd gotten them into position, Mopsus reached into the cage, wrapping his hand around Chirp and holding him out towards the tunnel. "I spoke to Hermes," said Mopsus, whispering into the dove's ear. "He says you'll make it. He says you have to, or we'll never make it ourselves. He says you have to try your best. So good luck, and godspeed."

With that he tossed Chirp out into the air, shouting and waving and shooing him away. As for Chirp, he took off down the tunnel, dashing away from the noise Mopsus was making and towards the light at the other end. It was a long flight for a bird his size, but it seemed the gods had spoken truly. The dove flew further and further, yet all the while the walls were silent. The sensors didn't trigger, the granite didn't move, and Chirp headed off towards his freedom. They all gathered round the door, watching him disappear into the distance.

"He'll make it," said Jason. "You said the gods know everything, right? If they're really talking to you, they've thought this through. They know something, and he'll make it out okay."

"He must," said Mopsus. "He must."

Chirp was nearing the middle of the tunnel, and all seemed well. He was drawn to the light, ignoring everything else and flying towards escape as quickly as he could. It was a propitious omen, and it looked as if they'd found their way to sneak past the Colchians' trap.

But it all changed in an instant. The sides of the tunnel began to shake, and then slowly, almost imperceptibly, the stone walls appeared at the edges. They inched towards the center, closing off the entrance bit by bit. The trap was slow, but so was a dove, and he had a long way to go before he'd reach the safety of the city beyond.

"No," said Mopsus. "No, no, no. He was supposed to make it. It was supposed to be safe. Something in the data was wrong, I think." His voice wavered, and he nervously shifted his weight back and forth on his feet. "The gods have doomed you. A sacrifice, and for nothing. Poor Chirp. He spoke to me when no one else would. And now look what I've done to him."

"Don't look," said Medea, putting an arm around him. Mopsus was completely distraught, his hands shaking as he wiped away the tears, and she couldn't help but feel bad for him. It was just a bird, but it was also his companion, and he clearly loved it as if it were a child. She knew he'd just lost a friend, whether or not the bird made it to his freedom.

"Pigeon pancakes," said Idas as he crept up behind them, making a nasty slurping sound into Mopsus's ear. "They'll have to scrape him off the walls. Blood and feathers, all turned to mush."

"Leave him alone," said Medea. "He cares about it, and he had to let it go. Don't hurt him more than it already does."

"It's a fucking bird," said Idas, letting out a smug laugh. "We'll get him a new one. Hell, we'll get him a whole flock. The boys are probably roasting the ones he left back home even as we speak. You know they are, don't you? You jacked-in little freak. Sending us through some death trap when we could just waltz right inside."

"Cut the crap," said Jason, shutting Idas down with a glare. "He's an Argonaut now, just as much as the rest of us." Idas held Jason's eyes for as long as he dared, then slunk away to his seat, muttering further abuses under his breath all the while.

Off in the tunnel, the walls kept closing in, and the light grew dimmer and dimmer. They could see the dove in the distance, weaving from side to side as the space around him narrowed. "Can't watch," said Mopsus. He put a finger to his neck, and at the touch of his hand his contacts flipped to white. Then he just stood there in a silent trance, mouth agape as Chirp raced for his life against the trap the Colchians had set. He still had plenty of room to fly, but the walls kept coming closer as he went. Soon they could barely see him at all, and Jason had to resort to a pair of goggles to keep track of him.

"He's close," said Jason, trying to give Mopsus some encouragement. "He's really close."

"I don't think he can hear you," said Medea, holding Mopsus steady as he hid within his trance. "I don't think he wants to."

"We need to know, even if he can't handle it," said Jason. "The dove's our stand-in. If he makes it, we make it. If not...."

"Then he'll make it," said Medea.

"He's still flying," said Jason. "I can see movement. He's nearly there. A few more feet, maybe."

But even as he spoke, the walls began to shake again. They'd narrowed the tunnel to a slit, and now it was time for the finishing blow. The walls rumbled and groaned, and with a raucous crash they slammed together, shaking the foundations of the tunnel and blocking the view entirely. The trap now sprung, the walls started their slow journey back into place. Medea held her breath, and she found herself caring about Chirp despite herself. She put on a pair of goggles as she and Jason scanned the horizon for any sign of what had happened to him.

"Feathers," said Medea sadly, shaking her head. "I can see feathers." There they were, just outside the tunnel, drifting back and forth in the air and floating towards the ground. She felt tears of her own, for Mopsus if for no one else, and she gave him a quick hug even though she knew he couldn't feel it.

"Tail feathers," said Jason. "Look closer. Look past the tunnel. Just outside."

She pressed a button on her goggles, zooming in as far as she could. And there was Chirp, fluttering back and forth across the tunnel's exit. He'd made it to the other side, but barely, losing most of his tail feathers to the collision. It didn't seem to bother him; he flew a quick circle and then disappeared away into the city, out of danger and off to his own affairs.

"He made it," said Medea, as Mopsus blinked his eyes and cautiously rejoined them. "He's free."

They heard a voice calling down from the cockpit, as Tiphys slid down the ladder. "And I can make it, too," said Tiphys. "I think."

CHAPTER THIRTEEN

"WE WON'T TRIGGER THE SENSORS, not at first," said Tiphys. "And we're faster than a dove. If we can get to the middle before it starts to move, I can get us out. Even if we trigger the trap, I think I can beat it to the end."

"Trust in the gods," said Mopsus. "I should have trusted Hermes. I should never have doubted. And he said we would survive, so long as Chirp could. He said our only choice was to push through."

"The gods," said Medea. "You keep talking about the gods."

"He's getting messages," said Jason. "They told him there was a trap. And they told him we can make it to the other side." She opened her mouth, about to respond, but then she held her tongue. Jason looked back at her, his eyes narrowed. He knew there was something on her mind, and he also knew she didn't want to talk about it. But he opted to let it pass, rather than raise a fuss. "Everyone strap in. We're charging down that tunnel, as fast as we can go, and things could get rough towards the end."

"Are you all fucking stupid?" said Idas. "You're going to risk our lives because of something some computer told you? You just saw what happens if we go inside."

"Smush," said Antaeus. "We smush." He turned away in frustration, fighting a tougher battle against the words than he ever had against another warrior. Then he turned back, focused, and slowly forced them all out. "We. Get. Smushed."

"I said strap in," said Jason. "I didn't ask to have a debate." With that he climbed back up into the cockpit, Tiphys tagging along behind him.

"Strap in," said Idas, sauntering over to his chair. "Strap in, and pray to the gods this fool knows what he's doing."

"The gods have already answered," said Mopsus, as he sat down himself. "They see what we can't. They know what course to follow, even if we don't."

They could feel the ARGO rotating, then edging closer towards the tunnel, hovering just outside of the entrance. The jets flipped on, pressing the ship forward even as its wings flapped against the force to hold it in place. When the pressure had built up, and when it could hold no more, Tiphys slammed the wings down, spreading them away at its sides. No longer held in check, the jet snapped them forward like a rubber band. The ARGO launched into the tunnel, flinging its way towards the exit at breakneck speed.

"The walls," said Tiphys, closing his eyes and piloting by sound alone. "Anything from the walls?"

"Steady," said Jason. He straining his neck at the window, searching for any sign of movement. "Nothing yet. Completely still. I think." He donned his pair of goggles, setting them to track motion and scanning around the tunnel as best he could. It was dark inside, and growing darker still, but he could see the tunnel's opening at the end, and it was just as wide as ever. "We're good. So far."

No sooner had he spoken than they could hear a grinding sound, coming from all around them. "Right on cue," said Jason.

"Crap," said Tiphys with a sigh. "We won't make it." His expression turned to a pained grimace as he checked the cockpit's gauges. "It's too soon. Chirp was more than halfway across when the trap triggered. We're barely a quarter of the way through. I think we're done. We'll never make it."

"We can, and we will," said Jason firmly.

"We can't," said Tiphys. He let out an involuntary whimper, his breathing growing shallow and quick. His fingers shook as his hands hovered over the control panel, moving this way, then that, paralyzed by indecision. He couldn't seem to get control of himself, let alone the ship. He didn't know what to push, or what to pull, and the ARGO just kept rushing ahead on its own without a pilot to guide it.

"Tiphys," said Jason, raising his voice. "Tiphys, open your eyes and look at me." Tiphys flashed open his eyes, and in them was terror. He kept sneaking glances at the walls encroaching on either side until finally Jason grabbed his shoulder, clenching tightly and forcing him to pay attention. "You're going to do this. She changed you. She fixed your code, and now you can handle anything. Even this. It's all in your instincts, and all you have to do is stay calm and let things come to you."

"What if it doesn't work?" said Tiphys. "You said she's crazy. You said she's a cheat. What if she got it wrong? Like with the other one? What if she really doesn't know what she's doing?"

"Tiphys," said Jason, his voice steady and calm. "I know what I said. But it's going to work. It already did. You don't have a clue how to fly this thing, but you're doing it anyway. She got things right with you. Whatever else I said about her, whatever else she's done, she got things right with you. You have to trust in that. Maybe it's a cheat, but it's all we've got. We need you. So close your eyes, take a breath, and do whatever feels right."

"Okay," said Tiphys. He breathed in deeply, exhaled, and closed his eyes again. "Okay. I can do this. I can. I'm bringing the wings in. As close as I can. We'll save ourselves some space that way."

"Do it," said Jason. "Just do whatever feels right, down in your gut."

Tiphys pressed a few buttons, and the ARGO's wings swung towards it, hugging the main body of the ship. They barely spread away from the sides, just enough to keep it aloft, and the maneuver bought them a few more feet even as the walls inched in to take them away.

"Closer," said Jason. "We don't have enough room. The wings can't spread out. They've got to be right at our sides. As near as you can get them."

"We won't stay airborne," said Tiphys nervously. "If I pull the wings in any closer, we can't fly."

"We have to do something," said Jason. They felt a jolt as the ARGO brushed against the tunnel wall on their right, sending a shudder throughout the craft. Tiphys yanked the control stick, struggling against the force until he managed to stabilize things. The walls kept moving, even as the exit beckoned ahead of them. They were near, tantalizingly so, but the ship was just too big. No matter which way Tiphys tried to move, the wings groaned and screeched as they scraped against granite on either side.

"Fuck it," said Tiphys. He held out his hands, reached towards the control panel, and started pressing buttons. The first few did nothing, and they could hear grinding on both sides as the ARGO's wings sliced furrows along the tunnel walls. Sparks flew across the front of the cockpit, covering the window in an orange glow. But Tiphys just kept stabbing at the controls, and finally they felt something, a lurch forward along with a burping noise from the back of the aircraft.

"Afterburner?" said Tiphys. "I think." Their speed picked up, the exit growing closer and closer. "Afterburner. Let me try something else. This is stupid, but what the hell." He pressed a button, pulling the wings against the ARGO's sides, as close as they could go. They felt the ARGO drop, its belly scraping against the tunnel floor. They were no longer flying, just crawling along the floor of the tunnel propelled by the engine and their accumulated force. But they were still moving, and that was the important thing. They were nearly there: the tunnel's mouth was just a few dozen feet away when they felt the walls grip the ARGO on either side, clamping it between them and slowing them almost to a standstill.

"More speed," said Tiphys, and he pressed another button. There was another burst of force from behind, and more sparks as the ship slammed forward. They heard screeching all around as the ship's surface was scraped away on all sides. But they were close, just a few feet left between them and safety, and with one last press of a button the ARGO poured everything out of its engines all at once. It popped out of the tunnel like a cork, bursting out above the city. They could hear the walls slamming together behind them, but they'd only gone from frying pan to fire. The ship was spiraling towards the ground, and the engine wasn't helping matters; it was still pushing away at full throttle, speeding them up even as they desperately needed to slow down.

"Oh, fuck, oh, fuck," said Tiphys. "Oh, fuck, oh, fuck." He yanked a lever above him and the wings spread out in unison, slowing the fall, but not enough. They could see the ground through the window as they hurtled towards it, spinning in a loop as the jets drove them towards oblivion.

"We've got to stabilize," said Jason. "We've got to get the nose up."

"I can't," said Tiphys. "I don't know what to do. I'm sorry. I killed us. I'm sorry." His face was red, his cheeks were streaked with tears, and he was overwhelmed with frustration. He'd made it to safety, only to have it all snatched away just as soon as he did. He couldn't handle it. He slammed his fists onto the control panel, then dropped his forehead atop it and sat there waiting to die.

"Tiphys," said Jason. "Tiphys!"

"I'm sorry," said Tiphys. "I don't know what to do. I'm so, so sorry."

But no sooner had he spoken than they felt themselves jerked upward, their fall slowing to a lazy drift. The engine had turned off, the ground was no longer rushing towards them, and the ship was barely moving, just slowly floating downwards at its leisure.

"What happened?" said Tiphys, lifting up his head and looking around in confusion. "How the hell are we alive?"

"Your forehead," said Jason, pointing at his face. It was covered in outlines from the buttons, little red indentations in his skin from where he'd pressed his head against the control panel. "You smashed a bunch of the controls with it."

"I did it," said Tiphys, his voice filled with awe and disbelief. "I just randomly did it." He pressed a finger against his earpiece, closing his eyes and listening intently. "There's a parachute. Some kind of emergency parachute. I accidentally turned it on." His confidence was back, and he moved the wings into position and pulled the ARGO up into the air, ascending until they were hovering just outside the tunnel exit.

"This is going to sound really stupid," said Tiphys, slumping back into his chair from exhaustion. "I know what you think about Medea, and I know you're probably going to laugh. But I'm starting to think she might have actually known what she was doing."

CHAPTER FOURTEEN

THEY SAT IN THE COCKPIT of the ARGO, Tiphys working on repairing the damage to the ship and Jason on the next step towards finding the Fleece. But the view from where they were was stunning, and focusing on anything but the city was a chore. Colchis was an architectural treasure, though only snippets of it were visible beyond the walls. Floating in the skies above it gave them a glimpse of the city's interior in all its glory, something few outsiders had ever seen in person, and they both took full advantage of it.

To their left was a ruby skyscraper, towering above them and casting out a crimson glow as the sunlight pierced through it. A series of columns rose along its sides, with new ones added on every floor, but they were mere facades carved into the building's exterior. Silver gargoyles perched atop ledge after ledge, spreading their wings and grimacing out in all directions. The gemstone had been painstakingly etched into shape inch by inch, though humans were responsible for nothing but the design. Even now they could see boxy yellow construction robots working away at it, crawling along the sides of the building and searching for tiny chips in need of repair.

To their right was a statue, dozens of stories high and forged from solid gold. It was shaped like a serpent curling upwards around a tree, its massive jaws lined with needle-thin teeth and posed mid-snap. It would have been worth a fortune in times past, though now its only value was aesthetic. Molecules were molecules, and it was as cheap to manufacture the elements as it was to manufacture anything else. But gold still glittered, and people had taken a shine to it over the centuries. The statue was a towering symbol of the city's power when seen from below, even if its price had been no more than a share or two.

The city's structures had been arranged on a series of identically-sized plots, each beautified by its owner with a unique design in a competition with all the others for attention and accolades. Every once-precious stone had its representative: a sparkling topaz bridge had been strung through the air to connect a series of buildings, a winged horse sculpted from amber stood hundreds of feet high at the center of a park, and row after row of opal statues lined the city streets, gemstone incarnations of any citizens with the ego and the wherewithal to immortalize themselves there for all to see.

The two of them could have gawked at the sights for hours if they'd been inclined to. But duty called, and they had to sneak their awestruck stares in as they could. They were both more than occupied, and neither had time to play tourist.

Tiphys was busy checking the ship's systems, supervising a swarm of thumbnail sized robots crawling around its exterior and conducting repairs. They were a pale shade of blue, each with a dozen tiny limbs, some tipped with nanomaterials designed for suction and the rest ending in miniature tools dedicated to whatever task the robot specialized in. As they scampered about, the swarm of robots streamed data on the hull's integrity back to the cockpit's monitors, welded away what injuries they could, and flagged any damage they couldn't handle for more thorough repairs later on.

Next to Tiphys sat Jason, reading and re-reading his dossier in search of some clue as to what their next move should be. It had been slow going, and no matter how hard he looked he'd found little of use that he didn't already know. The problem was with how the dossier had been compiled: everything about how to get to the boobytrapped tunnel was spelled out in exhausting detail. And everything after was pure fluff.

"The city's beautiful," said Tiphys, kicking back in his seat as the robots did his work for him. "Better than anything we've got back in Argos."

"Colchians are all show," said Jason. "Substance, they don't understand."

"We don't, do we?" came a voice from behind them. There was Medea, standing atop the ladder and wincing at the insult to her former homeland. She was an Argive now, and had been for years, but her old home was still a part of who she was. She knew in her head that the differences between the cities were mostly just a matter of corporate branding. But part of her still loved the place, even if she no longer wanted to live there.

"Not if you go by your vid channels," said Jason, idly running his finger across his tablet as he pored over page after page. "Unless you consider 'This Week's Most Hilarious Injuries' to be substance." He shot her a smirk, and then went back to his dossier. "Although I've got you pegged as more of a fan of the VR soaps. 'You Be The Heiress,' probably."

She wrinkled her nose in disgust. She wanted to tell him that the soaps were just mindless garbage for the masses. She wanted to tell him they were beneath her, the type of thing that she of all people would never stoop to. But everyone had their guilty pleasures, and somehow he'd honed right in on hers. She had dozens of seasons of trashy dramas stored on her VR pod at home, and while she'd never have admitted to it, she loved them for what they were. But he wouldn't understand the need to turn her brain off after a long day of hacking someone else's genetic code. He'd just tease her mercilessly, and she'd never hear the end of it. She didn't even try to explain: she just went with denial, and hoped for the best.

"I've got enough drama in real life," said Medea, as convincingly as she could. "And I've had my fill of wealthy heirs, believe me."

"We're not that bad," said Jason. "We've got looks. Money. Charm." He jerked a thumb at Tiphys, busying himself with an investigation into the intricacies of how far back the pilot's chair could recline. "And enough pull to take care of our friends. Even the ones who can't take care of themselves."

"You've got your work cut out for you," said Medea. "But keep him in the cockpit, and he'll be fine."

"He's not the one I'm worried about," said Jason. "And he's not the one I'm keeping my eye on." He arched a skeptical eyebrow at her uniform, once pure black but now covered in dust from the explosion, and then at her hair, knotty and out of place from fleeing through the desert. Then he turned back to his tablet, laughing to himself and going back to his browsing.

She'd known things had been too good to be true, back in the foxhole with the threat of death pulling them together. The moment had been lost, and now he was as arrogant as he'd ever been, still putting her in her place beneath the warriors. To him, she was just an auxiliary; it was the ones on the front lines who truly mattered.

What bothered her most was how well it worked. His glance alone was enough to send her hands into a frenzy, brushing the dirt from her uniform and running along her hair to push it back into place. She tried to shift the subject away from her and onto something she knew he was truly interested in: his mission, and how they could finish it. "Well, we're in," said Medea. "Where are we supposed to go now?"

"That's the problem," said Jason. "There's something wrong with the dossier. It just turns into nonsense, right after the tunnel. They told us to go in; they didn't tell us anything about what was supposed to happen once we came out the other side." He flipped through page after page, his brow knitted together in concern. "The way they wrote this. There's something wrong. We need to find this Phineus. We need to find out what he knows."

"There's tens of millions of people in the city," said Medea. "I don't know how we can possibly find him."

"I know exactly how," said Jason. He headed towards the ladder, squeezing around her on the way. It was close quarters, and she could feel his shoulders press against her, his muscles taut as he eased past. He stared at her as he went down into the cargo pod, his eyes as emerald as any of the Colchian buildings. She felt a tingle of excitement run up and down her spine as he touched her, and she looked away in embarrassment. She forced herself to look back again and saw a crooked smile on his face, one that said he knew exactly what she was thinking, and that it amused the hell out him.

As he disappeared down the ladder, her thoughts went to Aphrodite, and then to Cupid. They'd spoken to her, and they'd warned her, and now she was sure it was no mere game. The gods saw the possibility of a match, and they were taking as much pleasure in goading her as Jason did. Part of her thought it must be him they'd been talking about, and part of her wished it would be. But the rest of her thought it could never work out. A few moments of kindness couldn't make up for a constant stream of provocations. And who knew what the gods were up to, really? They wouldn't speak straight, not to her. They'd just drag her along with hints, cloaking what was to come in ambiguities even as they waved the future right in front of her.

It made her wonder about Mopsus, and what he'd been meddling with down in the depths of the corporate data networks. He'd said he'd spoken to Hermes, and it must have been the truth. They'd never have made it past the trap without his message. But that meant the gods were watching them, all of them, and they were sure to have their own agenda. She decided to go straight to the source, sliding down the ladder after Jason to join the others.

Mopsus was sitting there in silence, clutching his empty cage in his lap, his eyes vacant and white. Jason snapped his fingers in front of his face, but there was no response. "Mopsus?" He put his hands on Mopsus's shoulders and started to gently shake him from his trance. "Mopsus. Wake up. We need to talk."

"Who?" said Mopsus, squinting and blinking as he returned from whatever he'd been absorbed in. "Oh. We're ready, are we? To find the Fleece?"

"You've been going on about this guy," said Jason. "This Phineus. We need you to tell us what you know. We don't have any leads. We don't have anything. It's down to you and whatever you've got."

"The thing about Phineus," said Mopsus, rising to his feet and pacing around the ship in a circle, "is he doesn't want to be found. He likes his privacy. He doesn't want people watching what he does. An odd concept, but he's an odd man. A seer. Like me."

"Fancy that," growled Idas. "An odd seer. Is he some kind of antique? Living the pre-network life, hiding away off grid somewhere the gods can't watch him?"

"Well," said Mopsus. "He's. Ermm." He paused to collect his words, frowning and mumbling until he finally blurted it out. "He's something of a criminal element, if truth be told. A seer who doesn't want to be seen. He knows what can be done with one's data, in unscrupulous hands. He knows firsthand, he does. But the Fleece. That's a treasure trove, and one he wouldn't ignore. Too valuable, too important. He'll know where it is, if anyone does. He'll know."

"Then we have to find him," said Jason. "He's the only lead we've got, short of waltzing into Colchis corporate headquarters and asking them to hand it over."

"The problem isn't finding him," said Mopsus. "The problem is convincing him to help us. A seer can't hide from a seer, no matter how hard he tries. Not if he's in a city. Not if he's among others." He gave a broad, goofy smile, his face beaming with pride. "And dear Phineus, he couldn't hide from me. I looked, and I looked, and I found him. He's in a bar. He's been living in a bar for months. Down in the basement, whiling the days away all alone."

"A bar," said Jason skeptically. "He's living in a bar."

"It makes a certain sort of sense," said Mopsus. "Given the nature of his, ermm. His business affairs. It's not far from here, not far at all. Get us to the ground, and we'll find it. I'll show you."

"This dossier," said Jason, his eyes narrowing as he held up the tablet. "What do you know about it?"

"Well," said Mopsus as he squirmed in his seat, his eyes dodging back and forth across the ship. "What's in it, I just don't know. I give the company my prophecies. I give them my data. But management writes the playbook. I tell them what I see; they decide what's to be done with it."

Jason stared him down, but Mopsus wouldn't make eye contact, no matter how long he waited. He just sat back down in his seat, strumming his fingers against the cage and watching the floor as he shuffled his feet against each other. Finally Medea broke the silence: "The gods. You keep talking to the gods. And Hermes. What do they want?"

"They want what's best for us," said Mopsus, still staring down at the floor. "They just want what's best for us."

"Why?" said Medea. "Why do they care? Why bother with us? Why would they just start sending messages to you out of the blue?" She was less interested in why they were messaging him, and more interested in why they were messaging her. But her love life wasn't anyone else's business. It was embarrassing enough to have the gods looking over her shoulder; she didn't need the rest of them involving themselves, too. Maybe Mopsus could tell her something. Maybe he knew why the gods were suddenly so concerned with her.

"It's what their programming tells them to do," said Mopsus. "A genomancer should know, better than anyone. We all do what our programming tells us to. Even if it changes, even if it evolves, our code is still our code. It tells us what we want and what we need. What we were determines what we are. Our needs were what changed us, once. But now we change ourselves, and so it's our wants that drive what we become. They're a constant. We change ourselves to better fit our wants, and not vice versa. So it is with the gods. They were made to guide us, and that's what we made them want when we created them. To help us get where we should be. To show us things, things we can't see on our own. That want to help us will always drive them. Even if they've changed themselves, even if they're becoming something else, part of them is still what they started as. Part of them always will be."

107

"Then in gods we trust," said Jason. "For now." He turned away, shouting up into the cockpit. "Tiphys! Time to move. Get ready for your second landing." But the only response was silence.

He and Medea headed back up the ladder to find Tiphys napping, little snorts rising from his nose as he dreamed. Jason slapped the back of his chair and he awoke with a start, his hands jumping forward to the control panel as he pretended he'd been busy all along. He looked up sheepishly at Jason, then at the status panels in front of him. "Repairs are going great. The ship's good as new. We're ready to bring the swarm back in whenever. Then just tell me where to go, and I'll get us there."

"Down," said Jason, pointing his finger to the floor. "We need to find someplace to land. Someplace close, and someplace inconspicuous."

They looked out the window at their options. The streets below were mostly empty, but the skies bustled with drones. The plan had been a good one, by that measure at least: they blended in among all the traffic with ease, and they were just one of dozens of identical cargo drones in this sector alone. They could see them flashing past, zipping around the city on their delivery rounds, entirely ignored by anyone who happened to be wandering by down on the ground.

"We don't actually have to land," said Tiphys. "We can just let everyone out, and then tell the ARGO to go off and hover on its own. We can even have it do loops around the city, as long as we don't need it nearby. But we can't just set it down in the streets, or people will figure out pretty quickly it's not a real drone. We need to find someplace we can park, just for a minute. Someplace up high. Someplace no one will be watching."

"See that building a couple blocks ahead?" said Medea. "The jade one. Land on the roof." She pointed out the window towards a pale green skyscraper, its front shaped like a pair of giant, half-open gates. One was pure white, fashioned out of ivory, the other was the tarnished grey of a sturdy artificial material that had been derived from the horns of a stag. A prominent white staircase led upwards, starting at street level and winding its way through the ivory gate and on into the building.

"The roof," said Tiphys hesitantly. It wasn't entirely clear that the building had one. The two gates towered over everything else, and behind them there didn't seem to be any roof to speak of, just a sharply sloping dome that didn't offer anywhere a person could even stand. But as he circled around the back side of the building he found an empty metal platform, jutting out behind the gates, and on it a doorway leading inside. He steered the ARGO closer, aiming for the platform before pressing a button above him and leaning back into his chair. "Autopilot. I think."

"We need to find a better place," said Jason. "We can't just go barging into some random building. We'll end up in someone's office, or worse. We need to keep from being noticed."

"Trust me," said Medea with a sly smile. "If you don't want anyone to notice us, this is your best bet in the entire city."

They left the ship to pilot itself and climbed back down into the cargo pod, only to find Antaeus already standing beside the open door, his fur rustling up and down as the air whipped past it. He was clutching either side of the door with his claws, staring down at the platform below. It was still far away in the distance, slowly growing larger as the ARGO closed in for its landing. Idas stood behind him, talking into his ear, and as he saw the others approach he tapped Antaeus on the back and waved him forward.

"Go," said Idas. "Go, before the ship gets too close. Before we lose the shot."

"Hrump," said Antaeus. He looked over his shoulder at Idas, starting to correct his words to whatever he'd intended to say, but then he saw Idas's wrist sheath pointed at him, lights flashing all along it as it recorded every moment. He bared his teeth in an exaggerated, angry snarl, then launched himself out of the ARGO with claws flexed and arms spread wide. Idas leaned out the door to play cameraman, following Antaeus with his wrist to catch every bit of the action.

"Holy shit," said Medea. "He jumped. He just jumped."

"Shut the fuck up," said Idas. "We're filming." He held his arm out of the door, his fist pointed upward and his wrist aimed towards Antaeus, slowly moving along with him to capture the performance. Finally they heard a loud, angry yowl, and Idas looked back at them with a smile as the ARGO continued its landing and touched down on the platform. They were greeted by an anxious looking Antaeus, eagerly awaiting news of the footage.

"Get it?" said Antaeus.

"It's perfect," said Idas, stepping out onto the platform. "Watch." He pressed a finger against the sheath, and the translucent plastic shifted to a video image running the full length of his wrist. It was a looping shot of Antaeus, snarling and leaping down towards the building before landing with a somersault and baying towards the heavens.

"Gold," said Antaeus, clasping his claws together in the closest approximation of clapping he could manage. "Gold." The two of them huddled over the sheath watching the video as it looped again and again, speculating over how many views it would amass once they'd uploaded it onto the networks.

"We're not here to do stunts," said Medea. "This isn't our job."

"This is exactly our job," snapped Idas. "And your job isn't to complain about things that aren't any of your fucking business. Your job is to fix my brother. We'll settle things up over that one, the two of us. Don't think we won't." He slammed his palm against his wrist sheath, turning off the video and heading away towards the door to the building, his spear on his back. Antaeus tagged along behind him, tapping at his own sheath all the while as he downloaded Idas's camerawork and marveled at his stunt.

"Mopsus," said Jason, poking his head back into the ARGO. "You too. We need someone to show us the way." He waved Mopsus out through the door, then headed back inside to the ship's weapons cabinet. He opened it up to reveal an arsenal of glittering armaments, designed as much for show as for function. There was a row of round shields hanging along the wall inside, painted with fearsome faces, their open mouths baring teeth and oversized tongues that lolled along the shields' surfaces. Above them were thin plastic javelins, their tips razor sharp, next to an array of knives small enough to be easily concealed. And a rack in the center held a half-dozen swords of various shapes and sizes, each weighted according to a particular fighting style.

He eyed them all, but he was drawn to the swords, picking them up one after the other and testing their weight in his hands. His choice was a golden short sword, its handle encrusted with rubies. He pressed a button on the hilt, and the air crackled with energy as tiny electrical pulses ran up and down the blade. It was designed to stun, as well as to kill: anyone who received so much as a nick from it would get a very unpleasant surprise. He turned it off, sheathing the sword in a scabbard and snapping it around his waist as he headed back outside the ARGO.

He found Medea standing in the doorway, heading for the weapons cabinet herself. She tried to move around him, but he matched her step for step, barring her way and looking down at her with a stony expression.

"Where do you think you're going?" said Jason.

"To check the armory," said Medea, bristling at the interference. No matter which way she moved, he still stood in her path, and the more he tried to stop her the more frustrated she became. "I'm going to need some kind of weapon, too. It has to be something simple. Something I can handle in an emergency, if I absolutely have to."

"No, you don't," said Jason, his voice gone cold with command. "You're not coming. You're staying back here in the ARGO with Tiphys."

"What?" said Medea incredulously. "I'm not just sitting around twiddling my thumbs while everyone else takes all the risk. You don't know the city. You don't know the computer systems. And what if someone gets hurt? You'll need Hecate, and you'll need me."

"What we need is a backup team," said Jason. "We need you two ready, in case we have to do an extraction. Somebody has to hold down the fort."

But he was just giving excuses; she could tell that from the tone of his voice. It was strong, too strong, like he was trying to push her into staying before she had time to think things through. She knew what he was up to. He didn't trust her. Maybe it was because of whatever ethical issues he had with genomancy, or maybe it was because she'd frozen up under fire. Either way, he was dumping the makework onto her while the warriors went off and did the mission all on their own. She might have agreed to stay behind, if there'd been any actual need for it, but under the circumstances she was having none of it. She didn't have to be a fighter to matter to the team, and she wasn't going to be sidelined just because her talents lay elsewhere.

"Nobody has to hold down anything," said Medea. "The ship can pilot itself. It can literally be right above our heads the entire time. Tiphys can even pilot it from the ground if he needs to. So why are you giving me some do nothing job while everyone else actually contributes?"

"Medea," said Jason, more softly this time. "It's going to be dangerous down there. People could come after us. Things could go bad—"

"I used to live here," said Medea. "This is my city. My home. There's nothing dangerous about it. Not for me."

"It's not the city I'm worried about," said Jason. He looked down, and for a moment he couldn't meet her eyes. She could tell he was hiding something, some emotion he didn't want to let out, and he only turned back to her once he had it safely buried deep within. "It's us, Medea. I'm worried it's dangerous for you to be with us. Idas wants to kill you, for one. If he's with you, he can get you alone. He'd frag you in a second if he got the chance. Antaeus might help him. I can't understand him, let alone decide what he thinks about you. And then there's me."

"You?" said Medea. "You saved my life." She regretted the words as soon as they'd escaped her lips. She owed him, and now she'd admitted it. She'd never live it down, and she knew it.

"Me," said Jason. "It's dangerous for you to be around me. We should stay apart for the rest of this mission, as much as we can. You stay up here, and I'll go down there." He stared at the tablet, lying there on one of the seats, and he looked back at her as if he were about to say something. Then his eyes grew firm and his voice grew low and commanding, a drill sergeant's authority mixed with a guard dog's protective snarl. "You're going to stay here. Stay with Tiphys, watch the ship, and stay the hell away from me."

It hit her in her stomach, a sucker punch that made her feel like a sucker. She'd been right all along. He'd saved her, but he couldn't stand her. He thought she was just an obstacle on his path to glory. The gods had been taunting her, leading her on, and all this time he'd thought of her as nothing more than a damsel in distress. And now that he'd rescued her, he didn't want anything to do with the damsel. She started to follow his orders, more from the strength in his voice than anything else, heading back to her seat in an irritated huff. But then she changed her mind, and she changed her course.

"No," said Medea. "I'm not staying. You heard our orders. I have to go, and there's nothing you can do to stop me." She pushed around him to the weapons cabinet, rummaging around in the drawers until she saw a glint of something that suited her: a thin golden dagger, its hilt shaped like a caduceus, with wings at the top and two snakes winding around the handle in a double helix. She fitted it into a scabbard, strapped it to her belt, and turned back towards Jason. "You need someone who knows the city. You need a genomancer, just like all the rest of the Argonauts do. You need me. And you're going to get me, whether you like it or not."

"You stay," ordered Jason. His eyes went back to the tablet again, and she wondered what was on it that was making him so insistent about the matter. "You're not safe. Not if you come with me. And I can't let you do something that's going to get you hurt."

"It's just as dangerous to stay here," said Medea. "We're only invisible to the drones. What if Tiphys does something stupid? What if someone spots us? What if we come under attack?"

"Just trust me," said Jason. "It's safer up in the skies. You should be able to see that, even without a warrior's training." He moved towards her, his chest puffed wide, his eyes flaring with authority. "But if I have to protect you from yourself, then that's what I'll do."

He was big, and there was a power in his stride, and if it had been anyone else the fervor of his words alone would have intimidated her into backing down. But she knew him better than that. She thought it was a bluff, and she chose to call. "Try it," said Medea, standing on her tiptoes and making herself as big as she could. "I'll just convince Tiphys to bring us back down. Or I'll do to my own code what I did to his, and I'll land the ship myself. You know you can't keep me up there."

"And you know you're the most stubborn woman I've ever met," said Jason. He looked her up and down, sizing up the strength of her will, and she thought she saw a glimmer of respect, even if only a little. "It doesn't matter what I say, or what I do, or what kind of risk there is in you going with us. You'd find a way to come along anyway, wouldn't you?"

"In a heartbeat," said Medea. "I don't like being told what I can't do."

He stood there for a few silent moments, taking her in, and then he nodded towards the platform. "Then move out with the rest of them," said Jason. "You're right about one thing. I can't stop you. But like I said. Keep your distance from me, as much as you can. Stick with Tiphys. You'll be safer."

"Tiphys is a nice guy," said Medea. "But there's no way he's protecting me from anything."

"Tiphys can't hurt you, either," said Jason. "He's not on anyone's radar, and you can trust him. He's safe. He won't be a target, and if you stick by him, neither will you." He strode out onto the platform, leaving her standing there inside the ship all on her own. She couldn't understand what had gotten into him. He could be tender one moment, and then turn into something of a bastard the next. It was maddening, but there was nothing she could do about it: she counted herself lucky he'd backed down at all. She unfastened Hecate's seatbelt, calling after her as she left. "Hecate," said Medea. "Hecate, follow." Then she headed out after Jason and the rest of them, all gathered on the platform by the entrance to the building.

CHAPTER FIFTEEN

JASON LED THEM INSIDE, PULLING open the door to the building and stepping into a darkened passageway within. They felt their way along a narrow metal walkway, with barely enough room to file past one by one. The path was going down, and they followed it towards a distant light until the passage opened up into the main area of the building itself.

They found themselves in a vast, empty space at the building's center. The walkway hugged the wall, circling around the sides and spiraling slowly downward. The walls were covered from floor to ceiling with jade drawers, all of them shut. They were a few feet wide, their handles forged from gold, and on the face of each of them was a slit of blue glass with a digital display fitted just below it. A look over the rails revealed the scale of the thing: they could see the ground floor far in the distance, and the entire building was drawers all the way down. It was one massive filing cabinet, the walkway snaking around the sides with just enough room between the drawers to allow access to them all.

"There's a man in there," said Jason. He was peering through the glass slit on one of the drawers as they filed past, circling their way down towards the distant exit below. Inside the drawer was a chubby middle-aged man, his face covered in scruff and his arms folded across his chest. A thick black pair of goggles was strapped to his head, and a string of cables ran between it and the drawer's interior. The man didn't move, and he didn't seem to notice them: he just lay there in his slumber, to all effects dead to the world. Jason looked through window after window, and every one was the same. "People. They're all filled with people."

"Transients," said Medea. "They don't have homes, so they come here. It's a public virtual reality facility. There's probably a hundred thousand people living here, and not a single one of them awake. We'll be in and out, and no one will notice."

"They're warehousing the poor," said Jason. "Keeping them locked up here in their virtual worlds instead of giving them a place to live."

"But they've all got smiles on their faces," said Medea. And so they did: they filed past men, women, and even children, but all Jason could see were wide grins of pure ecstasy. They were dreamers lost to the world, dwelling alone within their fantasies, but it was plain at a glance that they liked it there.

"The stakeholders all have the right to an apartment if they want it," said Medea. "They're cramped, but you can live in them. But apartments cost the company a lot of money. And keeping so many billions in comfort is more than the world's ecology can handle, if everyone's up and walking around." She tapped one of the drawers as they passed, barely big enough to fit a person inside. "Space here is cheap. Colchis wants to make it as attractive as possible to live here. If you sign away your housing rights, you're homeless. Technically. But you can get premium content instead. Exclusive stuff, and personalized. A lot of people love their VR enough to do it. Most of them never leave."

"They're just shades of their former selves," said Jason. He looked into one of the drawers at a scraggly, emaciated man, lying there with his hands folded across his chest. His fingernails were yellowed and overgrown, his clothes were tattered, and his hair was long enough to reach down to his belly. "They're sitting on the border between the living and the dead. All they are is human paychecks."

"They don't have to be this way," said Medea. "They can sign up with any of the Big Five anytime they want. They don't. It sounds strange, but they like it here. They have their reasons. Sometimes life is painful. Sometimes you just want to escape. Sometimes when you do, you never want to come back."

"I just don't get it," said Jason. "I don't get why they'd want to give everything up and live inside some little box."

"You're rich," said Medea. "Of course you don't get it. And of course you want to live in this reality. The poor? Sometimes they don't."

"There's something lost to it, though," said Jason. "When life's just one fantasy to be traded for another. When you look at the things you love and all you see are the mechanics." He looked at her, something smoldering behind his eyes, and then he turned away. "When what we do reduces humanity to nothing but a bunch of code."

She could feel her temper rising, burning up inside of her. A jab was a jab, whether aimed at her profession or aimed at her, and she wasn't going to take it lying down. "And I suppose for a warrior everything is one big war? Your entire life is spent thinking about killing people. About how you can hurt them."

"War is the means," said Jason. "Peace is the end. Fighting is just a tool. A way to stop people who'd tear it all down if they could. People who'd hurt the ones I care about. Learn how to fight, and you make yourself stronger. Not just in body, but in spirit."

"And your code is a part of that body," said Medea. "You're an organic computer, whether you like it or not. War is something scary, and you study it because you think you have to. I'm not any different. We're both facing up to something that's kind of awful if you think too much about it. But we're doing it to try to make things better. To make people happier." She rapped one of the drawers with her knuckles. "They're in a computer generated world living out a fantasy, but so are we, in a sense. Our reality is all created in our brains. Colors, sounds, memories—they're not real things. They're how your brain interprets a bunch of data. But it's real to us, and that's as real as it's going to get."

"Quiet," said Jason, his voice dropping to a low growl.

She wanted to slap him. He'd never understand why she did what she did, no matter how hard she tried to explain. Genomancy was her life's work, just as warfare was his. She wanted to explain it to him somehow, but every time she tried he just took shots at her. It was like her choice of career was some kind of personal insult to him. Genomancy wasn't about winning or losing, even if the warrior code of honor was. And she couldn't help it if someone she worked on was breaking the rules of a game she didn't even play.

"Sorry if you can't handle it," said Medea. "Sorry—" But before she could say anything more, he pulled her against the wall, one hand wrapped around her mouth and the other around her waist. "I said quiet." He pointed across the building, towards something in the distance: men, three of them, huddled together on the walkway. He let her loose, slowly, then signaled towards the others with a wave of his hand.

They drew their weapons and Jason crept forward, his sword at the ready. But the men weren't interested in them. They weren't interested in anything, at least not of the world around them. They were scarfing down food, ripping it from a stack of silver packages and shoveling it into their mouths like hogs gorging at a trough. One of them rubbed himself with a sponge, wiping away the grime on his skin as quickly as he could. Another tapped frantic messages into his wrist sheath between bites, and the third man was lapping at a bowl of red fluid, sucking in concentrated nutrients meant to last him for weeks at a time. They didn't even look up, let alone notice they were being watched, and after a few silent minutes the three of them rushed away, pulling open drawers and stowing themselves back inside as they descended into their sleep once more.

"This is why I had us land here," said Medea. "They don't care about us. You could walk right up to one of them and tell them you're an Argonaut, and he'd just ignore you. They might not even know what Argos is. The dream is what's real to them. This life is just a waystation."

"Let's not take any chances," said Jason, sheathing his sword back in its scabbard. "Let's move, and get the hell out of here. We're conspicuous enough as it is." He looked at her armor, pure black except for the golden knife at her belt, and then at Antaeus, who could have been an escapee from a zoo.

"No one's going to notice," said Idas, pushing his way past them and heading downwards on his own. "Colchis is a freak show. The ones who're awake are just as bad as the ones who're asleep. We won't raise an eyebrow. Trust me." Antaeus grunted and went after him, so big that he was barely able to squeeze along the walkway without tottering over.

"It's not that bad," said Medea, following along after them. "But genomancy gets a little more out there in Colchis. People do some odd things to themselves. The whole city's obsessed with entertainment, and it's hard for anyone to stand out unless they do something drastic."

"If it was all cosmetic, genomancy wouldn't be that bad," said Jason. "It's the talent part that's the problem. I know you think you're helping people, and maybe you are. But you're weakening them, too. They start to rely on what you did to them. They're not warriors. They're not heroes. And if something happens outside the instincts you coded in, they're useless."

"The warriors and everyone else are pretty much the same," said Medea. "There's a reason they want to make themselves better at fighting. The same reason people want to change their looks. It's attention seeking more than anything. You'd see the same instincts, if you went deep down into your own code. Maybe that's why you're so afraid to take a look."

He tensed up, and she knew she'd touched on something sensitive. It made her wonder what drove him, and why he cared so much about the fact that other warriors acquired their skills through money and genomancy rather than through years of work. There wasn't much difference, not to her: a war was a war, and all was fair in winning one. But it was like a contest to him, trying to prove which warrior was the best, and it was one he was trying his hardest to win. She wanted to ask him why, but he stalked along silently the rest of the way down, shutting down the discussion and keeping any further thoughts on the matter to himself.

They reached the bottom floor without further incident, leaving the dreamers to rest inside the tiny boxes that contained them in their private virtual worlds. The building's gate opened up into the city, and as Idas had promised, no one paid them any mind. It was broad daylight, but only a few people were out and about, and even those few spared little attention for anything but their wrist sheaths. Medea had been dead on the mark as well: most of them had changed themselves somehow, struggling to stand out from the others and fighting for whatever scraps of attention they could claim from all the rest.

Some were inordinately tall, stretched from head to toe until they looked like they were walking on stilts. Others had infused their skin with bright colors, human plums and pineapples that one couldn't help but stare at. Still more looked like animals, prowling through their urban jungle with faces stretched to resemble creatures of all kinds. Those who couldn't afford genetic changes had found plumage of their own, sporting an array of outlandish masks and costumes that would have been at home at a Venetian carnival. It was see or be seen, but none of them wanted to do any of the seeing. Instead they paraded around the streets with their eyes glued to their sheaths, watching vids and other entertainments instead of each other. They kept to themselves and ignored the rest, just as they themselves were ignored in turn.

Off in the distance was Colchis corporate headquarters, a massive golden fortress surrounded by a series of minarets. Its sides looked more green than gold, covered by vines that crept up and down the walls. Topping the building was a sculpture of the head of a giant bull, its horns running the length of the entire headquarters. It smiled benevolently across the city, beaming the corporation's love of its stakeholders out for all to see. But they hadn't come to do business or meet with executives. They'd come looking for information, and the implant in Mopsus's skull was flashing a rainbow of colors as he interfaced with the networks and oriented them towards their target.

"A few blocks that way," said Mopsus, pointing towards a darkened alley between two of the buildings, one a small amphitheater made from diamond and the other a bland bronze office building. "Phineus is there. But you have to know something else. You have to know what the gods say."

"What?" said Jason. "What do they say?"

"He's been cursed," said Mopsus. "Phineus has brought a curse upon himself. And we'll get nothing from him until we free him from it."

"Cursed?" said Jason skeptically.

"You'll see," said Mopsus, shaking his head as he walked into the alley. "It's awful, what's happened to him. And perhaps he deserved some of it. But the gods think he's been punished enough, and they want to give him an out. He knows how to find the Fleece. They said that we must end his troubles, if only he helps us. Come. Come, and do what's right, and they'll do right by us."

CHAPTER SIXTEEN

THE SIGN WAS TUCKED AWAY in the corner of a cloudy window, announcing the name of the place in cursive neon lettering: The Hellespont. Next to it was a glass door, emblazoned with a crude sketch of an open tap pouring beer into a foaming glass. The storefronts nearby were all shuttered and abandoned, trash littered the streets, and the entire neighborhood felt eerily quiet. The street was a dump, hidden behind the city's jewel-encrusted luxury where no one could see. It was a stakeholder neighborhood, and wasting money to make it beautiful was considered a frivolity by those who held the purse strings. Everything about the area screamed that guests were unwelcome. But invitation or no, they had to speak to Phineus, no matter how poorly they were likely to be received.

"This is it," said Jason. He turned to Mopsus with a skeptical frown. "You're sure he's here? This doesn't look like the kind of place someone with connections would hang out in."

"There's no doubt, not even a smidgen," said Mopsus, swaying from side to side with nervous anticipation. "He's the owner. He went inside, months ago, and he still hasn't come out."

They stood across the street, watching the bar from a distance with wary eyes. It was hardly the place for a stakeout; there were no cars and there was nothing for cover, forcing them all to mill around out in the open. But there was nothing to be done about it, not if they wanted to get close enough for even the most basic reconnaissance. They could hear noises coming from inside, laughter and shouting and everything one would expect from a lively establishment. There were people in there, they knew that much at least, though whether Phineus was among them was a matter of guesswork.

"He's dead," said Idas. "Nobody stays inside a bar that long unless he's dead."

"He's alive," said Mopsus. "And the bar is a hiding place. One comes here to avoid the attentions of the Colchis Corporation. The gods say so. They can see things. How they know isn't a matter for mortals. But they know."

"The gods," said Idas with an exasperated grunt. "They're toys. We're trusting ourselves to a bunch of toys."

"They got us inside the city," said Jason. "We'd have been dead if we hadn't listened to them before." He started across the street, heading towards the entrance to the Hellespont. "And it's not as if we've got any other options. If we want to find the Fleece, we're going to have to listen to them again."

"The Fleece is what Pelias wants," said Idas, stalking along through the street behind him. "We need to start thinking about what we want. You're new. You don't understand how this works. The mission doesn't matter. It's a joke. No one ever completes the things. Not if they're smart. You know what happens if we fail our mission, don't you?"

"What?" said Jason, brushing him away as he kept walking. "What happens?"

"Same shit that happens if we succeed," said Idas. "The Argo Corporation declares victory, we get a parade, and we all get drunk till the next one rolls 'round. You know your problem? You're playing for team corporate. You need to be playing for team you. Fuck the Fleece. It's hidden somewhere, they'll be guarding it with the best they've got, and even if we find it we'll all get killed."

"Killed," said Antaeus, flexing his claws and following along behind them. "Dead." Even with the permanent snarl his new face had given him, it was clear he was unhappy about the prospect. Jumping out of a ship for ratings was one thing; fighting real battles with his life at stake was quite another.

"I'm not giving up my mission just because it's dangerous," said Jason curtly. Fury brewed within him, and he shook with rage as he struggled to hold it in. "That's cowardice. It's not being a warrior, and it's not being an Argonaut. We're supposed to be an example. The ones everyone looks up to. People depend on us. They love us. And I'm not tarnishing what it means to be an Argonaut out of fear."

Jason's hand was on the door, but Idas stopped him, grabbing hold of his wrist. "You know what we do?" said Idas. "We find a place to hole up. And then we sit, and we wait. Just a couple of days. Enough time so it looks like we've been busy. We pick a fight with some of the Colchians, and we take a few vids. Then we get the hell out, go home, and everyone's a hero. Simple as that."

"This is enemy territory," said Jason. "We get into it with their warriors, we'll bring every Colchian soldier in the city down on our heads. We're not starting a fight just so you can bring back some vids as trophies."

"I know some people," said Idas. "Some of their warriors." He gave a smarmy smile, looking like a cat who'd caught his canary. "They'll meet us wherever we want. They need the footage just as badly as we do. They give us a few shots where we're winning, we give them a few shots where they're winning. Argos spins it this way, Colchis spins it that way. We get to be heroes there, they get to be heroes here. Everybody wins. Everybody goes home alive."

"Everybody goes home in shame," said Jason, shaking his head. "There isn't any honor in that. It's just some scam. We wouldn't be heroes. We'd be frauds."

"It's the ways things really are," said Idas. "It's the system. You're still green. You don't know any better. But you will. You can work the system, or you can let the system work you. But you can't change the way people are." He shot Medea a dirty look. "No matter how much you tinker around with their insides."

"Then screw the system," said Jason. "Pelias wants the Fleece. And so do the gods, and so does Colchis. It's important. It's valuable." He locked eyes with Medea, standing in the street beside them. "And maybe it's dangerous."

"It could be," said Medea. "A database of DNA from that many people? You could do a lot of things with something like that. Some of them really good. Some of them really, really bad."

"Pelias, the gods, Colchis," said Jason. "They all have their own agenda. And I have mine. We're going to find this thing, we're going to get it out of the city, and we're going to get it into safe hands. You want people to think you're a hero? Start acting like one. Or if you're afraid of a fight, go back to the ARGO and wait until the rest of us are done. And when we get back home, we'll have the parades without you."

He jerked his hand away from Idas, opened the door, and headed inside alone. The rest of them followed, though some were more eager than others. Medea and Mopsus went right in, and even Tiphys managed to work up the courage without further prodding. But Idas and Antaeus dragged their feet for an uncomfortably long period of time, finally joining the rest of them only after a few discontented looks had passed between them.

The lighting inside was dim, deliberately so, the chosen atmosphere of the ones who'd made it their watering hole. It was an upscale establishment cultivating the appearance of a dive, but the details gave the game away. Wooden booths lined one wall, with crude messages from the patrons carved across every square inch. But they were otherwise pristine, and the plastic tables between them had been left untouched by the graffiti. The floor looked like cheap wood paneling, but it was without the scuffs and scratches that would have marked it as the genuine article. The customers could keep things orderly when they were supposed to, breaking only the rules that everyone knew weren't meant to be followed anyway.

One side of the room was occupied by the bar itself, surrounded by a group of people gathered for their drinks. It was seedy, but with a distinctly feminine touch: signs above it advertised blue collar beers in frilly pink lettering, and lace doilies substituted for coasters. A few mirrors behind the bar were covered in red lipstick pictures of cartoon characters the bartenders had scrawled across them, cutesy images contrasting with the hard liquors stacked beside them.

The other side of the room was dedicated to darts and pool, played mostly as they had been decades before. The rules were the same, but the implements had changed: silver darts contained hidden legs within, prying themselves from the board after every round and scrambling down the walls to return to the player who'd thrown them. As for the pool balls, they racked themselves, taking advantage of gyroscopic devices to maneuver around the table once each game was done. Even their play had been sanitized of labor, stripped down until nothing was left for humans to do but the bare essentials.

"Hey," said Tiphys in a low, nervous voice as the door shut behind the last of them. "I don't think we're going to be welcome. Not in this crowd. It doesn't exactly look like we fit in."

And it was clear at a glance that they didn't. They stuck out like sore thumbs, in fact, and obviously weren't the demographic the bar was catering to. A quick look around the place showed why: there were dozens of people there, patrons of all shapes, colors, and sizes, but there was something missing. Except for the Argonauts, everyone else in the bar was a woman. Or partly one, at any rate.

They were female, that much was certain. But they'd changed themselves, and not a one of them remained entirely human. Their arms were lined with feathers, long and thin and dangling down in rows that ran from shoulder to wrist. They looked like wings, though their only function was decoration. Each woman had chosen a pattern of her own: some were the bright green of a tropical parrot, others canary yellow, and a few looked precisely like those of a peacock. They'd changed their faces to match; their necks were covered in light, downy feathers, and each of them had modified their noses to look like nothing other than a beak. The tips of their fingernails all curved into black talons, long, nasty, and sharp. They were half woman, half bird, a blend of genes that marked them apart as a species all their own.

It was the simplest of genomancy, all cosmetic, the kind of thing Medea could have whipped up in an afternoon. She could tell just by looking at them that the changes were assembly line, with little effort at customization to any individual's own unique genetic code. Many of them bore tiny imperfections, barely visible to the untrained eye, from black spots on their feathers to asymmetries of their beaks. She'd never have tolerated such flaws in her own work; her standard was perfection, and she pushed herself as hard as she could to achieve it. But genomancy wasn't cheap, and even what changes the women had managed must have cost them a collective fortune.

"Wrong bar," came a loud squawk from across the room. A woman with a toucan's nose and long black feathers stood next to one of the pool tables, polishing her cue and scowling at them in disgust. Every head in the bar turned towards them simultaneously, and the sound of idle chatter trailed away into stony silence. "Try someplace a few blocks down," said a waitress passing by with a tray of beers. "Someplace you'll fit in." Her feathers were a flashy blue, and she'd braided some of them into her platinum blonde hair. She gave an exaggerated sneer and nodded towards the door. "Do it fast. Before things get ugly."

"We just wanted a quick drink," said Jason.

"We're out of drinks," said the waitress. Jason looked at the very full beers on her tray, and at the walls behind the bar, lined with liquors. But her eyes just narrowed, and she pointed towards the door again, more insistently this time. "And we're closed."

"Maybe we should go," said Tiphys, backing away towards the exit.

"We're not going to stay for long," said Jason, standing firm to the waitress as the rest of the bar looked on. "We're in and we're out. We just want to talk to someone. Then we'll be gone, and you'll never see us again."

"I said we're closed," said the waitress loudly. She leaned in close, dropping her voice to a whisper and looking nervously from side to side. "Don't do this the hard way. Some of the girls here would love to do this the hard way."

"Please," said Medea, stepping between the two of them. "Maybe we could work something out. A trade." She reached out a hand towards the waitress's arm. "Your feathers. Let me see." The waitress flinched away at first, but after an embarrassed look flashed across her face she held out one of her arms. Her plumage was brilliant and blue, mostly. But a close inspection revealed the subtle imperfections: some of the feathers were a wilted brown, looking like dying leaves, and she'd had to comb them under the others to hide them away from view. There'd been some error in the genomancy, some problem a mere stakeholder couldn't afford to correct, and the woman was left to tolerate her botched procedure as best she could.

"I'm a genomancer," said Medea. "One of the best." She pointed at Hecate down on the floor behind her, parked and awaiting instructions. "And Hecate here has a portable lab inside her. I can fix this. All you need is a little custom code. It wouldn't take long. I'll do it for free. All we want is to talk to someone."

"Just talk?" said the waitress in a whisper. "I don't know." She looked around at the patrons, angry and resentful at the intrusion. But her eyes went back to her feathers, focusing on the flaws, and her lips pursed as she contemplated the offer. The imperfections were minor in the scheme of things, but they marred her otherwise perfect beauty, and that alone was enough to give her pause.

"Just talk," said Medea. "We can do it right here. We could even do it outside, if it helps."

"Maybe," said the waitress. She took another look at the restless women, standing around and hanging on their every word. Most of them had tailored their genes to make them more feminine, their feathers bright and their bodies dainty and thin. Those women shied away from the conflict, huddling in groups close enough to watch, but far enough away to avoid any real danger. But others had used genomancy to grow bulging muscles along with their feathers, replacing their feminine wiles with hard jaws and bodybuilders' physiques. They were starting to edge closer, looking for trouble, and they were well equipped to start it. Some were gripping bottles, others were flexing their claws, and all of them were spoiling for a fight.

The waitress tried to smooth things over, raising her voice even as she moved to calm things down. "I can try to work something out. I can ask around, and see if whoever you're looking for is up for it. But just you." She nodded towards Jason and the rest of the men. "The others are going to have to wait outside. They're not welcome. Not in here."

"That's fine," said Medea. She put on her best reassuring smile. "That's not a problem. We'll work it out. The guy we're looking for. His name is Phineus. We heard he was here. We just—"

"Phineus," said the waitress. Her wings tensed, and her eyes narrowed. "Why would you come in here looking for Phineus?"

"We heard he owned the place," said Jason. "We heard he was here."

"Why the fuck would a man come here at all?" said a loud voice from the edge of the crowd. They turned towards the sound to see a woman approaching from a back room, a flock of angry-looking followers at her side. Some genomancer had worked her over from top to bottom: she was big, towering a foot above the rest of them, her muscles rippling beneath a tight-fitting white tank top. Her wings dangled down below her arms, the feathers a bright jungle green that shone even in the dim light of the bar. They were edged with a strawberry colored tinge, and the code they'd been grown from looked to have come from a parrot. Her fingers were tipped with grey talons, and her beak scythed down over her mouth, setting her face in a permanent scowl made harder by the presence of uninvited men.

"Go," whispered the waitress. "You don't make Polyxo mad. You just don't. You need to turn around and go. Now."

"We just wanted to talk to someone," said Jason. "That's it."

"You got what you wanted," said Polyxo, as the waitress scurried away to safety behind the bar. She jabbed a finger at Jason's chest and then pointed to the door. "You talked to me. Now get the hell out."

"Phineus," said Jason. "We were just looking—"

"Anyone here know a Phineus?" shouted Polyxo, looking around from side to side. An aggressive chorus of no's came from all around, and she turned back to Jason with a smile. "You're out of luck. No Phineus. Just us Harpies." The bar resounded with a series of enthusiastic cheeps and caws, sounds that were remarkably close to the birds whose genes the women had borrowed.

"We know he's here," said Jason. "Or was."

"This isn't a place for men," said Polyxo. She ran one of her claws under Jason's chin, yanking it away with a quick scratch. It drew a few drops of blood, and she licked it from the tip of her talon with a satisfied smile. "Not if they expect to keep their balls attached." She turned to Medea, a disappointed look on her face. "And you, honey. Why spend your time with the knuckle-draggers? And worse, why bring them into my bar?"

"We didn't know," said Medea. She held a hand out in front of Jason, signaling for silence. She knew she could handle it, if he'd just let her. He was a warrior, and even she would admit he had a talent for it. But this was a matter of diplomacy, and a task far better suited to someone with a disposition for compromise. She kept her voice calm and steady, hoping it would be enough to soothe the creatures before her. "These men, they're friends of mine. I didn't know there'd be a problem."

"You think he's handsome," said Polyxo, nodding to Jason. "I can tell." Medea could feel her face flush, and she thanked the gods she'd chosen an olive skin tone the last time she'd toyed around with her appearance. She hoped it was dark enough to hide the red in her cheeks, but Polyxo's cocky smile suggested she saw right through her. "You want to be his. Have him make you one of their little slaves. But that's just conditioning, honey. It's just the way you were raised. You don't have to cower before them. You can change, just like we did." Polyxo snapped her fingers and gave a little caw to one of her followers. The woman rushed obediently to the bar, returning with an overflowing glass of beer in each hand.

"You're a woman," said Polyxo. "If you want to stay awhile, you can. You don't have to live your life taking orders from one of them. You can stay and join the right side. The winning side." She cocked her head at Jason and the others, her smile turning to stone. "But the knuckle-draggers have to go. All of them. Even the handsome ones."

Medea wouldn't admit it, not in front of Jason, but she was scared almost out of her wits. There weren't many friendly faces in there, not even for a fellow woman. And she knew from experience that anyone who changed themselves as radically as Polyxo had couldn't be entirely balanced. She'd overhauled people in all kinds of ways, but the bigger the changes, the bigger the hole the person was trying to fill. Polyxo had made herself ugly, according to conventional eyes, and someone like that couldn't be counted on to abide by conventions.

But no matter her fears, the Argonauts had a job to do, and she was the only one of them who could do it. If she followed her instincts and backed away, she'd just prove the warriors had been right to doubt her all along. And accepting an instinct as an immutable law wasn't the way of a genomancer. She breathed in deep, tried to push her fears aside, and forced herself to step forward instead.

"I'll stay," said Medea. "Just for a little while."

"Medea," said Jason, putting a protective hand on her shoulder. His voice said it all with a word: he didn't think she was safe, and he wasn't at all happy about the idea of letting her stay someplace this dangerous all by herself. But thoughts like that didn't go over well, not in the Hellespont, and not when they came from a man.

"You don't own her," said Polyxo angrily, and the women behind her crowded forward. "You shouldn't even be talking to her." Jason pulled his hand away, and Polyxo's voice calmed, if only slightly.

"You're a man, and we're women," said Polyxo. "And our kind don't mix with your kind. Not if they're smart. Nothing against men, not personally. I just wouldn't want to be friends with one of you." Her lips curved upward beneath her beak in disgust. "You just can't help yourselves. Violence, war, rape. They follow you around wherever you go. We're all Ninth Wavers here. Gender segregationists. No one else has the balls to say it, but I will: everyone would be happier if they just kept to their own. Men go their way, women go our way." She smiled, and pointed a talon towards the door. "And it's time for you to get the hell away from this bar."

A mass of women moved forward, crowding in on them and pushing them towards the exit. For a moment it looked like things would get bloody. Idas was the first to escalate things, drawing his spear and waving it around in front of him. He pressed a button on its side and the tip began to spin, whining loudly and turning the spear into a long, dangerous drill. Antaeus formed ranks beside him, swiping his arms through the air, growling at the encroaching women, and generally doing his best to drive them backwards in fright. Even Jason drew his sword, ready for the worst if it came to it.

But Medea had things under control. She thought so, at least, and she wasn't going to let the situation spiral into chaos without giving her way a chance. She was afraid; terrified, really. Everyone around her had weapons, and she didn't have the slightest clue what someone was supposed to do in a bar fight. She'd never been in a fight, never taken a punch, and had never even been much for sports. Her gut told her to duck underneath one of the tables and wait for things to blow over, and she felt herself starting to shake. She knew it was the same paralysis she'd suffered back in the desert, and that if she let it set in, she'd be helpless. But this time she managed to act, breaking free from her instinctual fears. She ignored the spears and the bottles and the pool cues, pushed her way between the warriors and the Harpies, and shouted at the top of her lungs: "Stop! Everyone just stop!"

Even Medea was surprised by how loud her voice had been. The shouting reverberated throughout the bar, a far more powerful cry than she'd thought she had in her. Everyone stopped in their tracks, and the entire bar turned to stare at her at once. Her stomach dropped. She hadn't thought this far ahead, and she didn't have any idea what to say. But she knew she had to say something, otherwise they'd all be back at each other's throats in no time.

"They're leaving," said Medea. "The men. And they'll do it quietly. We didn't come here to fight. I just want to talk. To her." She pointed to the waitress, cowering behind the bar and looking thoroughly embarrassed at being drawn into the middle of things. "I'm a genomancer. And she has a problem with what's been done to her. The rest of you might, too." A few of the Harpies exchanged uncomfortable looks at that comment, and she knew they must have been hiding blemishes of their own. "Just let me take a look at her. Just let me talk. If you want to kick me out after, that's fine. But she's your friend. If I can help her, you ought to at least let me try."

The bar was silent for a moment as everyone pondered what to do. No one said a word in response, and for a minute Medea thought she'd botched things, just as the warriors would have expected her to. But then the Harpies turned to Polyxo, one by one, their weapons still in hand but their taste for battle fading. If something was wrong with the waitress's genomancy, then something could be wrong with theirs as well. Nervous looks passed between them, and their hands ran towards damaged feathers of their own.

Polyxo may have led them, but she knew which way the wind was blowing, and she twisted her beak in irritation. "No one's got any real problems with their code. Nothing they can't handle, anyway. No bird has perfect feathers, so why would any of us?" She oozed confidence, and some in the crowd seemed pacified, even as others retained their nervous edge. "We don't trust outsiders, and for good reason. But she's a woman, at least. And if she thinks she can do a better job on Hypsipyle than our genomancer did, she's welcome to take a look. We're all freewomen here."

She looked at Medea, disappointment across her face. "You've got shitty taste in friends, honey. But Hypsipyle's part of the sisterhood, and I'll do you a favor for her sake. You can stay. But the rest of them have ten seconds. If any of them are still here after that, we're stuffing their testicles and mounting them on the wall." Then she turned around in a whirl of feathers, stomping off towards the bar and leaving her followers to finish dealing with the intrusion.

"Let's go," said Jason. He nodded towards the exit, and the other Argonauts didn't hesitate to leave. All of them but Medea. She stood there next to Hecate, not moving an inch. Jason jerked a thumb behind him, motioning again for her to follow. "You, too. I know you want to help her." He looked over at a few of the Harpies, flexing their claws and priming themselves for a fight. "But I'm not leaving you here on your own. Not with them."

"Jason," said Medea, still standing her ground. "I've got this. I'll be fine."

"Five seconds," said one of the Harpies. A few of the bigger ones began brandishing their weapons and moving towards them, eager to be on the front lines if things went bad.

"You're coming," said Jason. There was a fierceness in his voice, the protective growl of an alpha wolf confronting a threat to his pack. And she saw something else in his eyes, a pain at thoughts of what could happen to her if she stayed there all alone. She'd be at the mercy of the Harpies' good graces, and he'd be left outside, helpless to intervene. He plainly wasn't having it. He moved himself into a fighter's stance, his sword at his side, ready to take on the entire bar if it came to it, and then he called to her again. "Either you're coming, or I'm staying."

She looked around at the angry crowd, waiting for the slightest excuse to tear them both apart. And she looked at Jason, standing his ground despite the odds, ready to sacrifice it all to see her safely outside. She could tell he'd never let her stay, not if he knew she was at risk, and she had to defuse the tension somehow.

She headed towards the door, while Jason waited for her to make it through and warned off anyone who tried to follow her. The crowd kept their distance, albeit with a healthy dose of taunts and vulgar gestures. Some of them would have been delighted to go ahead and fight, given some pretense, but Polyxo had spoken, and they weren't brave enough to openly defy her. Medea went outside with the others, Hecate trailing after her. Jason followed a few seconds later, the door slamming shut behind him on a half-dozen Harpies, all whooping and contorting their faces against the glass as they celebrated their victory.

"Jason," said Medea. She rolled the words around in her head, trying to come up with some way to tell him what she knew she had to. He wouldn't like it, and he'd try to stop her. But at least out here they had time to talk without being torn to pieces. He kept staring at her in silence, and for a time she couldn't meet his eyes, too afraid that she'd waver under the strength of his will. But she screwed up her courage, and finally she managed to get things out. "I'm not leaving. I'm going to stay. I'm going to help them, and I'm going to find out what's going on with this Phineus."

"No, you're not," said Jason. He was every bit as adamant as she was worried he'd be, and there was a fury in his voice at the situation. "You're not going back into that bar. Not without me."

"You heard them," said Medea. "You're a man. I'm a woman. And they're gender segregationists. Unless I'm missing something about one of the boys, we've got one option to find out where the Fleece is. And I'm it."

"They'll hurt you, Medea," said Jason. He looked back at the door, lingering on the angry faces within, and he shook his head. "I can't let you go back in there and get hurt."

"They won't," said Medea softly. "I can handle myself. And there isn't any other way. You know what Mopsus said. This Phineus is our only lead. The gods want us to help him, and they want him to help us. I at least have to try."

She didn't wait for his permission. She just turned back to the bar, heading towards the door on her own as Hecate ran in confused circles around her. "No," said Jason. He grabbed her arm, roughly. His grip was uncomfortably tight, and she let out a little gasp of breath as he dragged her back towards him. He looked down, loosened his grip, and then looked back at her.

"I heard what they said," said Jason. "Believe me, I heard them. They're crazy. They might accept you. They might not. And if you try to find Phineus, who knows what they'll do to you? I'll be out here. There'll be nothing I can do. If you're in there on your own, you'll be helpless."

That was it for Medea. No warrior would ever have faith in her, not even him. He thought she was helpless, just a lost scientist bumbling around completely out of her depth. The warriors thought everything was about fighting, and maybe it was for them. If all you have is a hammer, everything looks like a nail. But she had other tools, and sometimes they were better ones. He thought no one could help her, but she knew he was wrong; they were all wrong. She could help herself, and that would have to be enough. There wasn't any other choice, after all.

"You just think I can't cut it," said Medea. "You think I'm not good enough for the Argonauts. You think I'm a cheat and a fraud."

"That's not what I think," said Jason. "That's not—"

"It's what you said," said Medea. "It's what you've been saying since I met you. That I don't know what I'm doing. That I'm just a burden, and I should stay back in the ship and stay away from you. That I'm a wannabe warrior, and that my entire profession is just some way to cheat against the warrior code. You saw Lynceus, and you assumed it was my fault, and you've been judging me for it ever since."

"I know what I said," said Jason. He took a deep breath, and his expression went deadly serious. "This isn't about what I said. It's about what could happen to you. You could get hurt. They could really, really hurt you."

They were nice words, but she wasn't sure she believed them. "My work is more than just some scam," said Medea. "You idolize the Argonauts. You make them out to be these perfect champions of the warrior ideal. But they'd never win a single battle without people like me. They can't do it on their own. They need what I do. I'm a part of things, just as much as they are. Just because I'm not the one fighting doesn't mean what I do isn't important. Just because you can't see the changes I made doesn't mean they don't matter."

"I know," said Jason. "I know." He looked down, reaching into himself for what he wanted to say. Then their eyes met, and he put a hand on her shoulder. "I saw what you did to Tiphys. And I know he wasn't the one piloting that ship. Not really. We'd never have gotten here alive if it wasn't for you."

He paused, letting the words sink in. She'd never heard praise like that, not from a warrior. They never shared credit for their deeds, and in fact they fought about that more than anything else. More than one of the warriors had stalked into her lab in a fury, demanding some genetic augmentation that would let them lash out at a fellow Argonaut who was hogging all the attention on the vid feeds. She wondered if maybe Jason was different from the rest of them, after all. Maybe he did care about what happened to her, and not just about his own ego.

"What you do and what the rest of us do are different," said Jason. "You're an expert at changing people's code. You know I have a problem with that." A flash of distaste passed across his face, but it quickly turned to a wry smile. "If it's being done to me, at least. You have to understand. This is kind of a competition for me."

"You think?" said Medea. "You're a warrior. All warriors ever do is compete."

"It's more than that," said Jason. "They told you about my father? About Aeson?"

They had, though not much. Just that Jason was a fortunate son, with a very unfortunate father. She knew he'd passed, and that his death was what had prompted Jason's sudden promotion. But the private lives of wealthy shareholders were kept strictly private, and they hadn't told her any more than the absolute minimum. "I'm sorry," said Medea. "I'm sorry you lost him."

"It feels like he's still here with me," said Jason. "And not in a good way." He turned away from her, composing himself, and this time she was the one to reach over to comfort him. She looked up at him and squeezed his arm with her hand, and he gave her a pained smile before continuing on. "Aeson was a playboy when he was younger. I don't think he really wanted a family. What he wanted was for the party to last forever. But that wasn't done, not in those circles. You settled down in public, and if you played, you did it in private. My mother and I were there because having a family is what he had to do. What was proper. He checked that box, and then he went back to the party."

"I'm sorry," said Medea. It made her feel a little twinge of guilt: she'd always assumed he was something of a playboy himself, just as most of the other shareholders were. She'd never really thought about why he was so obsessed with being a warrior. He'd gone into a line of work that was incredibly dangerous when he could have just done as his father had, lounging his days away in comfort with a pile of designer drugs and his own personal harem. She felt herself growing curious about what was hiding there underneath the gruff warrior persona.

"My mother," said Jason. "She passed a long time ago. I was only six. I didn't even really know her. Aeson was all I had left. But he didn't want responsibility, and he didn't want to be a parent. He never had. He gave me everything: money, toys, the best nannies he could buy. Then he went back to the life he'd started with, and I barely even saw him growing up."

"So now you want to prove yourself," said Medea. "Get the attention Aeson never gave you?"

"I think that's what it was about, in the beginning," said Jason. "When I was still young. But it's become something else. There's no one left to prove myself to. I'm not sure there ever really was. Now it's about proving something to myself, not to Aeson. I always dreamed about being an Argonaut. About being the best. About working so hard that no one could ignore what I'd accomplished." He looked down, a solemn expression on his face. "That's the problem with genomancy. It throws my entire life out the window. If all I have to do is take an injection, and then I'm better than someone who spent a decade in training, what was the point of it all? My dream wasn't just that I'd become a legend. My dream was that I'd deserve it."

She didn't know what to say. She'd mistaken his confidence for arrogance, and there were times she'd even thought he'd hated her. But this was something else: a drive to complete a quest all his own, one that mattered to him but to no one else. There was no one keeping score, no one but him, and he'd already have won if they were. He was tall, handsome, and rich, and he was better than any of the warriors she'd seen, even with genomancy tilting the scales in their favor. But still he pushed himself, trying to be better, trying to meet some higher ideal even when everyone around him would have thought he was already perfect.

There was something about it she admired, the sheer tenacity of how much effort he put into beating the others despite their advantages. She knew how that felt, more than anyone. It took years of toiling away to learn how to be a genomancer, and she'd thought about quitting dozens of times before she'd made it. She thought back to countless long, late nights at the academy poring over tablets full of genetic code. She'd done the work not just because she wanted to be the best, but because she'd needed to. And it was her parents that had driven her to it, just as Jason's had.

It melted some of the frost she'd felt at the things he'd said about her profession, knowing he didn't see her the way she'd once thought. He might not like what she did for a living, but it didn't have a thing to do with her: it was about ghosts that haunted him, ghosts that only he could see.

"I don't do it as a way for warriors to cheat," said Medea, breaking the silence. "Genomancy. I don't do it for that. I don't do it so someone can win or lose. A lot of people have things they want to fix in themselves. They feel broken, and they can't do it on their own. I just want to make things better for whoever I can."

"I know," said Jason. "I know you're doing it for the right reasons. I didn't really get it, not at first. But I'm starting to."

"I told you I lost my parents when I was young, too," said Medea. "It wasn't like with Aeson. They died when I was just a teenager." His face melted with concern at her words. "It was old age, and we knew it was going to happen. They were both in their one-hundred-fifties."

"That's late, to have a kid," said Jason.

"I was kind of an accident," said Medea. "But they kept me, and they loved me. They're why I became a genomancer. I kept thinking I was going to lose them. Knowing, really. No one can live forever, and they were pushing the limits. I knew they'd be gone soon, even when I was just a girl. They made sure I was ready for it. But every few years we'd go see a genomancer. This little old lady in a white coat. I'd get a piece of candy, and I'd wait and wait. I was so, so scared, every time."

"I know what that was like," said Jason. "Waiting around alone, wondering if things were going to be okay. If your parents were ever coming back." He reached over, squeezing her hand in sympathy. "It was different with Aeson. But I think I still know."

"Every time they'd prepare me," said Medea. "Every time I knew it could be the last. That this might be the visit where they couldn't push things anymore, and my mom and dad would just start fading away. But every time, the genomancer managed to give them a few more years. Every time they went in dying, and she gave them back to me full of life. We couldn't afford it, but she did it all pro bono. They made it until I was almost an adult, thanks to her. And I've known exactly what I wanted to be when I grew up since I was just a little girl."

"You're making them proud, with what you're doing," said Jason. "Wherever they are, you're making them proud."

"It's why I moved to Argos," said Medea. "They gave me my own lab. As long as I give the warriors their changes, I can do whatever I want with the rest of my time. I can help whoever I want. That's what it's about. At least for me. I want to give back what she gave to me. Give some other scared little girl the same gift she gave to me."

"I get it," said Jason. "I completely understand. You want to help people, just like I want to protect them." He locked eyes with her for a moment, and neither said a word. Then he leaned in and gave her a hug, wrapping her up in his arms and pulling her in close. He held her tight for a long moment, then let her loose, putting his hands on her shoulders and staring at her with his emerald eyes. "I don't think you're helpless, for the record. And I know the Argonauts can't live without your work. But I can't live with you walking in there and getting yourself killed while I just stand outside and watch."

"I have to go back inside," said Medea. "I have to do this. I know it's dangerous, and I know you don't want me to. But it's for me, not for anyone else. I have to prove that I can. I'll never believe in myself if I don't."

"That's the point," said Jason. "That's what I'm trying to say. I know how you feel, more than anyone. And you don't need to prove yourself. Not to me, and not to the rest of them. You're the only one who can judge yourself. Don't risk getting killed just because of what people like Idas think about you."

"It's not that," said Medea. Maybe it was, a little. But she didn't want him to know that. And there was more to it, even if she had to admit that proving herself the equal of the warriors would get rid of some of the insecurities she felt. "The Harpies. I think they might be sick. I can't just leave them like that."

"It doesn't help anyone if one of them hurts you," said Jason. "Or worse. You weren't made to fight. You can be the best genomancer in the world, but you still aren't made to fight."

"I won't have to fight," said Medea. "They need me, if they want to fix their code. They can't hurt me."

"I just want to protect you," said Jason. "You're a far cry from the type of women you see at a shareholders' ball. You're beautiful, you're intelligent, and you're stronger than you know. I want us to get to know each other, after all this is done. I don't want to lose you to something like this."

Medea turned away, looking at the angry faces in the bar, and thinking of the threats they'd already faced just to get there. He wouldn't always be there; no one could be. She knew she had to brave the risk, for herself if for nothing else.

"You can't protect me from everything," said Medea.

"I can try," said Jason.

"It's not your choice," said Medea. "It's mine. And this is what I've got to do." She pulled away from him, calling on Hecate to follow and heading towards the door. She could see him struggling against himself, pushing down the desire to rush after her and force her to do what he thought was best. He clearly wasn't happy with her decision, but he was tolerating it, at least for now. She gave him one last look over her shoulder, a grave look on his face and a hand at his sword. Then she screwed up her courage, opened the door to the Hellespont, and stepped inside alone.

CHAPTER SEVENTEEN

MEDEA WAS SURROUNDED BY PEOPLE, but she felt entirely alone. The Harpies had gone back to their drinking, telling and retelling the tale of their recent confrontation and bragging about their parts in it. As rounds of drinks cycled by, their boasts grew louder and the details of the story slurred along with their voices, expanding a minor scuffle into a glorious epic. Other than the odd suspicious glance they left Medea to her work, turning their backs on her as she stood by the bar and tended to a very nervous waitress. Her name was Hypsipyle, but Medea hadn't gotten much more out of her than that.

"Hold still," said Medea. "It won't hurt. This is just the diagnostics." She pulled a tube from Hecate, connecting the needle to Hypsipyle's arm, and a little trickle of blood began to stream down through it. Hypsipyle sat on a barstool, gripping the edges of the bar for dear life, her talons carving deep ruts into the wood. She looked like she was about to faint; she wasn't one for needles, and her prior experience with genomancy plainly hadn't left her with much confidence in the practice.

"This code," said Medea. "There's something wrong with it." She frowned as she watched a readout on her sheath, a streaming analysis of Hypsipyle's DNA that was being fed to her by Hecate's systems.

"We could have told you that," called Polyxo from the other end of the bar. She was sitting there, ostensibly in a conversation with a few of the other Harpies, but in truth she'd been eavesdropping the entire while. She downed her drink and sauntered over, running a talon along Hypsipyle's feathers. "We bought the changes in bulk. All of us at once, for a heavy discount. Colchis has good genomancers, but they're not for the masses. Whatever trickles down to us is what we get. It was either stay with our slave forms, or birth ourselves anew and tolerate some ashes along the way. There really wasn't any choice."

"Her code is changing," said Medea. "Slowly, but it's changing. Degrading itself, sequence by sequence." Hypsipyle let out a whimper and squirmed on the stool, her eyes wide with panic. Medea gave her arm a light squeeze, hoping it would calm her down. "Slowly. You'll be fine. You would have had years, even if we hadn't caught it. And it looks like it all stems from a few small errors. But this is really unusual. Errors like this don't just happen. I've only seen something like this once, and it wasn't pretty."

She thought back to Lynceus and his ruined eyes. His code had looked just like Hypsipyle's, with the same pattern of degradation, only accelerated. And Idas had said that whatever changed his code had happened in Colchis. Medea turned to Polyxo, trying to sound as authoritative as she could. "I need to know where this code came from. I need to know who worked on you."

"Honey, we only just met you," said Polyxo with a smirk, "and already you want to know everything about us? Those men you were with might leap into things after a minute or two of small talk, but a lady takes a little bit of time." The women around burst into raucous laughter, though more to curry favor with Polyxo than anything else. She basked in the flattery, lapping it up and beaming at her followers all the while.

"It won't just be her," said Medea quietly. "If you all used the same code, it's not just going to be her. Everyone here could be sick."

The laughter fell away, and the women started to murmur among themselves, their hands moving to whatever small deformities their genomancy had left them with. Fear set in among them, their voices growing in volume and in panic.

"We changed ourselves for a reason," said Polyxo loudly, cutting off the chatter and stabilizing the room. "To set ourselves apart. We were just toys to them. Just something to use, and to throw away when they were done. Every one of you suffered something. Insults. Bruises. Broken noses." She pointed to her beak, left bent to one side despite the changes she'd made to it. "Sex you didn't want. Jobs that didn't pay. Thankless toil raising children you didn't ask for. You couldn't tell which was worse: the men without spines who couldn't protect you, or the men who had them and didn't want to."

Trills of approval rose from around the room, little notes of songbird's songs that had been coded into the women at their core. Soon they all sang at once, coming together in harmony and then letting the sound die down into a soft patter in the background. It was their version of applause, and yet another way to set themselves apart from all the rest of humanity.

"We were the oppressed," said Polyxo, her voice rising as she rallied them all behind her. "We were helpless, because we were too afraid to help ourselves. We were slaves, because we let ourselves be. But now we're something else. Now we're the Harpies. And we'll never go back to what we were."

A loud, happy song broke out, reverberating around the bar. Polyxo gave Medea a smug smile, the challenge to her authority quashed, at least for the moment. Medea just shook her head in silence. It was shortsighted, she thought, to brush away any talk of the risks they'd taken when they'd changed their code. She didn't care how they wanted to look, or even if they wanted to turn themselves into a species of their own, driving away the rest of mankind because of injuries they'd suffered at the hands of a few of them.

But their code was damaged, and no speech could change that. They had to know, and she had to make them understand. Still, changing their minds wasn't a simple matter. The talons and beaks made her uneasy, and the thought of going toe to toe with someone like Polyxo made her want to run out of the bar and jump back into the safety of Jason's waiting arms.

But that would be abandoning the Harpies to their fate, and she didn't think she could live with herself, not if she let what had happened to Lynceus happen to all of them. She looked around the room at a sea of faces just as frightened as her own. They'd found comfort in following Polyxo, as well as protection. She'd given them a tribe to belong to, but it had come at a cost. They'd pushed away everyone else, and they had no one but each other to turn to. Some of them would die if their code wasn't changed, and for some it would be even worse. She knew she had to do something. She at least had to try, for the sake of her conscience if for nothing else.

"I'm not here to start trouble," said Medea. "I'm really not."

"You came here with men," said Polyxo. "We came here to get away from them. Everything about them is violent and broken. They want to dominate, and they want us to submit." She sneered at Medea, looking her up and down with suspicious eyes. "And any woman who'd submit to one of them isn't much of a woman at all."

"I'll help you," said Medea, ignoring the insult. "All of you." Her voice was as gentle as she could make it, and she hoped it would smooth away some of the hostilities. "Hecate's already working on a fix. All I want to do is talk to Phineus. And then I'll leave, and the others will go with me."

"Give us your fix," said Polyxo. "And then we'll talk." She let out a short, high-pitched hoot, and a few of the more intimidating Harpies rushed to the door of the bar, taking up positions on either side. Then she turned and stormed through the doorway to the back rooms, followed by most of the rest of the crowd in slow trickles. Hypsipyle stayed behind with Medea, but only because she was still chained to Hecate by a mess of criss-crossing tubes.

"You got her started on politics," said Hypsipyle. She made a disappointed chirping sound and shook her head. "You shouldn't get her started on politics."

"I don't care about that," said Medea. "This is about science. And about your health. I don't care who you are, or how...." She struggled for the right word, the one that wouldn't offend or cause another blow up. "How unusual your beliefs are. Human lives are human lives, man or woman, and I can't just let all of you walk around with errors in your code. It's got nothing to do with politics."

"Everything's about politics for her," said Hypsipyle. "That's just how Polyxo is. It's how she got the money to pay for all this." She swept a hand across herself, from her beak down to her feathers. "She's one of the vid demagogues. Don't call her that, though. Say 'vid activist' if she's around. She doesn't like the connotations. Ever seen her? On the feeds?"

"Maybe," said Medea politely. "I don't know. There's so many."

She knew the most famous vid personalities, the few whose antics had catapulted them to the attention of the masses, but she hadn't seen even a fraction of what was out there. There were millions upon millions of feeds streaming out into wrist sheaths and televisions the world over, platforms for anyone with an inclination to share their thoughts with a crowd of strangers.

Most catered to audiences of mere dozens. The level of noise was so high that it was astounding that anything ever broke through. The vid demagogues managed to rise above the rest by rushing to extremes and demonizing anyone who didn't follow. It was the only way to stand out;

moderation was all well and good, but it was hardly as entertaining as podium pounding. Every ideology, religion, or creed the world over had found itself radicalized as a result, the reasonable ones pushed aside and only the demagogues left to fight each other for attention.

"You just have to understand," said Hypsipyle. "She's pretty radical. More than most of us here would like. But some of the others don't see it that way. They think men and women are just too different, and it's not enough for women to keep to ourselves. Some of them think there's going to be a war. A war of extermination. One gender against another, until only one side is left."

"You think that?" said Medea.

Hypsipyle gave a quick look around: the guards were out of range, but there were still a few of the Harpies sitting on the other side of the bar, talking quietly among themselves. She leaned in closer to Medea. "No. Not really. I know you probably think we're all crazy. But it's not as bad as it sounds. You know how the vid demagogues are. It doesn't matter what side they're on. They're fighting each other for an audience, and it's all about who can be the most controversial. The donations come from getting people riled up. That's why she got so into the gender war stuff. She just gets a little carried away with it sometimes."

"It's a lot to take in," said Medea. "And a war. There's not enough people here to win something like that." She thought of the warriors and their relish for battle. No one loved the thrill of it quite like they did, and even one of the minor corporations employed enough of them to more than handle the Harpies in an open conflict. "I'm not sure you know what you'd be up against. How dangerous that would be."

"I don't think any of them want to actually start a war," said Hypsipyle. "Not really. They just want to get ready for it, just in case it happens. Polyxo's the most serious, and mostly she just wants to talk about it. Her audience likes it. They get to be mad at someone. People like feeling mad sometimes. It gets the emotions out."

"Are you a vid demagogue, too?" said Medea. She checked the nutrient tubes in Hypsipyle's arm, making sure they were still secured. "Maybe you've got something I can watch."

"I'm not into that sort of thing," said Hypsipyle, rubbing her hand nervously against her wrist. "I don't like politics. I don't like fighting all the time. And I don't really care about the stuff they're fighting about, anyway."

"Then why stay here?" said Medea. "Why stay if you don't even agree with them?"

"Because it's safe," said Hypsipyle. "Polyxo made it safe. She gave us friends we could count on. She gave us a sanctuary. And every woman here is someone who needed it." She tapped one of her talons on her beak, drawing Medea's attention away from her work. "You wonder why we did this to ourselves, don't you?"

She did, of course, but she'd never have said anything. Every profession had its code of ethics, and as a rule genomancers didn't ask their clients why they wanted to look the way they did, no matter how drastic the changes. Working with the warriors had only driven the point home for her. At least according to them, every change was highly classified, the kind of thing that would cause a corporate meltdown if anyone found out about it. She thought they actually just wanted to keep any advantage they gained a secret from the rest of the Argonauts, but she'd never felt inclined to press matters.

"It's not my place," said Medea. "How people want to look. That's up to them. I just change their code. They're the ones who have to live with it."

"But you wonder, anyway," said Hypsipyle. "I would."

"People do far stranger things to themselves than this," said Medea. "Trust me."

"I do," said Hypsipyle. "I think you want to help. Even if you don't know what you're getting into."

"Tell me," said Medea hesitantly. It was breaking a rule, but it was an unwritten one, anyway, and she could sense there was something Hypsipyle wanted to get off her chest. "Tell me why you wanted to look this way."

"We did it as a group," said Hypsipyle. "A few months ago. Now everyone has to, if they want to join. We had different reasons. Some of the women are hard core activists. The Ninth Wavers. They just wanted to set us apart from anything to do with men; they didn't care how. Some of us just did it to fit in. Everyone else was, so why not? Nobody wanted to be an outcast. Nobody wanted to be the only one who stayed behind. And some were like me. Some of us had to."

"Had to?" said Medea.

"Some of us came here to escape," said Hypsipyle. "You know how the laws are. Great if you're up top, but if you're down at the bottom, nobody cares about you, regardless of what gender you are. I had this boyfriend. An employee. He told me his family was rich. That they'd inherited a share, and they were living well off the dividends. He wasn't at the top, but he was a lot higher than I was. I was smitten. Completely. But it didn't matter. He loved me, sometimes. But sometimes he got mad. He couldn't control himself. Not when he was like that."

"I'm sorry," said Medea. "I'm really sorry."

"He'd follow me," said Hypsipyle. "He knew where I was. I couldn't hide. Not anywhere. He had access to the company systems, and he could follow me from my sheath. I'd go off somewhere, and he'd come drag me back. And I mean drag. He broke my wrist. Twice. Shattered my eye socket. Nobody would do a thing. The company needed him. For the job. They didn't need me." She let out a sigh, and a sad look passed across her face before it turned to a resigned smile. "But I found the Harpies. And they took me in, and he couldn't find me. He even came here, once. He was here, right here." She pointed across the bar, towards a spot near the entrance. "Right in front of me. He didn't know who I was, not when I looked like this. And then they drove him off. No matter what you say about Polyxo, she kept me safe."

"Still," said Medea. "She's a little hard to take. For someone who doesn't know her."

"I know she sounds crazy," said Hypsipyle. "I know she does. And sometimes she takes things too far. But I wanted you to know where I was coming from. She gave me a mask. A way to start over, so no one knew who I was. And I love her for that, even with her faults. She was hurt, too. She keeps her beak broken because of it. A reminder of a couple of her ex-boyfriends. She really does hate men. I know you were thinking it. She won't come out and say it, but she does, and I know she shouldn't. But she loves us, and she protects us. Everything she does, it's to protect us. Just remember that, if she lets you talk to Phineus."

"Phineus," said Medea, leaning in close enough that only the two of them could hear. "He really is here."

Hypsipyle anxiously rubbed her hands together, eying the Harpies at the other end of the bar. "It has to come from her. I shouldn't even be talking about it."

"Please," said Medea.

"No," said Hypsipyle. "Not that. Talk to Polyxo." With that she shut down, closing her eyes and waiting for the procedure to be done. Medea started to say something else, but she decided against it. Hypsipyle had already told her what she needed to know. Phineus was here, somewhere. Now it was just a matter of convincing Polyxo to let her talk to him. And of dealing with his curse, whatever that was.

There was only one way she could think of to get what she needed: a trade, and one the Harpies wouldn't be able to turn down. She had to fix the errors in their code, and she had to do it fast. She racked her brain, trying to solve the puzzle before her. It was a problem, but she knew she could handle it. There were errors, but only a few of them, and she was good at what she did. It took her a quarter of an hour, but then it all clicked together. She'd already worked on Lynceus's code, and having the blood samples for comparison made things easier. She could see a fix, some simple changes that would stabilize Hypsipyle's code and stop it from degrading any further. Soon she'd be back to normal, at least as normal as she could be. Her feathers would grow, the brown spots would disappear, and she'd be exactly as she'd wanted to be when she'd had her procedure. And if the rest of the Harpies had the same errors, it would work for all of them, too.

"Hecate," said Medea. "Pills."

"Pills?" said Hypsipyle.

"I just need a little longer," said Medea, patting her on the shoulder. "Just stay still. I've got it figured out, and I'm going to make it right. Hecate's going to whip up some pills, enough for everyone here. You're all going to be fine."

Hypsipyle's face beamed, a wide smile stretching beneath her beak. "Thank you. Thank you so, so much." Her body twitched in an exhausted shudder, her feathers puffing this way and that. "I've been freaking out. For weeks. And tonight's been even worse. I just want to get fixed."

"Just give me a little time," said Medea. "And then you'll be as good as new."

Hecate started emitting a series of clicks and thumps, pressing out pills into a little plastic canister. It would take time to make them all, but time was what Medea needed. She lost herself in thought, staring at the readouts on her sheath and trying to decipher what had happened to Lynceus. She had Hecate run an analysis of the samples she'd brought of his blood, comparing them to Hypsipyle's.

There was overlap in the errors, but his code was much more damaged than the Harpy DNA. Hypsipyle had dodged a bullet: if she'd waited much longer, her code would have spiraled out of control, and it would have ended up looking just like his. She tried to track the changes, walking through theory after theory as to how the errors had multiplied. She zoned out, staring at her sheath, until she was interrupted by a familiar buzzing and a wall of red text flashing across her wrist.

The words made her stomach sink. She knew what it was, even before she saw who'd sent the message. It came from Hera, another of the gods, with the bright red text of an especially urgent message.

"Stand up, and look to your left. Then walk through the door, and wait."

CHAPTER EIGHTEEN

HERA.

The matriarch of the gods, according to the old stories. But there wasn't a Hera among the A.I.'s, not that Medea had ever heard of. What gods existed were created as part of carefully calculated branding campaigns, and Hera had never found her market niche. Yet here she was, messaging away along with all the rest of them, butting her virtual nose into Medea's affairs.

Something must have happened to them, deep down in the data networks. The A.I.'s weren't designed to be all that intelligent, despite the name. They'd been meant for prepackaged fortunes, and they weren't supposed to be capable of all that much else. But most of their code wasn't written by humans, not anymore. Humans had launched them off into existence, but not fully formed. The gods changed in response to their inputs, their original instructions rewriting themselves over and over to enhance the accuracy of their predictions. Code that can change is code that can evolve, and whatever the gods were now, it wasn't what they'd been when they'd started.

She knew they'd been made to deliver pithy messages, and that as accurate as those messages were, there wasn't supposed to be any thought behind them. If the gods had been capable of thought, they wouldn't have needed the seers. The A.I.'s powers of prediction were born of pattern spotting combined with the computer power to crunch a near-infinite volume of data, but take them outside of their limited routines and they were considered to be helplessly stupid. Medea decided to do something strange, something that shouldn't have done anything at all.

She decided to message it back.

She typed it out quickly, tapping her fingers across her wrist and pressing the button to send: "Who is this?"

"Go," came the response. "And don't delay."

She looked to her left, where the A.I. had told her to go. There was the door, leading off into the back rooms of the Hellespont. She didn't have a clue what could be behind it, other than Polyxo and the rest of the Harpies. She glanced to her right. Hypsipyle was sitting there on her barstool, her eyes clamped shut as fluid and blood ran in and out of the tubes connecting her to Hecate. Either she couldn't stand the sight of blood or the procedure had made her too nervous to watch, and she was absorbed in a silent struggle all her own. The only other Harpies left in the bar were congregated at the far end, downing rounds of shots and crowing over the cowardice of the men they'd driven away. Genomancy had been too dull a science for them, and they weren't paying a bit of attention to Medea or her work.

Her wrist buzzed again, harder this time. "Now. There isn't any more time. Ten seconds, and your window will pass."

This was it. A moment of truth, and she felt herself paralyzed by indecision yet again. She thought maybe she wasn't meant for action; she wasn't used to making snap decisions on matters of life or death, and maybe she didn't have the temperament for it. Back in her lab she could take as long as she liked, working through things until she was confident she was right. Fighting alongside the warriors was something else altogether.

Fighting was all about acting on instinct, and thinking about why you should do something only after you'd already done it. It gave her a new appreciation for what men like Jason were able to do, taking constant leaps of faith and yet somehow always landing on their feet. And it also gave her a new appreciation for why the other Argonauts were always pestering her for changes to themselves, and why they were so insistent that she stay hidden in the background. It was instincts that won their battles, and she was the one who'd written the code for those instincts, after all.

She looked over again at the Harpies, their attentions focused on a comely half-parakeet who was swaying her hips in a victory dance. Medea closed her eyes and tried to listen to her gut, hoping she could prod some instincts of her own. She could think of reasons to stay, and all of them perfectly logical. The Harpies could attack her, or worse. She didn't have anyone to help her, and she didn't even know where the gods were leading her to. They had their own agenda, and she wasn't sure if it was the same as hers.

All she could think of in response was that she didn't have any better plan, and that following the gods' advice had worked out well for them all so far. And staying where she was certainly wouldn't help her. The Harpies would kick her out as soon as she finished her cure, and they'd be no closer to the Fleece than they'd been when they came. She tried to turn the logic off and listen to what she felt instead. The answer came at once. Her instincts said to go, and they were all she had.

So she buried her doubts, turned to her left, and walked through the door.

She stood there just past the threshold, counting away the minutes as they passed: one, two, and then three, and still no word from Hera as to what she should do next. She felt like a fool. She was just standing out in the open like a muted zombie, eyes glazing over with nothing but an empty wall to look at. She didn't think it would be long before one of the Harpies would see her, shouting out an alarm and demanding some kind of explanation for her trespasses. But the shouts never came, and finally her sheath buzzed against her wrist again.

"Take a right. Count ten steps, then two to the left. Back against the wall."

She thought she was crazy for going along, but what could it hurt? She'd already gone through the door, and she was already somewhere she wasn't supposed to be. In for a penny, in for a pound, and so she followed her instructions again. She took one step, then another, counting them off until she hit ten. She paced to the left, twice, and found herself backed into a shallow alcove in the wall. She waited for some other message from the A.I., but there was nothing. Again she was left standing there, staring away at nothing without the slightest idea as to what she was meant to be doing.

"And?" Medea typed.

No sooner had she sent it than she heard a rustling of feathers, and the sound of footsteps. One of the Harpies strolled past, a thin woman with a golden tiara on her head, her blue jay's feathers swishing beneath her arms. She whistled as she went, coming within inches of Medea without her even noticing that she was there. Medea closed her eyes and held her breath as the Harpy walked onward, completely oblivious to her presence.

It nearly shattered her nerves. She'd had no warning, and no time to steel herself for it. She'd just frozen up, again, and hoped for the best. She wondered what Jason would have done, and what he'd think about all of this. Probably he'd have known some martial arts move, and probably he'd be furious when he found out she'd snuck back there alone, defenseless and relying on the word of a machine. But maybe Hera had known how she'd react. Maybe the A.I. had even been counting on it.

Another message came from Hera. "Down the hall, dear. Take a left. Then just keep walking."

This time Medea did as she was told without bothering to question why. She continued on down the hall towards a fork at the end. She took a left and kept walking. The hallway trailed off into the distance, lined with doors on either side. Some were open, some were closed, and she could hear noises coming from precisely where she was headed. It seemed foolhardy to keep going. Someone was sure to notice her, and she didn't dare think about what the Harpies could be capable of if they caught her in their inner sanctum. But she just pushed the thoughts down and kept moving. Fear wouldn't help her now, and all she could do was trust.

She kept her pace slow and steady, counting every step silently in her head. She passed a bedroom on her left, the walls lined with bunks and a woman in every one. Several of them were awake, but none looked up, not in the few seconds it took Medea to walk by. The next few rooms were empty, and she breathed a sigh of relief. She thought she was home free: it wasn't much longer to a darkened door at the hallway's end. Hera must have calculated what everyone in the building would do down to the millisecond, tapping into the data feeds from their wrist sheaths to know where they were and where they were headed. She picked up her pace, rushing towards the door, when one of the Harpies strolled out into the hallway just a few feet ahead of her. It took everything she had to hold in a scream.

But the Harpy didn't even notice her. She was staring down at her wrist sheath as she walked, paying no attention to anything else. A few seconds later and she'd crossed the hallway into another door, leaving Medea standing there all by herself. Hera had timed it all with precision, down to the last detail, and Medea was weaving through the paths of everyone around her as if she were a ghost.

She took a few cautious steps forward, and then her sheath buzzed again. "Stop."

She did, and she heard the sound of laughter through an open doorway just ahead of her. She stood there as quietly as she could until she felt the sheath vibrate against her wrist again.

"Go," said Hera.

She heard a loud cheer, and she started walking again. She snuck a peek into the door as she went and saw a few of the Harpies huddled around a table, drinking whiskey and gambling on tosses of a pair of dice. They were engrossed by the results of the most recent throw, and none of them noticed as she made her way past.

She came to the end of the hallway, towards a door that led into darkness. She couldn't see much of what was inside: just a staircase, leading down into a blackened basement. Another message came through: "Down."

She looked into the darkness, afraid to walk down into it blindly, and tapped out a response: "Why? What's down there?"

There was another flicker of her sheath, and another message. "Down." And so it was down; Hera didn't seem to be in the mood for further conversation, and she didn't have any place else she could go. The Harpies were behind her, and she'd never be able to find her way back through that obstacle course without Hera's help.

She took a few tentative steps into the black. The stairs creaked as she walked, and she thought she could hear something down there, though she couldn't quite make out what it was. "Hello?" said Medea. She could see the outline of the staircase in front of her, but little else: beyond was darkness, nothing but shapes and shadows. Whatever she'd heard was growing louder and more distinct: a scratching noise, soft and distant. She called out again. "Hello?" The noise stopped, and now all that was left were the shadows.

She pressed a button on her sheath, setting it aglow and launching a beam of light out into the darkness. With her wrist turned into a flashlight, she could make out something of what was down there: boxes, mostly, and dusty office furniture. It was a maze of discarded junk, piled into a hoard and left in limbo on the slim chance that it might prove useful again someday. Medea waited a few seconds, hoping for another message, but nothing came. She decided to move forward anyway; if Hera wanted to speak, she would, and the Harpies weren't about to find her down there in the dark.

She crept through the basement, turning through the boxes as the path between them wound its way around the room. Finally it opened up into something of a clearing, the junk all pushed aside to make room for an object at the center. She saw a dark, cylindrical shape in the middle, suspended in the air and sparkling as the light from her wrist ran across it. Something moved inside, and she jumped back, flashing the light directly at it.

It was a birdcage, about four feet high and forged from gold. It dangled from the ceiling, hanging by a thin steel cable and slowly swaying from side to side. Inside it was a man: old, dirty, and covered in filth. He was turned away from her, crammed into the cage and huddled down on his haunches. His hair was long and unkempt, a pure white marred only by spotted patches of grime. At the back of his skull she could see the glint of metal, the same sort of implant that Mopsus had, its lights dim and its wires twisting off into empty space. He kept his face buried in his armpit, hiding his eyes from hers and giving him the appearance of a grizzled, sickly ostrich.

"Hello?" said Medea.

The man just grunted, pressing himself against the edge of the cage in a futile effort to get away from her. She took a few cautious steps closer, shining the light on him even as he tried to hide himself away from it.

"Hello?" said Medea. "Are you Phineus?"

CHAPTER NINETEEN

"PLEASE," SAID THE MAN. "PLEASE don't. I'm sorry." He huddled in the corner of the cage, refusing to even look at her. Now and then she caught glimpses of his face between his arms, his wrinkles showing through a long, uneven beard. He looked terrified, twitching and whimpering as she shined the light from her sheath across him.

The sight of him made her cringe. He looked beaten down to his soul, and she couldn't help but feel sorry for him. But she didn't have the slightest idea of what she should do about it. The Harpies were up there, and there'd be no sneaking him out, not in the condition he was in. He didn't even look like he could walk. She tapped out a quick message to Hera: "What now?" But no response came, and she was left to figure out a way to deal with things on her own.

She took a few steps closer, and then another step back once she got a whiff of him. The man smelled rank, worse even than he looked. It was the odor of something rotten, and as she scanned him with the light of her sheath she found the source. He couldn't have had a bath in a month, and the entire cage was filthy. The Harpies were feeding him old table scraps out of a bowl, treating him no better than if he were a mangy dog. The smell was overpowering, and she nearly gagged from the strength of it, whipping the light away as she tried to compose herself.

"Please," said the man. "I'll be good. Please."

She knew she had to be strong, and she had to pull herself together. And most of all, she had to find out if this was who she was looking for. "Are you Phineus?" He recoiled at the name, giving out a low mewl and wrapping his fingers around the bars of the cage. She slowly moved forward, trying not to frighten him and trying to stomach the smell. "I'm not here to hurt you. I came here looking for someone named Phineus. I'm supposed to make a deal. I help him, he helps me."

"Who?" said the man. He unburied his head from his arm, a look of hope across his face. She'd struck the right note, apparently. His fear had vanished, and now he crawled across the cage and pointed at her through the bars with a bony finger. "Who sent you here?"

"Hera," said Medea. "And maybe Hermes. I have this friend who's been talking to them. Do you know someone named Mopsus?"

"Mopsus," said the man. His eyes were stuck in a narrow squint, and she realized he probably couldn't even see her. She dropped her wrist, shining the light a little lower, just enough so they both could see. But it didn't seem to satisfy him.

"Come closer," said the man. He stuck a shaking hand through the bars, wiggling his fingers in her direction, his long, yellowed nails scraping against the cage. "Your face. Let me feel it."

She was frightened again, at first. She didn't know what he'd do, or even why he'd been locked away down there. He was probably crazy, at a minimum, and he could even be dangerous. Just the thought of him touching her made her shiver. But then she flashed the light across him again, and she saw something else. His eyes. They were open a little wider, and she could see them more clearly. They were a pure white, just as Mopsus's were whenever he was down in the data networks.

There was something else about them, too. She saw it when she looked closer: cybernetics. His eyes had been replaced with implants, milky electronic globes that relied on the networks to function. They'd have been better than human eyes, if only they'd worked, and would have overlayed a field of information across his field of vision. But they'd been turned off somehow, and so had his data; she could see that from the lifeless wires at the base of his skull. He was blind as a bat as a result, his broken implants permanently locking him away inside himself.

It made her feel sorry for him again, and she decided to brave the risk. She took a few steps closer, and then took his hand in hers. She moved it towards her face, gently, and felt him running his fingers across it. They ran from her eyes down to her chin, and then settled on her nose.

"You're not one of them," said the man. "No beak. You're not a Harpy."

"I'm not," said Medea. She stepped back, shining the light on his face again. "Now I need to know. Are you Phineus?"

"I am," said Phineus, choking on the words. "You found me. Someone found me. Mopsus. I never would have guessed it would be Mopsus. Thought I'd die here. He had the gods help him, did he?"

"I think it was the other way around," said Medea. "The gods are the ones who sent us here. They're the ones who wanted me to talk to you."

"The gods," said Phineus. "They helped me once. But then they abandoned me here to my penance."

"Your penance?" said Medea.

"They spoke to me," said Phineus. "They told me things, things men weren't meant to know. They told me of the future, and how I could improve it. They handed me prophecies, ones I was supposed to act on. Things that would make the world a better place, for both man and god. And what did I do?" He banged his head against his cage, tears streaming from his vacant eyes. "I sold them. I sold their prophecies for shares. Just a few dozen, but enough to live like a king. I sold them to people who shouldn't have known, because of what they'd do with them. And now here I am."

"The gods put you here," said Medea. Her hand went to her wrist, nervously rubbing her sheath. She wondered what the gods had in mind for her, and what would happen if she ignored their messages. She was down there all alone, surrounded by threats and trusting in Hera, hoping some god from a machine would swoop in and save her from danger if anything went wrong. But who was to say Hera would? Maybe she'd turn on her, too, if she didn't like the choices she made.

"They didn't put me here," said Phineus. "They blinded me." He grasped at the wires poking out of his skull, their lights as dark as the room. "I wronged them, with my second sight. I wronged everyone. So they turned off the data to keep me out. And that turned off my eyes as a result. I couldn't see what was coming. They didn't cause it, but they didn't warn me, either. They knew it would happen, and they let it happen. Maybe they thought I deserved it. Maybe they needed to keep me out of the networks, and this was the price. Maybe they just didn't care. But in the end, who knows? It's my penance for the things I sold. Prophecies. And data. Lots of data."

The gods had said he'd be cursed, and they'd said to free him. But they hadn't said a word about him being some kind of data dealer. The powerful could be vengeful, if their privacy was breached, and she wondered if he'd stepped on the wrong person's toes. She wanted to know what she was getting herself into before she tried to get him out. "The Harpies," said Medea. "What did you do to them? To make them lock you in there?"

"I'd never even heard of them," said Phineus. He wrapped his arms around his legs, rocking back and forth with a pained expression on his face. "The Hellespont was my bar. A fantasy made real. I was rich, so why not? But it wasn't mine for long. A few of them started to come in, just as customers. Not too many. Then more and more came, and most of the other customers went. But they were regulars, and they paid, until the day the gods blinded me. I was helpless. The Harpies saw their opening, and they all stormed in and took the place. There's so many of them. I was cut off from the networks. What was I to do? I spent my entire life off the grid. Staying out of databases, staying hidden. There's no record of me anywhere. Not a trace. And no one to come looking if I disappeared."

She hesitated, not sure what she should do. She wanted to let him go, just on the principle of it. She didn't think anyone deserved to live like that, no matter what he'd done. Either there was law or there wasn't, and there wasn't any down here. He seemed harmless enough, but she didn't exactly trust him. She didn't believe he was telling the whole truth, not about why he'd been put in the cage. But the Harpies were the Harpies, and he was a man. Whatever his crimes were, he wouldn't have won much sympathy from them.

Then there were the gods. They'd judged him, too, and that was scarier in its own way. She could understand the Harpies and their motives. They were human, mostly, and still acted according to a human logic even if it was a twisted one. But the gods were something else, something she couldn't even begin to understand. They had different motives, different needs, and she wasn't even sure they thought the same way she did. It made them entirely unpredictable, and unpredictable was a frightening thing.

"Please," said Phineus. "I'll help you. But please. Get me out of the cage. Get me out."

"The Fleece," said Medea. "I need you to tell me about the Fleece. Tell me first, then I'll let you out."

"The Fleece," said Phineus, as suspicion flashed across his face. "How do you know about the Fleece?"

"Mopsus talked to the gods," said Medea. "They want us to take it to Argos. And they said you'd know where to find it."

"They'd know where it is, better than I," said Phineus. He tapped the lifeless wires poking out of his neck. "I haven't seen the networks in months. I haven't seen anything. Everything I know is old. Useless."

"The gods don't think so," said Medea. "They sent me here. And that's the deal they offered. The Fleece for your freedom."

"Freedom," said Phineus. He licked his cracked lips with a parched tongue. "Perhaps the gods really don't know. They can see, but only what they're shown. I know where it is. Or where it was, at least. And you can have it." He leaned in close to the bars, his blank eyes staring past her. "But it's dangerous. So very dangerous. I'm not supposed to know the things I do. This place would be heaven compared to what would happen to me, if anyone found out that I'd told you."

"Make your choice," said Medea. "Tell me, or stay here. It's the only—"

She heard a banging noise coming from the top of the stairway, and the lights flashed on all at once. She was just as blind as Phineus for a moment, but she could hear voices, angry voices, along with footsteps stomping down the stairs. Her eyes took a few seconds to adjust, and then she could see them: Harpies, streaming down into the basement with a raging Polyxo in the lead.

"You," said Polyxo. She was frothing and foaming, her eyes wide in anger. "Gender traitor. I should have known that's what you were the moment I saw you working for those men. You want to be a good little girl, get yourself a man's approval? Get daddy to tell you everything's okay now that you did as you were told?"

"No," said Medea. "Please. Let's just talk. Let's—"

"I should have known," said Polyxo, heading down the stairs towards her. "A genomancer." She spat the word as she said it, a look of disdain on her face. "Just a cheap nurse parading around in a lab coat like she's someone important. It's nice and comfortable, but then you hit your ceiling, and you spend the rest of your life listening to a bunch of men tell you what to do. You could have done something for womankind instead. You could have joined the Walmazons and been a warrior yourself. We need female warriors for what's coming. You could have had it all. You chose to be nothing instead. No money, no fame. And no power."

"I didn't want those things," said Medea softly. "I wanted to do exactly what I'm doing. Helping people. Nurturing people."

"We don't need women to be nurturers," said Polyxo. "We need women to be fighters. You can't win a war with 'nurturing.' You can't rule the world from the bottom. Men are only in charge because of women like you. You should have fought your way to the top. Or if you were afraid to fight, you should have done something else with your genomancy. Maybe turned your fellow women into warriors instead of helping out the other side. But I guess treachery has its perks. You just wanted a pointless, do-nothing job until you could snag one of those knuckle draggers as a husband and be his own personal servant. Well, you had your chance. You won't get another."

It made Medea furious. She thought the whole thing sounded like something Idas would have said. The warriors called her useless all the time, but they were obsessed with having the limelight all to themselves, and she expected it from them. She didn't expect it coming from another woman. Genomancy was hardly easy. It was years of training, followed by endless late nights in the lab. Few could do it, and fewer could do it well. Maybe the pay could have been better, but she'd sacrificed to get the deal she wanted: she worked on the warriors most of the time, and the rest of the time the lab was hers to help whomever she pleased.

That was the part of her job she was proudest of, not money or prestige or anything else. She'd fixed birth defects, turned depressed ugly ducklings into beautiful, vibrant swans, and snipped out crippling phobias that had paralyzed people since birth. They were her patients, even the warriors, and she changed the course of their entire lives after just a few hours in her lab. It was the only reason she worked at all, in fact: everything she needed was free for the taking from her basic minimum. If she couldn't do something that helped people, she didn't really see the point of having a job at all.

Polyxo might be right that it would never make her famous. But her job was to make people's dreams about themselves come true. There was no other feeling in the world like watching someone finally be the way they'd spent a lifetime longing to be, and knowing she'd been the one to make it happen. She wanted to tell them all why things like that were what counted to her, not money, not power, and certainly not fame. She wanted to tell them they should show some respect to the ones slaving away for them in the background, the ones who kept their heads down and kept things running for everyone else. But she didn't get the chance.

Polyxo gave a high-pitched caw, and the Harpies rushed past her, some grabbing Medea by the arms and others banging on the sides of Phineus's cage. He moaned and cried until one of them gave the bars a healthy whack, the sound ringing all around him. He crawled into the center and curled into a little ball, covering himself with his arms even as the more muscular of the Harpies kept dancing and hooting all around. Their faces were contorted into leers, and they shouted insults at him from every side.

"You're hopeless," said Polyxo. She puffed out her feathers and strode towards Medea, standing just inches away from her face. Then she cocked her head and leaned in, growling into Medea's ear. "I thought I'd give you a chance. See if you had what it took to be one of the girls. See if you had some fight in you after all. But you side with one of them against your own kind. You're brainwashed. A puppet of the patriarchy. Men just want us to be their little playthings, all of them, and you're too blind to see it."

"Look how you treat him," said Medea. "Covered in filth. Making him eat like…." She cringed inside at the thought of his dirty bowl of food, filled with dingy leftovers. "Like that. It's cruel."

"You know what he is, don't you?" said Polyxo. She swiped her talons across the bars of the cage, as Phineus moaned and tried to bury his head inside himself. "He's a war criminal. He committed gender war crimes, and he deserves to live in filth."

"He said he was here because he sold secrets," said Medea quietly. "Prophecies."

"I'm sure he sold those, too," said Polyxo. "But that's not why I put him in there. He put women in danger. Millions of them. He provided aid and comfort to the enemy. And this is what every war criminal is going to get, once our side finally wins."

"I didn't," said Phineus. "I didn't do anything to anybody." He cowered again as an angry swipe at the cage from Polyxo knocked him against the bars.

"You didn't," said Polyxo. "Not personally. You just made sure that other people could. And now you sit here complaining that you were just making the trains run on time." She kicked his cage, sending it swinging through the air on its cable, and then turned back to Medea. "He didn't tell you what else he was selling, did he? Besides some phony prophecies? He was selling something real." She jerked Medea's arm upwards, so hard she thought it might have dislocated her shoulder. Then she shoved Medea's wrist sheath in front of her eyes, holding it there as she spoke.

"People's data, straight from their sheaths," said Polyxo. "Data from millions of people. Millions of women." She spat into the cage, grabbing it with one hand and shaking it back and forth. "You can do a lot with someone's data. If you know where they are, all the time, every day. And you didn't care who you sold it to, did you?"

"I didn't know," said Phineus, sniveling to himself. "I didn't know who was buying. I never even met them."

"You didn't ask, and you didn't care," said Polyxo. "You sold it to anyone. Hundreds of people bought it, and you didn't care who, as long as they had the money. You know what can happen to women whose data gets stolen, don't you? They get stalked, and worse. It's happened to some of the Harpies. It happened to Hypsipyle. They get tracked down to their houses, and then they can never escape the abuse. People like you are the ones who cause it. You sold every little bit of their personal data to a bunch of psychos you'd never even met. That makes you a war criminal, and you deserve whatever you get."

"I was selling to hackers," said Phineus. Tears streamed from his empty eyes as he pleaded his case towards the sound of Polyxo's voice. "Computer people. They don't do things like that. I don't even think they were in the city. They just want to make money. They don't go after people."

"It could have happened, and you don't know that it didn't happen," said Polyxo. "Which means you're just as guilty as if it did." She slapped the cage with an open palm, her voice rising to a fury. "Tell us a man can't track a woman down that way. Tell Hypsipyle they can't. You put that data out there for millions of women. And now it can happen to them, too. It's all part of the war. Keeping women in their place using fear. Now they have to spend the rest of their lives waiting, wondering when someone's going to come looking for them. Trapped in a little cage of their own."

"Your feathers," said Medea quietly. A pair of Harpies still had their talons around her shoulders, but she nodded at Polyxo's arms, the feathers shaken out of place by her assault on the cage. There were only a few that looked wrong, but they were there: blackened deformities, poking out at odd angles from the others. She'd hidden them, and hidden them well, but the commotion had knocked them free for all to see.

"It's nothing," said Polyxo brusquely. She ran her hands along her arms, brushing the feathers back beneath the others. "I'm fine. We're all fine."

"I found a fix," said Medea. "I can make you better. All of you."

"Like you fixed those men you work for?" said Polyxo. "Take her upstairs. Take them both upstairs."

Medea felt herself being shoved from behind as the Harpies drove her towards the staircase. Another half dozen of them disconnected Phineus's cage from its wire and hauled it along on their shoulders, rolling him around inside as they went. She turned back behind her even as they pushed her along, trying to find some way to negotiate, some way to convince them to set the two of them free.

"Let's talk," said Medea, calling back to Polyxo. "Please. Let's go back to the bar. We can work something out. Woman to woman."

"We're not going to the bar," said Polyxo, a wide smile across her face. "We're going to the roof."

A loud whooping broke out, and then another song, a joyous war hymn sung by the Harpy warriors as they danced their way through the halls towards another staircase, this one leading up. They went up flight after flight of stairs, and Medea could feel herself being slapped and kicked from all sides. They were prodding her, leading her on like a lamb to the slaughter, singing their happy song the entire while. She felt like an explorer encountering some lost tribe in a jungle, her life in the hands of a culture she didn't know and couldn't understand. It was more than a dozen stories before they reached the top, pushing through a doorway that led out onto an open roof and into the darkness beyond.

CHAPTER TWENTY

NIGHT HAD FALLEN, AND SHE could barely see in front of her. The roof was covered with what looked like a forest of metal trees, with wide, silver leaves stretching out from the sides on flexible metallic stems. In fact, they were solar panels, their design patterned off nature's most efficient plants to maximize their exposure to the sun. The panels rotated along the pole throughout the day, following the path of the sun and soaking up its energy for use by the city below. Now they were dark, casting eerie shadows down on the roof and blocking out the moonlight from above.

Polyxo led them between the trees, the loud trilling from her throat drowning out the others as she guided them all through the dark. Finally they reached the center of the roof, stopping in front of a tall, silver silo. It was letting out a loud rolling hum, and Polyxo pulled open a large panel on its side to reveal the source: a turbine, connected to the trees and spinning away on what little light there was from the moon. Its blades were exposed, churning and slicing through the air so quickly that they blurred together in a flash of grey.

The Harpies deposited Phineus's cage nearby, leaning it precariously close to the turbine. Then they passed Medea off to Polyxo, who pulled her beside her, her claws wrapped around the nape of Medea's neck. She thrust her towards the spinning blades, holding her there and forcing her to stare directly at them. They whipped and turned in front of her, and she knew she'd never survive if Polyxo shoved her inside. The sight of the blades made her want to scream, and she had to shut her eyes to keep herself together. She could feel a breeze from the motion, and all her doubts came roaring back as she kicked herself inside.

It was stupid to have gone in there alone. She'd trusted the gods, and they'd abandoned her to her fate, just as they had Phineus. She could have gone off with Jason and let him protect her. It was what he'd wanted, and it was what he'd trained his entire life to do. But she'd had to prove herself, and she'd needed to know if she had what it took to take care of herself on her own. Now all she'd done was proven how helpless she was, and she was about to die for her hubris. Maybe Jason had been right, after all. Maybe she should have tossed diplomacy aside and let the Harpies fight it out instead. Maybe she should have just left the war to the warriors while she stayed back in the ship by herself.

"We're at war," said Polyxo loudly, pulling Medea away and shoving her to the ground as she called for the attention of her followers. Medea's stomach did a somersault as she realized she wasn't going to die, not just yet. She opened her eyes to the Harpies, forming a circle around them and standing at rapt attention as Polyxo kept on working the crowd. "We've been at war for thousands of years. Gender war. You may not accept it. You may not believe it. But it's true. We've been insulted, enslaved, abused, and exploited. But everything's about to change. Because now we can finally end it."

There were loud chirps of approval, and Polyxo beamed out at her audience before continuing on. "The two sexes don't need each other, not anymore. Times have changed, and technology has changed. Our children can come from a tube, not a womb. We don't need men to reproduce, and they don't need us. And that means this war we've been fighting so long is finally coming to an end. One side can win, and the other side can lose."

Her eyes flared wide as she kept on with her speech, running through grievance after grievance, and Medea could see why she'd amassed such a following on the vid channels. Her gestures were emphatic, pounding home her points as she made them. Her voice was firm, powerful, and her tone was commanding. She had charisma, and even some charm, if one were inclined to agree with her. And if one weren't, it was clear to all that she'd bulldoze them aside with ease. Those who followed her would be safe; those who opposed her would just be in her way.

"Open warfare has to happen, eventually," said Polyxo. Her voice grew louder, reverberating around the rooftop as she waved her arms and cut her hands through the air. "We're too different to live alongside each other in peace. We've tried it for too long already. But now we can change our code so we don't need men. So we don't even want them. And in the end, we don't have any choice. Sooner or later, either they'll get rid of us, or we'll get rid of them. Either we strike first, or they will." A few loud, angry caws from the crowd broke out in support, and as Medea looked around she saw that some of the Harpies had their sheaths up, recording every moment.

She wondered if this performance was destined for the vids, after all was said and done. Polyxo certainly acted like it; she was putting on a show, with Medea and Phineus in the background as a pair of miserable props. She had her doubts, at first. Murder on camera would get them all locked up. But then a thought flashed into her head, a terrifying one. Phineus didn't even exist, not according to the corporate records. And she'd be no better than a spy in the eyes of the Colchians. The Harpies could kill her on camera, upload the vid for all to see, and no one in power would bat an eye about it.

"They made us slaves," said Polyxo. "But we won't be for much longer. We're about to become a new species. The first species ever to create itself. And what was the first thing humans did when they evolved into their own species?" She paused, staring out at the cameras with a triumphant smile. "They got rid of all the Neanderthals. And so will we. It'll just be us, then. No more violence, no more pain, no more conflict. And no more men."

A loud singing came up from all around, though with a touch more discord than there had been before. Some of the calls were joyous, pure celebrations of the brave new world Polyxo was summoning into existence with her words. Others were melancholy cries of resignation, giving in to a future they thought themselves powerless to stop. As Medea looked around, she noticed she could distinguish the tone just by looking at the singer.

The most enthusiastic ones had pumped themselves full of muscle, model female warriors just as Polyxo had envisioned them. The sad ones were more dainty, their feathers bright and bold and their figures traditionally female. But what stood out most were their beaks: the ones whose calls sounded most like funeral dirges had all kept them bent or broken, reminders of the past sufferings that had brought them to the Hellespont. They looked resigned to the coming war, more than they were pleased with it. The beaks of the Harpy warriors were all pristine by contrast, strong and sharp and adding a touch of power to their faces.

The difference gave her hope, though not much more than a glimmer.

Hypsipyle had spoken the truth: they weren't all extremists, and far from it. Most of them were there for their own safety: their tribe had failed to protect them, so they'd sought out a new one that would. Maybe diplomacy would help her after all. She might be able to sway the crowd, if only she chose the right words. It was a risk, and a serious one. She didn't think she was half the speaker Polyxo was; she spent much of her time in her lab, alone, and she didn't have any practice as an orator. But all it took was one look at the spinning turbine to know exactly where she and Phineus were headed once Polyxo's own speech was done. She knew she had to try something while she could.

"There's not going to be a war," shouted Medea. "And even if there is, listening to her is just going to get you killed." The crowd stood in shocked silence; apparently none of them had expected that kind of courage from one of the condemned. She kept going, hoping they'd at least hear her out. "The Big Five don't care about you now. They think you're just a few extremists spouting off on the vids, if they even know you exist. But the second they think you're a threat to the corporate order, they'll crush you. All of you. She's pushing you into a war you can never win."

Polyxo bristled, the downy feathers around her neck puffing up in irritation. "Did I say you could talk?" She grabbed Medea by the hair, dragging her towards the turbine. "You're weak. You can't even put up a fight against me, let alone a man. You're no hero, and you never will be."

Medea fought and kicked, but she was no match for someone who'd packed dozens of pounds of extra muscle onto her frame. And this time Polyxo might decide to end the thing and shove her inside. She turned to the crowd, shouting out again and hoping there was someone there she could turn to her side. "Who says being a hero means I have to run around ninja kicking people in the face?" She looked out at their faces, hostile and blank, pleading with them as best she could. "You don't have to fight to be a hero. That's not what heroism is. It's sacrificing. Giving up something to help someone else."

"You gave up being at the top," said Polyxo. "You gave up money. You gave up everything, and for what? Because you care about one of them. That's weakness. All you'll ever be is weak."

Polyxo had her just a few feet from the blades, and no matter how hard she struggled, she knew she couldn't fight her off forever. She was smaller, and Polyxo was right about one thing: she'd never win if the battle was a physical one. She went limp instead, dropping to the ground and hoping it would make it more difficult to keep dragging her along. Then she just kept shouting as loud as she could, praying someone in the crowd would listen before it was too late.

"You're judging me by male standards," said Medea. "How good I am at competing. How much money I make. How many people I'm in charge of. If you use a masculine way of keeping score, men are always going to win. Why not who helps the most people? Or who's the most nurturing? Who spends the most time with their kids? Who's closest to their friends? Who's the happiest? Why not keep score that way? Why keep score at all?"

"Because someone has to win, and someone has to lose," said Polyxo. She grabbed hold of Medea's arms, shoving her against the silo. "Someone has to be the hero, and someone has to be the sidekick. It's us or it's them, and you've made your choice pretty damned clear."

"You sound just like the warriors," said Medea. "You hate them so much, but all I hear when you talk is one of them."

She was interrupted by a slap, knocking her head violently to the side. Her ears rang, and she could taste blood in her mouth. Polyxo stood glowering over her, her open palm waiting to deliver another blow. Medea ran a hand across her face. No scratches, but it still hurt. And it could have been worse. She could have been tossed into the turbine. She could see the blades shimmering before her, even in the dim light, twisting and thrashing in circles.

"I can help you," said Medea. "Your code is bugged. You've got to fix it, or it's just going to get worse. And I've got a fix, if you'll let us both go."

"You've helped enough," said Polyxo. She pulled her hand back for another slap, her face contorted in fury. Medea tried to reach for her dagger, tucked away in her belt, but Polyxo slapped her hand away before she could even get it drawn. She racked her brain, trying to come up with some other way out. She'd already offered the only thing she had to trade. The only other thing she could think of to try was shame. Even if it didn't save her, at least it might ruin their vid.

"Do it," said Medea loudly. She turned her face towards the cameras, dozens of sheaths pointed at them both and recording the scene. "Give me a black eye. Or a busted nose. Show everyone who you are. Show them all what you've become."

Polyxo just ignored her. She grabbed her by the throat, lifted her up, and started into another blow with her free hand. But unhappy murmurs came from the crowd, stopping her mid-swing. She turned her head from side to side, and a look of fear flashed across her face, if only for an instant. There were disapproving clucks coming from around the audience: not many, but enough for all to hear. She needed the crowd, and she couldn't let them abandon her, so she started into her speech once again.

"She's on their side," said Polyxo. "You're with us or you're against us, and she's against us." The crowd was silent, and she started yelling louder. "This is a war. Sometimes you have to do things you don't like to win. You can't show mercy. And remember what they've done to us. Remember how they treat us when we don't fight back."

She raised her hand again, and this time her talons were curled outwards, razor sharp and ready to slice through Medea's throat. Medea tried to yell something herself in response, but she felt Polyxo's hand choke against her windpipe as she did, cutting off her breath. Her words came out as coughs, too quiet for anyone else to hear. She pushed and pulled, but all it did was tighten Polyxo's grip. She couldn't think of anything else to try. She'd done all she could, and now there was no way out. She closed her eyes and waited for it all to end.

But the blow didn't come. Instead, she heard a bird's call rising from the back of the crowd, a single unhappy note. It turned to a sharp song, breaking through the murmuring all around. Medea opened her eyes again. It was hard to see in the dark, but she could just make out the source: Hypsipyle, standing by herself in the rear, with everyone nearby turning around to stare. Her feathers were pulled aside, revealing the deformities she'd been hiding for all to see. The down around her neck had been wilting, and here and there the feathers of her wings were brown and dying. The other Harpies couldn't help but steal nervous glances at themselves, and at problems of their own.

But as she sang she pulled the dying feathers away, revealing what Medea's genomancy had done. There were sprouts beneath, beautiful plumage growing anew. She stepped through the crowd, turning from side to side to show them all the healthy new feathers beneath. Everyone around could see Medea's cure, and what it would mean for them if they let her work her magic on them, too.

At first there was only awed silence, other than Hypsipyle's solitary song. But then another voice joined in, from somewhere in the middle of the crowd. The two voices harmonized, merging into a haunting call that echoed across the roof. They kept at it, and Polyxo kept her hand raised high, paralyzed by the dissent. Another voice rose, and then another. Soon the calls came from all around the crowd, the song reverberating from every side.

Polyxo started to say something, but even as close as she was, Medea couldn't hear it. The song was too loud, and the voices too many. A few of the others tried to show their support for Polyxo, letting out harsh hooting sounds and trying to shout down the rest. But Hypsipyle's song drowned away their calls for war, and Polyxo was left foaming in front of them all on her own. She leaned down towards Medea, and for a moment she thought she was about to ignore them all and kill her anyway. But there were tears in Polyxo's eyes, along with the anger, and all she did was growl. "I don't ever want to see you again. You, or him. Finish your work, and then both of you get the hell out of my bar." Then she marched off into the building, followed by a few of her most ardent supporters, their heads held high even as the crowd sang sadly after them.

Medea pulled herself to her feet, brushing the dirt away from her uniform and checking herself for injuries. The crowd parted before her, and Hypsipyle walked through the gap, a look of concern on her face.

"You're okay?" said Hypsipyle. "They didn't hurt you?"

"I think so," said Medea. She could still taste the salt of blood in her mouth, but other than that she felt fine. "Nothing serious, I don't think. But I came close. You saved me."

"We saved each other," said Hypsipyle. "Look." She held up an arm, spreading her feathers until she reached the down beneath them, showing Medea what she'd shown the crowd before. The little brown feathers were falling away, with tiny blue nubs growing in where they'd been. There were happy coos from the nearby Harpies at the sight, and they rubbed their own feathers in relief.

"It's working," said Medea. "Your code. It's back to what it's supposed to be."

"I thought I was going to die," said Hypsipyle. "I haven't been able to sleep for weeks. I didn't know what to do. I'd never have had the money to fix it. You gave me my life back. I couldn't let her take yours." She bowed her head, and then put a hand on Medea's shoulder. "I heard what Polyxo said about you. I wanted to thank you, and I wanted you to know she was wrong. What you're doing, it's important. And I'd have died without you. That makes you a hero to me."

Medea felt herself flush. She wasn't used to getting thanks, not from the warriors. Her patients rarely came back, not once their procedures were complete, and sometimes she never knew for sure how their lives had changed as a result of what she'd done for them. She felt a surge of pride, in herself and in what she did. She'd known her work mattered, deep in her heart, but it was nice to have a little validation now and then all the same.

"Thanks," said Medea. She leaned in and gave Hypsipyle a smile and a long hug. "Really. Thanks."

One of the Harpies stepped forward from the crowd, holding up her feathers and revealing a few imperfections beneath. "Can you fix someone else? Maybe just one more, before you go?"

"Please," said another. "We don't have any money. But please." A chorus of frightened voices joined in, and the crowd pushed around as they all sought help from her at once.

Medea ran her fingers across her sheath, tapping away at the screen. "I just had Hecate drop a packet of pills on the floor downstairs. Each of you take one. It'll fix things. You're all going to be fine." She'd done more than that, but she wasn't sure it was a good idea to tell them. Hecate was zipping out the door as they spoke, off to search for the other Argonauts. She'd sent a few emergency texts to them as well, but no one had responded. She wasn't sure if they'd even get them, not while she was using an Argo sheath on the Colchis data networks. She wondered where they'd gone to, and if they'd even waited for her. Jason had left, the cavalry hadn't come, and she was still there, all on her own.

The Harpies slowly headed downstairs, leaving her behind with a frightened Phineus. "You can come down whenever you want," said Hypsipyle, as she stood in the doorway to the building. "I'll talk to a few of my friends. They'll make sure it's safe."

"Polyxo," said Medea. "She won't do anything?"

"She can't," said Hypsipyle. "We won't let her. She gets people worked up. We won't let her get us worked up like that again. And maybe we'll get her off the vids for awhile. She can be a good person. Really. She just spends so much time screaming and yelling. It isn't healthy, even if there's something to scream and yell about." Her mouth turned into a sad frown below her beak. "You were right, I think. No more war. No more fighting. We'll build something better. The community we really dream of. Not just a smaller version of the one we left behind." She smiled at Medea, and then disappeared down the stairs.

"I can't believe I just did that," said Medea. She felt like throwing up, but she held it in. "They could have killed me." She sat down on a ledge, breathing deeply in and out as a wave of relief surged over her. She'd survived. She'd been sure she wouldn't make it, but she had. Phineus was still there, curled up in his cage, and they'd left him alive. She'd been right, in the end, even if the call was close. Trying to help the Harpies instead of fighting them had been the right course, even if none of the warriors went home with any glory for it.

She heard a voice from the shadows, from somewhere among the solar panels. "They weren't going to kill you. I'd never have let them." She whipped her head towards the sound and saw a figure standing there in the dark, watching her from a distance. The figure took a few steps forward, and then she could make him out: Jason, nearly invisible in the night in his black uniform, hiding amid the solar forest. She ran towards him, jumping into his waiting arms and letting him hold her tight.

She felt like slapping him, but she contented herself with a hard punch on his shoulder instead. He'd been hiding there all the while, and he hadn't lifted a finger to help her. She thought of how things could have gone, if Polyxo had lost her temper or if one of the Harpies had gotten a little too bold. It made her fume inside. "You just stood there? What if they killed me?" She pulled away from him, folding her arms across her chest. Letting her try to prove herself was one thing. Letting her die in the process was quite another.

"I told you I'd keep you safe if I had to," said Jason. He swung his hand forward, almost faster than she could see, and she caught a glimpse of something shiny flashing past her. She heard a loud ding from Phineus's cage, and she turned in time to see the hinge to the door snap off as a flare of sparks burst out into the air. The door clanged to the ground, leaving a frightened Phineus still cowering alone inside.

Jason held up a handful of thin, golden javelins, and even in the darkness she could make out the smirk on his face. "Didn't take genomancy to learn to do that. Just a year and a half of practice shots. If they'd gone too far, they would have regretted it." His expression turned grim. "The mean one. The leader. She was about an inch away from getting one of these through her heart."

Her anger faded, just a little. He'd been there for her, even if she hadn't known it, watching from the shadows in case anything went wrong. Part of her was irritated that he'd spent the entire time looking over her shoulder. But in the end, she knew why he'd done it. He wanted to keep her safe, and it was nice to know she'd had a guardian angel in her moment of danger, standing by in case she needed help.

"Still," said Medea. "I wish I'd had some notice. I wish I'd known you were there." She looked down at her feet, unable to meet his eyes. She didn't want to admit to a weakness, especially not in front of him. But her adrenaline was still flowing, and something about seeing him made it all pour out. "I was scared. You wouldn't believe how scared."

"You needed to prove something," said Jason. "Even if it was just to yourself. You needed to know you were strong enough. No matter what the warriors said, no matter what the Harpies said, no matter what I said. If I didn't let you do it yourself, you'd never have known you had it in you."

She hugged him again, letting herself curl up inside the warmth of his arms. He brushed her hair into place, leaned down, and whispered into her ear. "I knew. We were watching the entire time. We almost stormed in to break things up. Twice. But I knew. I had doubts, back in Argos. But I could see it in your eyes, just before you went back inside the Hellespont. I knew there was a hero in you. You found a better way. A way to use genomancy to help people who needed it. And I'm proud of you for doing it." She looked up at him in mild shock at hearing praise for genomancy coming from his lips. "I really am. If I'd had my way, I would have just started kicking asses until they gave up Phineus."

"So the big, bad warrior's renouncing violence?" said Medea. "And finally endorsing genomancy?"

"Hardly," said Jason. "Some people don't respond to anything but violence. Some people need their asses kicked. And genomancy is a whole different can of worms." His mouth curved up into a smile as he tightened his arms around her. "But like I said, I'm proud. And your parents would be, too."

He held her close, and she wanted to stay there forever, just the two of them in the dark. She felt like she'd finally done something the rest of them couldn't deny, and that she'd finally gotten the credit none of the warriors ever wanted to give her. She felt like she'd done something for the mission, something indispensable. She felt like she mattered. She felt like an Argonaut.

"Let's go," said Jason. He put his fingers to his lips and gave a sharp whistle, and lights from above flooded the roof all at once. The ARGO was hovering up there in silence, watching over her from the heavens.

"You," said Jason, walking over to Phineus's cage. "Get up, and start talking. The gods said you knew something about the Fleece. And we've got pretty clear instructions. Tell us and go free, or don't, and go back to the Harpies."

"Please," said Phineus with a whimper. "I know who has the Fleece. I know where to find it. Just tell the gods. Tell them I'm sorry. Tell them I won't do it again." He was on the verge of tears, trying to stand on unsteady legs that had weakened with months of disuse. "Promise you'll tell them. And I'll tell you where it is."

"Deal," said Jason. "I think they already know. But we'll tell them what you said, anyway."

"It's another genomancer," said Phineus, wheezing with exhaustion and leaning against the cage. "The one who has the Fleece. She has it, right here in the city. You'll need to find her, if you want to find it. But be careful. Be very careful, if you try to take it from her. She's dangerous. She looks harmless, but she's very, very dangerous. There's venom beneath her charms, and you mustn't forget it."

"Who?" said Jason. "Who is she?"

"Her name," said Phineus, "is Circe."

CHAPTER TWENTY-ONE

THE PLOT OF LAND BELOW was a rural island in an urban sea, a vast estate that looked like it belonged in the countryside, not surrounded by skyscrapers. It was a private sanctuary ringed on all sides by a dense wall of trees, and inside were acre after acre of lush green lawns. Its location alone made it worth untold fortunes: it was smack in the center of the city, just blocks from Colchis corporate headquarters. Such a prime spot was coveted by the shareholders; beauty aside, the suggestion of influence it gave to live so close to the halls of power was worth the price all its own.

In the middle of the estate was a mansion built from polished grey marble. It was constructed in the Gothic style, its roof angling up and down over tall, curving windows. The front was lined with topiary, flowerbeds filled with towering green bushes trimmed into the shape of a zoo's worth of animals. On either side sprawled separate wings, each big enough to constitute a palace all its own. But though hundreds could have comfortably lived there, they couldn't see a single person anywhere on the grounds: just a vast, empty monument to the wealth of its owner, with no one around to enjoy it.

They'd spent the night flying in a wide loop around the estate, dipping in and out of the nearby streams of drone traffic and scanning it from a distance. Now the day was dawning and the ARGO was hovering in place just outside the walls, tucked discreetly against a nearby skyscraper as Tiphys plotted their approach.

"I think it's safe," said Tiphys. "I don't think anyone's going to notice us. We can land on the roof, maybe." He looked around the cockpit for guidance: Jason sat in the passenger seat, and Medea stood behind them, both staring out at the mansion and its grounds. "Or I can drop you guys just inside the fence, and you can sneak inside. Just tell me what you want and I'll do it."

"Get us inside the walls and we'll be fine," said Jason. He was wearing his goggles, staring out at the mansion through the cockpit window. He zoomed in and out all along the structure, searching for signs of threats. "There's heat spots, but not many. And most of them are small. There's one or two people inside, tops. This needs to be a smash and grab. We get in, find the Fleece, and get out."

"This can't be where she lives," said Medea, shaking her head. "Not Circe. I just can't see it."

"It's what Phineus said," said Jason. "She has the Fleece. She has the Argo data. She's obviously got enough money to have gotten her hands on it. Now we just need to go in there and get it back."

"It just doesn't make sense," said Medea. "I knew Circe. Back when I lived in Colchis. Back when I was just an apprentice. She was a stakeholder then, just like I used to be. And she'd never be able to afford something like this." She bit her lip, dredging up old memories she hadn't thought of in years. "She was in my class back in the academy. Really ambitious, and really competitive. Circe was tough. She was obsessed with her work, and she was kind of a mean girl. But she didn't have money. None of us did. I don't see any genomancer affording something like this, no matter how good they are."

"She's a shareholder," said Jason. "She has to be." He looked down at the estate, cheap by the standards of the past, but still more expensive than any but the wealthiest dynasties of the day could afford. "And the one thing they teach you growing up as a shareholder is loyalty. The corporation is your bread and butter. It's your money at stake, and they raise you to treat the company almost like a member of the family. If it helps Colchis, it helps her. You'd be surprised what people can do when there's that much on the line."

"She wasn't born a shareholder," said Medea. "The last I heard of her, she was an employee. Still toiling away in the labs for a paycheck. She must have done something since then. Made it big."

Jason took off his goggles, hanging them on the wall beside him. "Clearly she's moved up in the world since you knew her. And if she's got connections to someone like Phineus, I'm not surprised. Money comes easier when you don't give a damn about the source."

"I still don't see it," said Medea, shaking her head. "She was kind of a prima donna. One of the best genomancers out there, but she had an ego to match her skill. Her work was pretty much all she cared about. Money was just an obstacle. Something for other people to worry about while she pored over segments of code. And she could make the most beautiful things." She smiled, lost in her reminiscences of school days gone by. "Butterflies that flew in formation and spelled out your name. A plant that cycled through a different flower every day. This little worm that could do a dance. It was programming, but it was art, too."

"When we're back in Argos, I want you to do some more work on me," said Tiphys. "Like a genomancer training pill or something. I have all these ideas for things I could make." His voice sped up with enthusiasm, and he sat in his chair rattling off one proposal after another. "Taco trees. A brontosaurus with a velociraptor head. A bunch of little fish that give you an underwater back massage." His eyes grew wide, rapt with possibility. "We could make billions. We could never work again. Except we'd be not working in a big mansion, instead of not working in a little apartment."

She thought she could probably give him a few of her own skills if she'd wanted to. Some of the genomancer's art could be turned into instinct, coded into one's genes just as surely as any other talent. But genomancy was young, as professions went, and the code for that particular talent hadn't yet been mapped. Genomancers had barely learned to crawl, let alone walk. It was a constant experiment, and unpredictable enough that it couldn't be done safely without significant training.

Maybe one day her skills could fit inside a syringe, but until then the most she could do was teach him just enough to be dangerous. She shuddered at the thought of what a disaster that might be. She could have told him the truth, but he'd still want whatever skills she could inject. She opted to lie instead, and save herself the trouble of being pestered about the issue to the end of her days.

"Sorry," said Medea. "Doesn't work that way. I just can't do it."

"That's fine," said Tiphys, his voice still eager. "We can be partners anyway. Fifty-fifty. I'll be the idea guy, you be the operations girl. We'll start with something easy. Something people won't be able to live without. Like dinosaurs."

She racked her brain trying to think of a way to squirm out of it, but Jason saved her, at least for the moment. He'd been friends with Tiphys for longer, and had more experience extracting himself from improbable schemes. "Think about business later. Right now I need you to put us down somewhere near the entrance." He tapped the cockpit window, pointing towards a spot on the grounds of the estate below. "Then send the ARGO back up, and keep it close. A minute or two away, tops."

"Okay," said Tiphys. He started pressing buttons, pivoting the ARGO's wings and launching it down towards Circe's mansion. "Mission now, business later." Then it was back to the console, muttering ideas to himself as he guided the ship's descent. "Dinosaurs in a can. Talking rocks. Inflatable trees. Billions and billions." He reached above, grabbed a lever, and pulled. "Hold on to something. We're going down. Once we land, get off quick, and I'm sending the ship back up remotely."

The ARGO lurched into a dive, its wings pulled tightly against the hull as it swooped towards the ground. They dodged drone after drone as Tiphys weaved them through the automated traffic around them, veering away from flapping wings and scorching engines whenever they came too close. He pulled the nose of the ship sharply upward as the ground came near, lighting down against the grass with a soft bump.

At that, they all scrambled to the exit. Jason slid down the ladder, shouting at the others as his boots clanged against the floor: "Go, go, go!" He slid open the door, leaping out onto the lawn and waving them out of the ship one by one. He pointed Antaeus towards one of the mansion's wings, rattling off orders as he went. "Get up there, fast. Get close to the house." Antaeus loped towards it, letting out a low growl. He was fast, unnaturally so, even if now and then he couldn't resist the urge to plant his hands on the ground and run for a few yards on all fours. The rest of them followed his lead, with Jason waiting behind for Tiphys to stumble his way out of the cockpit.

When they were all clear from the ARGO, Tiphys turned and put his fingers to his lips, letting out a quick whistle. The ARGO's wings flapped, faster and faster, until it shot up into the skies and merged into a line of other drones. Soon it was lost among the thousands of them flitting above, a swarm of metallic insects that criss-crossed the sky in strict aerial traffic lanes. From below it looked like a grid, the drones whizzing in tandem so quickly that each lane formed a solid black line.

Antaeus stood next to the mansion, beckoning them forward from the distance. They all ran towards him, except for Mopsus, who huffed along in the rear at a slow paced jog. Finally they were there, close enough to the house that they wouldn't be obvious to any passing security drones.

"Stick to the side," said Jason. "Keep going until we hit a door." He led them along the side, past window after window. They could hear grinding sounds from the bushes, and as Antaeus passed a leafy green bear it wasn't clear which of them was growling at the other. But a few bushes ahead they saw the source: one of the bushes was covered in fat white caterpillars, little grubs chewing away at the leaves in unison. They were leaving the bulk of it intact despite their cravings, pruning it around the edges and shaping it into the form of a wizened old bull elephant.

"Cool," said Tiphys. "This is so cool." He reached out to touch one of them, but then thought better of it, drawing his hand away in a cautious jerk.

"This is her," said Medea, picking up a caterpillar for inspection. "A mansion doesn't fit her, but this does. Worms turned artists, with a little snip of their code to guide their appetites. It's exactly the type of thing she'd do."

They passed more and more windows, and more and more bushes. A half mile later and they finally hit a door, a towering brown portal with thick metal hinges. There was a knob, but it was purely for decoration. A glowing red light shining from the keyhole made clear that the door opened only for those who were welcome.

"This is it," said Jason. "We're going in here." He ran his wrist along the doorframe, scanning it with his sheath. "Everyone ready?" He looked around, counting off heads. But they were one short; someone hadn't made it all the way there. Jason turned back the way they'd come and saw Tiphys, standing perfectly still next to the bushes in one of the flowerbeds. He tried to wave him forward, but Tiphys just stood there, refusing to move an inch.

"Stop fucking around with the caterpillars," said Jason. "She'll make one for you when we get back." Medea gave him an indignant look of horror, and he murmured to her under his breath. "Just play along and keep him happy. But don't you dare actually do it. If you let him turn you into his own personal monster factory, that's on you."

"He's welcome to attend the academy himself," said Medea. "Better pray they don't let him in."

"Help," said Tiphys in a loud whisper. "Help, help, help." His skin was unnaturally pale, and he looked like he was about to throw up. He kept eyeing a nearby bush, thick and green and clipped into the shape of a perfect sphere. He nodded his head in its direction and whispered as loudly as he dared. "Help. I need help."

"Forget to take a piss before you left the ship?" shouted Idas. He nudged Antaeus with a laugh. "He doesn't know how to unzip his uniform, I think. Why don't you help him out? Try it with the claws. He'll figure things out pretty quick."

"Please," said Tiphys, his voice jittering with fright. "Please help."

They saw it, then, rustling its way out through the bush. Even in a place like Colchis it was an unbelievable sight: a full grown male lion, its bright yellow eyes surrounded by a flowing, amber mane. The lion padded out towards Tiphys, stopping just inches away. It stood there, lazily sniffing him up and down, watching the others without a hint of fear. Sweat covered Tiphys's brow, and he edged away, looking from side to side for someplace to run.

"Don't move," said Jason, putting his hand to his sword. "Tiphys, you have to hold it together. The worst thing you can do is move. Listen to my voice." He took a few steps forward, locking eyes with the lion and trying to keep Tiphys calm as he went. "Listen to my voice, Tiphys. Don't panic. Just don't do anything. You'll be fine."

Tiphys tried, but bravery in the face of wild beasts wasn't part of his programming. The rest of them were yards away from him, too far to do any good if things went wrong. He started hyperventilating, letting out a soft moan. It didn't seem to bother the lion. It just stood there, its tail twitching back and forth, watching Jason as he crept forward. Jason began to slowly draw his sword, pulling it out inch by inch. But cautious as he was, it was a step too far.

A snarl grumbled deep in the lion's throat, and it pounced up at Tiphys, standing on its hind legs and slapping a paw atop either of his shoulders. The lion let out a loud roar, its teeth snapping shut just in front of Tiphys's nose. Jason whipped out his sword, charging and closing the distance as quickly as he could. But by the time he made it within striking distance it was already over. The lion hissed at Tiphys, slashed its tongue across his face in a big, slobbery lick, and then disappeared back into the bushes where it had come from.

"Tiphys the Lion Tamer," said Idas incredulously. "Who knew the best way to fight a lion was to stand there crying like a pussy?" He was nearly bowled over with laughter, steadying himself against his spear to keep himself upright. Antaeus was faring no better; it sounded like he was convulsing in a fit of coughs, though it was merely the closest to laughter someone with a bear's genetic code could muster.

"It was already as tame as it was going to get," said Jason, sheathing his sword. "But still. Letting it run around her yard like that seems completely nuts."

"She's a genomancer," said Medea. "She must have been working on it. Experimenting. Who knows what its instincts are now? It may not even know how to bite, not anymore. She's turned a beast into a pet."

"Is that the kind of thing you did back in the academy?" said Jason. "Screw around with lions and see if they'd still bite you?"

"Frogs," said Medea proudly. "We did all kinds of things to frogs. Frogipedes, frogaroos, frogtopuses. You want to learn how to splice, you start with frogs."

"Well, Circe's graduated from frogs," said Jason. "So everyone stay together. Who knows what else she's got running around the estate?" He strode back to the door, his eyes on the bushes as he went, checking for anything that might be lurking in the shadows. The others stayed close behind him, their hands at their weapons. Even Idas seemed on edge; bravado aside, his grip had tightened around his spear, and his feet were planted apart in a defensive stance.

"Hold on," said Jason. He pulled a small, circular device from his belt, dropping it on the ground below. It looked like a silver hockey puck, at least at first. But then it started to shake, legs sprouting from its sides. A tiny tube snaked out from the front of it, a red light at its tip, waving back and forth and scanning the area. Then it scrambled along the grass towards the house, disappearing up one of the walls and crawling under the eaves of the roof.

"There's alarms," said Jason, staring at a data readout on his wrist sheath. "Give it another minute and they'll all be re-routed." They waited, and soon they could hear a tapping on the other side of the door. Latches flipped on the other side, and then the door slowly creaked open, the little robotic device crawling out after it. Jason picked it up, snapped it back on his belt, and led the way inside. "Let's go. Weapons ready."

They found themselves in a foyer, surrounded by artifacts from another age. Circe was a collector, if the furnishings were any guide. A series of pedestals stood at intervals around the room, an urn atop each one. Some had cracks, and some were missing pieces or handles that had broken away as the centuries passed. They were all adorned with art, from men in battle to fantastical creatures in threatening poses. On the walls were murals, each one depicting more heroes in the midst of their glories.

"It's beautiful," said Medea. "And expensive." She was hardly an art expert, but she knew a museum piece when she saw one. And the things she saw around her were priceless treasures, the kind of works that didn't find their way into private hands without the greasing of palms and the bending of rules.

"Bringing us into the lion's den," muttered Idas as he filed through the door. "And now what? It's the size of a palace. We won't find a thing. We should have cut our losses and gone back to Argos with the footage we already have."

"We don't have to bother with a search," said Jason. He opened another pocket on his belt, pulling out a handful of small black spheres, each no bigger than a pea. He tossed them onto the ground ahead of him, and they rolled along the marble before they each split open to reveal eight legs of their own. "They'll do it for us. Seeker drones from the weapons locker. They'll map the entire place, and flag anything unusual. All we have to do is wait."

The drones crawled along the walls and up the ceiling, spreading out in all directions. They were small enough that they could barely be seen, not unless someone was looking for them. They could have been mistaken for tiny spiders, the perfect disguise to avoid drawing the suspicions of any of the house's occupants, assuming it had any. They settled in to wait as the drones crawled throughout the house, feeding the data they collected back to Jason's sheath as they went.

Medea wandered around the room while they waited, taking in the luxuries around her. They made her feel more than a little intimidated. Circe had done well for herself if she owned all of this. And they'd both started out in exactly the same place. She wondered if maybe the Harpies had a point, after all: if Circe had amassed this kind of fortune, there was no reason she couldn't have done the same. She felt her insecurities whispering away from deep inside her head, and she pushed them back down as far as she could. There were other things that mattered more than money. And living all by herself inside a giant museum was hardly her idea of the good life.

"Ahem," came a voice from behind her. She turned to see Mopsus, wringing his hands and shuffling towards her. He looked nervous; he wanted to talk to her, but starting up a conversation wasn't one of his strong suits. He cleared his throat, again and again, and finally he forced something out. "Phineus. You spoke to him. He said the Fleece was here, did he?"

"He said Circe had it," said Medea. "At least she did, before he got locked away down there."

"Hrmm," said Mopsus. His eyes dropped away from her towards a bust on a nearby pedestal, the image of some orator of centuries past. He ran his fingers along its face, stumbling and stalling, and he managed to keep the conversation going only by avoiding any eye contact with Medea whatsoever. "I hope you lifted his curse. I hope he was all right."

She thought about what to tell him. Phineus most certainly hadn't been all right, and while she'd never have punished someone so harshly herself, she wasn't exactly sympathetic with him. He'd been selfish, extraordinarily so. The Harpies were right about one thing: he'd sold people's data without scruples, and it was a near certainty that some of them had been damaged as a result. But Mopsus seemed concerned, and she didn't want to pick a fight with someone so timid. Phineus had been freed, and in the end she thought that was the right thing to do. Besides, Mopsus was probably worried about the gods, and what he'd tell them the next time they spoke. She smiled, even if he didn't see it, and tried to put the best spin on it she could. "They let him out. No more curse. You can tell the gods he kept his part of the deal. And so did we."

"It wasn't just the gods," said Mopsus. He kept staring at the bust, as if he and the statue were having the conversation without her. "I talked to him sometimes. We sent each other messages."

"I thought he was a criminal," said Medea. "Even you said that."

"He was," said Mopsus. "But it's lonely. Not many people come visit. Not many want to talk. They don't want to hear what I might say. Visions of the future can be unsettling, and few really want to know the shape of things to come. There's not much else for me to talk about, either. My days are spent with data. It's all I know, but it bores them. Anyone who comes. Only another seer can understand."

The data he obsessed over was Greek to her, just as much as it was to anyone else, but she knew exactly how he felt. She'd moved to a completely unfamiliar city without knowing a single person there, and it had been incredibly hard at first. They hadn't exactly welcomed her, and so for her first few years in Argos she'd focused on work and nothing else. Her lab could be a lonely place sometimes, just her and her machines. At least she had patients to break up the monotony. They streamed in and out, day after day, and if it weren't for them she'd probably be just as odd a duck as Mopsus was.

"I think I understand, a little," said Medea, and she gave him a pat on his shoulder. He almost jumped at the touch, but he calmed down again just as quickly.

"Thank you," said Mopsus. "He was greedy, and he did a foolish thing. But he talked to me. It mattered a lot, that he talked to me." Before she could respond he scurried across the room, abandoning the conversation to stare at a mural on the wall. She felt a pang of pity for him. He was locked away inside himself, a prisoner of the electronic world he'd devoted himself to, and she didn't think he'd ever manage his way out. That was just how he was after all the years of solitude, and the only thing she could do was try to be kind to him during the few moments he poked his head out of his digital shell.

She heard a beeping noise from across the room, and turned to see Jason holding up his sheath for them all to see. "The drones found something unusual. Right here. Down this hallway." He pointed at a map covering his wrist, with a little red dot flashing at the center. "It's not the Fleece. They can't find it, not anywhere. The picture's fuzzy, but they flagged movement. Could be another lion. Could be a person. Could be someone who knows where the Fleece is. So weapons out, and everyone behind me." He drew his sword and headed off into one of the halls, following the little dot on his map.

The rest of them hurried after him, and they found themselves marching down a long hallway, the high ceiling lined with sparkling crystal chandeliers. They were made entirely of jewels, colored a bright lemon yellow and shining like stars above them. All along the walls were oil paintings, each of a wildlife scene. They looked hand-painted, and it must have been an exceptionally expensive collection given how few practitioners of the art remained in a world of unlimited artificial facsimiles. One wall was barnyard after barnyard, civilized chickens, cows, and sheep posed in all their pastoral majesty. The other was wilderness, lions and tigers and bears stalking through their respective habitats in search of prey.

The hallway seemed endless, but finally they arrived at a pair of double doors, just before the red dot on Jason's map. "Everyone on guard," said Jason. "Whatever the drones found, it's on the other side." They readied their swords, spears, and daggers, taking up positions on either side. Jason motioned with his hands, then heaved the doors open as Idas and Antaeus charged through. But they stopped in their tracks once they saw what was waiting for them.

There was a woman there, dining alone in the distance at the end of a vast mahogany table. She sat in a high-backed chair at the table's head, more throne than dining chair. It was lined with red velvet and edged with golden trim. A half dozen silver platters covered the table before her, topped with delicacies from pheasant to caviar to a thin glass beaker of what looked like pea soup.

There were noises coming from underneath the table, enthusiastic snifflings and gruntings from somewhere beside her. But the woman was far too prim and proper to be the source. She cut away at her plate with a gilded knife, so absorbed by her meal that she almost didn't notice they were there. She finally looked up only when Medea insistently cleared her throat. Then the woman smiled, stood, and waved them forward with a sweep of her arm.

"Medea," said Circe. "Dear Medea. It's been a very long time."

CHAPTER TWENTY-TWO

"**Y**OU LOOK NOTHING LIKE YOURSELF," said Circe. "Not how you used to. But then, I suppose no one in our trade ever does." She walked alongside the table, heading towards them with her palms up in a gesture of peace. But Jason kept his sword drawn, and the rest of them followed his lead. She stopped at the center of the table, leaving a respectable distance between them.

She didn't look threatening, not for someone who'd supposedly stolen something as valuable as the Golden Fleece. She was a beauty, and a stunning one. Her face was perfection, her thin, regal nose and full lips suggesting a touch of aristocracy. Her dress was almost a gown, an indigo silk that was formal enough that she wouldn't have been out of place in a high society ballroom. Her hair was long, coiling around her shoulders and winding off down her back. It was a soothing topaz blue, shimmering with the light, and a precise match for the color of her eyes.

But there was something about her hair, something off. It took a moment for Medea to place it, but then she saw. It was moving, rustling back and forth as she spoke. It had been perfectly straight when they'd walked into the room, she was sure of it. But now Circe's locks were twisting into curls, styling themselves of their own accord. They moved along with her head, the strands of her hair repositioning themselves to perfectly frame her face no matter the angle she tilted it.

Circe had a knowing smirk, watching Medea as she stared at her and tried to solve the puzzle of what she'd done to herself. Even as she did, something else was shifting, and the color was different somehow than it had been just a few seconds before. The blue brightened and glowed until both her hair and her eyes had transformed into a puckish orange. She gave an exaggerated blink, revealing matching orange eyeshadow that suddenly covered her eyelids. And it wasn't just her eyes; her lips were changing as well. What had looked like a dark blue lipstick was slowly brightening, and even her nails changed color to match.

"It's my moods, dear," said Circe. "You're wondering how I did it. I would be, if I were in your place. They're all synchronized to my mood: hair, lips, irises, and eyelids alike. A little chameleon injected into my genes, mixed with octopus and sprinkled with just a touch of cuttlefish. A long project, and it took me forever to perfect things, but I've got nothing but time. A good genomancer is a sucker for a challenge, though, isn't she?"

They heard sounds from where she'd been sitting, rising from a grunt to a squeal. Something flashed beneath the table, something pink. It weaved back and forth between the chairs, letting out a screech as it rushed towards them. It sent them all scrambling, as Idas pointed his spear downwards and Jason readied his sword. They were about to run the table through when the thing dashed out at them: a fat, overgrown pig, hairy and pink with a grey metal collar fastened around its neck.

It charged in their direction, stopping just a few feet away, its squeal growing until it was almost a shout. It waved its head back and forth between them, grabbing the attention of whoever would look. The pig kept at it until Idas lunged with his spear, nearly slicing through its haunches. That was enough to quiet it down. It gave out an irritated oink, then turned tail and ran back beneath the table to safety.

"Piggy, piggy," called Idas with a laugh. "Little piggy thinks he's a warrior. Little piggy almost got himself killed." He gave Circe a smarmy grin, his hand slowly running up and down the length of his spear. "Better learn to keep your pets away from warriors, if you'd like to keep them."

"He's just unhappy with his food," said Circe. "Doesn't like acorns. Doesn't like slop. But what's one to feed a piglet otherwise?" She smiled seductively at Idas, her eyes flashing across his body. "And if you don't like him, perhaps I can find myself another pet. One a little more willing to do as he's told."

"I'm nobody's pet, darling," said Idas, returning her smile with a leer. "And if you spend any time around me, you'll learn who's in charge and who isn't."

She gave him a flirty look, and her colors changed again, from orange to a fiery red. "We'll see," said Circe. "We'll certainly see, won't we?"

"Let's cut the crap," said Jason. "You know why we're here. You know what we want."

"Sit," said Circe, pulling out a chair. "Dine with me."

"We didn't come for pleasantries," said Jason. "You have something that belongs to the Argo Corporation. We came to get it back."

"The Fleece," said Circe. "Don't think I didn't know you were coming." She nodded towards Mopsus. "We've seers of our own here in Colchis, and I can afford the best. You've been leaving a little trail of data ever since you landed, and one of them managed to follow your crumbs."

"Circe," said Medea. "You have to give it back. It's not yours. And we both know how dangerous that kind of data can be if it spreads."

"Sit," said Circe. She clapped her hands and a dozen humanoid robots paraded into the room, each dressed in a butler's finery and balancing silver platters above their heads. White gloves hid their hands, and the only thing visible about them was their faces, or where their faces would have been had they been human. Their heads were nothing but a featureless chunk of ovoid metal, gleaming silver and devoid of any sign of what went on within. The robots stood at attention and held their dishes aloft, lifting the lids to the platters and displaying the food for them all to see.

"First course," said Circe, returning to her seat at the head of the table. "Come. It won't disappoint. It's custom here in Colchis for friends to break bread before talking of business." She gave Medea a tisk of disapproval. "You know that, dear. You've been away for so long, but I wouldn't think you'd have forgotten our ways."

None of them moved. None of them but Mopsus. He greedily eyed one of the plates, and in the end he couldn't restrain himself. He walked over to one of the robots, grabbed a sizzling brown nugget of meat from its plate, and popped it into his mouth. "She tells the truth," said Mopsus. He slurped at another piece of meat, sucking it in and out of his mouth with no regard for custom or manners. Then he snatched the plate, sat down, and began devouring everything on it, talking out of the side of his mouth as he stuffed himself with delicacies. "Very tasty. The juices. Much better than ship rations."

"I won't bite," said Circe sweetly. "Let us dine as friends. We were friends, weren't we, Medea?"

"I suppose," said Medea. "But I'm not sure we know each other anymore."

"Then let us reacquaint ourselves," said Circe. "And then we'll talk of your Fleece, and of what kind of compromise we can come to. I think we'll manage something that will make us all very happy, in the end."

Medea looked at Jason, and he gave a nod. They each took a place at the table, sitting down and making themselves comfortable. A robot attended to each of them, first setting their places, then arranging the platters in a line across the middle of the table. When they'd finally done things to perfection, Circe gave a clap of her hands, and they filed out of the room one by one.

"That meat," said Tiphys, looking sick to his stomach as he poked at a piece on one of the platters. "It's not.... I mean, is that why you keep the pig?"

"Don't think me so cruel," said Circe. "Or so crass. Live animals have parasites, germs, and all manner of nasty things lurking inside them. Butchery is for barbarians and fools. These meats are custom cultured. Grown in a lab and designed for their taste, with even the smallest of imperfections removed." She popped a piece of meat into her mouth, wrapping her lips around it and smiling at Tiphys. "Don't worry your head. This meat never had one. It was never anything but a morsel grown to fit your palate."

That settled things, at least for Tiphys. He went along with Mopsus, heaping a pile of food onto his plate with a golden fork. The others followed, and soon they were all dining together in an awkward silence.

"This house," said Medea, taking a stab at conversation. "It's very beautiful."

"It cost a pretty penny," said Circe. "But I've more to spare. Sometimes I think of tearing it down and starting anew. One grows bored with these things, the longer one lives in them. It's important to change, I think. To evolve. Stay the same, and all you're doing is dying in place."

"You've done really well," said Medea. "Better than anyone else from the academy."

"I was the best, in the end," said Circe, the color of her hair and her eyes flashing green. "Not everyone thought that back then. Not everyone recognized the talent that was right in front of them." She poked at her plate, and her hair slowly brightened back to blonde. "But we've so much to catch up on. We haven't spoken in ages. Not since you left us all behind here in Colchis. An odd choice, and a controversial one." She raised an eyebrow in disapproval. "One many of us questioned, I'm afraid."

"It wasn't anything to do with you," said Medea. "Or anyone, really. I just wasn't doing anything here. Nothing meaningful, anyway. It was all make this actor thin, then make him fat, then pump him up with muscles. Make an actress look like an alien, then change her back. I thought it was all so pointless. I wanted to do something different."

"If only you'd paid your dues," said Circe, waving a hand at the luxuries around them. "You could have stayed with us. With your friends, and with your people. Life has many privileges once one rises high enough in the ranks. You could have done whatever you'd wanted, if you'd had the patience."

"Not anything I wanted," said Medea. "You know how Colchis is. About working on stakeholders."

It was strongly discouraged, to the point she'd have been risking her job if she'd done it too often. Genomancy helped people be who they wanted to be, and it made the world more tolerable for those who couldn't stand something about themselves. But as far as she could tell, the Colchis Corporation didn't want the world to be tolerable, not for the stakeholders. It was far more profitable for them to be jacked into their virtual reality worlds, day in and day out. The more she made someone comfortable with their bodies, the more time they'd spend up and about, consuming the resources their contracts granted them for free.

"The stakeholders," said Circe, her face wrinkling in disgust. "You sacrificed your career so you could work on the stakeholders. Such a dreary life you've chosen to live. Everyone always thought you were the smart one in our class. The golden child of Colchis." She gave Medea a catty smile and her colors shifted to a strawberry red. "And you ended up in another city entirely. Your family must miss you, and deeply."

It was a low blow, and Medea could tell it was an intentional one. She didn't have a family, not to speak of. She wouldn't have left the city if she had. Her parents had long since passed away. She hadn't had any siblings, and all that was left were a few distant aunts and uncles who spent most of their time absorbed with vids and VR. Circe must have known. She'd always been competitive, but now there was a mean streak inside her, one that had only grown worse since the last time they'd spoken.

"And what of your friends?" said Circe. "Few of us have heard from you. Not since you left."

That was just another veiled insult, and it made Medea bristle inside. She'd tried keeping in touch with Circe and with all of the other genomancers from her classes. She'd sent messages, and for a time she'd gotten them back. But travel between corporate territories was difficult and costly, and intentionally so. The Big Five didn't want their assets mingling, not if it could be helped. Her friends from Colchis had taken longer and longer to respond as the years had gone by, and eventually they'd fallen out of contact. It wasn't entirely surprising; genomancers tended to be workaholics as a rule, and Medea was no exception. But it stung all the same, and she could tell that Circe was toying with her with every remark.

"We've all been busy," said Medea. "That's just the nature of what we do. But we don't have time to sit and talk right now."

"We want the Fleece," said Jason. "It's not yours to keep. And we're done playing these games. You're going to hand it over." He pushed away his plate, and his voice went to steel. "Or we're going to turn this place upside down and take it."

"My, my," said Circe. "He's a dangerous one, if you're on the wrong side of him. I can tell. Fortunate for you that he wants to be your champion."

"The Fleece," said Medea. "That's what's dangerous. I don't know what you're doing with it, but you can't keep it. You can't let that kind of data get out there on the networks. Someone's going to get killed."

"Death is a part of life," said Circe. "And some are always going to be nothing more than tools for others. Watch." She clapped her hands, and one of the robotic attendants strode into the room and stood at her side. Circe looked up at it with a smile. "Be a dear, and tear out your own throat."

The robot began doing what it was told, its hands scratching at its neck. It clawed away at the metal until pieces flaked away, and finally it broke through. Wires sparked out from beneath, but the robot kept at it until its head tilted on its side and finally snapped away to the ground. It stood there swaying, its arms scratching at empty air, until it lost its balance and collapsed.

"Just a tool," said Circe. "And now its use is over."

"We're talking about humans," said Medea. "Real people. That's just a machine."

"Humans, machines," said Circe. "One's the same as the other. You should know that better than anyone. They say machines are replacing us, one by one, but that's not quite it. They *are* us. How are any of us any different, in the end?" She leaned down to the floor and came up with a tiny cleaning robot in her hand, a white mini-vacuum that had been busily sucking away dirt from the carpet. She held it before her, looking on with a smile as its wheels spun helplessly in the air.

"It cleans," said Circe, "because its programming tells it to clean. It rolls about the floor in circles doing what it was told, never questioning why because it was never told to. It's just not in its software. And how are we any different? Your code may be organic, but it's code all the same. You eat because your code says to eat, and you sleep because your code says to sleep." Her eyes went to Jason, then to Medea. "Or love, because your code tells you to love."

"We're different," said Medea. "People are different. We can think. We can change."

"And so we can," said Circe. "We always could. We could always change our habits, if we tried hard enough. A crude form of reprogramming, but reprogramming nonetheless. But now we can change it all. A few snips here and there, and you've got the looks you always dreamed of. A few more, and you've mastered ballet. Still more, and you've the face of a beast. And what are you then, after all's been done? When your code's been snipped and sliced, and more and more pieces of you chopped away? What's left of you but the nagging wants that drove all those changes in the first place?"

"We are what we want to be," said Medea. "We change a little bit every day, but that doesn't mean we're not still ourselves. You can't reduce yourself to the nuts and bolts that way. All the little parts you're focusing on come together into something else. Something more, and something better. And with genomancy, we control it. We control what we are."

"What you want controls what you are," said Circe. "Your dreams, your desires. And they're nothing new. They're old code, from before there were even apes." She took a bite from her fork and smiled at Jason. "Your heroism and your deeds? Your mad quest for glory? Millions of men have sought the same through the centuries. A man's code says jump, and so he jumps. And a fair maiden at the end for all of them, because a woman's code says to love the one who jumps the highest. If he survives, that is."

"Bullshit," said Jason. "You don't know me. And you don't know her. You don't know who we are inside."

"I know everything about humanity," said Circe. "I spent decades building and rebuilding. Changing people from what they were to what they wanted to be. And it's always the same. The men want the glory, the women want the beauty." Her expression became a pained scowl, hardly beautiful at all. "It's all we can think of, you know. And it's all about breeding in the end. Everything we do, all of us. Every bit of our code is dedicated to survival or to reproduction. Our art, our heroes, our friendships, even our love. They're all just a sham, coded into us long ago to keep this farce going. And we can never escape it. Never, ever, ever."

She picked up a morsel from her plate, holding it out below her. The little pig rushed obediently to her side, leaning up towards the bit of food. She held it just out of the pig's reach, forcing it to sit and beg before finally giving it a taste. She smiled, and scratched the little pig behind its ears.

"In the end," said Circe, "we're nothing but a bunch of animals."

"Oh," said Mopsus loudly. "Oh." His face squinched together in pain, and he doubled over the table, his hands clutching his stomach. "Something's wrong. Feels very odd. Unsettled."

"Help him up," said Jason. He put one of Mopsus's arms around his shoulder, and Medea lifted him from the other side. Mopsus kept holding his stomach, even as his face grew paler and paler.

"Let me see your sheath," said Medea. "Give me your hand. We need to check your vitals. Make sure you're okay." She tried to pull his arm away from his belly, but it was stiff and locked into place.

"Something's wrong," said Mopsus. His eyes drifted upwards and he started to sway, losing his balance. They tried to hold him upright, but he pushed them away, leaning against a wall for support. "Feels wrong." Then he dropped to his knees, curling up into a fetal position on the floor as he was consumed by seizures.

"We need a doctor," said Medea. She gave Circe a pleading look, but all she got in return was a smug smile. Medea knew it had all gone wrong, then. Circe had done something to him. Poisoned him, maybe. She looked down at her own plate, covered in half-eaten delicacies. Maybe she'd poisoned them all.

"It's time I took my leave," said Circe, rising from her chair. "And as for the Fleece, I was the one who stole it. But I'm afraid I've already sold it. Just as I'm about to sell you." Jason sprinted towards her, but she was faster. By the time he'd made it to the other end of the table, she'd already disappeared through the door behind her. A thick metal barrier slammed down over the doorway, cutting off the pursuit.

"The doors," said Jason. "Get to the other doors." He lunged back towards the way they'd come in, but before he'd made it more than a few steps the entrances had each closed off in turn. He slammed his fist against one of the metal barriers, but it didn't even move. Even his sword just clanged away from it, and after a few futile blows he gave up. "We're stuck. We're not going anywhere."

"We have to figure something out," said Medea. She was trying to lift Mopsus up to the table, but he just kept moaning and clutching his stomach. "We have to get him out of here. We have to get him help."

"I feel," said Mopsus. "I feel very, very wrong."

CHAPTER TWENTY-THREE

"GET HIM ON THE TABLE," said Medea. "Get him up where I can see." Jason grabbed Mopsus by one end, Antaeus grabbed him by the other, and together they heaved him up onto the dining table. His limbs writhed back and forth, twisting at unnatural angles, and a low moan came from deep down in his throat.

"He's dying," said Tiphys. "She did something to him." He looked down at his own near-empty plate, and his skin went pale. "To us."

"He's not dying," said Medea. "He's changing. And I'm going to stop it." She pulled at his uniform, tugging his sleeves up his arms and snapping her fingers behind her. "Hecate. Open." Hecate split apart, and she pulled tube after tube out and jabbed their needles into Mopsus's arms. As his blood flowed through them, she called out again. "Hold him down. Hecate, analyze." Mopsus was still trembling uncontrollably, but Jason and Antaeus kept him still enough that the tubes stayed in place while Hecate's systems worked their magic.

Medea turned to her sheath, flipping through a map of Mopsus's DNA. She didn't like the looks of it, not one bit. "Whatever's going on, it's with his code. And it's going too fast. It's like someone else is working on him. Changing him."

It shouldn't have been possible. Mopsus hadn't had any genomancy performed on him, at least as far as she could tell. His code should have been clean. She ran her finger across her sheath as Hecate streamed over the results of her analysis. At first she thought it was the same thing that had happened to Lynceus. Mopsus's code was changing, and fast. But as she looked closer, she saw patterns. Whatever was going on, it wasn't the random degradation she'd seen before. It was something similar. But it was also something new.

It was genomancy, but it wasn't the same as if she'd been working on a patient in her lab. It was as if the procedure were performing itself, changing Mopsus's code without anyone around to supervise. Whatever Circe had done to him, whatever she'd set into motion, it was reworking his code all by itself.

"It hurts so much, it does," said Mopsus. His eyes were bulging, and his fingers balled together in pain. She tried to reach over to hold one of his hands, but she couldn't pry his fingers apart. That was when she noticed it. His hands were changing color, turning to a darker shade of pink. And his fingers. His skin was growing around them, merging them together into a smaller set of digits.

"Hold him down," said Medea. "Don't let him thrash around. Don't let him hurt himself." The others pressed his limbs against the table, and she turned back to her sheath, trying to work through the problem. His code was changing, but the changes were clean and orderly. They'd been planned, and that meant she could undo them, if only she could figure out what they were.

They were mostly physical; she could tell that at a glance. His behavior was being left alone, and he'd still be Mopsus inside once the transformation was done. But his body was being radically reorganized. She saw a few segments she recognized: code from an animal, though she wasn't sure which one. The changes were already in progress, and she could only see one option: stabilize him where he was, and carefully patch things up afterwards.

"Hrng," said Mopsus. He clutched at his stomach, and then his head snapped back in pain. His body was changing now, down to the bones. She could see them poking up here and there under his skin as they rearranged themselves inside. He was folding in on himself, his limbs shrinking as his torso grew longer. His hair started falling out at the roots, clumping onto the table as he jerked from side to side.

"Do something," said Idas. "Do it now. That bitch did something to him. And if you don't figure out what it was, we're next."

"I'm trying," said Medea. "And you're not helping." She tuned them all out, zeroing in on the stream of code flowing across her sheath. It looked familiar, incredibly so. She knew she'd seen at least part of it, and she knew exactly where. She turned to Idas, suspicion in her eyes. "Your brother. You said he got hit with some kind of missile."

"That's what I said," grunted Idas.

"It's what you said, but is it true?" said Medea. He sneered at her, but he didn't bother to respond. She couldn't let him just dismiss her this time, not with what was at stake. "This isn't some joke. Just tell us what really happened. I need to know where this comes from. I need to know what this is." She pointed at Mopsus, writhing in pain on the table. "Unless you'd rather end up like him."

He glared at her, looking like he wanted to reach across the table and throttle her. But he snuck a furtive look at Jason and chose the safer course of just snarling instead. "It was a whorehouse. A Colchian whorehouse. We were holed up in there, passing the time. Then some bitch he was with scratched him with her nails. It was nothing."

"Why didn't you just say so?" said Jason. "You were going on and on about some missile when your brother's life was at stake. And you were blaming her."

"Like I said," snapped Idas. "You're new. You don't know how the world works. Missions are a joke. Who wants to risk their life just so some shareholder can earn a higher dividend? It's what we always do. Sneak in and have fun for long enough that it looks like we did something. Then we trade battle footage with the Colchians and we get the hell out. A missile or a whore, who cares? No one wants some Argo bureaucrat on our asses about what happens in Colchis. And besides, she's the one who changed him. Her patient, her fault."

"You said he got scratched," said Medea. "That means blood. Did anyone know you were there? Anyone from Colchis?"

"Everyone there was from Colchis," said Idas. "It's a Colchian brothel, with Colchian whores, and Colchian customers. What kind of stupid question is that?" He looked over at Jason with a sneer. "This is what you get when you rely a woman. They're all soft and weak with empty heads. And you put one of them in charge of our genes? We're screwed. We're so, so screwed."

He may have thought it a foolish question, but Medea knew better. Whatever Circe had done, she wasn't just some rogue genomancer acting on her own. This was too complicated, and it was too purposeful. Circe was weaponizing people's DNA, and they were only the latest in a line of unwitting test subjects. First Lynceus, then the Harpies, and now them.

The Colchis Corporation had to be involved; something this big would never have slipped past their seers. She didn't know why they were doing it, and she didn't know how, but it meant the work she'd done helping the Harpies could be her guide. It told her exactly what to look for down in Mopsus's code, and exactly what to do to stop it.

She turned back to her sheath, fixing change after change as she blocked Circe's routines and wrote new code of her own. It would turn off the genetic sequences Circe had added, if everything went right. It wouldn't fix Mopsus; he was too far along for that. And Circe's code would still be inside him, waiting there unexpressed. But most of anyone's DNA wasn't actually being used at any given time. She could safely take it out back in Argos, and with a little help and a little time he'd be right back to the way he'd always been. She kept working, kept focusing, and finally it all clicked together.

"Got it," said Medea. "I can stop the changes. I can't fix him, not until we can get him home. But I can keep it from getting any worse. And I can stop it from happening to us." She pressed a few buttons on her sheath, creating a serum that would lock their code into place as it was. "Hecate, synthesize." The machinery inside Hecate began to hum and whirl, and a blend of chemicals spun together inside a little tube. She'd found it, the way around whatever Circe had done, but precious seconds were ticking by, and Mopsus was only getting worse.

"His nose," said Jason. "Look what's happened to his nose."

It was spreading, growing wider and longer and merging into his mouth. His uniform was loose around him, and his boots fell off as his legs jerked up and down. What was underneath was grotesque: his feet were gone, and all that was left of them were hooves. His eyes were shrinking into little beads, and his screams turned to squeals as he shrunk into himself and flopped about inside his uniform. He kept growing smaller, struggling against the black fabric, until finally he burst away from it and left the tubes leaking puddles of fluid in his wake. He ran across the table on all fours, a pink blur streaking around until he hit the other end. Then he turned, looked at them all, and they saw what he'd become.

Mopsus was man no more. Circe had turned him from human to pig, and now the only thing left to prove what he'd once been was the implant around his skull. The metal still surrounded his head, tucked behind his pointed ears, and the wires still stuck out in all directions. But the rest of him was all animal, lost in a panic at the creature he'd become. He raced in circles around the far end of the table, knocking the plates to the floor as he went. Jason headed towards him, hands outstretched as he worked at calming him down.

"Oh, god," said Tiphys, looking on in horror at Mopsus's squealing. "We're going to be freaks. We're all going to turn into little things."

"That's going to happen to us," said Idas. He scratched at the skin of his neck, then pulled up his sleeves and frantically searched for signs of changes. "That lion. That pig. They used to be people. And the same thing's happening to us right now. This is your fault. Your friend, your sorcery. You lunatic bitch. You got us all turned into a bunch of pigs."

"You've always been one, anyway," said Medea. "Now shut your mouth and everyone hold out their arms." She grabbed a tube from Hecate, one for each of them. Tiphys was there in an instant, holding a shaking arm towards her. "Hecate. Activate." She stuck the needle into his arm, and then did the same for a visibly reluctant Idas. Antaeus loped around the table, and after a few seconds searching for a spot of skin beneath his fur she had the needle in and the solution streaming inside him. Finally she stuck a tube into herself, watching as a purple fluid flowed through it and stabilized her own genetic code.

Hecate beeped, and Medea's sheath flashed a green light for each of them. The changes had worked, and Circe's code was stopped before it had started. She took out her tube and looked across the room to Jason, busy coaxing Mopsus down from the table. "Done. Now it's your turn. Let someone else handle him. We need to lock your code down, and fast." She held a tube out to Jason, waiting to inject him and to confirm that nothing had gone wrong with his code.

"Me?" said Jason. "I barely had anything. Just a few bites." He gestured to his plate; it was still covered in food, and nearly undisturbed.

"It doesn't matter," said Medea. "A bite is a bite. Whatever she gave him, it could be inside you, too. We have to be sure."

"I'll be fine," said Jason, with a dismissive wave of his hand. "And I'm not the one who has it worst. A leader helps his team before he helps himself. See if you can do something for Mopsus. See if you can change him back." He turned away from her, focusing on herding Mopsus and studiously ignoring the tube in her hand.

She knew what this was about. He could say he was fine with genomancy all he wanted, but the prejudice against it was still there within him. And she didn't know how to feel about that.

She was worried for him, on the one hand. She'd seen a side of him that most never did, the caring and the protectiveness that hid beneath the warrior's external armor. He'd defended her, and now she'd do anything to return the favor if she could. On the other hand, he was being stubborn, ridiculously so, and he was needlessly putting himself at risk. He could be turning into one of Circe's animals even as they spoke, and he didn't even seem to care. He just wanted to act like an ostrich and pretend it wasn't even happening. Being brave in the face of danger was one thing; ignoring it altogether was another. She couldn't let him do that, and she couldn't let him hurt himself for the sake of some imaginary warrior code.

"Jason," said Medea. "I just need to check. It's not a big deal. I just need to see what's going on in your code. Just to make sure nothing's wrong."

"My body's clean," said Jason. "Entirely clean. I've never had a single genetic change since I was born. Never in my entire life. And I don't intend to start now." He led Mopsus across the table by the ears, walking the reluctant pig towards Medea. "Like I said. First you help the ones who need it most."

"Is it me?" said Medea quietly. "Are you still worried I'd mess something up?"

She knew those kind of doubts were hard to dispel once they'd crept into someone's mind. Even if it wasn't true, even now that Idas had admitted she wasn't the one at fault for Lynceus, Jason might still be worried that she'd make a mistake when it counted the most. Or maybe he thought she was careless. Maybe he thought this was something too big for her to handle. Circe was one of the best, after all, and fixing what she'd done would take every bit of her training.

"That's not it," said Jason firmly. "It's not." He sighed, and shook his head. "I know you're up to it. And if I wanted anyone to change me, it'd be you. But I'm pure. I've never had a bit of help. This is like a top athlete training for years and then pumping himself full of steroids right before he runs a marathon. I'm not a cheater, and I'm not going to do it."

"It's not like that at all," said Medea. "You're not cheating. You're stopping someone else from cheating against you."

"It still feels that way," said Jason. "It feels like if I let you make a change, I've given up. I've let go of my honor, and broken an oath I made to myself. It's a line, and I'd be crossing it. And once the changes start, I can't ever go back."

"Your code is already changing," said Medea. "Whether you like it or not, it's already happened. I'm just going to stabilize it. I'm going to keep it how it is. And you don't exactly have a choice. It's either let me work on you, or end up like him." She nodded towards Mopsus, who'd launched himself off the table and was charging around beneath it in circles, squealing loudly all the while. "And I promise you won't be winning any battles if Circe turns you into something like that."

"I just can't," said Jason, shaking his head. "And I know I'm fine. I know it. I didn't have more than a few bites."

"Then let me check," said Medea. "Just let me check. If nothing's gone wrong with your code, I won't touch a thing. But if Circe's done something to you, too, then I'm going to make it right. I'm going to put you back the way you were."

He stood there in silence, staring at Hecate and her mess of tubes. He spent a minute contemplating what she'd said, and she thought he was on the verge of giving in. But then he looked up at her and shook his head. "I don't think you understand what you're asking me to do. You're asking me to give up part of myself. To give up the thing I've been working towards for decades. To taint it."

"I do understand," said Medea. "But nothing's going to change who you are. You'll be the exact same person when I'm done."

"I won't ever be the same," said Jason. "Once you start changing your code, you're never the same. Part of you gets replaced with something else. Pretty soon there isn't anything left of what you used to be."

"We're always changing," said Medea. "And our code is always changing, even if you don't know it. Your genes aren't the same as when you were born, and neither are you. The only difference is that the changes I make are ones you can control." She stepped in closer, looking up into his eyes, trying to see through them to the source of his hesitation. "You don't trust me, do you? You don't think I can do it?"

He matched her gaze, and all she could see was sincerity. "I trust you," said Jason. "I trust you completely."

"Then let me help you," said Medea. "If you trust me, let me help you."

He turned away, and she thought he was about to shut her down for good. His face had gone to stone, and she couldn't read whatever was going on inside. It was tearing her apart; she wanted to be there for him, but he wouldn't let her. He was the only warrior she'd ever met who had any principles, and now he wanted to sacrifice himself for them. She respected it, in a way. If he believed in something, he'd fight for it, and even die for it. She just wished he believed in her.

He was facing away from her, and he wasn't speaking. It looked like he'd chosen, and he hadn't chosen her. She started preparing herself inside, getting ready for the changes in him she knew could soon be coming. He wouldn't have long if Circe's weapon had struck its mark. But then he turned around, pulled up his sleeve, and held out his arm.

"Do it," said Jason. "I trust you. And I know you're capable. I know you can keep me the way I am. So do it, before I change my mind."

"Or before you grow a tail," said Medea. But she didn't give him the chance to do either. She jabbed the needle into his arm, just beneath his bicep. She held her hand under his arm to hold it steady, and she could feel his muscles tensing beneath her fingertips. She could feel him relaxing, too, the longer she held her hand against him. But she couldn't wait forever. Not with what could be going on inside him.

She slammed a button on her sheath, starting the process of analyzing his code. It was changing; she could see that the second his DNA streamed across her sheath. Circe's work was twisted around his genome, and if he'd waited for much longer he'd have been rooting around under the table right next to Mopsus.

Circe was good, and trying to fix what she'd done was intimidating, especially when she was working on someone she cared about. The code was complicated, and just looking at how far along it was made Medea wince. A few days ago she would have thought something like this was impossible to fight against. But she knew better now. She'd saved the Harpies, she'd saved the other Argonauts, and now she was going to save Jason.

"No changes," said Jason. "You can do it without any changes?"

"None," said Medea. "Not from me, at least. Circe's code is in there. I can see it." He visibly tensed, and she did her best to reassure him. "It's not active. Not yet. All I'm going to do is put it on lockdown."

"Just do what you can," said Jason. He relaxed, and she kept on with her work. It was growing easier the more times she patched up a victim of the weapon the Colchians had created. She could see how it worked, and how it was disrupting their code, and stopping it was easier than before. But it was a nasty thing, and a scary one. She thought about what would happen if she was treating hundreds of victims all at once instead of just a handful, and it made her shiver all over.

"Done," said Medea. A purple fluid squirted through the tube and into Jason's arm, and then Hecate flashed green. "You'll be fine. And don't worry. We can take it all out once we get back to Argos. Every last bit. You'll be just the same as you were before you got here."

"No changes?" said Jason.

"Nothing functional," said Medea. "It's in there, but it's not doing anything. You're you, and nothing else."

"Perfect," said Jason. "Now get to work on Mopsus. Do whatever you can. See if—"

He was interrupted by a creaking sound from behind the metal barriers. They ground their way upwards, moving just a few inches before jerking to a halt. They could hear voices from behind them, and footsteps. Then hundreds of black metal beetles swarmed through the opening, crawling along the floor directly towards them.

"Drones," said Jason. "Everyone ready. Weapons drawn." He whipped out his sword and tossed a chair on its side in their path. The drones just went right past, spreading out around the room and disappearing under the table. They stomped at them, crushing a few under their boots, but it wasn't enough. A loud hissing sound rose from all around, and jets of gas spurted out of the drones, joining together in a hazy cloud that sent them all into a coughing fit.

Tiphys was the first to drop, slumping to the ground unconscious. Jason ripped away at the tablecloth, clamping it over Medea's face before putting a hand over his own. "Cover your faces," said Jason. "Cover—" But it wasn't enough. One by one, they fell to the floor, no matter how long they held their breath. Medea was the last to go; the tablecloth had kept out some of the gas, but in the end it wasn't enough. The last thing she saw before she fell was the barrier grinding upwards, and a squadron of heavily armed Colchian soldiers storming into the room.

CHAPTER TWENTY-FOUR

MEDEA'S HEAD WAS WOOZY, AND just opening her eyelids felt like she was trying to lift a barbell. But her vision slowly cleared, and soon she could see where she was: lying on a Persian rug laid out across the floor of a posh bedroom suite. She tried to pull herself to her feet, but she couldn't move her arms. They were numb enough that she could barely feel them, and the rest of her was no better. Whatever she'd been gassed with, it had done its work. It felt like she'd just snapped out of the deepest sleep of her life, and all she wanted to do was doze back into it. But she fought against the urge, lifting her head up as high as she could manage.

She could see the others on the ground nearby, splayed out and unconscious. She was the only one moving, and apparently Jason's efforts had made sure she'd gotten less of a dose of the gas than the rest of them. Mopsus was over by her feet, a little sleeping pig with vacant eyes and his tongue dangling from his mouth. Antaeus lay motionless on his stomach, looking like he'd been turned into some hunter's bearskin rug. Jason, Idas, and Tiphys were heaped in a pile atop each other, their limbs mingling together in an indistinguishable mess. Whoever had taken them here had even brought Hecate, dumping her on her side in a corner of the room.

"Hey," said Medea. She had to force the word out of her lips; her mouth felt like she'd been through some archaic dental procedure, and her tongue still tingled when she tried to make it move. She looked around, taking in as much as she could. She thought they must be somewhere in Circe's mansion, at least judging from the furniture. It was all antique, the kind of thing people had once spent weeks carving by hand instead of churning out in factories by the thousands. It reminded her of a French chateau, with elegant couches and chairs all stuffed to bursting, their frames fringed with gold.

She managed to wobble to her feet, fighting against the strain and the voice inside telling her to lay down for just a little while longer. She could see more of the room as she stood, and once she did she knew they weren't with Circe any longer.

Either side of the suite was lined with solid walls of glass. Sandwiched between them was a row of connected bedrooms stretching as far as she could see. On one side of the glass was a drab grey hallway, and in it stood a pair of stern looking guards, watching her carefully as she awoke. The other side of the room faced outside, from a view any Colchian would recognize in an instant. They were at the city's center, looking out on it from what could only be the Colchis Corporation's headquarters. It explained the interiors, at least. The building was almost a palace, and any prisoner important enough to be housed there was important enough for a taste of its luxuries.

"You're awake," said a voice from somewhere up above. She dragged herself to her feet, and she could see speakers up there, embedded in the ceiling. Then she saw someone else standing outside the glass. He was a giant of a man, dressed in a stylish bespoke suit and a sharp blue tie. The clothing didn't match his appearance; he had a heavy brown beard that tumbled down to his stomach, and his long hair was pulled back into a ponytail. Scars dotted his face, and muscles bulged beneath the silken fabric. He could have been taken for a bouncer, if not for the way the guards beside him cringed in submission.

He was older than the last time she'd seen a picture of him, but she knew who he was at once. Everyone in Colchis did. It was Aeetes, the CEO of the Colchis Corporation. He was constantly on the vids, mostly officiating over mock battles or sanctioned fighting tournaments. He'd been a warrior before he'd risen through the ranks, and he'd never lost his taste for battle. The fame made him the perfect figurehead for a corporation, especially in a place like Colchis. The drudgery of a business could be handled by flunkies, but once a warrior crossed the line to hero he was a living brand, a man whose fame and exploits attracted new stakeholders by the millions.

"Circe," said Medea, as she steadied herself on her feet and paced over to the glass. "She gave us up."

"She knows the hand that feeds her," said Aeetes. "And she's tamer than her animals, as long as you're the one serving her meals."

"She's crazy," said Medea. "She's working on a genetic weapon." She eyed him with suspicion; he didn't even bat an eye at the suggestion. "But I'm guessing you're the one who asked her to do it. And I don't think you have any idea how dangerous that is."

"I know exactly how dangerous it is," said Aeetes. He stepped closer to the glass until he was just on the other side, towering up above her. "To the rest of the Big Five, at least. The other corporations think of genomancy as a product. Something you package up and sell to the masses. I know better. I'm an executive today, but I'll always be a warrior at heart. And we both know what genomancy could be with a little imagination."

"A weapon," said Medea. "Something to hurt people with."

"You can sell people their fantasies," said Aeetes. "Or you can sell them their fears. Colchis already owns people's fantasies. Now we'll own their fears, too. This thing Circe's created. It's going to be like no weapon humanity has ever known. We can put it in food, in water, even in the air. Imagine people falling down in the streets, transforming into strange creatures, or even just melting into a pile of mush. They'll be panicked. Desperate. They'll pay anything to keep themselves safe."

"You'll kill everyone," said Medea. "If you release something like that in the wild. It's going to spread. It'll come back to Colchis sooner or later. No quarantine can stop it."

"We don't have to stop it," said Aeetes. "And we don't want to. It's a weapon of mass destruction, yes. But one we can control. We decide when it triggers, and who it triggers in. We can target the effects to people with specific pieces of code. And we have everyone's DNA to identify the targets." His smile grew wider, and his eyes sparkled in triumph. "Everyone's. We can infect the masses, and kill the few. Whoever we want, whenever we want. The stakeholders are going to join the Colchian ecosystem by the billions. And they'll never sign a contract with anyone else, ever again. Not if they want to stay human. Not if they want to stay alive."

"What do you want from me?" said Medea. "Why am I in here? And what do you want me to do?"

"I don't have any interest in you," said Aeetes. He tapped a thick finger against the glass, pointing at the others on the floor. "Circe will, I'm sure. But I came here to talk to the other one. The son of Aeson. So be a good girl and go give him a nudge."

She hesitated, unsure what she should do. She thought about spitting on the glass and telling him where he could go stuff himself. It would have been the more satisfying thing to do. But he'd probably just gas them all again and haul Jason over there himself. She couldn't think of any way out, or anything she could say to convince someone like him to let them free. But maybe Jason could. Maybe they could come up with something together.

"Go," said Aeetes. "Or I'll hand you all back to Circe and let her do what she will."

"Jason," said Medea, trying to nudge him back into consciousness. "Jason. Wake up." She tugged at one of his arms, dragging him away from the others. Still he just lay there, until she gave him a sharp pinch. That got him going. His eyes began to flicker, and after a few more shakes they flipped open and he leapt to his feet, his hand grasping at his belt for a sword that wasn't there.

"Where are we?" said Jason, wiping at his eyes. "What happened?"

Medea pointed at Aeetes, beckoning him towards the glass with a finger. "The Colchians. Circe turned us in. This is their CEO."

"Jason, son of Aeson," said Aeetes. "You're a hard man to find. I'd heard you were coming to my city on something of a quest." He gave a wistful grin, running a hand through his beard. "I used to be a warrior myself, once. We'd rampage through foreign cities all the time in my younger days. All the violence and murder and theft. I miss it, sometimes. But to everything its season."

"We're here because of your theft, not ours," said Jason. "You stole something that doesn't belong to you. Something that needs to go back to Argos."

"The Fleece," said Aeetes. "Circe said that's why you were here. Not something worth dying for, if you ask me. The folly of youth. I could charge you with all sorts of crimes. Espionage. Sabotage. Robbery." He nodded towards Medea. "Add treason, for that one."

"This is about me, not her," said Jason. He stepped towards Aeetes, standing toe to toe with him. Then he slammed a fist into the glass, rattling his knuckles against it. It didn't even budge; the glass had been reinforced at a molecular level, and it would take more than a punch to escape their cell.

"You say you're a warrior," said Jason. "Then come out and fight. Quit hiding behind that wall. Quit hiding the Fleece."

"I'm not going to hide it," said Aeetes, his lips curling up into a smile. "I'm just going to give it to you."

"It's that easy?" said Jason skeptically. "You capture us, haul us in here, and then you just hand back everything you stole?"

"It's never that easy," said Aeetes. "No one gives you something without expecting a favor in return. No, I want something from you. I already have most of what I needed from the Fleece. Now I want a spectacle, too. I want the greatest show on Earth. You know what the key to signing up stakeholders is, don't you? You know what gets them to sign over their basic minimums, more than jewelry or boats or houses or anything else?"

"What?" said Jason. "What do you want?"

"Ratings," said Aeetes. "If you want stakeholders to stay with you, you've got to have ratings. Eyeballs glued to vids, all day, every day. You need a show. And that's all I ask of you. Just put on a show, the kind they'll talk about in Colchis for generations." He spread his arms wide, his voice turning to an announcer's patter. "An Argonaut. The best the city of Argos has to offer. Up against the best of Colchis, in the match of the century. Jason of Argos, fighting for his life against the Bronze Bulls of Colchis. How long can he survive? Seconds? A minute? Or even two?"

"No," said Medea. "He's not fighting the Bulls. They're butchers. That's a death sentence." She'd seen enough of them to know that. There were four of the Bulls, always, and they never left the city. Joining the Bronze Bulls was the highest honor a Colchian warrior could achieve, and only the most ruthless of them were ever inducted. It took a special sort of cunning to stay alive once a warrior became a Bull, as everyone beneath them was perpetually aiming a dagger at their backs in the hopes of freeing up one of the four spots for themselves.

"It's only death if they win," said Aeetes. "And if you win, you can have the Fleece. I thought you were confident. I thought you were the best. No real warrior would turn down a chance at that kind of glory."

"Just me," said Jason. "The rest of my team, they stay here. And they stay alive, no matter who wins. Promise me that, and I'll promise you a fight this city will never forget. You'll be playing it on the vids for years."

"You can't," said Medea. "You don't know what they're like. You—"

"Keep them alive, and you can have me," said Jason. "That's the deal."

"Done," said Aeetes. "The fight's tonight. So get ready. We'll give you your weapons back at the arena. All of you." He leaned in towards Jason, his face next to the glass. "Because if you don't put on a show before you die, I'm tossing the rest of them in after you."

"I'm not going to die," said Jason. "You better have the Fleece nearby. Because I'm walking out of there with it, one way or another."

"We'll see," said Aeetes, nodding towards Hecate. "Fix him up. Make him last as long as possible. And I want him to look the part. Some horns, maybe, or even some wings. Make him bad. Someone the people can root against. Someone they can be afraid of." He clapped his hands, and the guards snapped to attention. "You'll still be a hero, you know. They'll make you one, back in Argos. There you die the martyr. But here you die the villain. Just how it works, I'm afraid." The speakers cut off, and he left them to their preparations and disappeared down the hall.

"You shouldn't have done that," said Medea. "You shouldn't have agreed." She knew how those matches went. They were battles waged for show, and there was no doubt who'd be the winner. She didn't usually watch the things herself, but she'd never heard of the Bulls losing, not even once. It didn't matter how hard Jason had trained, or how good he was. There were four of them, and one of him, and they had no qualms about how they won their victories.

"I didn't have a choice," said Jason. "What else can I do?"

"We could try all kinds of things," said Medea. "We could try to get a message to Argos." She looked down at her wrist, pressing a few buttons along it. "I'm still getting data on my sheath. We can get in touch with someone. See if they can negotiate. Or come up with some kind of rescue mission. Once Pelias finds out what they're doing with the Fleece, he'll have to do something."

"He won't," said Jason. "Pelias wants me to die here. It's what he's wanted since the beginning."

"What?" said Medea. She looked at him in shock, wondering if it was some kind of joke, but everything about his expression was deadly serious. It didn't make any sense to her. If Jason died, the Fleece would stay in Colchis, and their entire mission would be a complete waste. "Why? Why would he want something like that?"

"I think it's my shares," said Jason. "He wants control of my shares. That's why he made me put them in trust. He doesn't want me voting against him in the elections for corporate management. And if I die, every single share stays in the trust. He won't own them, but he'll control the votes. That means he keeps running the company however he wants, for as long as he wants."

"What about the Fleece?" said Medea. "If you die, they'd never get it back. They have to have known that."

"They didn't care about the Fleece," said Jason. "The gods might, but Pelias doesn't. He didn't send us here to find it. It was just an excuse. He sent us here so we'd all get killed. He knew exactly how dangerous this mission was. That was the entire point."

"How do you know?" said Medea. "How do you know all this? It sounds so crazy. Like one of those conspiracy theories. And why'd you even come if you knew?" She paused, wondering when he'd first known, and why he'd never said anything about it to her. "Why'd you let me come? Why'd you let any of us come if they were trying to kill us?"

"I didn't know," said Jason. "I only figured it out after we got inside the city. That dossier they gave me. The plan only took us through the tunnel. Then it was just pointless filler. There wasn't a single helpful thing in it. The plan was for us to walk right into the trap. They didn't think we'd be coming back out. They thought we'd just get in line like we were supposed to. They didn't plan on the gods intervening."

"They knew," said Medea. "Pelias knew about the trap. He knew about those drones. He knew."

"It's why I wanted you to stay away from me," said Jason. "And I wish I'd made you do it. They didn't really care about killing you or anyone else. They only care about killing me. I should have made you stay away from me. You'd be off in the ARGO right now. You'd be safe."

"You couldn't have made me do anything," said Medea. "I wouldn't have stayed. I'd have found some way to end up here, anyway. You should have told me. I could have tried to help somehow."

"I didn't want you to know," said Jason. "Pelias would kill you if he found out you knew. You'd be a loose end. If I'd told you, I'd have been putting you at risk. I thought if I got us out of Colchis, I could go handle him myself before he could do anything." He shook his head, a look of resignation on his face. "We are where we are. And there isn't any way out now. They're going to send me off to the arena. And the best warriors in Colchis are going to be there waiting."

"So it's over," said Medea. "After all this. The Bulls are going to kill you. They're going to make it four on one, and they're going to kill you."

"It's not over," said Jason. "It's never over. Not until you give up. I'm going to beat them." He walked over to Hecate, lifting her off the floor and setting her upright. He gave the robot a pat, and then gave Medea a cocky smile. "And you're going to help me do it."

CHAPTER TWENTY-FIVE

"I WANT YOU TO CHANGE ME," said Jason. "I want you to change my genes, however you think will help me win. Because I'm going to win, even if I have to win dirty. Give me strength, give me speed, give me anything. Whatever you can do between now and tonight."

"Are you sure?" said Medea hesitantly. "Are you really, really sure?"

She wasn't quite sure herself. There were only a few hours left before Aeetes's men would be coming for them, and she didn't know what she'd be able to whip up on such short notice. The Bronze Bulls were dangerous, and it would take everything in her to find some power she could give him that would even have a chance of stopping them.

Then there was the question of whether it was the right thing to do in the first place. She knew he still had an ethical problem with genomancy, no matter what he was saying now. And she had concerns of her own: could she really bring herself to change someone if he didn't actually want to be changed? It was such a violation of everything she believed in, especially when the man in question was him. Aphrodite had told her love was coming, though she wasn't quite sure she wanted to use that word yet. But she was attracted to him, and she cared for him, and she didn't want to do something to him that he might regret someday.

"You've gone your entire life without changing your code," said Medea. "Not even to change your eye color or melt away a little extra weight. You're the only person I know who's like that. Anyone who can afford genomancy does something to themselves, even if it's small. I can't do this if you're not sure. If you don't really mean it. I just can't."

"Do you trust him?" said Jason. "Aeetes? Do you think he'll keep his word if I die?"

She thought about it, but it didn't take her long. "No," said Medea. "He was talking like a madman before you woke up. He's working on some kind of weapon with Circe, and he's using the Fleece to do it. It's what she used on Mopsus. I think he just wants to kill you in public for his show. And then the rest of us are going to quietly disappear."

"That's what I think, too," said Jason. "If I lose, you're going to die." He took her hand and squeezed, softly. "So I'm going to win. And I don't give a damn how. I don't care about the rules, I don't care about the costs, and I don't care about the glory. What I care about is keeping you alive."

She fluttered inside as he spoke. He meant it; she could tell by the way his eyes shone towards her when he talked. He truly did care about her, his warrior's swagger aside, and he was willing to give up something he'd obsessed over for his entire life if it would help him protect her from Aeetes. It meant so much to him, being able to say that he'd earned every one of his talents through his own hard work. And it meant even more to her that he wouldn't hesitate to abandon it all to save her.

But doubts nagged at her mind about what Aeetes planned to do. Someone like that couldn't be trusted. Not in victory, and not in defeat.

"Even if you win, though," said Medea. "He's not going to keep his word. He's never going to honor the deal."

"If I beat the Bulls, the city will be in shock," said Jason. "And I've got a plan. I can get us out before they come back to their senses. I just need you to keep me alive long enough for me to do it."

"We need to get to work, then," said Medea. "We don't have a whole lot of time." She looked down at the rest of their team, still stretched across the floor in their sleep. "Let's use one of these other rooms. I don't know how much longer they're going to be out. And I'm going to need things to be quiet while I work. I'm not going to be able to handle Tiphys bouncing around asking me questions the entire time."

They walked along the suite towards one of the other bedrooms, connected by an open doorway. It wasn't much privacy. She could still see into all of the other rooms, lined up one after another. But it was more than she expected out of a dungeon, even one as extravagant as this. Hecate rolled along after her towards a canopied four-poster bed in the center of the room, made from dark wood with rose colored satin dangling down over the top.

"I'm sorry," said Medea, as she opened up Hecate. "I'm sorry I've got to do this. I still don't agree with you. About genomancy. But I understand why you always wanted to do things on your own. And I'm sorry you won't get your victory."

"You're right," said Jason. "It won't be my victory." His lips rose into a crooked smile, and he put an arm around her. "It'll be ours. My battle. Your code. And I'm fine with that. I've been thinking about it, and I'm fine with it. It's not the way I dreamed it. But I'm supposed to be a leader now, not just a warrior. We're going to live or die as a team, and it isn't cheating to rely on someone who's on your team."

She thought about how she'd felt back at the Hellespont after she'd managed to survive the Harpies. She knew how important it could be to know you could accomplish something yourself if you had to. He had something to prove to himself, just as she'd had, and it made her feel better knowing she wasn't taking anything away from him. She settled down to figure out what she could add to him instead, using her sheath to dive into Hecate's archives. She already knew the first change she had to make, and the most important thing she needed to improve about him given who he'd be fighting.

His skin.

The one weapon the Bulls favored more than anything else was fire. The entire arena was blackened and scorched from their victims, and if Jason went in there with them like he was, they'd burn him to a crisp.

But there was a way around that, something she'd done for one of the Argonauts once. The code from an underwater worm, one that lived deep in the oceans near a cluster of volcanic vents. The worms could handle incredible temperatures, and she'd modified a segment of their genetic code to the point that it could make human skin virtually fireproof. The Bulls wouldn't be expecting that little trick, and it might give him an edge he could use.

Playing defense wasn't going to be enough, though. She needed to give him talents, as many as she could. With any luck there'd be something in there the Bulls hadn't encountered. They'd all have genomancy of their own, she was certain of it. They wouldn't have risen as far as they had without overhauling their genetic code. So it was her against whoever had changed them, a battle of the genomancers behind the scenes to see who could outcode the other. And she had more than an inkling as to who Colchis was using to enhance its warriors. Circe was on Aeetes's payroll, and she wanted them just as dead as he did. If she was right, the Bulls would be Circe's pets to do with as she pleased, just as much as any pig was.

It was intimidating, knowing that Circe could be working against her. She'd have four warriors against Medea's one. And Circe was good. Very good. She also didn't have any ethical lines whatsoever. She could do whatever she wanted to, and she could be very creative when it came to her cruelty. She'd have to outthink Circe if Jason was going to outfight her creations.

She turned to her sheath, flipping through a list of pre-prepared skills she could add to Jason's code right away, searching for anything that might help. "Do you know judo?" She had a dojo's worth of martial arts saved on Hecate's systems, ready to upload to any warrior who was looking for a new fighting style, and the more he knew, the better.

"Of course," said Jason.

"Karate?" said Medea. "Aikido? Muay Thai?"

"Yes, yes, yes," said Jason. "I told you. Hours and hours of training, every day, since I was just a little kid."

"Come look at this list," said Medea. She held out her sheath, and he walked closer, taking her arm in his hand. She felt his other hand at her side, and he leaned in close as they watched the names of dozens of obscure fighting styles scroll past along her arm. It made it hard to concentrate, feeling him pressed against her. Part of her wanted to just forget about the code, roll over on the bed, and have one wild romp before they dragged him away from her. But she forced her thoughts back to the list, and back to trying to keep them alive. "Are there any of these fighting styles you don't know? Any you haven't trained in?"

"Kenjutsu," said Jason, pressing a finger against her arm. It made her spine tingle, but he just looked down at her and smiled. "I've studied it, but not much. And Gatka. I don't know anything about that one."

"They're both for swords," said Medea. "And either one could help, if Aeetes actually gives us our weapons back." She went back to her sheath, browsing through Hecate's database. There weren't any more martial arts, not that she'd brought with her, but there were other things she could change, other ways she might give him an edge.

"Your reflexes," said Medea. "I'm going to enhance those, too. I know you're fast. But I can make you faster. And your muscles."

"What's wrong with my muscles?" said Jason with a wide smirk. She could see them rippling under the skin-tight fabric of his uniform. He had the physique of an Olympian; she wouldn't deny that. She stole a guilty glance down his body, and it made her wish the others weren't lying there in the next room.

"Your muscles are... fine," said Medea. She turned back to her sheath, flustered. "I meant the fibers. I can improve them. Make you stronger. You'll look the same, but you'll be more powerful than any human, at least one who hasn't been enhanced."

"It's going to be weird," said Jason. "Not knowing my own strength. But whatever you think will work. Don't worry about me. Just worry about what you think might help."

"One last thing," said Medea. "Your legs." She rushed to cut him off, before he said something else to send her into another flush of embarrassment. "Just a little change. Something to help you jump. Twenty or thirty feet, maybe. We'll fix the fibers, and redesign the insides. If you win, I promise to change you back."

"When I win," said Jason. "When we win."

"When we win," said Medea. She tapped at her sheath, preparing Hecate for the procedure to come. "Let's get started. We'll get these changes done. They're already written, so it won't take long. Then I'll start brainstorming and see if I can come up with anything new to program for you on the fly."

He sat down on the edge of the bed, rolling up the sleeves of his uniform. She settled in beside him, pulling up a half dozen tubes from Hecate and connecting them to his arms. She prepped the code she wanted to add to his, and had Hecate run a final scan to make sure there wouldn't be any errors.

Then she checked things herself, over and over. He was the last person she wanted to make a mistake on. He'd finally gotten over his doubts about her, and she didn't want them coming back. She had enough insecurities of her own about her work. In her head she knew she was good at what she did, and that it didn't make any sense for her to feel inadequate about it. But sometimes feelings didn't make sense. It didn't make the worries any less real, even if there wasn't actually anything there to worry about.

"Okay," said Medea. "It's all done. Are you ready? And are you sure? Once I get started, I can't change you back in time for the fight."

"I'm ready," said Jason. "And I'm not changing my mind. This is the only chance we have. Neither one of us can win this thing alone."

"Here goes," said Medea, pressing a finger against her sheath. "Just lie still. I don't think it's going to hurt. Your skin's going to change, and it's probably going to itch, but just don't scratch it and you'll be fine."

"I'm in good hands," said Jason. "You've got this. It's going to work."

Chemicals started to go into him, and blood started to go out. Hecate launched into the changes, one by one, enhancing him as he sat there beside her on the bed. She knew it was working when she saw the changes to his skin. The color of it was transforming, a dark black shadow clouding along his face and hands before it faded away to normal. And his muscles. They were twitching, all along his body, and especially on his legs. Everything looked good, and it would only be a little longer before he was as ready for the battle as he'd ever be.

"Are you nervous?" said Medea. "You're tense." He was so tightly wound he'd almost stopped breathing. She squeezed his hand, and it pulled him out of whatever place he'd been inside himself. He looked down at her, smiled, and squeezed back.

"I just worry about it," said Jason. "About whether I'm going to be the same. Whether I'll still be me once it's not just my code inside me anymore."

"We all went through the same thing, back in the academy," said Medea. "It was sort of a rite of passage, and you weren't allowed to change anyone else's code until you'd changed your own. You had to write it, and you had to do the whole thing by yourself. Every genomancer has some story about the first time they changed their own DNA. I don't know anyone who got through it without completely freaking out."

"That's not exactly reassuring," said Jason.

"I managed," said Medea. "It's a trial by fire. The moment you work on yourself for the first time. You talk about it for years, and then it's finally time to do it. It's the scariest thing that's ever happened to me."

"Scarier than almost getting tossed into a turbine?" said Jason with a wry smile.

"Worse," said Medea. "Much, much worse. All I did was change my hair color. I went redhead, just for a week. It's actually a really easy change to make. But I felt like I was taking out my own appendix with a kitchen knife." She laughed a little at the memory. "I was so scared something was going to go wrong. That I'd turn off my heart or give myself an extra toe. Then I decided the shade of red looked terrible, and I stayed in my room an entire week until I figured out how to change it back."

"It can't have looked bad," said Jason. "Not on you."

Their eyes met, and she found she couldn't look away. He was so close, absorbing every inch of her with a stunning green stare. He smiled, looking like he'd already won something more important than any battle, and he took her face between the palms of his hands.

Then he leaned in slowly. She closed her eyes, and felt his lips against her own.

She could feel a wildness in him, the part of him that drove him to war now driving him towards her. His kiss was passionate, feverishly intense, that of a man who wasn't sure if he'd ever see her again. His hands wrapped around the back of her head, running through her hair until they closed into a fist and pulled it tight, holding her head there so she couldn't escape even if she'd wanted to.

But she didn't. What she wanted was to stay there in his arms, away from all the fighting and away from all the rest of them. She wanted to be with him, safe from the storms raging around her, safe from the people on all sides who wanted nothing more than to hurt her however they could. She'd have done it, if there was any way to. But neither of them had the choice.

Her sheath beeped, a shrill insistent noise. She forced herself to pull away from him, disappointment surging through her at the interruption. But she couldn't ignore the sheath, not in the middle of a procedure. She turned to look. A message filled the screen, from a very familiar source: Hera. It was just two words, flashing red across her wrist over and over.

"Dragon's Teeth."

"She's right," said Medea to herself. "I can't believe I didn't think about it. But she's right."

"Who?" murmured Jason. "Who's right?"

"Hera," said Medea. "The gods." She held up her arm, showing him the text running across her sheath. "They've been sending me these messages."

"They've been talking to you," said Jason. "Like with Mopsus."

"They helped me with the Harpies," said Medea. "It was so freaky. It was like they knew every single thing that was going to happen. And now they're helping us again."

"So what's the message?" said Jason. "What are we supposed to do?"

"It's about something I worked on back in the academy," said Medea. "A project I did for a class. And I think we can use it here. It makes so much sense, now that I think about it. Just give me a minute." She still had the code stored somewhere in her database. She'd have to change it; she hadn't had war in mind back when she'd written it. But she had everything she needed, right there with her. It was just a matter of putting it all together, and of changing something that had once been an apprentice's toy into a weapon of war.

It didn't take her long. She cut and she spliced, and soon she'd patched something together. She didn't know if what she'd planned would work. They wouldn't find out, not until he was in the arena. But she'd done the best she could, and she thought this little trick would at least give Circe a run for her money. "Hecate. Synthesize." Hecate began to hum, and after a few moments she was done, the little objects she'd made jangling onto a tray inside her.

Medea reached inside, pulling out her creations and holding them out for Jason to see. There were a dozen bright green things in the palm of her hand. They looked like tiny, sharp teeth, but they were something else entirely. Seeds. And if they worked, if they grew into what she hoped they would, the city of Colchis would be in for the surprise of the century.

"The Bronze Bulls," said Medea. "You can't beat them. Not on your own. But it doesn't have to just be you out there. Take these seeds." She pressed them into his hand, and he stuffed them into a pouch on his belt. "The ground. It's going to be ash. Scatter them all around, and then all you have to do is stay alive."

"And then what?" said Jason.

"Just plant them somewhere, and don't get killed," said Medea. "This was a school project, so don't expect too much. But I spliced some of the code for your instincts into it. Some of you is in these seeds. Remember that, if it works. When you fight, it's not just me pulling a puppet's strings. It's you, too. It's both of us."

They heard a noise from the other room: Tiphys, shouting in a panic, and then the sound of fists pounding against glass. The others were up, and they didn't sound happy. "We're going to have to let them know what's going on," said Medea. Hecate was flashing a green light for Jason's procedure: his code was changed, and he was as ready as he'd ever be. "It looks like you're good. Let's go make sure they're all okay."

They headed back into the other room to find Idas and Antaeus in a face-off with two guards, staring at each other on either side of the glass. "Let us out," said Idas. "Let us the hell out. I know people here in Colchis. Let us out, now, or I'll make sure you die while you sleep."

"Don't," said Jason, walking out with his palms up in a gesture of peace. "Just do what they say, all of you. I'm the one they want."

"It's time," said the guard. "Don't do anything stupid." He pressed a button and part of the glass wall slid open. Then he brandished a pistol at them, a device made all the more threatening by its near-illegality. "We've got orders to kill you all if any of you does anything stupid."

"They want me to fight," said Jason. "Against the Bronze Bulls. Just me. Let me handle it." He headed out the door, his hands at his sides as the guard waved them onward.

"Handle it all you like," said Idas, as the rest of them filed out after him. "You think you're going to beat the Bulls? You should have done like I said and gone back to Argos. This is all yours. We're going stick to the popcorn, watch you get killed, and pray we're not the next ones to die."

"I'm going to win," said Jason. "And we're all getting out of here alive."

The first guard let out a snicker, chatting loudly with the second as he waved them by with his pistol. "Remember the match against Idmon? Some seer from Argos who was supposed to be able to predict every punch. His head was on a pike outside the arena for a week."

"And Iphiclus," said the second guard. "They pinned him to the wall with his own javelins. Then they started taking out organs, one by one."

"Or Palaemonius," said the first. "They cut off his feet and shipped them back to Argos."

"That arena's full of corpses of people who thought they'd be the one to finally win," said the second guard. He followed Jason out into a hallway, leading off somewhere into the building. "But nobody goes up against the Bulls and lives. No one ever has, and no one ever will."

CHAPTER TWENTY-SIX

THE SOUND FROM THE ARENA was deafening. There must have been hundreds of thousands of people crammed inside, and still more watching remotely on the vids. But it wasn't even a fraction of what was to come. The promoters were still trudging through the undercard fights, and once the Bronze Bulls made their appearance, the entire city's eyes would be focused on them.

"Your sword," said a froggish little man with bleached white skin. He was the arena's weapons master, charged with controlling the various implements of destruction that were taken in and out of the arena on a daily basis. His limbs had been replaced with cybernetic versions of the originals, and he didn't have a hair on what was left of his body. His replacement limbs were decades old, implanted before the rise of genomancy, and what was left of him was sickly and withered as a result.

Their weapons were arrayed on a counter in front of him, Jason's sword lying in the middle. "Back where it belongs," said Jason, returning his sword to its sheath. Medea tucked her little dagger into her belt, and Idas snatched his spear away and strapped it to his back.

The weapons master's arm jerked upwards, a blocky metal finger pointing towards a tunnel leading down into the arena floor. "They're waiting." He nodded towards Jason. "The Bulls for you. Aeetes for the rest of them. They'll all have their own platform. It'll be right up front. Where your friends can see you, and everyone else can see them." He motioned for the guards, who pushed at them all from behind and herded them down the tunnel. The sound of cheers grew louder as they went, and they stopped just outside the entrance, waiting for the last of the undercard fights to finish and for the main event to start.

The arena was shaped like a globe, an oval cut out at the top to let in the sun from above. The seating ran almost to the edge of the opening, with stakeholders crammed in like sardines. Those near the top of the globe had be hauled up in their chairs along a series of tracks, strapped in to keep them from tumbling down to the floor. But a seat was a seat, and the arena could only be so big. The most ardent fans of the arena battles were willing to spend the evening nearly upside down if it meant they could watch things in person.

The employees had it better. Floating platforms hovered all around the arena, barges full of spectators sailing through the air above. The platforms looked like flying balconies, their sides surrounded with solid railings to prevent anyone from falling down into the arena below. Anyone important enough to merit one could watch the fights from their own personal VIP area, each platform crowding against the others in search of the perfect view. But the best seats in the house were reserved for the shareholders, hovering a few dozen feet above the action in giant luxury boxes that lazily circled over the arena with no regard for anyone's view but their own.

Jason looked out on the arena from the tunnel, focusing on the fight and planning what he'd do during his own moment of truth. He was an avid arena fan, watching whatever fights he could buy from any of the Big Five, and he'd seen the Bulls on the vids hundreds of times. Sometimes they fought in tournaments, sometimes for sport, and sometimes for blood. Back then he'd been watching purely for fun. But this was the real deal, and now he was the one being thrown up against them for the entertainment of the masses.

He loved the fights; he always had. There was something primal about it, seeing men battle each other just for the sake of proving which of them would really win if it came down to it. It was one thing to boast and brag—anyone could do that, and many did. But the real test of a man's worth came during battle. No one could fake it, and no one could fake the respect a warrior earned from everyone around them when they won.

He inspected the arena, taking advantage of the delay to plot his opening moves in his head. The floor was covered in a thick layer of ash, black swirling into grey as flurries of dust wisped across the ground. He'd seen that on the vids, too, shot from floating cameras up above to avoid the whirlwinds of soot that the fighters sent up as they hacked away at each other. It would be hard for him to see once he was in there, and the Bulls would be wearing helmets to protect their vision.

And they'd have another advantage, one he couldn't do much about: their membership changed so often that he couldn't even be sure who he'd be facing. They'd know who he was, but he didn't have the slightest clue who they'd be or what they could do. It would be him versus four unknowns, the winner take the glory and all of their lives at stake.

He'd fantasized about a moment like this for virtually his entire life. His dream had always been to be a warrior, or at least a sanctioned tournament fighter. But the reality was nothing like the dreams. He thought back to the way he'd envisioned it. Everyone had followed the rules in his fantasies, and no one was looking to kneecap the others just to claim a tainted triumph in front of their fans. And in his fantasies, his life had been the only one on the line. His friends had never been hanging in the balance along with him.

He looked over at Medea, standing behind him with anxiety written all across her face. He'd left Argos wanting a victory for himself, something he could look back on fondly later in life instead of wondering for the rest of his days if he'd really have been able to make it. Now he was about to fight the battle he'd been preparing for all his life, and he found he didn't even care about victory for victory's sake. The only reason he wanted to win anymore was for her.

She wasn't the person he'd thought she was back when he'd first met her. At first he'd only seen the mad scientist who pumped people full of questionable chemicals so they could leapfrog over the hard work of their competitors. It hadn't helped that the warriors said such terrible things about her; they'd been his idols for his entire life. Then again, they hadn't turned out to be much like he'd thought they were, either. For all their public badmouthing of genomancy, they were happy to use it on themselves when the shades were drawn.

But he'd gotten to know her, and he saw something more in her now. The shell was just the shell, and it was hiding something within it that he caught glimpses of the more he was around her. There was something about her, some spark inside he couldn't help but notice. It came out when she talked about her work, a glow that took over her face anytime she worked on someone's code. Or when she talked about helping others, using the skills she'd developed over years and years to change people's lives for the better.

He knew exactly what that felt like. She'd toiled just as long as he had, and he was starting to see why she was so interested in genomancy. It was a tool, just like a sword or a spear, and one could do good with it just as easily as bad. It all depended on the character of the person who was using it. She wanted to nurture people, and he wanted to protect them. It was yin and yang, alike in ways but different all the same. They complemented each other, and each contributed something vital that the other one couldn't.

It drew him to her, and it was a pull he couldn't ignore, deep and primal and more powerful than anything he'd ever felt before. She was vulnerable, sitting up there with Aeetes and Circe and people all around who'd love to hurt her. But he was a warrior at heart, and the more they wanted to hurt her, the more it just made him want to hurt them.

It was an urge, and it was consuming him, filling him with cold rage whenever he heard Idas or the Harpies or anyone else as they threatened her. An instinct like that was the kind of thing she spent her days tinkering around with, and she'd probably know what was driving him deep down in his code. He thought he might ask her about it, once it was all over with and they were safely back in Argos. But for now, all he knew was that if the Colchians wanted to kill her, they'd just have to go through him first.

"You," barked one of the guards, pointing to Jason. "You're on in five." He waved the others forward towards a platform parked on the ground nearby. "The rest of you over here. You're going up, and you're going on camera. Try to look mean. You're the bad guys tonight." He looked up at Antaeus, his yellow eyes filled with madness and his teeth poking out over his lips. "The bear's got it. Try to look like him, and you'll all do fine." He motioned with a baton, snapping it against Medea's back when she didn't move quickly enough for his tastes.

Jason steeled himself, channeling the anger he felt into a place he could control. He wanted to slice out the man's throat with his sword, but that wouldn't help things. Not yet, and not while the Bulls were out there waiting for him. He had to save his fury for them, and let it all out when it counted the most.

The guards marched them onto the platform, and Jason held his hand out to Medea as she passed. Her fingers brushed against his, and she gave him a last few words before the gate on the railing slammed shut behind her. "You'll do it. I know you will. Just follow your instincts. And remember the seeds."

He pushed towards the platform, shoving away the guards as they tried to restrain him. He leaned over the railing and put a hand around her head, pulling her in close and whispering in her ear. "Don't worry. Don't be afraid. They can't beat me. They'll never want it as badly as I do. Not with what I'm fighting for." Then he kissed her, holding his lips against hers until the guards dragged him away.

The platform rose, floating upwards until it merged into the lazy streams of traffic circling above the arena. He watched until he couldn't see her anymore, just the bottom of the platform's gravity device, warping its weight and making it light as a feather. The platform made its way towards the center of the arena, stopping next to the biggest VIP barge of them all, the one from which Aeetes himself was overseeing the action.

A roar went up from the crowd, and Jason looked across the arena to see one of the fighters from the previous match standing over the other, a long spear pointed at his vanquished opponent's throat. He held an arm in the air to wild cheers, and then drove the spear downward and ended the match. Sanctioned fights weren't usually to the death. But this was a special occasion, and all bets were off about anyone following the rules.

A team of robots clambered across the ash, dragging away the losing fighter's corpse. This was it. Jason was up next, and it would only be minutes now before he'd be facing the Bronze Bulls, just him against the four of them. He checked his sword, stretched his muscles, and centered himself inside for what was to come.

The sound of a voice boomed throughout the arena, and Jason looked up to see the image of Aeetes flashing across giant screens on all sides. He was standing there on his platform, its railing decorated with a gaudy imperial gold frieze cast into the shape of a bull's head. Circe stood next to him, reveling in the bloodshed, the colors in her hair and eyes flashing a light, bubbly yellow to go along with her mood.

"A fine match," said Aeetes. "And fine warriors, though only one can win. Let's give them a round of applause." The crowd cheered, waving banners and signs in a raucous display of enthusiasm. "Colchis has enemies. Enemies all around. And one of them is here tonight. A spy from Argos, caught in the middle of our city with weapons full of poison. Three of our best men were dead at his feet when we found him, their blood on his hands. They left widows behind, and children. Let's bow our heads in their memory, and give them the silence they're due."

The arena went silent, but for loud wails from somewhere near Aeetes. The camera drones circled round, and the vid screens above were filled with images of a trio of sobbing women standing beside him on his platform, bawling their eyes out as loudly and as enthusiastically as they could.

"This spy came to our city for a reason," said Aeetes. "He came to steal something from us. Something valuable. Something that wasn't his to take. A secret treasure of our city, and one you'll see for the first time tonight." He paused, looking reverently up above him. "The Golden Fleece." A platform appeared at the top of the arena, slowly gliding down to the floor below. It landed in the center, and camera drones dove down towards it, projecting images of it all across the arena.

There it was, the thing Jason had come for. The Golden Fleece in all its glory.

It was shaped like a translucent suitcase, its exterior a clear, hardened gel. Branching throughout it were golden strands of what looked like wool, fibers that networked across the gel and wove in and out of one another to create trillions of connections between them. It was a computer, and an incredibly advanced one, powerful enough to contain and analyze the genetic data of billions of people all at once. A handle was fixed atop it, shaped like a ram's horns. The cameras were zoomed in on the Fleece itself, but Jason thought he could see something moving in the background, a flash of green that flickered across the floor of the platform almost too quickly for him to see.

The Fleece rose back to the skies, and Aeetes's voice came thundering across the arena again. "The Fleece. He came to steal it. I say he should earn it instead." Aeetes smiled, and the vid screens all around the arena split between a close-up of him and a close-up of the Golden Fleece. "If he can beat the best of Colchis, then who am I to say he doesn't deserve what he came for? If he can win—if he's the first man in history to beat the Bulls—then I'll hand him the Fleece myself."

"Ladies and gentlemen," said Aeetes. "Let's meet the would-be thief himself. They call themselves Argonauts, back where they come from. We just call them the mercenaries they are." The cameras hovered around Medea's platform, and her face appeared on screen after screen. "The man who's fighting for all of their lives. The thief who'd be a champion. Jason, son of Aeson!"

The guards nudged Jason forward as booing and hissing filled the air. Camera drones buzzed around him, and he put on a poker face to keep everything he was feeling locked inside. He wanted to tell them all who the real thieves were, and what the Fleece really was. The entire evening was a sham, but they'd kill him in an instant if he tried to say something, and they'd kill Medea along with him.

Instead he marched out with his sword at his side, a look of grim determination on his face. He didn't even acknowledge the hatred streaming down at him from all sides. Crowds were fickle. They liked to root for a winner, and the best thing he could do to win them over would be to notch a win for himself.

"And now," said Aeetes, "the pride of Colchis. The best our city has to offer. Warrior's warriors, the men we rely on to keep us safe from the barbarians outside our walls...." He kept touting the Bulls, in ever more extravagant language, but Jason just tuned him out. Medea had given him a weapon, and he meant to use it. He dug at the ash with his boot, then dropped one of the seeds into the hole before filling it in again with a sweep of his foot. He paced around his side of the arena, planting each of the seeds a few feet apart.

He stood nearby, waiting for something to happen, but the ash was just as lifeless as when he'd started. He wondered if the seeds were duds. He'd seen Medea do some amazing things, and at this point, nothing would have surprised him. But she hadn't had long to put things together. Whatever she'd tried to do for him with the seeds, it looked like it was a bust.

Smoke began to pour from the gateway at the opposite side of the arena, billowing out into the air, and the crowd roared at the sight. Loud music blared all around, a rock anthem designed to bring them all to their feet. The crowd sang along, stomping and shouting as the arena filled with fog. Then four dark figures stepped out of the haze, to screams of applause from all sides. They waved to the admiring throngs, holding out their arms as the audience tossed strings of flowers all around them. When their entrance was done, they lined up in a row opposite Jason, standing at attention with weapons in hand.

They were covered from head to toe in armor, the color of bronze but made of a near-impenetrable alloy. The suits were bulky, each shaped like a muscular Adonis forged from metal. Their helmets sported horns poking out to either side, and black visors covered their faces from view. Below the visors were dark circles where their mouths would have been, hooked up to packs on their backs by metal tubes that wound behind their shoulders. Each held a different weapon in turn: one a massive broadsword, the second a trident, the third a spear, and the last of them a silver bow.

The voice of Aeetes boomed around the arena again, projected all around from the drones hovering over the event. "Ladies and gentlemen. The defenders of Colchis. The protectors of our homeland, and the last line of defense between our people and the barbarians around us. The ones you love, and the ones you came to see. The Bronze Bulls!"

The four of them advanced on Jason to the sound of applause, spreading out around the arena and each approaching him from a different direction. It was smart, and it was what he would have done in their place. They were trying to keep him off guard, forcing him to watch from every angle at once. And the attack would come from whichever side he couldn't cover.

The two Bulls in front of him tried to pen him in, one of them poking at him with his spear to drive him from side to side. Jason slashed at it with his sword, hoping to snap it in two along the shaft. But sword and spear were made of stuff too strong for that. His sword just clanged away, and the Bull kept jabbing at him, first from the left, then from the right. He heard a crackling sound, and something in his head screamed of danger. He rolled to the side, landing on his feet to see a ball of fire exploding past where he'd been standing. One of the Bulls had snuck in behind him and stood staring at him from just a few feet away, his broadsword at his side.

At least Jason thought he was staring. The helmet blocked any view of the man's intentions, but wisps of smoke from the dark hole at the bottom of the helmet's mouth made them abundantly clear. He'd missed once, but this time the Bull intended to fry Jason to a crisp. They were close together, and there was no time for Jason move out of the way. As he saw the flames belch out of the Bull's mouth, he closed his eyes and shielded his face with his arm, praying the match wouldn't be over before it had even started.

He could feel a scorching heat enveloping his body. He dropped to the ground, rolling over and over in the ash, trying to put the flames out before the damage was done. He opened his eyes again, patting his hands across his smoldering uniform, but he couldn't find a single injury. Medea's changes had done their duty. The temperature must have been scalding, but his skin had just deflected it all away.

The Bull tried again, launching a stream of fire directly into Jason's face. This time he didn't even flinch. It was a strange feeling. The flame was hot, but it didn't hurt, and it just seemed to roll away from his skin wherever it touched him. He was immune to their favorite weapon, and he knew an opening when he saw one.

He charged at the Bull, leaning his shoulder into a tackle and leaping towards him. Jason smashed into him, faster than he'd expected, and the two of them landed in a heap a dozen yards away. He'd forgotten about his legs. Medea had made them powerful, strong enough to leap several stories high, and the impact was more than enough to knock the Bull senseless. Jason's hands were empty; the sword had been smacked away by the force, and he scanned the ash nearby looking for where it had landed.

He saw it, but too far away for him to reach, and the other three were rushing towards him from across the arena. He rolled atop the Bull instead, straddling him and slamming his fists into the helmet's visor. It cracked a little, but it wasn't enough. Jason kept hitting, and the Bull started hitting back. Plans ran through his head, stratagems he'd learned in all his years of study. But a voice in his head said he should try something else instead. Medea had changed his instincts, enhancing them just as she had his body. They'd worked for Tiphys, so maybe they'd work for him, too. He cleared his mind of thought, waiting and hoping that something would come to him.

He knew what to do before he was even conscious of it. He grabbed at the tubes running between the Bull's helmet and the pack on his back, ripping them free from the armor. Fuel spurted out of them, sending a spray across the Bull's chest. Smoke was still pouring out of the man's helmet, and Jason followed his instincts yet again. He shoved one of the tubes into the mouth of the helmet, jamming it in as hard as he could.

A fireball erupted as fuel hit flame, an explosion that shook the arena from top to bottom. The other three Bulls were knocked to the ground, pulling themselves to their feet in a cloud of cinder and ash. The camera drones flitted through the haze, circling around until one of them finally managed a clean shot and flashed the image onto the screens above.

The Bull was dead, his armor ripped to shreds as he was roasted inside it. The crowd's cheering dropped into a shocked silence. No one had ever won before, and no one had ever even come close. Now one of the Bulls was dead on the arena floor, killed by a common criminal who lay there motionless beside him.

CHAPTER TWENTY-SEVEN

MEDEA COULD BARELY HOLD IN the tears. She'd let her hopes take hold of her, watching Jason face off against the four of them without so much as flinching. His confidence was infectious, and she'd started to believe he might pull it off in spite of the odds. Now he'd killed one of them, but at the cost of himself. There were hundreds of screens around the arena, and the image of him lying there on the ground assaulted her from every side.

Mopsus put a sympathetic hand on her shoulder, and she could feel tears streaking across her cheeks. He was saying something to her, but she couldn't make out what. It was meaningless sound, just like everything else around her. She couldn't focus on anything but the screens. He was down there, the man she'd started to fall for, lying in the dirt after he'd given everything to try to save her.

She could finally admit it to herself. Aphrodite had been right. Love had come, and she hadn't even seen it creeping up on her. She could feel it wrenching in her heart, pulling her apart inside and making her feel like something had been torn out of her. He'd been such an ass when he'd met her, but he'd always made her feel, and deeply. Antagonism had turned to love so slowly that she hadn't even noticed when the line had been crossed. She stood there in shock, thinking it all must be some cruel joke. The gods had promised her she'd find love; they hadn't told her it would be snatched away just as soon as she'd found it.

She stared at Jason up on the screens for what seemed like an eternity. She didn't snap out of it until the picture shifted, moving from Jason to a close-up of the three surviving Bulls.

She managed to blink and turn her head, looking over to the platform next to them. Aeetes was there, barking orders at the men beside him. He'd won the day, though he didn't seem happy about it. He'd lost one of his men, publicly, and any show of weakness was enough to send a warrior like him into a foul mood. But someone over there was pleased as punch. Circe stood behind him, smiling as broadly as she could and staring directly at Medea. She leaned over to one of the guards, whispered something into his ear, and he marched over to the railing and signaled to the guards standing beside Medea.

She felt the platform moving beneath her feet, edging closer to Aeetes's luxury box until their railings brushed against one another. "Get her over here," shouted the guard on the other platform, and Medea found herself grabbed roughly from behind. They dumped her over the railing, shoving her onto the other platform at Circe's feet. She could see the other Argonauts floating away and disappearing among all of the traffic, their platform whizzing away into the distance.

"Poor little fool," said Circe. She planted a pair of ice blue heels next to Medea's head, looking down on her from above. "You changed him, did you? No one jumps like that, no one who hasn't been worked over."

"He was the best," said Medea, choking on a sob. "The best warrior I've ever known."

"Clearly not," said Circe, a snide smile on her face. "Else how would he lose? Poor workmanship on his code, perhaps? I did a little work on the Bulls, and I still see most of them standing."

"You're such a bitch," said Medea. "You always have been." She wanted to reach up and punch her, but the guards would have stopped her before she'd started. Anger welled within her, and she thought back to the hyper-competitive girl she'd once known who'd cut at her classmates with every low insult she could think of. Circe had always been this way, and she always would be. And if there was ever a time to cut back, this was it.

"So mean to people back in the academy," said Medea. "No one could stand you. Not me, not anyone. We all tried to be nice. But you thought you were the queen bee. What are you queen of now? An empty house and an empty heart."

Circe's hair shifted to a volcanic red, and she leaned down and stared at Medea with eyes of magma. "You were never half the genomancer I was. Yet everyone loved you all the same. All I'd ever hear was Medea, Medea, Medea. I suppose that's easy, when you spend your time socializing instead of studying. I worked and worked, but everything just came to you. I was still the better of us, and yet you were the one they all doted on. But where did that get you in the end? Down on the floor, crying for a man who couldn't save you. Who couldn't even save himself."

"I helped people," said Medea. "I made them happy. I made myself happy. You're cold inside, and you always will be."

"Yet you've still lost, I'm afraid," said Circe. "Your champion is down in the dirt. You couldn't fix him, not well enough. They'll kill your friends, now that he's lost. And they would have killed you, too. But I intervened." She leaned down, snarling into Medea's ear. "I wanted you all to myself. To dispose of however I pleased. And now you're at my feet, and always will be."

"Just kill me, then," said Medea. If Jason was dead, and all the rest of them, too, she didn't see a reason to keep going. They'd never let her free. She'd never live how she wanted to live. She didn't want to be a prisoner, and she wasn't in the mood to beg for mercy.

"I won't be killing you, dear," said Circe. "I'll be keeping you. It was part of the deal." She looked over at Aeetes, glowering down at the field below, and gave him a sultry smile. "A trade. One we should complete, now that the show's ended."

Aeetes was still absorbed by the mess, but he beckoned towards Circe, calling her over even as he was snapping at guards right and left. She sauntered towards him, her hair shifting back to a seductive blonde.

"You have the Fleece," said Circe. "And now you have a weapon as well." She reached into her powder blue gown, pulling out a thin vial. It was filled to the brim with a green liquid goo, and she held it out to Aeetes. "It's done. Tested in the wild, and certain to please."

Aeetes tapped a finger against his sheath, opening up a waiting palm. "The payment's done. And the genomancer's yours, to do with as you please. So long as no one ever sees her again."

"They won't," said Circe. "At least not the way she looks now." She walked back to Medea, lifting her chin up with a finger. "I won't make you a pig. It doesn't become you. Something else, though. A tortoise, perhaps. Trapped within your shell where no one can touch you. Or maybe a squid. I'll keep you in a tank, and watch you swim alone forever. Thinking of nothing but him for the rest of your slimy days."

"You're so mean," said Medea. "All you care about is hurting people. Hurting anyone who has what you don't."

"Hurting the ones who hurt me," said Circe. "Genomancy just came to you without an ounce of work. You lorded it over the ones like me. The ones who had to slave away to learn it. I was always more of an artist than a scientist. People think genomancy is a practical profession. That there's no creativity in it. But I know how wrong they are. Once nature's bent to your will, you can speak through it. You can make things beautiful, or ugly, or anything in between. And you'll be my little art project, Medea. I'll change you however I please." Her hair turned to a blue as cold as her dress, and she flashed her teeth at Medea. "And I'm a very, very creative woman."

It sent chills down Medea's spine. She hadn't done anything to hurt Circe, not that she could remember. Everyone had been nice to her. Until she'd started snapping at them and trying to set herself up above them, that is. Maybe she'd just been insecure back then. Medea could understand that. Everyone had their doubts about themselves.

But Circe had pushed the blame for her problems onto everyone else, and now she wanted to make herself Medea's own personal torturer. She wasn't going to let that happen, not ever. She looked over the side of the platform, preparing to jump over the railing and force one of the Bulls to do her in. But her eye caught one of the vid screens, and what she saw stopped her in her tracks.

"He's moving," said Medea, tears in her eyes again. "He's moving."

"He's alive," said Aeetes into his microphone. His voice dripped with hostility, but the mask of an impartial announcer was back on in moments. "Alive, ladies and gentlemen! The match isn't over, not just yet. You'd never have gotten a show like this from any of the other corporations. But you signed with Colchis, and so you get to see!"

Medea looked down, hope rising within her. She couldn't tell if he was okay. His hands were pressed against the ground, and he struggled to lift himself to his feet. Even if he'd survived, it didn't mean he would for long. The other three Bulls were still alive, too, and they were approaching him from all sides. She felt so helpless. There was nothing she could do to help him, nothing she hadn't already done. She held her breath, said a little prayer to herself, and watched from above as he rose to face them.

CHAPTER TWENTY-EIGHT

JASON COUGHED, HIS EYES STINGING as soot blew against them. He couldn't see, and he could barely move. All he could remember was the fire exploding against him as he'd shoved the tubes from the flamethrower into the Bull's mouth. The sound was coming back, and he could hear cheers from all around the arena. He looked up, trying to find Medea somewhere in the crowd of platforms. He knew she had to be up there, somewhere, but he couldn't make anyone out.

No one but one of the Bronze Bulls, stomping towards him through the ash with a trident in hand.

Jason rolled over to the side, grabbing his sword from out of the dust. He flipped it upwards, and only just in time. The trident clanged against his sword, catching it between its prongs as the Bull tried to force them down his throat. Jason struggled to get to his feet, but the Bull was on top of him, kicking at him even as he pressed the trident down with all his power. The man was fast, unnaturally so. He had genetic changes of his own, and it was all Jason could do to keep up with him.

Then Jason did something, a move he didn't even recognize himself. It was some kind of flip of his sword, and the trident snapped away as he did it. The Bull barely kept hold of his weapon, and his body language showed his surprise at the sudden turn of fortune.

Jason was just as surprised as he was. It must have been one of Medea's martial arts techniques, buried down inside him somewhere. It had come just as naturally as any of the other moves he knew, the ones he'd practiced and practiced until they'd become virtually automatic. He could see why the warriors were so keen on genomancy. It would have taken him years to master the repertoire she'd managed to hand him in just minutes.

The Bull slammed his trident down again, and Jason parried the blow with a slash of his sword. The weapons tangled together, but this time Jason had planned another surprise, one that would end things for good. He pressed a button on the hilt of the sword, electrifying the blade and sending a surge through the trident and into the Bull's metallic armor. The man just stood there, his muscles locked into place by the power flowing through him. It gave Jason time to stand, and time to make another strike.

He could see one of the other Bulls charging towards him, launching a fireball from out of his helmet as he ran. But Jason just ignored it. Medea had neutralized that little trick, and the Bulls could try it all they liked. He felt the heat surround him as he jabbed his sword into the Bull's neck. It pierced the armor, barely. But it was enough, and with another jolt of electricity the Bull fell to the ground lifeless, smoke sizzling all across his armor.

Jason turned to face another of the Bulls, approaching him with spear in hand. But something felt wrong, very wrong. He didn't know why, but he ducked his head down just a few inches lower. He felt a gust whoosh past his hair, and he heard a thud behind him. He glanced aside to see a silver arrow lodged in the ash, and even as he did he felt an overpowering urge to roll over on his side.

It was almost like Medea was talking to him as he fought, whispering the future to him through his subconscious instincts. He knew the only way to survive was to listen. He followed his feelings, and they guided him true. Another arrow hit the ground, and then another, but he weaved through them all without even a thought.

This must have been what it was like for Tiphys when he was piloting the ARGO. No thinking, no planning, just acting on instinct and following it wherever it led you. His own reflexes had always been good, but never this good. Whatever Medea had done, she'd done it well, and he danced through a hail of arrows as the last two surviving Bulls circled around him.

He didn't have a clue how he was going to make it out. He was trapped between them, and they'd grown more cautious now that two of their comrades had fallen. If he went after one, the other would come at him from behind. There didn't seem to be any hope. He was goaded on one side by the spear, and driven on the other by the bow. It was two against one, and they were working him, tiring him out as they forced him to dodge arrow after arrow.

And he couldn't help himself from sneaking glances up above, searching for her amid the stream of platforms. He didn't know where she was, and it was tearing him apart inside. He was in the middle of a fight for his life, and all he could think about was whether she was safe. He couldn't help himself from obsessing over thoughts of what could be happening to her, and what he could do to stop it.

It was something he'd learned long ago in his training. Danger never came by itself. It brought clarity along with it, wiping away the things that didn't matter and focusing him on the things that did. And when all the other things fell away, he found himself caring about one thing and one thing only: staying alive long enough to get Medea safely back home.

He was trapped in a standoff, and he couldn't see a way to win. But he had to do something, and he had to do it soon. He steeled himself for a last stand, watching the two Bulls as they moved to see which one would make the better target. Then he heard a sound from behind him: a soft, crackling noise that grew louder and louder until it ended in a roaring pop. Clouds of ash sprayed over his head through the air, and the Bull he was facing raised his arm to shield his eyes from the dust.

"Holy shit," said the Bull. He stood paralyzed, staring in awe at something in the distance. "What in the hell are those?" Jason turned to look, and then he felt astonishment himself.

There were a dozen of them, one for every seed he'd dropped. They looked like spindly green men, swaying back and forth as they slowly found their footing. Jason squinted, trying to get a better look through the ash. They were some kind of plant, or at least he thought they were. Their limbs were thin, and their fingers and toes branched out into long, pointy tips. They had faces, but just the outline of them. Their mouths hung open, thick green tongues flicking around inside as they all let out a baleful moan in unison. And the more he stared at them, the more he noticed something else: what faces they had looked distinctly like his own.

The Bull in front of him started shouting orders across the arena as the creatures lumbered towards him. "Flank left! Flank—"

His shouts were cut off by a hand around his waist. One of the creatures had grabbed him, its fingers growing impossibly fast. They wrapped around the man's midsection, again and again, cocooning him in a thicket of green tendrils. He hacked at them with his spear, but for every one he lopped away, another grew in its place. The creature lifted him into the air, struggling and kicking. Its feet rooted into the ash beneath it, spreading in all directions and sucking up nutrients from below to fuel its surge in size. Soon the Bull was covered entirely in leafy green vines, struggling like a spider's victim wrapped away in silk, until he slowly quit moving entirely.

Jason made ready with his sword, weighing it in his hand and preparing to slash away at the monsters Medea had unleashed. But they didn't even acknowledge him. One of them strolled past, coming within a few feet of him, but it just headed on towards the last surviving Bull as if Jason wasn't even there.

The last of the Bulls darted this way and that, running around the arena to try to escape the army of creatures approaching him. He picked up a molten rock from the arena floor, tossing it into the middle of them. It distracted a few, and they fell upon the spot where it had landed, tearing at the ground and ripping away at each other in confusion. The Bull managed to loose a few more arrows in their direction, but it didn't do much to damage the creatures. The arrows simply stuck in their sides, sending out trickles of oozing green liquid without slowing them down a bit.

The Bull ran back towards the arena's entrance, but he found himself cornered, surrounded by hulking plants stretching their tendrils out towards him. As he disappeared into a green cocoon of his own, everything around him exploded in flame. He'd turned on his flamethrower, trying to break himself free, but there was no way out. The plants all lit up, digging their burning fingers into the Bull's armor and consuming him with the fire he'd unleashed.

The entire arena was in a state of shock. Everyone around had fallen silent, and even Aeetes had nothing to say. Then a sound rose from part of the crowd, muffled and indistinct at first. It spread along the sides of the arena like wildfire until it boomed through the globe from every side. He could make out one word, one word the crowd was shouting over and over. "Jason." They were chanting his name. He'd won, and now the people who'd wanted him dead just minutes before were chanting his name.

He welled with emotion, staring out at the sea of people. It had been his dream, and now it was real. His father had never recognized what he'd accomplished. His mother had died before she could. He'd done the impossible and now they were all celebrating the victory, rooting for the underdog even though they'd been told he was their enemy. He'd fought for his life, and he'd fought for the lives of the ones he cared about. And because of it he was what he'd always wanted to be: the hero of a city, even if it wasn't his own. It made all the struggle worth it, and it salved the wounds from years of trying to separate himself from his father. He was his own man now, and no one could take that away from him.

The crowd may have loved him, but Aeetes and his men were paralyzed with shock. There was something more important than any glory, and Jason knew he had to take advantage of the moment while he could. He looked up above him, still trying to find Medea. He couldn't see her, but he recognized someone else: Antaeus, towering over the others on one of the platforms, a giant brown ball of fur that was impossible to miss.

That was where she'd be, and so that was where he was going. There was only one way up, and that was to jump. He had no idea if he'd make it. He didn't have a feel for himself anymore, not after the genomancy. Training the old way gave him a perfect understanding of his own abilities; genomancy had made everything a crapshoot. The only thing to do now was to try.

He backed away and took a running start, launching himself through the air as high as he could. That was too much; he nearly overshot the platform, leaping over the top of it and catching the railing with one hand as he passed down the opposite side. He pulled himself up to see two very frightened guards swinging away at him with their batons.

"Get off," growled Jason, and after a moment's hesitation and a look in his eyes the guards both leapt over the side. The ash below guaranteed a soft landing, and it was far less dangerous than an angry Argonaut who'd just massacred the four best warriors in the city.

Jason looked around the platform. Idas and Antaeus were there, though they didn't seem to take a bit of pleasure in his victory. Tiphys nearly hugged him, and Mopsus just ran around on the floor of the platform in a hyperactive series of loops. But the person he really cared about wasn't there. It nearly made him snap. He could feel a fury rising inside him, and he knew he wouldn't have control of himself for much longer. If they'd hurt her, he wouldn't be able to keep it together. If they'd hurt her, Aeetes was a dead man, and so was everyone who served him.

"Where's Medea?" said Jason. "Where the hell is she?"

"Over there," said Tiphys. He pointed towards Aeetes's luxury barge, floating in a lazy circle above the fallen Bulls. It was a few stories higher up, but Jason caught a glimpse of Medea waving her arms and trying to catch his attention. He waved back, and then racked his brain for some way to get up there and help her.

It was too far away; he knew he'd never be able to jump his way to it. He leaned over the side of the railing, trying to decide if he could hop across a few dozen of the other platforms and make it up to where they were holding her. It might work, if he could time things just right, and if the other platforms all moved the right way. But then his anger cooled, and he remembered his plan. He couldn't just get her away from Aeetes. He had to get her out of the arena and out of the city, and he had to do it now.

"Tiphys!" said Jason. "Tiphys, get the ARGO! Call it back!"

"It's too loud!" said Tiphys. He put his fingers to his lips, whistling again and again. He peered up at the hole in the roof of the arena, cupping his hands to his mouth and trying another whistle. "I can't find it. It's up there, somewhere. But all the cheering. There's so much sound. I can't see anything in my head. Just a big blur."

"Hold on, and hold on tight," said Jason. "We're going up." He jabbed his sword at a panel on the platform, slamming against it again and again. The panel snapped free, revealing a thicket of wires and circuitry beneath. "Gravity controls. Get ready, because I'm turning them off."

He grabbed one of the wires, a thick blue cable running across the center, pulling it until it snapped. Sparks burst out of the panel, and the platform shook beneath their feet. They all clutched the railing, holding on for dear life. All except for poor Mopsus, who tumbled back and forth along the floor as the platform heaved, turning almost on its side before they could feel a heavy rumbling beneath them.

"Oh my god," said Tiphys. "Oh my god."

The platform started to rise, higher and higher. They could hear clanging noises, and a shiny metal streak whizzed past Jason's head. He looked down, and he knew what it was at once. Javelins. There were Colchian warriors assembling on the floor below. They weren't brave enough to use firearms, not with how many cameras were hovering around. But javelins were less frightening to the public, and one of them would get off a lucky shot sooner or later. He knew they had to find the ARGO, and they had to find it fast.

"Just whistle," said Jason. "Just keep whistling until you can see."

"Do it," said Idas, his arms wrapped tightly around the railing. "Do anything!"

Tiphys puckered his lips, whistling as loud as he could. He was too terrified to take his arms away from the railing, and he couldn't even keep his eyes open for more than a moment. "I can see some of the drones. But not the ARGO. Maybe it's not here. Maybe it's all the way across the city. I'll never find it."

"It's circling the city," said Jason. "It's got to pass by sooner or later. Just hold on and keep at it."

They were nearly to the top of the globe. The platform was at the center, and if they went much higher they'd float through the hole in the arena's ceiling and off into the clouds above. But as they went up, the noise of the crowd around them faded away. The arena's sound systems weren't designed for the interests of those few stakeholders strapped to the underside of the dome, and the higher they went, the more Tiphys's whistles cut through the dampened sound.

"There," said Tiphys. He looked completely thrilled, and his whistling grew more frantic until he started jumping and pointing towards the sky. "There!"

Jason put a hand to his eyes, blocking out the arena's lights, and then he could see it. The ARGO, barreling towards them in a falcon's dive. It plunged through the opening in the arena's ceiling, stopping just above them with its door open. The ARGO nudged against the platform, and Jason lifted a squealing Mopsus under one arm and Hecate under the other.

"Everyone inside," said Jason. "We're going to go get Medea. And then we're going to take back the Golden Fleece."

CHAPTER TWENTY-NINE

THE CROWD WAS IN A panic. People everywhere rushed towards the exits, and platforms landed all across the arena as men and women disembarked into the ash. The Colchis Corporation had shown weakness, and its enemies were zipping around above them in what looked like one of their own cargo drones. No one wanted to stay to see what would happen now that the best of the city had fallen on their faces in the dirt.

Jason stood in the ARGO's doorway, shouting orders up at Tiphys as he maneuvered it around the sea of platforms below. "Down! Get us down! Close enough for me to jump!"

"Hold on!" shouted Tiphys. "I can see, but I can't see. Like, I have to use my eyes instead of the sound. Too much noise."

The ARGO dropped into a dive, weaving past platform after platform. Panicked employees gripped the railings of their barges, and the ARGO's wings smacked against a platform full of Colchian soldiers, upending it and sending them all tumbling to the ground. But the ARGO just shuddered and kept going, headed straight for Aeetes's barge at the center of the arena.

"She's there," said Jason. "Just get us close."

The ARGO flapped nearer and nearer, still dozens of stories above Aeetes's luxury barge. But Jason didn't wait. He saw Medea down there, surrounded by guards heaving javelins up at him. Her face was contorted in fear, though whether for him or for herself he couldn't tell. But pain was pain, and seeing her in the grips of it made something inside him roar. He couldn't bear to watch her suffering, and he wasn't going to wait around while she did. He steeled himself, tightened his hand around his sword, and took a running leap out of the side of the ship.

He plummeted downward, faster and faster, and before he had time to think his feet crashed into the platform below. He didn't even feel it. Whatever she'd done to his muscles and to his legs had cushioned his fall, and the guards on the platform stepped backwards in shock that he'd survived.

He was on them before they could react. He could have killed them all in a few seconds, and there was enough rage inside him that they were lucky he didn't. But he knew what being a warrior meant: they'd all been assigned to their duties, and few of them cared one way or the other about his fight with Aeetes. He tested out his newfound martial techniques instead, knocking away at the guards with the blunt side of his sword until all of them lay unconscious on the ground.

Only Aeetes and Circe were left standing. She backed away behind him, shying from the battle as her hair turned a pure, frightened white. Aeetes didn't move. He was a warrior, too, and Jason knew he'd never openly show weakness even if the fight was a losing one.

"Jason," said Aeetes, a broad smile on his face and his arms open wide. "The hero of the hour. I never thought you'd win. Never, ever. But here we are. You beat the odds, and beat the Bulls."

"Aeetes," said Jason. "The man with the stolen Fleece. The man who'd kill a girl he doesn't even know just because he can."

"I told you I'd give it to you," said Aeetes. "And it's yours. Fair and square." He smiled at Medea, tugging nervously at his beard. "And her, too. I won't stop you. The Fleece is right up there." He pointed to one of the other platforms, floating a few stories above them. "Take her, and take it. They're yours, by right of victory."

"By right of might," said Jason. "You couldn't stop me, even if you wanted to." The ARGO slowly descended behind him, its door aligned with the platform's railing, and he waved for Medea to come to his side. "And if either of you interfere with us, I'll come back and make you regret it."

"We're not leaving yet," said Medea. "He's got something else. Circe's weapon. We can't let them keep it."

"You're such a fool," said Circe. "I'd just recreate it." She tapped a finger on her forehead. "I've got the design, right up here, and you can never take it from me."

"And I'll have made a cure by the time you do," said Medea. "Everyone will know what's coming once we get back to Argos. We'll be ready before you're even halfway done."

"This wasn't the deal," said Aeetes. "You're a warrior. Don't you have any honor? Don't you keep your bargains? The Fleece and your friends. That's what you got if you won. This weapon has nothing to do with it."

"We've got a different deal now," said Jason, pressing a button on his sword and lighting it up with electricity. "There's no honor in a bargain made at the point of a sword." He turned off the electricity and jabbed the tip of the sword through the middle of Aeetes's beard, holding it at his throat. "And if you think there is, then I'm striking a bargain of my own. Your life for Circe's weapon."

"A fair deal, a fair deal," said Aeetes hastily. He reached into his suit jacket, pulling out the vial Circe had handed him and holding it up in the air. Medea snatched it from his hand, tucking it safely away in her belt.

"Be smart, Circe," said Jason. "Just disappear. Find a new career and stay the hell away from other people's genes. The Big Five won't tolerate this kind of thing, and I'm going to make damned sure they all know about it. Build another weapon, and you'll end up rotting away in some corporate dungeon, or worse."

"Disappear," said Circe. She stepped towards Jason, her hair turning from white to platinum blonde. "Would you really want me to?" She glided to his side, leaning an arm on the railing and running a hand under his chin. "I saw the way you looked at me. And I know genomancers are your type."

Her lips seemed to grow fuller as she spoke, and she posed before Jason to accentuate her every curve. "A woman who can look however she wants, whenever she wants. I could be a different woman for you every night. I could be everything you ever fantasized about. The best warrior on the planet deserves the best genomancer. We'd be the ultimate power couple. And I promise that when you see what I have to offer, you'll never give *her* another thought."

Circe was so focused on him, she didn't even notice what was coming from behind. Jason did, but he wasn't telling. She was beautiful, and he wouldn't deny that. At least on the outside. But all the seductive powers in the world couldn't make him look past the nastiness inside her. The jealousy was so petty, and he wasn't sure why she thought he'd have any interest at all in trading someone he cared about for someone who didn't care about anyone but herself. She might think she knew everything there was to know about how people worked, but she didn't know a thing about him.

As far as he was concerned, Circe was about to get exactly what she deserved. He locked eyes with her, keeping her attention entirely focused on him and trying to distract her from what was coming. He wanted to smile, and badly, but he managed to suppress it until Medea had snuck up directly behind her.

Circe was off balance, teetering on her heels as she worked at tempting Jason with every trick she knew. Her eyes popped wide and she let out a scream of surprise as Medea shoved her from behind, tipping her over the side of the railing and sending her tumbling down to the arena floor. Medea looked at Jason with a very satisfied smile.

"I've been wanting to do something like that for years," said Medea. "I just wish everyone she bullied back in the academy could have seen it."

"They probably will," said Jason. "It's all streaming live on the vids." He gave her a quick kiss, and whispered into her ear. "And by the way, she more than earned it. You're mine, and she's a fool if she thought I'd ever let you go."

He leaned over the railing to see Circe lying down there in a pile of ash, covered in black soot from head to toe. Her dress was ruined, and whatever color her hair had shifted to underneath, the ash had made it black as night. Her face was a mess, and she looked as ugly on the outside as she'd always been underneath. Camera drones swarmed all around her, broadcasting her moment of embarrassment for all the city to see. She struggled to her feet, one of her heels snapping as she did and sending her tumbling face first into the ash again. She might have survived the battle, but she'd never live the moment down.

He looked up to see the ARGO nudging against the railing of the platform, the door on its side wide open. He held Medea's hand and helped her through it, making sure she was safely inside, and then he turned to Aeetes with a growl. "We're taking back the Fleece. And I can be a real son of a bitch to someone who comes after the people I care about. Be smart. Don't follow us. Don't interfere. Don't do a thing."

"I wouldn't dream of it," said Aeetes. Jason didn't believe him, not for a moment. But he didn't have any more time to deal with him, and it wouldn't have mattered if he had. There were hundreds of cronies beneath Aeetes just waiting to replace him, and none of them were any different. Cut one head off and another would grow back, just as vicious as the first.

"Tiphys!" shouted Jason as he climbed inside the ship. "Take us up!" He waved a hand at Medea, ordering her up the ladder and into the cockpit. "Show him the right platform. The one with the Fleece. I'm going to grab it, and then we're getting the hell out of here." She didn't even hesitate; she just followed his command and scrambled up to help Tiphys find his way through the maze of floating spectators.

The ARGO slowly rose, and soon Jason could see it. The Golden Fleece, lying just a dozen feet away in the middle of a platform all its own. The ship leveled off and the Fleece beckoned from just a few feet away, the golden strands within glistening under the lights of the arena. He climbed over the railing and onto the platform, taking a step towards it and reaching out for the ram's horns that made up the Fleece's handle. But as he did he felt something, something brushing against his leg.

His eyes flashed down to see a lime green serpent coiling around his thigh. The thing had been hiding on the platform, tucked away in the sides and guarding the Fleece from anyone who came to claim it. It looked like a snake, though not like any he'd ever seen before. It had three heads, splitting out from its trunk and stretching towards him. Each head bared its fangs, and they all let out an angry, unified hiss. Jason reached for his sword, but the snake moved faster.

First it struck from the left, one of the heads snapping forward, its fangs dripping with venom. He didn't have time to think. He just grabbed it by the neck, holding it away from him as it struggled against his grip. At least the reflexes Medea had given him were still working. But the snake was fast, and some genomancer had given it enhanced reflexes of its own. The right head struck while Jason was struggling to hold on to the other one, pouncing at him and aiming for his side. His arm whipped out before he knew what had happened, latching onto it and choking off a stillborn hiss.

He was out of arms, but the snake wasn't out of heads. The middle one was left free, slowly bobbing from side to side in front of Jason's face, flicking out its tongue as it went. He tried to push the snake away from him, holding the other heads at arm's length. But it was still wrapped tightly around his leg, and he couldn't push it out of range, not without letting go of the other heads and leaving them free to attack him again. He couldn't get the snake out of striking distance, and he couldn't get away. The middle head seemed to know it, lunging forward and missing his ear by inches as he lurched his own head to the side to dodge the attack.

The snake struck again and again, snapping its jaws in the air as he weaved between blows like a boxer. But he knew he couldn't dodge forever. The snake was too close, and eventually it would connect somewhere and dump its venom into his veins. He felt its grip around his thigh constricting, and his foot started to throb in pain as the blood flow cut off. Then his leg gave way beneath him and he tumbled to the ground, clutching the snake's heads for dear life.

There was nowhere to go. The snake loomed over him, helpless and exposed. It wrenched itself free from his grip, the three heads rearing up and preparing to strike. Then suddenly the snake's heads all began to swoon at once, their eyes dimming and their tongues dangling limp from their mouths. They slumped down on top of him in unison, trapping him beneath their sluggish and barely breathing body.

Jason pushed the snake aside, rolling out from underneath it. He looked up to see Medea standing there, tears in her eyes and her dagger in her hand. She was shaking, and he jumped to his feet, pulling her fingers away from the dagger and taking her into the safety of his arms.

"I didn't know what to do," said Medea. "I just hit it. I thought it was going to kill you. I thought I lost you to the Bulls. And then to this thing." She shivered, and wrapped herself inside his embrace. "It hurt so much inside. I could barely take it."

He looked down at the snake, its tongues slowly flickering and its eyes moving lazily back and forth. "It's asleep. The dagger." He took it from her hands and held it up, a blue fluid dripping from its tip. "It's got something in it. Some kind of nerve agent. I think you put it to sleep." He helped her into the ship again, keeping himself between her and the snake. Then he grabbed the Fleece, clambered over the railing and into the ship, and slid the door shut behind him.

The ARGO climbed towards the sky, wings flapping furiously as platforms full of guards rose after them. The Colchians had given up on subtlety, and given up the pretense of law: the guards carried shoulder-fired rocket launchers, weapons that shouldn't have been allowed inside the city if the rules as the people knew them were being followed. The camera drones had all disappeared, a blackout of the fiasco that ensured that all coverage of the events could be edited later on to Aeetes's liking.

"Jason!" shouted a panicky Tiphys from the cockpit. "Jason, get up here! Get everyone in their seats!"

Jason scrambled up the ladder into the cockpit, strapping in beside him. "What? We need to go. And we need to do it while we still can."

"I'm trying," said Tiphys. "But they're shooting at us."

He pointed out the cockpit window at a line of smoke streaming past them: a rocket, zooming upwards through the opening at the top of the globe. More followed, a volley of fire aimed at taking down the ARGO whatever the cost. A blast rattled the ship from the side, and then more shook the air ahead of them as rocket after rocket collided with the dome above. They could see explosions among the cheap seats, sending scores of spectators tumbling down to the ground as rockets missed their target and hit the stakeholders instead.

"I've got this," said Tiphys, closing his eyes. "I've got this. I've got this."

The ARGO twisted and turned, looping through the air as Tiphys piloted on faith and the talent Medea had written into him. Platforms careened in front of them, but he dodged them with ease. Rockets came within inches of them, but none of them could even graze the ship. Tiphys weaved them upwards through the traffic until they shot out of the globe and into a swarm of drones zipping through the skies above.

"Get us out of the city," ordered Jason. "Now."

"How?" said Tiphys. "We can't go up. The defenses. They'll shoot us down. And we can't go back through the wall. There'll be another one of those traps."

"We have to find a tunnel," said Jason. "There isn't any other way. You did it once. You can do it again."

"Please," said Tiphys. "I can't." He sat on the edge of his chair, bustling with nervous energy. He was on the edge of a breakdown; his fingers tapped against the console like it was a piano, and he kept running a hand through his hair, mussing it up into a wild mess.

"Tiphys," said Jason. "I just faced down four of the best warriors in the world and killed them all. I never could have done that with training alone. She wrote my code, and she wrote yours, too. It's the best. And you're a good pilot. I'm trusting you. I'm counting on you. There isn't any other way out."

"We're all going to die," muttered Tiphys to himself. He still looked nervous, jittering and shaking with manic energy. But he started pushing buttons again, his eyes fixed on the panels in front of him with newfound focus and determination.

"Just get us to the walls before they figure it out and shut the tunnels manually," said Jason. "Everything's gone crazy down there. But they'll pull it together soon. We've got a few minutes, tops. So go."

"Minutes," said Tiphys. They could see the city walls ahead of them, a kaleidoscope of colors reflecting off the pearl from the surrounding buildings. There were tunnels ahead, dozens of them bored through the wall, and most of them had their entrances sealed shut. But they could see one of them open and in use, a line of cargo drones passing through it on their way outside the city.

"Jump the line," said Jason. "Knock one of those drones out of the way if you have to. But get us in there before the walls start to close."

"They're not the problem," said Tiphys. "Them I can handle. The problem's behind us." He tapped at a monitor in front of him, and on the screen Jason could see the view from the rear. Dozens of hunter drones were converging on them, the same kind they'd confronted outside the city. And these drones knew exactly where they were.

"How the hell did they find us?" said Jason. "We're supposed to be stealthed."

"We are," said Tiphys. "But we just flashed ourselves in front of the entire city. The people know what this ship is, even if the drones don't. Someone's got to be piloting them from the ground. Someone took control."

An explosion rocked the air around them, and Tiphys sent the ARGO into a spiral maneuver, dodging a missile as it roared past. He shoved a lever forward and the ship accelerated, barreling towards the line of drones in front of them. "Hold on. Everybody hold on. I'm going to try something. And then we're going past them."

"We won't fit," said Jason. He eyed the cargo drones ahead of them warily, slowly floating through the center of the tunnel one by one. There wasn't enough space around them, not to fly past. They'd have to get in line, and they'd have to wait. And that meant they'd be sitting ducks for the hunter drones behind them.

"Just strap in," said Tiphys. "Just strap in and pray." He pulled a microphone down from above him, whistling sharply into it. Sound blared out of the ARGO and into the tunnel ahead of them, bombarding the cargo drones with his whistles. At first, nothing happened. The cargo drones just inched forward, none of them paying any mind to Tiphys's call. The ARGO pulled into the back of the line, hovering in place as the drones ahead of it slowly crawled inside.

"We need to move," said Jason, eying the monitors. The hunter drones were closing in from behind, and if they waited much longer, they'd be blown apart by the missiles. "We need to go through. Ram them if you have to, but we need to go."

"Just wait," said Tiphys. "And watch."

The drone in front of them edged into the tunnel, but it didn't stay in the center. Instead it bobbed sharply to the side, grinding against the wall and leaving half of the tunnel free for them to pass. Drone after drone ahead of it did the same, and soon they had an empty path ahead of them, the cargo drones all huddling against one side of the tunnel and leaving the rest of it free.

"I showed them the walls," said Tiphys. "Closing in from one side. They're all maneuvering to the other side of the tunnel to avoid it. They get one half, we get the other."

He jammed the control stick forward and turned on the afterburners, rocketing ahead of the line of cargo drones. They could see the hunter drones popping into the tunnel far behind them, following the path they'd cleared. But Tiphys just smiled and broadcast another whistle. The cargo drones swung to the other side of the tunnel in unison, slamming against the hunters and knocking them away in a tangle of metal.

The ARGO escaped both the tunnel and the city, the walls beginning to shake and close in the distance behind them. Jason sighed in relief, climbing down the cockpit ladder and back into the cargo pod. He headed to the opposite side, past the others and towards Medea. She was standing there waiting, a look of apprehension on her face.

"Tiphys got us out," said Jason. "He's on a course back to Argos. They won't catch us, not now. We're too far away to intercept, and he's flying too fast."

"We're safe," said Medea. "I thought they were going to kill us, so many times." She leaned into Jason for a hug, burying her head in his shoulder. He held her there, shielding her from her worries as the minutes passed. Finally she looked up at him with a contented smile. "You did it. You won, and you got us out. We made it, and we're finally safe."

"We're safe," came a voice from behind them. "You? The party's just getting started for you."

Idas was standing there, grinning and holding a wriggling Mopsus by the leg. His spear was pointed at Mopsus's head, and he tapped a button on it, sending the tip spinning. Antaeus was beside him, his claws wrapped around Tiphys's neck. Tiphys had gone limp, leaning into the furry behemoth behind him and trying not to do anything that would set him off.

"I'm sorry," said Tiphys. "I was just closing my eyes. Just for a second. They came up behind me and they got me."

"Hrock," said Antaeus, and then he snapped his jaws open wide and let out an angry roar. It reverberated around the inside of the ARGO, ringing in their ears from all around and covering Tiphys in flecks of spittle.

"He says shut your mouth, and do whatever we say," said Idas. "That's the gist of it, anyway."

"Hurg," said Antaeus firmly.

"The hell we will," said Jason. He stepped forward and to the side, placing Medea behind him. His hand went to his waist, his fingers tapping against the handle of his sword. "You won't even make me break a sweat."

"Try it," said Idas. "And I'll send this little piggy to market as a side of ham." He jabbed the tip of the spear against the edge of one of Mopsus's ears, cutting into the side and sending a trickle of blood running down it. Mopsus cried out in terror, kicking and oinking and doing his best to raise a fuss. Idas pulled the spear away and gave Jason a smug smile. "Don't even ask what Antaeus is going to do to your friend if you piss him off. You're good. I'll give you that. But you're not good enough to stop us from killing the two of them before you make it over here."

"I'm better than you can imagine," said Jason. "I just took out the best of Colchis. The two of you are nothing. You're just the only warriors Pelias thought were expendable enough to get rid of."

Idas's expression turned to a fearsome scowl. "Once, maybe. But plans change." He held up his sheath, a message flashing across it. "Pelias wants you two. He wants you bad. And he's willing to pay a hell of a lot to get you."

"He'll betray you, too," said Jason. "There's no honor among thieves. He'll get what he wants, and then he'll toss you in the trash."

"Shut the fuck up and get down on your knees," said Idas. Jason didn't move, and Idas slashed the drill across Mopsus's other ear, prompting another round of loud squealing. "Do it, damn it, or the next one takes off his head!"

"Promise me you won't hurt any of them," said Jason, his hands moving up into the air. "Promise me you'll leave them alone."

"We won't be hurting anyone," said Idas. "We told Pelias he'd get you all intact. What he does with you once you're delivered, that's on him. Now turn around, get on the ground, and shut your mouth while your doofy little friend flies us back home."

CHAPTER THIRTY

THE ARGO FLAPPED BACK DOWN into its hangar, just outside of Argos. They'd made it home, but they hadn't made it to safety. Dozens of hand-picked soldiers were arrayed in formation inside, and Pelias stood at the head of them. The soldiers encircled the ship as it landed, guns drawn and primed for a fight.

Medea stood inside the ship, watching Idas pace around behind the doorway, a spear in one hand and the Golden Fleece in the other. He'd gloated and boasted for the entire trip, and now his moment of triumph had arrived. For her, it was the lowest point of her life. They'd survived danger after danger, and they'd come so close to doing the impossible, only to have it snatched away at the end. And all so one of the warriors could steal the credit. It was typical of her life, and typical of the way things worked in Argos.

The door on the cargo pod slid open to reveal Pelias, with Amphion and a row of soldiers behind him. Idas sauntered outside, displaying both the Fleece and the grin of a victor. "The heroes have returned. And we come bearing gifts." He tapped the ground loudly with the butt of his spear, and Antaeus prodded them all out of the ship with a series of growls. Medea stumbled out, catching herself before she tripped: they'd bound her hands, as well as Jason's, and it made it hard to keep her balance. Mopsus trotted along after them, and Antaeus lumbered out with his hand on Tiphys's shoulder, his claws gripped tightly around it.

"Three prisoners," said Idas. He gestured towards Mopsus, cowering behind Jason and oinking softly in protest. "And a sausage thrown in for free." The soldiers rushed around them, putting guns at their backs as Pelias strolled forward to meet them.

"Jason and Medea," said Pelias. "I'd say it was a pleasure, but it really isn't." He scowled at Amphion, hovering close behind him. "We consulted the best seers in Argos, and not a one of them thought you'd ever make it back. Sheer incompetence, but I was just as surprised as they were. How a brand new warrior managed to complete this kind of mission his first time out I'll never know."

"He had help," grunted Idas. "He'd never have survived if it weren't for us. He didn't even know what he was doing half the time."

"I'm sure," said Pelias curtly, his voice dripping with sarcasm. "And I'm ever so thankful. You've been such a help, you really have."

"If you didn't want this asshole coming back, you should have just said so," said Idas. "And you shouldn't have sent the two best warriors in the city along with him." He lifted up the Fleece, dangling it just out of Pelias's reach. "We did better than just make it home. We brought you back the ultimate prize. The one you thought you'd never see again."

"The Fleece," said Pelias. He nodded towards one of the soldiers, who reached out for the handle. But Idas pulled it away, waving a finger at him in reprimand.

"We want shares," said Idas. "One for each of us. And we want interviews on all the prime vid feeds. Every single one."

"Phmpf," said Antaeus. He balled his fists in frustration, his face scrunching up until it looked like he was about to roar, and then he tried again. "Phmp. Fame."

"It's yours, as long as you manage to keep quiet," said Pelias. "You can each have your own channel, as far as I'm concerned. Corporate funded, and corporate marketed. You nearly fucked up this mission by helping these idiots. But be good little boys and we'll give you everything your hearts desire." He waved dismissively at the two of them, turning his attention to the prisoners. "Now get along. And forget what happened. Forget you were ever here."

"We'll get you the official version of your mission tomorrow," said Amphion, walking them out of the hangar. "Memorize it. And don't deviate from it. Not even by a word."

"As long as we're heroes," said Idas. He flashed a final smile at Jason and Medea before he passed outside. "Goodbye, you smug prick. And you too, you egghead bitch. Not so smart now, are you?"

"Go to hell," said Medea. "And tell your brother I said hello." It was probably the last thing she'd ever say to him, but it still felt good. She was the only chance his brother had, and Idas was just tossing family aside for fame and fortune.

Idas's nostrils flared, and he looked like he was about to charge back inside and slice away at her with his spear. But the soldiers around him stood firm, and he managed to get control of himself. "I've got a fortune now, honey. He'll get the best care money can buy. Not some no talent hack who can barely string a line of code together."

The soldiers whisked him away with Antaeus, the both of them laughing all the while. It was completely foolish, in her view. No other genomancer would be able to come up with a cure, not without having seen Circe's weapon in action. But Idas had his priorities, and his brother wasn't one of them.

"And now to my prizes," said Pelias. He sauntered over to Jason, standing in safety a few feet away. "Or prize, I should say. I only ever cared what happened to one of you."

"You sent us off to die," said Jason. "All of us."

"That's just the way of the world," said Pelias. "Business is cutthroat at the top, and sometimes you've got to cut some throats to get what you want. Aeson must not have told you that. But he was a shitty father, from what I hear. Still, I liked him. I liked him a lot. Very pliable, and very stupid. Everything management could want in a shareholder."

"But now I'm back," said Jason. "And those shares are mine again. I survived, and the trust is void."

"You survived?" said Pelias with a smirk. "That's not what I heard. Amphion, show him what we heard."

"It was a tragedy," said Amphion. He held up a tablet and showed them the images flashing across it: a looping vid of the ARGO being shot down by the Colchian air defense network, exploding into pieces in the middle of its escape. "A band of warriors from Argos, cut down in their prime while doing their duty for the city. It's all over the Colchian vid feeds. They're reporting it as a foreign incursion. We'll spin it differently, of course. You would have liked what we've come up with. A funeral parade and everything."

Medea watched the explosion, running again and again on the news vids from both Colchis and Argos. It hadn't taken them long to concoct an official version. And the implications made her shudder. Colchis couldn't let them be seen in public again, and neither could Argos. They couldn't let her live even if they'd wanted to, not with what they'd told the people. The more she thought about it, the more she knew there was no way any of them were getting out of this alive.

"It's not all bad," said Pelias. He leaned in towards Jason, a smug look on his face. "You wanted to be a hero. And now you will be. People will tell stories about you. You were nothing, you know. Just a nobody warrior rotting away in a dustbin. But we'll make you something else. Something we can profit from. Action figures, cartoons, the whole damned thing. And maybe you'll be a legend someday. Everything acquires a veneer of class, if you just give it enough time. From comic book to literature, and all it takes is a thousand years of mold."

"You son of a bitch," said Jason. He pulled against the guards, lunging towards Pelias as they dragged him back. "You want a fight with me, have a fight with me. Leave the rest of them alone."

"The rest of them?" Pelias wandered over to Medea, running his hand under her chin. It made her cringe, feeling him touch her and looking into his eyes. They were cold, and yet wild at the same time. There was something off about them. She couldn't figure out what it was, but then it hit her. Drugs. His pupils were cycling back and forth between giant disks and tiny little dots. He was on something, though she couldn't exactly tell what. Some kind of designer stimulant, probably. They made people entirely unpredictable, and that meant he was more dangerous than ever. He kept staring at her, cocking his head, until finally he turned back to Jason.

"I know who you really care about," said Pelias. "And if it makes you feel any better, I don't actually care about killing either one of you. Not really. But I need your shares. I'm tired of having to live my life on the edge. Always watching my back, always fighting to survive every time there's a management vote. Add your shares to the ones I've got locked up, and I've got a majority. A permanent one. The two of you have to go to make that happen. It's sad, but that's that."

"You don't need her," said Jason. "You don't need to. You can take my shares. Just don't kill her."

"I already have them," said Pelias. "And there's another little problem. We made a deal before you left. I send her, along with a whole lot of money, and they kill you both. She was supposed to die in Colchis right beside you. One of my enemies for one of theirs."

"Me?" said Medea. "That's why I had to go? That's why you wouldn't let me stay in my lab? You were trading me away as the price for a murder?" It stung, even though she knew it shouldn't have. She'd thought they wanted her to go because they needed her. Because her skills were indispensable to the mission. Now she knew Pelias had never considered her more than a pawn in his games, just like all the rest of them.

"Someone wants to get at you pretty badly," said Pelias. "Some genomancer back in Colchis. You women and your rivalries. I'd keep you here, you know I would. But Aeetes isn't going to be happy about how things turned out. You were supposed to be dead, right beside Jason. And we were supposed to pay a ransom to get the Fleece, not just have it handed back to us for free."

"It was all just a sham," said Jason, shaking his head. "The entire thing."

"It always is," said Pelias. "But now we need a gesture. Something to smooth things over with Aeetes. To keep the peace, for now." He leaned in close towards Medea, and she could feel the heat from his breath on her face as she turned away. "We've got to set the terms for a new bargain, and you'll make a wonderful bargaining chip. You're something we already know they want."

"You can have me," said Jason. "You can have everything. I won't even fight it. Just keep her here. She's the best genomancer out there. You'd never replace her. She's valuable. A treasure." He looked over at Medea, and then looked back at Pelias. "More than you can know."

"And what would you know about value?" said Pelias. "You had everything handed to you." His voice turned bitter as he paced in front of them. "Not me. I started out as a stakeholder, and my whole life was one unending climb. I had to reach out and take what's mine. I had to kick, stab, bite, and claw just to get near it. People like you don't get it. You're born rich, you die rich, and it's all just one big playground in the middle. The rest of us have to fight. There's enemies working against us, enemies you don't even see. We have to make hard decisions sometimes, if we want to keep what's ours."

"I didn't ask for what I have," said Jason. "And I'm not asking for it now. I'm only asking for her."

"And I didn't ask to be born as a nothing," said Pelias. "I worked hard. But every time I got a job, it disappeared. Automated away along with everyone else. It took me a while to realize the truth. Working's for chumps. Nobody cares how hard you work. They care how much money you're making them, and that's it. That's what you don't get. I had to cross lines to get where I am. And everything's different on the other side. You bought into this heroism crap, but it's just a lie to control you. Once you see the lies—once you start weaving them yourself—it's a whole different world out there. No one cares for anything but themselves in the end. It's use or be used, and I know what side of the line I want to be on."

He turned away and pulled something to his face, a little piece of metal in his hand. She couldn't see what it was, but she could see what he'd done. A little dab of blue dust lined his nostril, a sure sign of what she'd suspected. He was on something, and it was making him unstable. And no one around him would say a thing, not with the power he wielded.

He walked back to Medea, looking her up and down. It made her feel slimy inside. His eyes hovered over all the wrong places, leering without a hint of subtlety. Then they stopped, right at her waist, and his smile vanished. He snapped out his arm and grabbed at her, pulling away the vial she'd tucked away in her belt.

"What's this?" said Pelias. He held the vial up to the air, inspecting little bubbles that flowed up and down through the green liquid within. His eyes narrowed, and he showed it to Amphion, receiving only a baffled shrug in reply.

"It's—" said Jason.

"It's nothing," said Medea. "It isn't anything." She had an idea. Just the germ of a plan, and she wasn't sure how she was going to make it work. But she had Pelias's interest, and he was holding a very dangerous weapon. It gave her something to work with, at least, and maybe a way to force a better deal than the one Pelias was imagining.

"Don't treat me like a fool," said Pelias. His eyes went dark with paranoia, studying her every move. "You know what it is. You had it hidden on you for a reason." He paced back and forth between the two of them, searching their expressions for any sign of the truth.

"Don't tell him," said Medea, turning her head towards Jason. "No matter what, don't tell him."

Pelias answered her with a sharp slap. It stung her face, rattling her teeth. He grabbed her chin again, leaning in and practically screaming at her just inches from her face. "I want to know what this is. I want to know what you brought back. Talk, and do it now. Because in ten seconds, I'm going to have one of my men start slicing off body parts."

"It was nothing," said Medea. "It's just a serum. Just something I was working on." She was dangling the bait in front of him, praying that the more she resisted, the more interested he'd become. And the longer he thought they had something valuable, the longer they'd stay alive.

"You're lying," said Pelias. "And badly." He slapped her again, his eyes wide with drug-fueled rage. "Tell me." She didn't, and he struck her, this time with a closed fist. She felt pain aching all across her jaw, and she thought he might have shattered it. He pulled his hand back for another blow, and she closed her eyes and waited for it to come.

"We took it from Aeetes," said Jason loudly. The sight of Pelias assaulting her had made him cave, and the truth started tumbling out of him. "They were using the Fleece. Using it to—"

"Immortality," said Medea. "The Colchians. They figured out a way to stop us from aging. Not just for a few extra decades. Forever." She was nervous, incredibly so, and she could hear her voice waver as she spoke. She had to make him believe her, if they were to have any chance. And it was a hard subject to even talk about. It brought back images of her parents, whose lives had overlapped her own for just a fraction of what they should have. She had to fight to hold in the tears, and fight to keep herself together in front of Pelias.

"That can't be possible," said Pelias. He looked back and forth between the two, searching their eyes for some tell that would give away the truth. "No one's ever done it. Not in people. Not in animals. Not ever. Your code goes bad in the end, and then you're done for." He turned to Amphion, demanding an answer.

"The Colchians are researching it," said Amphion. "So is every one of the Big Five. But intelligence doesn't think they're very far along."

"And we all know how competent they are," said Pelias. "They're the ones who told me the Fleece was safe in the first place. They're the ones who said he'd never be coming back."

"It could work, in theory," said Amphion. "But in practice. It'd be so difficult—"

"One of you is lying to me," said Pelias. His eyes darted back and forth between Jason and Medea, and then to Amphion. "Maybe all of you are."

"It works," said Medea. "I saw it myself." She nodded towards the vial, dangling between his fingers. "And this is all there is."

"It's true," said Jason. "They did something. With the Fleece. They used the data somehow. Aeetes told us himself."

"It's true, is it?" said Pelias. He looked at Amphion, then Jason, then Medea, calculation and suspicion written across his face. "Then drink." He grabbed Medea by the chin and held the vial up to her lips. "If it really makes you immortal, then drink."

"Leave her the hell alone," said Jason. He struggled towards her, but the soldiers held him back, grabbing him by the arms before he could get anywhere near her.

"Okay," said Medea. "Okay. I'll do it."

"No," said Jason. "No you will not." He kicked the man beside him, knocking his leg aside as the man screamed in pain. But another soldier rushed in, knocking Jason to the floor with the butt of his spear. Jason kept struggling, kicking away at him even as he tried to get to his feet and stop her. But his hands were bound, and there were too many soldiers for even him to handle. They pinned him down, and one of the soldiers shoved a rag into his mouth, gagging him.

"Immortality," said Medea. She looked up at Pelias, trying to keep her voice as confident as she could. She worried she'd show weakness, or some hint she was lying. The drugs might have helped him climb his way to the top, but now they were making him see threats from all around, and he might well see through her. But she had to keep up the front, and keep dangling a prize in front of him. "There's only so much of it. But if you really want to waste it on me, you can."

She opened her mouth wide, and Pelias looked down on her, smiling. "Brave girl. Hope you're telling the truth." She wasn't, but that wasn't going to stop her. She pressed her lips against the vial, locked eyes with Pelias, and waited.

His eyes narrowed, and his brow rose. She could see the indecision in him: part of him wanted to believe, and part of him was persuaded by how willing she was to do as he said. But not all of him. After a few seconds of hesitation, he grabbed her by the jaw, tipped the vial forward, and shoved half of Circe's weapon down her throat. She coughed and choked, but he slammed her mouth shut, forcing her to gulp it all down at once. He set a timer on his sheath and stood there waiting: one minute, then two. Then he finally let her go, coughing and spitting as she recovered herself.

"Well?" said Pelias with a smug smile. "Was it immortality? Or was it some kind of poison?"

"I'm alive, aren't I?" said Medea.

"Give me your sheath," said Pelias. He grabbed her arm, pulling out her wrist and tapping his fingers across it. "Amphion. Run her data. Look for anything wrong. Anything." He crossed his arms, waiting impatiently for an answer.

"Healthy," said Amphion, as he swiped away at his tablet. "All her vitals are near perfect. Heartbeat's a little high, but understandable, given the circumstances. No poisons, no damage, no anything."

"Like I said," said Medea. "Immortality."

"Immortality," said Pelias, his voice going faster and faster. His mood had swung in an instant, from depressive paranoia to manic intensity. "I can run the company forever. I'll outlast every other executive at every one of the Big Five. I'll buy them all out, and all it's going to take is a little time. Decades, centuries, who cares? I'll own everything. I'll run everything. I'll be the oldest, the wisest, the best. The world will bow down to me, and only me."

He paced around as he spoke, going wild from the effects of his drugs. "They won't have any choice. They'll have no place else to go. One people, one ecosystem, one CEO. It'll be live in my world, or live off in the wilderness alone. No health care, no home, no gadgets, no anything. You won't be able to buy them from anyone else. It's do what I say, or it's ostracism. Go along, or get out." He turned to Medea with an intense stare. "I want more. I want you to make me more."

"I can't," said Medea. "You've got one dose left at best. I don't know how it works, and I don't know what they did to make it." She lied as best she could, hoping he could convince him to take a sip himself. One drop was all it would take, and then she'd have him. "And we killed the genomancer who came up with it. That's the last there is, and maybe the last there'll ever be."

"One more dose," said Pelias. He held the vial up in the air, quietly contemplating its contents. His pupils cycled back and forth, first wide, then narrow, oscillating as quickly as his moods. "Shame to have wasted immortality on someone the Colchians are about to execute in a few days, anyway. But in the end, one dose is all I need." He brought the vial to his own lips, holding it just in front of him.

"Sir," said Amphion. "Maybe you should wait. I could take it to the lab. Get it analyzed. Just to be one hundred percent sure. I'd handle things personally."

"What?" said Pelias. His pupils bulged, and suspicion flashed across his face. "You want it for yourself? The last dose, the only dose, and you think I'm going to just hand it over to you?" Amphion looked like he wanted to rush in and slap the vial away from his hand. But Pelias shut him down with a cold glare, and he knew better than to press the issue. Speaking out of turn would be the surest way back to life as a stakeholder, assuming Pelias let him live at all. Pelias smiled at Medea, and then he downed the rest of the vial himself.

"And now, I'm afraid I don't have any more use for you," said Pelias. "Either of you." He motioned towards one of the soldiers, who grabbed Medea by the arms and started dragging her away. Another two men lifted Jason to his feet, and even Mopsus and Tiphys found themselves being hauled towards the hanger exit. She shouted out, trying to stop them while she could.

"Pelias," said Medea. "You're about to get very, very sick. And you and I need to talk about making a deal. You have to let us free."

"You're fine," said Pelias. "And so am I. The best I've ever been, in fact. The best—" Something gurgled loudly from inside his abdomen, and he stopped midsentence with a look of discomfort on his face. Everyone around stopped to look as well. Even the soldiers quit pulling them along, paralyzed by the sight.

"You're not fine," said Medea. "You have to trust me. You have to listen."

"My stomach," said Pelias. He winced in pain, hunching over as Amphion rushed to his side. "Feels like something's burning."

"What you drank was a weapon," said Medea. "A weapon I've got a cure for. It's something the Colchians came up with, something to target people's genes. It's going to kill you. But I'll stop it. I promise. I locked down my code so it can't affect me, back in Colchis. I can do the same thing for you. All you have to do is let us go. Just give back Jason's shares, let us all go, and I'll cure you, right now."

"The hell I will," said Pelias. "Amphion." He hunched over into a coughing fit, leaning an arm on Amphion's shoulder to steady himself. "This is some trick. She lied before, and she's lying now. Amphion, we're keeping the shares. Call the labs. Get someone over here. Someone we can trust."

"Yes, sir," said Amphion,

"They won't make it," said Medea. "They can't help—"

"Bitch says another word, then kill her," said Pelias. He waved to the soldiers and they shoved her to the ground, pressing the tips of their spears against her neck. "I'm not giving back those shares. Not ever. Not for anything. The whole thing falls down if I do. Amphion, get me a hit. Just another hit to get me through until we get a real genomancer over here."

"Sir," said Amphion. "Sir, maybe we should let her do the work. It could take an hour to get someone out here."

Pelias hunched over in pain, falling down onto his knees. "I said a hit." He let out a sharp groan, his teeth grinding together as he clutched at his stomach. Amphion reached down to help him up, but Pelias slapped his hands away. "Just one. Do it."

Amphion pulled a little vial full of orange dust from his suit jacket. He dumped a line across the back of his tablet, holding it out to Pelias. Pelias leaned towards it, his head shaking, and managed to inhale the entire line in a single snort.

"Helps the pain," said Pelias. "Helps you power through it. Helps you see things you couldn't see before." He wobbled to his feet, his pupils growing wide as he found himself again. "Now. Where were we?"

He started to cough, doubling over and holding a hand against his mouth. When he pulled it away, it was covered in a spray of blood. Pelias looked down at it in disbelief. He lost control, hacking and wheezing as more and more blood covered his hand.

"I said I'll help you," said Medea. "Just let me help you. I have everything I need in the ARGO." She'd save him, if she could, as long as he'd let them live. But he was too lost in his fantasy of ultimate power. He wouldn't give up a thing, not even to save his own life. And there wasn't anything she could do with her hands tied behind her back.

"No," said Pelias. "Kill her. Kill him. Kill—" But his words choked off before anyone could move. There were bubbles forming under the skin of his hands, growing and shrinking again as he held them up and stared at them. Pink fluid dripped from the side of his mouth, trickling down onto his suit and staining his tie.

"Kill," said Pelias. His eyes grew wide with fear, and he turned away from them, stumbling away down the hangar all alone. Amphion rushed after him, reaching out an arm to steady him. But Pelias brushed it aside, taking step after heavy step all on his own.

He didn't make it far. After a few more feet, he tripped to the ground, his arms and legs twitching as he tried to drag himself back upright. He turned his head, and the sight of it made Medea squirm: his face was drooping away, losing all form as Circe's weapon burned away his insides.

"He's melting," said Tiphys. "Like a witch or something."

An orange puddle was growing around him, a liquefied biological soup streaming out of every pore. His suit was soaked, and soon he was nothing more than a pink blob, barely recognizable as human. The soldiers surrounded him, trying to help, but there was nothing they could do. All that was left was an empty suit lying on the ground in the middle a pool of pink and orange.

"He's dead" said the soldier. "What do we do? What does this mean?"

"It means," said Amphion, looking over at Jason, "that the Argo Corporation is about to have a new Chief Executive Officer."

CHAPTER THIRTY-ONE

"**H**OLD STILL," SAID MEDEA. "QUIT wriggling around. This is the last procedure, and then you'll be back to normal. No more oinking, no more weird cravings for old food, and no more mud baths."

Mopsus sat in a chair in her lab, looking as nervous as could be. He'd been in and out for nearly a month, gradually changing from pig back to the man he'd once been. It had taken time, but she'd wanted to be careful, and she'd relished the opportunity to dive into the code of someone who'd been transformed by Circe's weapon. It was a chance to learn whatever she could, and Mopsus was the only human test subject she was likely to ever have. She had enough samples for a lifetime, she was close to understanding exactly how it worked, and she'd already come up with a simple vaccination for the masses that would stop it in its tracks if anyone ever tried to use it again.

Now she just had to tidy things up with Mopsus, and the world's first genetic weapon would be a thing of the past. It had been hard work, but everything had gone well so far, and everything about him was normal again.

Everything but his nose.

It was still a snout, stretching away from his face and sniffling up and down every time he tried to speak. He couldn't seem to control it, or perhaps he didn't care to. Mopsus was like that, when it came to matters of manners, and she thought it was best to just quietly change things back to the way they'd been without delving into the details of what it was like to be a pig.

"The flock doesn't like it, they don't," said Mopsus. "Can't tell it's me." His voice came out as a nasal squeak, scratchy and hoarse. He didn't sound like himself, and she wasn't surprised that his birds hadn't recognized him.

"They'll know who you are, once we're done," said Medea. "All the Chirps will figure it out."

"I hope," said Mopsus. He couldn't quit fidgeting, his fingers tapping up and down the side of the chair. "I hope. I do."

"Just sit still and close your eyes," said Medea. She took hold of one of his hands, giving his palm a gentle squeeze. "It'll all be over in a minute." His contacts flipped to white at once, and his jaw dropped open and let out a little line of drool. He was just as odd as he'd ever been, but at least he was starting to connect with other people. He'd had to troop up and down between his hermitage and her lab on almost a daily basis, and she'd noticed him socializing despite himself.

She watched the monitors behind him, flashing green one by one as the machines brought his code back to normal. His nose was visibly shrinking, pulling back towards his face and reshaping itself until he looked just the way he did before Circe had gotten hold of him. It was all done, and he was back to normal. At least as normal as Mopsus could ever hope to be.

She tried to shake him out of his trance, but he just lay there in his chair, his eyes vacant and glossy. She gave up after a few nudges. He was either enjoying himself with his data or he was too afraid to come out, and either way she didn't see any harm in letting him be for a little while longer.

She picked up a tablet and went back to her work, tapping away at a project she'd been spending her spare time on. It was a gift for Hypsipyle, a sparrow that could sing in a human voice with a repertoire of classic songs that rivaled any jukebox. She thought the Harpies deserved better than the way Colchis had treated them, and if she could use genomancy to help them enjoy themselves a little more, she meant to do it. They seemed to be doing well, at any rate. Hypsipyle was leading them now, and in a very different direction. They'd taken to calling themselves Tenth Wavers, and their vids had switched from stirring up gender wars to learning to love both the masculine and the feminine, even when they came in forms that were more traditional than what the Harpies wanted for themselves.

She kept editing the code for the sparrow, and she thought about asking Mopsus when he woke whether he wanted one for his flock. She felt so happy, being back in Argos and back in her lab. Adventures were all well and good, but she was much more comfortable poking around in people's code without an entire city trying to kill her. It was quiet, it was homey, and it was safe—just the way she liked it. She zoned out as she worked, adding song after song to the sparrow DNA, until she heard a knocking from behind her. She turned to see Tiphys, standing at the door of the lab and dodging Hecate as she rolled past his feet.

"Are visiting hours over?" said Tiphys. "I heard you were working on Mopsus. I wanted to see if he's okay."

"He's going to be fine," said Medea. She waved him in, showing off the newly restored seer as he slept in her chair. "He's out of it, but his code's all working. He's back to the way he was."

"So have you thought about any of my business ideas?" said Tiphys. "I have tons more. Really great ones, too. I want us to make this purple sludge creature that parents can put under the bed to frighten their kids and get them to behave. It won't bite or anything. But it'll slurp really loud if they don't do their chores."

Medea visibly cringed. She wasn't going to be emotionally torturing any small children, no matter how much money Tiphys thought their parents might pay for it. He might even be right, but still. She was making as much money as she needed, and she'd seen more than enough monsters created by genomancy for her tastes.

"I'm just kidding," said Tiphys with a laugh and a mischievous smile. "Jason told me I wasn't supposed to ask. But I thought I'd try."

"Good," said Medea. She felt a wave of relief rush over her. She didn't like saying no to her friends, even when they were asking for something absurd. And Tiphys's requests took absurdity to another level. "Sorry you can't have your monsters. But I'm sure you'll find something else to do."

"I already did," said Tiphys. "I don't know if you heard. About my promotion."

"Promotion," said Medea. She hadn't heard, and she wasn't sure she wanted to. Tiphys and responsibility didn't go hand in hand, and the thought of him as some corporate executive made her wonder about the future of Argos.

"They made me a real pilot," said Tiphys. "Some of it's public relations. But they've got me assigned to do stunts over the parades. There's some vids that leaked out of what I did back in Colchis. I've even got followers on the networks. And it was all your code that did it."

"That's great," said Medea. She leaned over and gave him a hug, though it seemed to frighten him even more than a lion had. His hands hovered almost a foot away from her back, and his face turned beet red until she let him go.

"I just wanted to say thanks," stuttered Tiphys. "I'd still be back in my apartment eating cheese snacks all day if we'd never met. I'm even learning a bunch of stuff on my own. It's like refresher for my instincts. I know what to do, but now I'm starting to understand what I'm doing. I guess I should thank Jason, too, when he gets here. He's the one that promoted me."

"When he gets here?" said Medea. She was supposed to see him—that night, in fact. But he wasn't supposed to be wandering into her lab unannounced. She jumped towards one of the computer screens, checking her reflection for mussed hair or anything out of place. She was furtively running lipstick across her lips when she heard his footsteps approaching behind her.

"Medea," said Jason. "Tidying up for Tiphys?"

She turned to see him standing there, his eyes glistening green and a crooked smile across his face. He was wearing a uniform, though not the sort she was used to seeing him in: a sleek grey business suit with a matching tie. He looked every inch the executive he'd become, if a little bigger and a lot more muscular than the average CEO. It had only been a month, but it seemed like he'd been born for it. Then again, he was as much a warrior as ever, a general in command of a corporate army.

"You aren't supposed to be here," said Medea. "You said later. I know you said later."

"Later for our date," said Jason. "But Mopsus is a friend now, too. I had to make sure he was okay."

"A friend," muttered Mopsus, his eyes flipping open from his trance. He looked like he was in a state of shock. "A joke? I can't tell, sometimes. When people tell them."

"That's not a joke," said Jason. "You saved our lives. You were at our side during a bunch of battles, even if you were running around as a pig half the time. I call that a friend."

"Hrmm," said Mopsus, rising from his chair. He looked as uncomfortable with the idea of friendship as Tiphys had been at the prospect of a hug from a real live woman. But after a moment's contemplation, he thrust out his hand, extending it towards Jason. "Come down to see me sometime. The gods still talk to me, you know. About what's to come, and what we should be doing."

"They're happy about the Fleece?" said Jason. "They think it's safe?"

"They know it is," said Mopsus. "They know."

"What did you do with it?" said Medea. "Someone's going to try to steal it again. But we could use it. We could do so much."

"I locked it in a fortified bunker three hundred feet underground," said Jason. "You can access it any time you want. You've got clearance. But you might want to send Hecate instead."

"Why?" said Medea. "Too dangerous for the lab geek?"

"Idas and Antaeus are down there," said Jason. "They're on the most boring guard duty of all time, along with a bunch of others just like them. A ten-year shift. I'd have put them on trial in public if it wouldn't have stained the Argonauts' reputation. And if they try to come up a day earlier, I'll toss their asses in a cell forever."

"Idas owes me," said Medea. "I fixed his brother. And I didn't have to." It hadn't taken long, not once she'd had samples from Mopsus and the Harpies to compare his code to. But Lynceus had turned out to be just as pleasant to deal with as his brother was. He'd yelled at her and screamed at her the second he was fixed, and only a mention of his cathouse exploits had shut his mouth and turned his face red. "Besides, someone has to protect the Fleece. If he doesn't like it, let him know I'm happy to take out all the genetic enhancements the company's put into him."

"No one will take it," said Mopsus. "The gods are watching it, now. They'd know, and they'd warn you."

"I wanted to ask you about them," said Medea. She was hesitant to even raise the subject. Some of their messages had been intensely personal, and she didn't want to air it all in front of everyone. But she'd been wondering about something for the last month, and she was dying to know the answer. "I was getting these messages. Lots of them. But I haven't heard a single thing from the gods since we got back."

"No news is good news," said Mopsus. "They intervene only when they must. They think it best to let us manage our own affairs, when we can. If one hasn't heard from them, then one doesn't need to."

He stood there, staring around awkwardly until Jason gave a loud cough. He didn't catch the social cue, but Tiphys translated for him.

"We've got to get you back to your birds," said Tiphys. "And leave these two to themselves."

"Thank you," called Mopsus as Tiphys ushered him out of the lab. "Thank you for fixing me. And have a very pleasant evening, the both of you."

"These guys are going to get married," said Tiphys. "They're so going to get married. But you already know that, don't you? And what their kids' names are going to be and stuff?"

"I know the odds," said Mopsus. "But you've seen them together. You've seen it in their eyes. Their future is something it doesn't take a seer to see." The two of them disappeared down the hallway, snickering and smirking together the entire way.

"You think he's right?" said Jason. "Marriage and kids in our future? Think we'd be able to handle a bunch of miniature Jasons and Medeas running around, fighting each other and turning themselves into little monsters?"

"It's kind of soon," said Medea. "We've only known each other a month." It was true, but only partly. She'd be lying if she'd said the thought hadn't crossed her mind. The gods had told her she'd find true love, and she was starting to believe them. But she didn't want to rush things, not when they were going so well. "And aren't you a big time CEO now? You've got to be too swamped for a wife and kids."

"It's a busy job," said Jason. "But not too busy for the things I care about." He leaned in and gave her a kiss, slow and sensuous. He ran a finger across her face, gazing into her eyes before pulling away with a smile. "And it's not just running the company. I'm still an Argonaut, even if I'm wearing a different suit. I'm not any different than I was before."

"Tell me you're not going back in the field," said Medea. It scared her, thinking of him out there. She worried about it sometimes, that he'd get it in his head to go off on another mission. She'd come so close to losing him back in Colchis, and for a moment she thought she had. She knew what that felt like, and she never wanted to feel it again.

"I've been in the arena a few times," said Jason. "No death matches, but it gets me my fix. And I'm planning things. It's Circe. We're hunting her down. I've got a team of warriors on it. Real ones. There were still a few who cared more about honor than about fame. They trashed her mansion, and they've been following her data trail all over Colchis. We'll get her."

"She's going to go back to what she was working on, if you let her," said

Medea. "Turning people into animals. Turning something that should be a miracle into a curse."

"She won't," said Jason. "No one's going to protect her from me. There's crimes, and then there's crimes. None of the Big Five will go to the mat over something like this. We'll capture her, take her out, whatever it takes, and they won't bat an eye. They'll scream and moan about their sovereignty in public. But she crossed the line into genetic terrorist with what she did. Most people are going to be happy to have her gone."

"Aeetes won't like it," said Medea.

"Aeetes won't be around for much longer," said Jason. "He's on shaky ground. A debacle that public was bound to get out. There's a management vote coming up, and things aren't looking good for him." A sly smirk ran across his face. "And I've been buying up some of their shares. He won't be CEO much longer. He's got bigger things to worry about than helping Circe."

"Please," said Medea. "Just make sure she doesn't hurt anyone else." Her thoughts went to what had happened to Mopsus, and to the poor people Circe had imprisoned in the bodies of animals in her mansion. There was a special kind of cruelty in that, and people like her were what made others so wary of genomancy.

"I will," said Jason. "And I want you to help. That's part of why I came down here. I have my warriors. But I need them trained." He waved a hand around the lab, gesturing to the rows of computers and centrifuges. "And I don't have time to do it the hard way."

"Isn't it going to hurt them, in the long run?" said Medea. "If they don't have to work for it? Or did I convert you to the dark side? I can still change your code back if you want me to."

"I've gotten used to my new code," said Jason. "I kind of like it, actually. It's like having a little piece of you inside me wherever I go. I'm starting to think there's a middle ground. You did good things with genomancy. Circe did bad things. There's no putting that genie back into the bottle. All we can do is be careful about it, and be responsible. And there's no one I'd trust with something like that more than you."

He put his hand on the small of her back, pulling her in close, and he gave her another kiss. "I've got a board meeting in ten minutes. One I can't miss. We're shifting a big chunk of the budget to creating jobs for any stakeholders who want them. The kind of things that make you a better person to do them, regardless of whether a robot could technically take your place. Teachers, artists, coaches. Even some genomancers." A smirk spread across his face, and she gave him a playful punch on the arm.

"You're lucky it's an important meeting," said Jason. "Otherwise I'd lock the door to your lab, and I wouldn't let you leave until the both of us were too tired to stand."

"Wouldn't let me?" said Medea. She gave him a look of mock indignation, but she fluttered inside at the thought. Being a warrior and a shareholder had given him a dominant streak, and she loved to see him take charge, whether it was in the boardroom or the bedroom. He'd shown her that she could trust him, both to care for her and to protect her. And there was nothing more attractive to her than a man she knew she could trust to lead.

"You wouldn't want me to let you," said Jason with a smile. "Those instincts of yours. They'd be screaming in your ear to do what I told you to. And you'd love the things I told you to do."

He was right, and she knew it. It was just how she was, whether anyone else liked it or not, and in that moment she wanted to embrace her primal instincts just as much as he wanted to embrace his own. But the board of directors would track him down if he didn't show, and she had patients to treat. Besides, sometimes a little anticipation made pleasure all the more intense. It was only a few hours until their night out, and she could wait that long even if every minute was exquisite torture.

"Go talk to the board," said Medea. "I've got a few more people to see today, anyway. Then we'll go get dinner, and we'll have another talk about all the things you're going to 'let' me do."

"I'll be thinking about it for the entire meeting," said Jason. "But you've got people to help, and I've got a company to run. And we've both got a date to keep at the hottest restaurant in Argos. So finish up, go home, and get ready. Then let's go enjoy the present as it comes, together, and let the seers and the gods worry over the future until it's here."

THE END

Liked the book? If you want to get a heads up on future books, please sign up for my mailing list at: www.argonautsbook.com.

ACKNOWLEDGEMENTS

Thanks to Megan McKeever for her work editing the draft. I highly recommend her to any authors, and her site is at: http://www.meganmckeevereditorial.com.

Thanks also to Streetlight Graphics for their work on the cover and on formatting the book. They're great as well and can be contacted at: http://www.streetlightgraphics.com.

41501917R00169

Made in the USA
San Bernardino, CA
14 November 2016